Thief of the Night Guild
(Queen of Thieves Book 2)

By Andy Peloquin

Acknowledgements

To all the people who played a vital role in the creation of this book: Suzan, Maura, Claire, Matt, Patricia, Donna, Lavern, Lily, Heidi, and many more. I cannot thank you enough!

Table of Contents

Chapter One

The dagger twitched in Ilanna's fingers as she watched Lord Ulimar's chest rise and fall. A quick cut and the foolish noble would never wake. The sleeping draught she'd dripped into his gaping mouth would keep him in the realm of dreams even as he bled out.

But if the Night Guild wanted Lord Ulimar dead, they'd have sent a Serpent. Clean and quiet. Or messy, as the job demanded. Ilanna was a Hawk; she'd come for another reason.

She drove the dagger into the bedside table with a *thunk*. Moonlight glinted off the silver skull pommel, the ruby eyes twinkling. When Lord Ulimar awoke, a headache from the sleeping draught would be the least of his concerns. The dagger sent a message: the Night Guild had marked him for death.

Ilanna almost pitied him. *Poor bastard has no idea the real reason it's here.* He'd work himself into a panic struggling to understand what he'd done to earn the Guild's ire. Little did he know, the Guild had no reason to wish him dead; they cared only for his money.

If that doesn't drive him into the Crown's arms, he's braver than most.

Turning her back on the sleeping nobleman, Ilanna drew two miniature glass orbs from her pouch; quickfire globes, a Hawk's best friend in the darkness. Light glimmered as she touched them together. Holding them high, she ran a practiced eye over the ornate armoire, the iron-bound chest at the foot of the canopied bed, and the tapestries on the wall.

Now where would you hide your true valuables, Lord Ulimar?

She paced the room on soft-soled boots, her keen ears listening for any sound. She snorted at the telltale creak of a floorboard. Drawing a dagger from her bracer, she slipped it into the crack and pried the wood loose. Within lay half a dozen velvet purses.

She grinned. *And it's not even my nameday!*

Ilanna counted out twenty golden imperials and slipped them inside her belt pouch, then replaced them with ten of her special lead coins. They weighed significantly less than gold specie, but Lord Ulimar would only notice the

1

missing money if he tried to spend the coins. She stuffed the purse into the bottom of the hoard. Unless the nobleman's finances took a *very* hard hit, he'd never discover the theft.

Replacing the floorboard, she drew a vial of dust and sprinkled some on the floor. Just enough to hide the fact the board had been moved. Her miniature rake combed the threads of the plush Al Hani rug into place behind her, obscuring her bootprints.

Lord Ulimar would find no trace of anyone entering his house, save for the dagger a hand's breadth from his nose.

Ilanna slipped out of the nobleman's bedroom and glanced down the hall. One floor down, the lantern of the night watchman drove back the shadows and the *tromp, tromp* of heavy booted feet sounded loud in the silent house.

She tensed as the sound grew louder. The watchman was supposed to head downstairs, not up! Stifling a curse, she slipped behind a pillar and held her breath. The light of a lantern spilled down the hallway. Her shoulders tightened as the beam pointed toward the door of Lord Ulimar's bedroom. She ran her thumb along the hilt of one of the four daggers in her bracer. If he didn't move along…

The lantern drifted away and the watchman whistled a mournful tune as he descended the stairs. Ilanna let out her breath in a slow exhale.

Too close. I'm lucky he's too lazy to check every room.

She moved when the light disappeared, slipping into Lord Ulimar's study. She didn't bother closing the door but shimmied up her black rope without a sound. A few seconds later, she stood atop the mansion roof.

Ilanna ran over everything that had happened since she'd entered half an hour earlier. Had she forgotten anything? She never did. It was what made her different from the other Hawks, what made her the best.

All Hawks carried out these assignments for the Night Guild; "shanking the fool" Lem called them. Some liked to ransack a mark's home and steal anything they could get their hands on. Ilanna thought that nonsense. Yes, any man would feel fear upon finding his house raided, but her way had proven far more effective.

No one ever saw her enter or leave, she left no sign of her passage. Lord Ulimar's guards could search the mansion top to bottom and find only the dagger. Humans couldn't walk through walls, couldn't enter without a trace. Ghosts could. And if ghosts served the Night Guild, Lord Ulimar would have no choice but to beg the Crown to protect him. The vulnerability, betrayal, and paranoia engendered by the message from the Night Guild would send any nobleman running to whoever offered protection.

Two hours of work had earned the Guild a hundred imperials a month, paid by King Ohilmos himself. House Hawk and the Crown had a beautiful partnership, one that earned her a cool ten percent of the profits—and that didn't count the imperials she'd stolen from Lord Ulimar.

A good night, indeed.

Kneeling, Ilanna replaced the pane of glass she'd removed earlier and applied a thin line of Darreth's quick-drying caulk. It would hold out the rain but she'd have no trouble scraping it away next time she wanted to enter Lord Ulimar's mansion. He had many, many more purses for her to empty.

Of course, she'd have to do it without the Guild finding out. Nobles who paid for the Crown's protection were exempt from depredation. King Ohilmos more than compensated the Guild to keep its Journeymen in line. If caught, she'd hang. Worse, she'd face punishment at the hands of her own House. No one broke the Guild's laws.

But Ilanna knew better. The Guild had only one law she needed to remember: don't get caught. She'd learned that the hard way. She fingered the leather strap curled around her right wrist; it brought back the painful memory of Ethen. He'd taught her how to use the sling. She couldn't bring herself to use it, not after that night, but she kept it close. She wanted it to remember him, to remember what had happened and what she'd done to the bastard who'd laid his hands on her.

Padding across the rooftop, Ilanna slipped into her harness and threw herself off the edge of the mansion. The metal rings sang as she sped across the aerial runway. The world flashed past at a tremendous speed and she bit back a delighted laugh. Years roaming the rooftops of Praamis hadn't dulled the thrill of flying. No one but a Hawk knew the true joy of seeing the world from above.

Her harness jerked as the metal rings snagged on the secondary rope. With deft movements, Ilanna unclipped the carabiner from the rope. She slid out of the harness and stuffed it into a satchel left beneath the eaves of a nearby roof. Jarl or one of the other Pathfinders would be along soon to remove the rope that bridged the gap to Lord Ulimar's mansion.

Now to return to the Guild and let Master Hawk know the mission was a success.

After the stealth and silence of Lord Ulimar's mansion, Ilanna couldn't resist the urge to run free. She raced across the rooftops of Praamis, vaulting obstacles and swinging through open air. Muscles strengthened by years of training cushioned the impact of long drops and pulled her lithe, compact body up walls twice her height. Her leather harness, bracer, and boots made no sound as she raced along the Hawk's Highway.

The wind tugged a few strands of her long, dark hair free of its tight tail. Her grey cloak streamed behind her. She felt like a bird flying through the night. Up here, she was alone with the moon, stars, and sky.

She hesitated at the entrance to House Hawk. The oppressive air of the Guild tunnels held little appeal after the cool breeze and star-filled heavens. But it was more than that. Down in the maze of passages, she would have to face people. She would have to face *men*.

Just a few more minutes.

She sat on the edge of the roof, legs dangling. The first rays of sunlight trickled over the horizon. The dull grey of dawn crept closer with every heartbeat.

As ever, her eyes sought out the towering Black Spire that rose high above Praamis. Once, the tower had challenged the Night Guild, mocked the thieves with its impregnability. Since Master Gold's success many years ago, every Guild member who wanted to make a name for themselves had attempted to break in. All had failed. All but *her*.

For her Undertaking, she had defeated the Black Spire. It had nearly killed her, but she'd survived the ascent and descent of the tower and brought back proof of her success—a golden pin that once belonged to Journeyman Callidis, a Hawk who'd died in a failed attempt. She had proven herself worthy of the Hawk name. She'd earned her place as a Journeyman.

Now, the Black Spire looked small, almost pitiful. The monument—a remnant of the ancient Serenii, some said—no longer mocked her with its impossible heights. It stood as testament to Ilanna's skill and ingenuity. Any time members of the Night Guild looked up at the obsidian tower, they would think of her.

Taking a deep breath, Ilanna climbed to her feet and ducked through the window that led to the Aerie. Lanterns shining far below illuminated the familiar maze of ropes, ladders, and wooden walkways of the Perch.

She'd spent countless hours high above the packed earth floor of House Hawk. In the Aerie, she'd found a home, friends, something that came close to replacing the family she'd lost the day her mother and baby Rose died. The Aerie held many good memories. Bad ones, too.

She swooped through the Perch at a speed Ilanna the apprentice would have found terrifying. That girl had been young, scared, weak. Journeyman Ilanna of House Hawk was none of those things. She'd proven her strength when she defeated the Black Spire, when she hacked Sabat to pieces with the same blade he used on her friend.

She fingered the leather strap around her wrist. Ilanna the scared little girl had died the same day as Ethen.

Chapter Two

"…which leaves us with just enough to cover House Hawk's dues to the Guild, plus a surplus to invest in new gear. Of course, that calls into question the decision of what to…"

Ilanna didn't bother to stifle her yawn. *Good gods! Will he ever shut up?* Journeyman Bryden had a tendency to drone on. Even after a full night of sleep—and those had become as rare as a clever idea in a Bloodbear's brain— he had a near-magical ability to put her to sleep. Judging by the slumped posture of the other Journeymen, she wasn't the only one to find Bryden tedious on his better days.

Bryden, a middle-aged Hawk going soft in the gut and grey at the temples, trailed off mid-sentence and fixed her with an irritated glare. "Sorry, Ilanna, is all this boring you? I apologize for interrupting one so important as yourself with the inconsequential matters of keeping this House running!"

Once, Ilanna would have wilted beneath the scorn of Master Hawk's second-in-command. Her composure didn't crack as she gave a lazy wave. "Truly, Bryden, I couldn't be more interested in discussing what material you'll choose for our clothing or what shade of brown thread will be stitched into the Hawk insignia. I simply speak out of concern for the others, some of whom may find this conversation falls squarely in the realm of inane. Unless you need reassurance that you're doing your job properly, of course."

"Ilanna!" Master Hawk's voice cut off Bryden's retort. He narrowed his dark eyes and leaned forward in his chair. "Do us the courtesy of showing your fellow Journeymen the respect they are due."

"Of course, Master Hawk." Ilanna inclined her head at the House Master and gave Bryden an elaborate seated bow. "By all means, Bryden, enchant us with your tales of accountancy and stewardship."

Bryden scowled at her but Master Hawk held up a hand. "If you please, Bryden, skip to any matters of *real* importance." His voice held a note of weariness matched by the droop of his slim eyebrows. "Those that must be discussed by *all* Hawks."

"Of course." Bryden gave a stiff nod and flipped through his book. "Ah." He ran a finger down the page. "I have tallied the monthly haul, and you'll be pleased to know House Hawk is wealthier than ever. Payoffs from the Crown have increased ten percent since this time last year. Our nights are proving more lucrative as well."

His lips twisted into a grimace and he studiously avoided glancing at Ilanna. He knew—as did everyone else in the room—that she brought in more coin than any other Hawk. Her earnings had surpassed the rest of her House every month for the last two years.

"That is welcome news, Bryden." Master Hawk rubbed his grizzled, angular face. "If that is all…?"

With a bow, Bryden limped back to his seat beside Master Hawk.

The House Master gazed around the room. "Does anyone else have any business of importance to the House?"

None of the twenty-odd Journeymen spoke. *They're only too glad to be free of Bryden's inanities!*

"So be it." Master Hawk drew a scroll from within his robes and turned to Ilanna. "Lord Ulimar has received the message?"

She nodded. "By this time tomorrow, he'll be licking the King's feet in exchange for the Crown's protection."

"Good." The House Master studied his scroll. "That's one more name off the list. Four more nobles to…convince before the month's out. King Ohilmos is very concerned for the safety of his wealthiest citizens."

A collective chuckle ran around the circle of seated Hawks. King Ohilmos paid the Guild to *encourage* his nobles to request royal protection—for a fee, of course. Ilanna still found the notion of Crown-sanctioned thievery odd, but if it earned her the coin she needed, she could live with it.

Most Houses despised the Hawks for their wealth. Ilanna hadn't noticed it until she'd sat in the Guild Council for the first time. House Serpent's assassinations earned them coin on par with House Hawk, but not even House Scorpion's poisons and potions or House Hound's bounties fully covered the cost of their Guild fees. The thugs of House Bloodbear wore their rough vests and tunics with pride, and House Fox's members seemed more comfortable in their homespun wool, threadbare cloaks, and boots with more holes than a wheel of Nyslian cheese. The Journeymen and tyros of House Grubber looked one missed meal from the Long Keeper's embrace.

All the other Houses—save, perhaps, for House Serpent—envied the wealth of House Hawk. Ilanna had broken more than a few bones after hearing the names some Journeymen and apprentices gave the Hawks. The Crown's gold meant little to her, but she wouldn't let anyone slander *her* House.

At a motion from Master Hawk, Journeymen Ellick—a short, slim man in his fourth decade—stood and handed the House Master a steel case. From within, Master Hawk drew four of the skull-headed daggers.

"Four names, four messages to deliver. Lord Kannassas, Lord Illiran, Count Chatham, and Lord Vorrel."

Ilanna leapt to her feet. "I'll take Lord Vorrel."

The nobleman owned the only silver mine in the south of Einan. More than a few Foxes had found themselves short a hand thanks to Vorrel's keen-eyed guards. Her gaze flashed to the empty chair across from her. Journeymen Rothur had been a clever Hawk, but he'd danced the hangman's shuffle the previous year after a failed attempt to steal into Vorrel's home. She would relish the opportunity to thumb her nose at the nobleman's security measures.

"*I'll* take Lord Vorrel." Bryden stood, wearing an expression just short of a sneer.

Ilanna took a step forward. "He's mine, Bryden." Her hand dropped toward her belt.

Bryden gave her a caustic grin. "Seniority rules, Ilanna." Her name rolled off his lips with the same tone he'd use to converse with a carcass. "Isn't that right, Master Hawk?" He spoke without looking at the House Master.

Master Hawk passed the dagger to Bryden. "It is. You have until the full moon to send the message."

"Three weeks?" Bryden snorted. "I'll have it done by week's end."

Ilanna scowled, but Master Hawk handed her another dagger. "Count Chatham, Ilanna."

She gave a curt nod and took a seat, heat burning in her chest. *Of course Bryden would want Lord Vorrel. Any chance to spite me, as always.*

Denber stood. "I'll have Illiran." Accepting the dagger from Master Hawk, he returned to his seat and winked at Ilanna. He tilted his head as if to say, *Next time.*

Journeyman Sayk, a quiet Hawk with more grey than black in his beard, took the last dagger.

Master Hawk folded his arms across his chest and bowed. "The Watcher guide you in your paths, my friends."

The Journeymen echoed the ceremonial words and the meeting adjourned. *Not a moment too soon!* Ilanna had no desire to spend any more time than necessary in the stuffy Guild tunnels.

She stood, but Master Hawk's hand gripped her arm with surprising strength for his slight build. "Best avoid provoking Bryden further, Ilanna." He spoke for her ears only. "Not even your reputation can protect you from the wrath of a petty bureaucrat."

Ice ran through Ilanna's veins at the touch. She wanted to jerk away, but forced herself to nod. "Understood, Master Hawk." Her nails dug into her palms.

He released her. "Good job with Lord Ulimar. Best of luck with Count Chatham."

Ilanna sniffed. "You had to give me the poorest of the lot."

Master Hawk shrugged. "You already sit at my left hand, a place reserved for a more senior Journeyman. No one says anything, but I've seen their faces when they look at you. I can't be seen showing you any more preference than you're due."

Ilanna didn't like it but she understood. She'd claimed her seat in defiance of the unspoken rule of seniority. None of the Journeymen had spoken out, and she hadn't bothered to care what they thought of her. She'd earned her place, protocol or custom be damned. If any Hawk wanted to oust her, they had only to prove their superiority. *Not much chance of that happening.*

Master Hawk released her arm and she inclined her head. "Watcher guide you, Master Hawk."

"And you, Ilanna." A smile tugged at the House Master's lips as Ilanna turned and followed the others from the Hawk Council Chamber.

* * *

"Ilanna!"

Ilanna's shoulders tensed at the familiar voice but she forced a smile as she turned. "It's good to see you, Denber."

His smile came easy. "You, too. Judging by the way you baited Bryden, Lord Ulimar's went off without a hitch?"

Ilanna quirked an eyebrow.

"What?" He raised his hands in a defensive gesture. "You always get cocky when you pull off a big job. I know you, remember?"

"You heading out somewhere?"

Denber glanced down at the dark grey outfit he only wore when he went on a job. "Lord Illiran's first, to get a quick look at the place. Then the twins and I have set up a way into Lord Morrin's. We'll have a few hours before daylight to get in and out."

Werrin came up behind Denber. "Come on, mate, we've gotta run. Lord Morrin's valuables won't steal themselves."

Denber nodded. "You and Lem head up top. I'll meet you in a minute."

"Right." Werrin grinned at Ilanna. "Good to see you again, 'Lanna. Been a while."

"Don't get yourself killed out there, Werrin. You and me'll have to get a drink after you're done."

"Deal." Werrin raced away.

Ilanna watched the Hawk go. "He hasn't changed much. Still has that same mischievous twinkle in his eye."

"Lem's about the same, too." Denber stroked the dark beard he'd allowed to grow on his broad, handsome face. "Way they act, it's hard to believe they're only a few years older than you."

"Just not half as clever. That's the real difference."

Denber chuckled. "No argument from me."

Neither of them spoke for seconds that seemed unnaturally long. Ilanna didn't know what to say. Being around Denber—around any of the Hawks she'd grown up with—made her uncomfortable. She hated the fact that she owed them a debt, one she could never truly repay. After what they'd done for her…

"You want to come with?" Denber jerked his head toward the Aerie. "Sun won't set for another few hours, which gives us plenty of time to get the lay of the land. We could always use another set of eyes." He grinned. "'Specially ones attached to a brain like yours."

Ilanna returned the smile. "Thanks, but I've got another dragon to slay." She thrust a chin at Bryden's door. "Turning in my haul from Lord Ulimar's."

Denber groaned. "The way you went off on him in the meeting, you'll be lucky to get out of there alive."

"I can handle myself."

He rested a hand on her shoulder. "I know you can."

Ilanna forced herself not to tense at the friendly touch. She kept her face a mask of calm. Over the years she'd learned to hide the instinctive shudder of revulsion, to not let her true feelings show as long as *she* had control, could anticipate the contact. It did little to calm the roiling of her stomach, but she no longer jerked away.

He means well, she told herself.

"Be well, Denber." She turned and strode down the tunnel.

"And you, Ilanna." His voice rang out. "I'll be taking you up on that drink when I get back."

Ilanna didn't relax until a corner in the tunnel hid Denber from view. Her forearms ached from her clenched fists and her fingernails had deepened the ever-present indentations in her palms.

At the next intersection, she found Conn deep in conversation with Jarl. Jarl nodded at her as she passed—as loquacious a greeting as he could manage—but Conn ignored her. Her relationship with the older Hawk hadn't improved over the years. She hated his haughty demeanor. He, like many other Hawks, resented her success. Unlike the others, he'd made no secret of his feelings.

Jealousy makes ugly men.

Reaching Bryden's door, she took a deep breath, drew herself up, and knocked.

"Come."

She pushed the door open and strode into what Bryden liked to call his office. The rooms were spacious, as befitted a senior member of House Hawk, but filled with heavily-laden shelves and cabinets. An enormous wooden desk occupied a full quarter of the room. Behind it, Bryden sat in the plush chair he'd ordered from Malandria.

"I've—"

Bryden raised a finger but didn't look up from the stack of parchments in his hand for long moments.

Ilanna's lip curled. She fought down the urge to scatter Bryden's papers across the room. That wouldn't get her anywhere.

Finally, Bryden lifted his gaze. "Ahh, Ilanna." He adjusted his spectacles and peered down his nose at her. "Is there something I can help you with?" His honeyed tone turned her stomach. His words held as much warmth as the Frozen Sea.

"I've brought the haul from Lord Ulimar's." She reached into her purse and drew out ten golden coins. "Ten imperials."

Bryden stared down at the coins as if she'd deposited a fresh horse apple on his desk. "That's *it?*"

"You think I'm holding out on you, Bryden?"

He looked like he wanted to say yes, but managed to restrain himself.

"Do you need to search me?" She held out her arms. "I know you'll enjoy that." She had nothing to hide. The other ten imperials lay in a secret purse in her rooms.

He rolled his eyes, a shade of hazel not quite as dark as his thinning hair. "I expected more from you, that's all."

"Add that to the kickback from the Crown and you've nothing to complain about."

He gave a dismissive wave. "Oh, I make no protest about your earnings. You've done well enough for yourself." He waggled a finger at the ten golden coins. "But surely even *you* could have come away with a bit more for your trouble."

Ilanna ignored the jab. "What do I always tell you, Bryden?"

Bryden parroted her voice. "*Never let them know you're there.*" He snorted. "Seems a foolish way to operate."

"But that's *my* way. And have you had any reason to complain thus far?"

Reluctantly, Bryden gave a stiff shake of his head.

"Then let me do things my way. Now, do you want those imperials or should I keep them?"

Bryden's leg, injured in a fall a decade earlier, slowed his steps but not his hands. The coins disappeared into his desk with a speed any Fox would envy. He scribbled in a ledger and handed her a golden imperial. "Your share of the take."

Ilanna pocketed the coin. "I'll need more pennyweighters."

"I gave you *ten* of them just a—"

She pointed to the drawer where he'd stowed the coins. "Ten imperials, Bryden."

The Hawk shook his head, but drew out a purse from another drawer. "How many?" He made no effort to hide his exasperation.

"Ten'll do." She held out a hand.

Muttering under his breath about "waste", Bryden passed her ten of the gold-plated lead coins.

The door opened and three Hawks entered the office. The second-in-command couldn't carry out the jobs himself, so he'd convinced these Hawks—not the brightest in the House, but skilled enough to serve his purposes—to do his footwork. Much as she disliked the man personally, she couldn't fault his intellect. He'd kept these men alive thus far, an accomplishment in itself.

"Setting up the Lord Vorrel job, eh?" Ilanna looked down at Bryden's twisted leg, stretched under the table. "D'you plan to be there yourself, or is this another one you'll leave to your crew?"

Scowling, Bryden climbed to his feet. "I've had enough of you." He stood a full head taller than her, though his leg ruined his attempts to loom. "Some of us have actual *work* to do."

With an angelic smile, she turned and nodded to the Hawks standing behind her. "Good thing the gods gave him a brain as well as two working legs, eh?"

Bryden's growl was music to her ears as she slipped from the office. The door closed behind her with enough force to stir up dust. Chuckling, Ilanna strode through the Aerie and into the tunnels toward her rooms.

Just one more thing to get out of the way...

Chapter Three

Ilanna swallowed the acid surging to her throat and gave a suggestive moan. Allon lay on his back, eyes closed, his breath coming in short gasps of delight. The stink of sex hung thick in the air and his grunting echoed from the walls of her chamber in House Hawk.

She kept the undulations of her hips slow and steady to build the tension. Allon's breathing quickened and he reached up to grope at her breasts. She seized his wrists and pressed his hands onto the bed. He yielded with a delighted grin.

She continued her moaning; it convinced him she enjoyed it and hastened the end of the unpleasant affair. *Anything to be done with this.*

When the force of his thrusts increased, she rolled off him. He was properly primed; she could let him drive to completion. The begging, pleading look in his eyes filled her with disdain and revulsion, but she only smiled and beckoned him. She could put up with physical contact—even *this* sort—provided she remained in control of the situation.

Red-faced, shoulders knotted with exertion, he whispered inanities into her ear and writhed atop her like a ship in a storm. The heat of his body on hers sent ice trickling through her veins. Her stomach churned as she gripped the sheets, but she forced herself to move in time with Allon's frantic pumping. She resisted the urge to wipe the sweat dripping from his forehead.

To Ilanna, it seemed she watched everything from behind her own eyes. Allon touched someone else—she was simply cursed to be present. She gave the right responses, encouraging him with a touch, a movement. Yet nothing but a hollow numbness filled her, amplifying her disgust as he slid in and out of her.

His eyes went wide, his gasping grew loud and fast, and the muscles in his face tightened. Ilanna let out a simulated cry of pleasure as Allon jerked and spasmed in his final exertion.

Groaning, he rolled onto the bed beside her. With a feigned moan, Ilanna stretched her arms over her head and uncurled her toes.

"Sweet gods of Einan!" Allon clutched his chest. "How in the fiery hell do you do that to me every time?"

Ilanna plastered a smile of mock contentment on her face. "What can I say? You're just that good." He would never notice the rigidity of her spine or the way her stomach twisted at his touch.

Allon sighed and rolled onto his side. "With you, Ilanna, a man can never have enough." He leaned in for a kiss but she quickly sat upright.

"I'll bet you say that to all the girls." She clenched her jaw as his finger traced a line down her spine. Her stomach lurched, rejecting the very essence of his presence.

"You know you're the only one for me."

She hid a shiver beneath a sultry smile and climbed to her feet to face him, hands planted on her hips. As always, his gaze explored her form. There was a time she might have felt uncomfortable, self-conscious even, standing in front of him like this, her body on display. She'd learned better; her form was just one more tool to get what she wanted.

Allon slumped back, his breath coming fast. Ilanna's gaze fell on the vein pulsing in his neck. Men were always so vulnerable after they got what they wanted. Her fingers twitched, aching to grab one of the daggers in her bracer. She could kill him before his befuddled mind realized the danger.

Her right hand strayed to the bracer, her thumb tracing the outline of her favorite push-dagger. "Comfortable?"

Allon chuckled. "Best bed in the Guild."

"Been in that many, eh?" Ilanna scowled. "A Hound's gotta keep warm on those cold nights."

"Now that's not fair." Allon pouted—he no doubt thought it cute, but it made him look foolish. "You know I only like it because *you're* in it." He reached for her. "Or should be." His eyes dropped to her lithe form and his body stirred in response.

"None of that!" She snapped her fingers, her voice hard and commanding. "Time for you to be getting back to your House."

Disappointment flashed across his face. "Come on, Ilanna." His voice turned wheedling. "Surely you—"

"Need a good night of rest in my own bed? Absolutely." She strode to the chair and seized his clothes. "I always sleep better when I'm *alone*." She dropped his pants, tunic, and belt onto his chest.

Allon grunted as the Hound-engraved buckle of his belt slapped his face. "You sure know how to make a fellow feel welcome." He climbed to his feet, making no attempt to hide his nakedness, and slipped into his clothes.

Ilanna took in his sinewy chest and shoulders with the dispassion of a butcher examining a hung carcass. She snorted. "After what we just did, you've nothing to complain about." She reclined in a nearby chair and reached for the pitcher of Nyslian red he'd brought. The velvet vintage slid down her throat, the taste of oak, blackberries, and cloves lingering on her palate. She couldn't complain about his taste in wines.

He winced as he pulled his tunic over his head. He peered over his shoulder in an attempt to see the red lines her nails had carved into his back. "That good, eh?"

Ilanna gave him an encouraging smile and tilt of her head. "What can I say?" Experience had taught her to tell men what they *wanted* to hear rather than the truth. Nothing would put an end to his usefulness faster than learning of her true feelings about their encounters.

Allon grinned. "Maybe next time you'll take the bracer off."

"And be defenseless around a man with such dishonorable intentions?" She drew a throwing knife from the bracer. "A woman has to protect her honor and reputation."

"Is that why I always have to sneak in?" He raised an eyebrow. "And why you never come to House Hound?"

Ilanna gave him a smile sweet and thick as honey. "You sneak in to keep your skills sharp. A Hound who can't avoid detection is no better than a Grubber."

He grimaced and mimed a dagger to the chest. "Cold, Ilanna." His face grew serious. "My uncle knows about us, so what's the problem? Why do you want to keep it from the rest of House Hawk?"

"Because my business is my own." She crossed her arms beneath her breasts, emphasizing their roundness. His eyes dropped from her face. "Besides, just because my House Master knows I'm…entertaining his nephew, that doesn't mean the whole Guild has to find out."

Allon's mind, occupied with her nakedness, failed to muster a response.

"Off with you, Hound." She waved him away.

"Until next time, Hawk." With a grin, he opened her door, peered into the hall, and slipped out without a sound.

Ilanna remained motionless for ten thundering heartbeats, then darted into the small bathing chamber. Shuddering, she splashed water over her body, scrubbing her chest, face, neck, and between her legs to be rid of any traces of him. Her skin crawled at the memory of his touch, his sweat, his breath, as if infected by a disease that went bone deep.

The smell of Allon's pleasure twisted her stomach into knots. She tore off the bedsheets and hurled them into a corner. Reaching into the chest at the foot of her bed, she drew out a vial, uncorked it, and downed the contents in a single gulp. She'd learned to make the contraceptive potion years ago, a few months after Sabat.

Stomach burning, she slid to a seat, back against the wall, legs drawn to her chest. She reached for a dagger and clutched it in a death-grip. Closing her eyes, she took deep breaths and tried to drive off the sensations washing over her: the agony of her hip, injured in a fall from the Black Spire; the taste of blood and dust in her mouth as Sabat smashed her face against the floor; the fetid smell and the heat of his breath on her face.

She gritted her teeth against a surge of acid. *I will do what I must!* She repeated the words, clinging to them as she had that night. As she had when she lay in bed recovering from Sabat's vicious attack, and again when Journeyman Tyman presented her with the tea that would end her pregnancy.

She'd survived. She'd had her vengeance on the Bloodbear apprentice. The image of his death still kept her awake at night, just as the memory of him forcing his way inside her. She'd vowed never again to be weak. Everything she'd done since that day had ensured she kept that promise.

Sabat had shown her the truth that night: she had to be harder, crueler if she wanted to survive. She wouldn't let herself be used; she would use others first. No matter how much it made her cringe to do it.

The words of Croquembouche, a courtesan from The Arms of Heaven in Voramis, rang in her mind. *"You think I like doing this? The feeling of those grubby hands in all the wrong places? Not a bleedin' chance, girl. But it gets me what I want."* The fact that Croquembouche had become the madame of the house—buying her former madame's share of the brothel—proved she knew her business.

Ilanna had discovered the truth of the courtesan's words on multiple occasions. Allon was just the latest in a string of people who served her purposes. He wasn't the first who'd fallen prey to the allures of her body. He wouldn't be the last. Once he stopped being useful, she would find someone else.

He had his uses, for now. As Master Hawk's nephew, he elevated her status in the House Master's eyes. As a Hound, he could procure things she couldn't. His skills as a tracker and hunter had come in handy on more than one occasion. It was why she had allowed him to touch her in the first place. She'd found the right incentive. All she had to do was moan and pretend to enjoy his touch at the right times, and he'd do whatever she wanted.

At that moment, she wanted nothing to do with the man—with any of the Guild. She ached to be free of the stuffy underground warren and the stink of sweat permeating her cramped chamber. She had to flee everything that reminded her of the life her father had condemned her to.

She just wanted to be home.

Midnight shadows swallowed Ilanna as she dropped from the rooftops into the narrow alleyway. With a quick glance around, she slipped down the empty streets. The silence of Old Town Market after dark set her nerves on edge. Something prickled in the back of her neck, as if eyes tracked her movements.

Impossible. She'd taken a circuitous route across the rooftops to reach her destination. Few in her House had the skill to follow her along the Hawk's Highway. *Besides, the only people with any reason to follow me are the Bloodbears, and they have as much stealth as a Royal Parade. It has to be my imagination.*

Pulling her dark cloak tighter, she hurried along the familiar cobblestone roads. She leapt the wall and crept across the muddy ground without a sound. Testing the door, she found it locked.

Again, Ria?

Kneeling, she drew her lockpicks from her bracer and inserted them into the lock. Her fingers moved with dexterity as she teased the tumblers open. The lodestone on her bracer held the multiple picks and rakes she needed for the job. After a few minutes, the lock opened with a *click* that echoed loud in the darkness.

The door opened and closed on well-oiled hinges, and Ilanna shot the deadbolt behind her. She crept up the stairs in silence.

The sound of heavy breathing filled the upstairs room. A sliver of moonlight shone on smooth ebony skin, a thick nose, and full lips. Dark eyes opened, and the girl in the bed jerked upright as she caught sight of Ilanna standing in the doorway.

"Easy, Ria!" Ilanna held up her hands. "It's just me."

"Ilanna?" Ria removed her hand from beneath her pillow—from the dagger she kept hidden.

"The doors are locked. You're safe."

Ria pulled the covers to her chest. Her eyes followed Ilanna's movements with their usual wariness.

Ilanna studied the sleeping form huddled beneath the pile of blankets. She smiled at the quiet snore that rose from the boy. From her pouch, she drew a small tin figurine: a hawk with wings spread wide. She bent and kissed her child's forehead. *For you, my little hawk.* The scent of his sweat-soaked hair and face drove all thoughts of the Guild from her mind.

Ria made to stand but Ilanna held out a hand. "Stay with him, please. Kodyn always sleeps better when you're here."

With a nod, Ria curled up beside the boy. Her hand slipped under the pillow, to the blade she never slept without.

Aware of Ria's eyes tracking her movements, Ilanna draped a blanket over the nearby stuffed chair and sat. She closed her eyes and leaned her head against the chair's back as her fingers toyed with one of Kodyn's black curls. The boy's presence felt like a soothing balm that erased all trace of disgust at Allon's touch.

This child—*her* child—gave her a reason to endure Allon's pawing and grunting, to face danger every time she crept into another mansion. She would do what she must, for his sake.

Chapter Four

Ilanna jerked awake. Her right hand flashed toward her bracer, and she'd half-drawn the dagger before she recognized her surroundings. Motes of dust danced in the sunlight streaming through the window. Blankets and pillows lay in disorder on the now empty bed. The sound of childish laughter drifted up the stairs.

She sat up and groaned at the twinge in her neck. Standing, she rolled her shoulders to loosen the kinks. *I've got to get Ria to start sleeping somewhere other than my bed, at least on those few nights I can make it home.*

Shielding her eyes from the too-bright daylight, she threw the blankets, sheets, and pillows into place on her bed. She hadn't slept there in months—not since Ria—but it belonged to her nonetheless.

Ilanna stretched and her arms brushed the low ceiling. *Funny how it felt so much larger when I was young.* Her eyes fell on the mirror that still sat on the table where she'd brushed her hair the day her father sold her to the Night Guild fifteen long years before.

She smiled at the familiar creak of the stairs as she descended. *So many memories.*

The sitting room below looked cheerier than it had when she lived here. Carved wooden toys littered the floor and Ria had draped colorful blankets over the plush armchair where Ilanna had spent hours sewing clothes to earn the few coins her father had spent on liquor.

The bright Voramian rug in the center of the room hid bloodstains—all that remained of Sabat. That, and the memories of his shrieks as she hacked and slashed at him with the same knife he'd used to kill Ethen, his grunts as he forced himself on her. The cruel Bloodbear apprentice tormented her even from the grave. She slept little. Her duties as a Hawk kept her busy, but whenever she closed her eyes, she saw his face, heard his screams. She'd relived Sabat's death countless times in the last five years. It woke her in the middle of the night, soaked in sweat, gasping for breath. It brought a hard, cold smile to her face, served as a reminder of her weakness. She would never be weak again.

Through the open door, she caught a glimpse of Kodyn playing with his carved hawks in the muddy garden. Ria sat beside him, clad in a comfortable, long-sleeved shirt, her finger trailing in the soil as Kodyn chattered like a sparrow.

Ilanna studied the dark-skinned girl in the garden. *She's looking more relaxed these days.* Ria sat straight, her shoulders free of the hunch that had plagued her for months. Her eyes still had the guarded look Ilanna knew only too well, but the tension in her face and mouth had lessened. *Hard to believe she's the same girl I found in that brothel almost a year ago.* She'd actually begun to smile when talking with Kodyn.

Ilanna's stomach tightened as she strode into the kitchen. Her gaze darted to the head of the table. Once, her father's moldering corpse had occupied the seat of honor. She'd replaced the furniture, hurled his rotted remains into a pile of debris, but she would never truly erase that faint, lingering musk of death from her memory.

She plucked an apple from the bowl on the table, drew one of her knives, and sliced the fruit into pieces. The herbs hanging by the windowsill filled the room with a clean, fresh smell. Taking a deep breath, Ilanna sat back and savored the tart apple.

She had to get back to the Guild, had to start planning her entry to Count Chatham's mansion. But for a few moments, she wanted to sit and bask in the quiet peace of her home.

Such an odd thought. My *home.*

She'd spent the first eight years of her life in this house with her father, mother, and sister. Baby Rose had died the same day as Mama. Her father had blamed her for the deaths. A year before, he'd borrowed from the Night Guild to pay the physicker's fees when she broke her arm. When he couldn't pay the debt, the Guild came calling. The beating left him unable to work and the pain drove him to drink. He hadn't *stopped* drinking. The memory of her father's bloated, rotting corpse disturbed her far less than it should. He'd deserved the miserable death after what he did to her, selling his own daughter to thugs, murderers, and thieves.

Finding the deed to the house had proven impossible. She had the skill to break into every money-lender's office in the city. But without knowing who claimed the property after her father's death, she had no idea where to begin the search.

She'd turned to House Hound—specifically, Journeyman Allon, Master Hawk's nephew. Allon had done in two weeks what she'd failed to do in three months. Upon presenting her with the deed, he'd refused payment for his services. Instead, he insisted he wanted nothing more than to share a drink with the most beautiful woman in the Night Guild. Of course, he'd intended to turn one drink into many, but Ilanna held him to his word. With a roguish grin, he kissed her hand and bade her goodnight.

Master Hawk held affection for few, but his Hound nephew counted among them. At the next House meeting, he'd assigned her first skull-headed dagger. She had a way to raise her standing in her House Master's eyes.

Allon had pursued her with fierce determination that almost matched her resistance to his advances. But even a man had his limits. After being rebuffed over and over—always with a flirtatious smile—he'd turned his eyes elsewhere. The other women in the Guild made no secret of their desire for the lean man with a charming smile and nimble fingers.

Ilanna wouldn't be parted from so valuable a tool. He'd proven useful on many occasions, tracking hard-to-acquire items vital for her jobs, planning secret ways to enter well-guarded mansions, and even locating people she needed found. She could endure his desire for her. She'd survived far worse. Indeed, that desire gave her sway over him. Every time she allowed him to her bed, she gained greater control. The more he wanted her, the more he would consent to being used by her.

Little feet pounded on the wooden floorboards of the main room and a bundle of muddy clothes and messy hair hurled itself into her lap. "Mama!"

Ilanna wrapped her arms around the child and planted a kiss on his cheek. "Hello, baby." She wiped mud from her lips. "You're a mess!"

"Ria and I were playing in the garden." Kodyn thrust a chubby finger toward the open door. "We were building castles and towers and bridges and palaces and…"

Ilanna listened patiently as he explained about the kingdom he had constructed from mud and the princess trapped in a tower. His words grew harder to understand the more excited he became, but Ilanna tried to follow along.

"Are you hungry? Want a piece of Mama's apple?"

Kodyn snatched the fruit in muddy hands and stuffed it into his mouth. Ilanna gathered him into her arms as he chattered around the mouthful of apple. She had so little time with him—she would make each minute count.

"Did you bring me a new birdie, Mama?"

Ilanna nodded. "It's on the table beside your bed. For my little hawk."

The midwife, an ancient, wizened woman with dark skin and stories of her life in a place called the Twelve Kingdoms, had suggested the name *Khodein*— "hawk" in the language of her people. As a child, he'd spent hours staring at the hawk stitched into her leather vest. For his first toy, she'd sewn scraps of cloth into the shape of the bird and stuffed it with wool. Every time she came, she brought him a new bit of wood, scrimshaw, or stone carved into the likeness of a hawk.

"Did you see my new birdie, Ria?" His warbling voice grew more animated as the dark-skinned girl entered the kitchen. "Mama said she brought me one. Can we play when we come back from the market? You promised we'd go."

The girl nodded and held out a hand. Kodyn wriggled down from Ilanna's lap, leaving muddy splotches on her clothes, and raced toward Ria.

"Be careful, Ria." Ilanna fought back the anxiety building in her chest. "Don't let anything happen to him."

Ria twitched open her coat, revealing a slim dagger hidden in her waistband. With a nod, she allowed the boy to drag her out the door.

Ilanna drew in a deep breath and let it out slowly. The nearby Old Town Market was the territory of the Fifth Claw, the toughest, cruelest of the Bloodbear apprentices. Sabat's gang. Yet she couldn't keep Kodyn locked in the house. She knew what dangers lurked in the city but could only do so much to protect him. She had to leave the rest to Ria.

Her heart ached every time she left Kodyn, yet she had no choice. People would grow suspicious if she spent too long away from the Guild. She had to earn her keep. That meant she had to trust the girl to look after Kodyn.

Ria had proven herself trustworthy. After what the girl had endured, Ilanna knew she would die before letting anything happen to her son.

Forcing the worries from her mind, Ilanna stood and reached for the earthen jar on the shelf beside the window. Within lay a purse. She spilled the contents into her palm and counted the handful of silver drakes.

Enough for a few more weeks, but it can't hurt to add more.

She drew out two of the golden imperials she'd stolen from Lord Ulimar and dropped them into the purse. Replacing the jar, she strode to the sitting room, knelt beside the fireplace, and pried up the three loose floorboards beneath the rug.

An iron-bound chest nestled in the small space she'd hollowed out in the foundation. She loosened the knots holding her forearm bracer in place enough to pluck out the hidden key, inserted it, and twisted. The lock opened with a *click* that sounded oddly loud in the silence of her house. Lifting the lid, she peered at the pile of glimmering metal within.

Eight thousand, four hundred, and twenty-two imperials. Eight golden coins clinked as she added them to the pile. *Make that eight thousand, four hundred, and thirty.*

It was a hefty fortune by the standards of a common Praamian, but nowhere near enough for her. If she wanted to be free of the Night Guild, she'd need at least four or five times that.

She closed and locked the lid, replaced the floorboards, and smoothed the rug. She scanned the hiding place with a critical eye. No one, not even Ria, could know about it. Its existence broke Guild law.

As a Hawk, she was duty-bound to report everything she earned to the Night Guild. Each House kept accounts of their Journeymen's earnings: each coin stolen, each piece of jewelry fenced. The Guild's official receiver actually issued receipts she had to deliver to Bryden. The Guild required control over every copper bit of illicit activity in the city. It took the lion's share of her earnings, leaving her with a meager ten percent.

Bryden's accounts held a record of Ilanna's official wealth: four thousand, six hundred and fifty imperials. The amount grew each month courtesy of kickbacks from the Crown. She added to it every time she went out on a job.

If she followed Guild law, she would never earn enough money to be free. So she failed to report *all* her income to Bryden. A risky gamble, but she had no choice. She wouldn't let Kodyn fall into the Guild's clutches. She had only a few more years to take him—and herself—away from Praamis. For that, she needed money.

Time to get back to the Guild. As a full Journeyman, she could come and go as she pleased, but she had to keep up appearances.

She paused in the garden to study Kodyn's mud pile. As always, her eyes drifted toward the tree growing beside the creek that flowed through the property. The tree had flourished since she added Sabat's body to the soil. A few young flower buds appeared among the dark green leaves. With a cold smile, she vaulted the wall.

Instead of returning to Old Town Market, she took the longer way around. She wouldn't risk any Fox or Bloodbear spotting her.

She slipped into an alley and, with a quick glance to make sure no one saw her, climbed a stack of pallets. She shimmied up a reinforced drainpipe, slipped beneath an overhanging eave, and ducked through a small crack between two buildings. A rope ladder hung from a rooftop two stories above. Within a minute, Ilanna stood on the Hawk's Highway.

She filled her lungs with the warm mid-morning air, savored its freshness. She had no reason to rush back to the Guild. Count Chatham's mansion could wait until tonight. She would enjoy the trek across the rooftops.

"Ilanna!" The sound drifted toward her.

She spun, searching for the source, and caught sight of Willem racing across the rooftops. He moved with a wild recklessness that surpassed his usual temerity. She stifled a cry as he stumbled, but he caught himself and charged toward her. Something about him reeked of urgency.

She sprinted toward him. "What's wrong, Lem?"

Fear filled his wide eyes and horror turned his face pale. "I-It's Denber and Werrin!"

Chapter Five

"Citizens of Praamis, I stand before you as Chief Justiciar, servant of the Watcher." Duke Elodon Phonnis' words rang out across the hushed crowd filling Watcher's Square. The Royal Palace rose behind him, a solid bulwark that lent authority to his voice. "For generations, the line of Keadanis has endeavored to keep the peace in our fair city. King Ohilmos, first of his name, has toiled day and night to guarantee the safety, prosperity, and well-being of each and every one of you."

The Duke's brow furrowed as he leaned forward. "But there are those who would defy our King, the anointed of Kiro, the Master." He swept an arm to the side. "Behold the enemies of justice and peace!"

Heart lurching, Ilanna's gaze followed the pointing finger. Two Journeymen—one wearing the white of House Hound, the other clad in Fox orange—stood with hands bound behind their backs. Beside them, Werrin coughed and spat blood. A dark bruise spread across his right side and he winced with each breath. Denber fared worst of all. Blood trickled from his split lip and his right eye had swollen closed. His clothing hung in tatters. He rested his weight on his left leg; a gash in his right thigh oozed crimson.

Nooses hung above the Journeymen's heads.

"These four stand accused of the heinous crime of entering Lord Morrin's home while he slept. I have here proof of their murderous intention." He held Denber and Werrin's daggers aloft.

A murmur ran through the crowd. Ilanna clenched her jaw and gripped Willem's hand tighter.

"There is no greater threat to a man's life and livelihood than these men. Imagine, if you will, the horror of being roused from sound slumber to find a vicious cutthroat in your home, your place of refuge! Our King has promised you safety, yet these men betray it for the promise of gold." He slammed a fist on the wooden railing. "Such a violation will not stand! The King's justice—nay, the *Watcher's* justice—will be carried out."

Ilanna tensed at the cries of "Justice!" The chant swelled to a roar as hundreds of throats joined in. Dread pierced her like a knife to the gut. *No! Not Denber.*

Duke Phonnis held up his hands and the crowd quieted. "The Watcher is the god of vengeance, and there are none more deserving of punishment than these. Yet he is also a god of justice and, as such, he has given us a way to put the guilt or innocence of these men to the test. Behold, the Field of Mercy."

The crowd cheered as the Duke thrust a finger at an empty field on the far side of Watcher's Square. He turned to the four prisoners. "You have defied the laws of Praamis, spurned your King's offer of peace. Thus, you are condemned to face the judgment of the Long Keeper himself. But you are given a choice: the noose, or the Watcher's justice. Which do you choose?"

Willem went rigid and Ilanna squeezed his hand with all her strength. "Don't do anything stupid!" she hissed.

He met her gaze. Fire raged in his eyes. The same inferno blazed in her gut, but she had to be rational. Forty guards stood between the crowd and the hanging platform. She couldn't let Lem throw his life away in the vain hope of saving Werrin or Denber.

The Duke stood before the Fox. "What is your choice?"

The Fox spoke in a quiet voice. "The noose."

The crowd groaned, but Duke Phonnis held up his hand and moved down the line. "What is your choice?"

"I choose…" The Hound's voice cracked. "…the Field of Mercy."

A delighted roar swelled in the square.

"I'll take my chances with the Field of Mercy," Werrin said before the Duke could ask him. Confidence filled his eyes and he spat blood at the Duke's feet.

Duke Phonnis didn't flinch. "So be it." He came to stand before Denber. "What say you? How do you choose to greet the Long Keeper?"

Denber straightened, wincing. He met the Duke's gaze and spoke in a clear, strong voice. "The noose."

Ilanna's heart sank. In the Field of Mercy, he had a chance. *Why, Denber?*

"You say you offer mercy." Denber's harsh laughter carried through the square. "But it is nothing more than a mockery." His face hardened in defiance. "I will face the Keeper with both eyes open, not drowning in mud."

The Duke gave a solemn nod and turned to the crowd. "The condemned have chosen. Let the Watcher's justice be carried out."

A squad of Praamian Guards marched up the steps and seized Werrin and the Hound's arms. The crowd cheered as the olive-clad guards dragged the two thieves through the square toward the Field of Mercy. Rotten fruit pelted Werrin, and the Hound sagged as a rock struck his head.

"Peace!" Duke Phonnis cried. "Peace, good people of Praamis. They will face the justice of the gods, not ours."

Willem jerked forward as Werrin passed within a few paces. Ilanna wrapped her arms around his throat and pulled him back. "Don't do it, Lem! Don't get yourself killed, too."

Willem fought for a moment then sagged in her arms. She clung to him—as much to restrain him as to anchor herself in the midst of this insanity.

The Praamian Guards shoved Werrin and the Hound into the Field of Mercy. Werrin spat blood at one, and the man backhanded him with a mailed fist. Werrin staggered but caught himself.

Duke Phonnis' voice rang out behind her. "Let the Watcher's justice be served."

The Praamian Guard prodded Werrin and the Hound with their spears. Snarling curses, Werrin started across the expanse. The Hound moved off to the right.

"Reach the far side of the Field and the Watcher has judged you not guilty."

The Field of Mercy stretched a hundred paces to the right and left, but only forty across. Such a short distance over such innocuous-looking terrain, yet everyone in Praamis knew the truth.

The Hound met the Watcher's justice first. The earth cracked beneath his foot and he sank to his knee. He struggled to break free but the ground devoured him with a relentless inevitability. The cheering of the crowd soon drowned out his cries.

Ilanna's gut twisted as she watched Werrin. He moved at a steady pace, placing his feet with caution. They'd spent years learning to read the surfaces of the Praamian rooftops. If anyone had a chance, it was—

She sucked in a breath as Werrin's heel sank into a depression in the earth. The Hawk leaped backward just as the ground caved beneath him. Mud swirled and clutched at his toes. He cast a glance over his shoulder. His face had gone pale and the wild light of desperation filled his eyes.

Willem gripped her hand with bone-crushing strength. He held his breath, his eyes never leaving Werrin.

Come on, Werrin! You can do this. A dozen paces and he'd be free.

Werrin moved more slowly now. A palpable tension hung thick over the Watcher's Square as the crowd watched the Hawk. Gasps rose from a few throats as he evaded another patch of hidden mud.

Dread knotted Ilanna's gut in the heartbeat before Werrin took his next step. The patch of grass he stepped on looked too thin, too spindly to be growing on solid ground. Her breath caught in her throat as he sank to his thigh in the mud. Werrin struggled and twisted, spreading out his weight to stop the quicksand from dragging him under. But the Hawk fought the earth itself. He had no hope of winning.

Ilanna's blood pounded in her ears. She couldn't watch it yet couldn't look away. He sank with a terrifying slowness. Fingers of mud crawled up his hips, his torso, his chest, working up to his shoulders and neck. Panic twisted his features as he battled the inexorable. Yet he refused to cry out. Even as the ground swallowed him whole, he summoned the strength for one last defiant shout.

A deafening roar swelled from the crowd as Werrin's hair disappeared beneath the mud. Her hand ached from Willem's grip, but she didn't release him. Ice seeped into her veins as she turned back to the platform where Denber stood. His eyes remained fixed on the Field of Mercy, and his face had grown hard, grim. Beside him, the Fox wept.

Duke Phonnis spoke with a solemn voice and a sorrowful expression. "The Watcher's justice has been served. They now stand before the Long Keeper."

At his gesture, two Praamian Guards brought buckets onto the stage and placed them before Denber and the Fox.

"These two have chosen the noose. But before their sentence is carried out, I would speak to their comrades hiding among you."

His hand dropped to the sword of the Chief Justiciar on his belt. "To any of you vermin who are watching—and make no mistake, there are those among you who strive against peace—let this message ring clear: we will no longer abide lawlessness. For too long, criminals have filled our city with their poison, bringing death, despair, and misery to the innocent, hard-working citizens of Praamis. That ends this day."

He surveyed the crowd, then continued. "No longer will we tolerate the thieves and murderers that fill our city. I, Duke Elodon Phonnis, Chief Justiciar, servant of the Watcher, give you my pledge: I will eradicate this plague that rots our fair Praamis from within. There will be no quarter given, no leniency." He thrust a finger toward Denber and the Fox. "As with these, so it shall be with every one of the lawless scum who would flout the laws of our King. This I swear."

The Duke's gaze swept the crowd. For a moment, his eyes seemed to rest on her, piercing to her very core.

"You know who you are. You know what you have done." His face hardened. "You will not escape me. You will not escape justice. I will find you."

She pressed her lips tight against a scream of anger and sorrow. Beside her, Willem trembled with rage. Hopelessness washed over her, rendered her immobile, as the Praamian Guards prodded Denber and the Fox forward.

The Fox climbed onto the overturned bucket and a guard draped a noose over his head. Denber tried to step up but sagged as his right leg gave out. He coughed, spraying blood. Two guards lifted him from the ground and supported his weight on the bucket. Two more olive-clad soldiers hung weighted belts around their ankles.

Ilanna understood. Denber wouldn't manage five steps across the Field of Mercy. He'd chosen to die with dignity. Despite the weakness in his legs and the visible agony etched on his face, he held his head high as the noose encircled his throat. His eyes met hers and a smile tugged on his split lips.

Duke Phonnis' voice echoed as if from a vast distance. "Let the Watcher's justice be served."

She held Denber's eyes for a heartbeat. The guards kicked the bucket from beneath him.

He jerked as the rope tightened. His eyes went wide, his tongue protruding from his mouth. Ilanna's horror grew with every frantic spasm. Minutes ticked by, and the crowd murmured as the condemned men gasped for breath. Their faces reddened and turned purple as the ropes starved their bodies of oxygen.

Ilanna couldn't tear her eyes from the swinging figure. The swollen, twisted features familiar yet so alien. All that remained of the man who had trained her, befriended her, tried his best to protect her.

With horrible, agonizing slowness, the twitching of Denber's legs stilled.

Chapter Six

The liquor burned Ilanna's throat and gut but she swallowed and took another long pull. The foul reek of the alcohol brought back stomach-twisting memories of her father. Right now, she welcomed them; anything to get the agonized face of her friend out of her thoughts.

She'd watched him die a hundred times in her mind. She didn't dare close her eyes for fear of seeing Denber again: silent, gasping for breath, legs jerking as he kicked his last. His unseeing stare when life finally faded from his eyes.

No tears came. She hadn't cried since Ethen, not even when the torment of birthing Kodyn had stolen her senses. She felt hollow and could find no way to fill the void.

Death followed her like a shadow. She'd lost too many people. Her mother and baby Rose, stolen by illness before her seventh nameday. Bert, killed in an accident she'd caused. Ethen, murdered by Sabat. No one had heard from Prynn in two years. The Night Guild had sent Hounds to track his whereabouts in vain. They counted him dead.

And now Denber and Werrin.

The loss of Werrin hit Willem hardest. He hadn't spoken a word since the Watcher's Square. He'd lain in his bed for hours, silent as Denber's corpse, eyes unseeing, the only sign of life the rise and fall of his chest. Had she lost him, too?

She took another pull at the liquor. *Damn you, Denber!* The glass bottle trembled in her fingers. She wanted to hurl it against the wall, wanted to hurl *herself* against the wall if it gave her an escape from the nightmare of her reality. A reality without the one person in the Guild who had genuinely cared for her.

Denber had been the first person to greet her in House Hawk. He'd stood up to Conn for her, encouraged her in her training, taken her under his wing. The Night Guild hadn't broken his spirit, hadn't stolen his easy smile and friendly, open manner. After Ethen's death, he'd been a quiet presence, solid as the stone walls around her. He never spoke a word but the worry in his eyes had shown his concern for her.

She'd hated that concern, resented him for it. She was Ilanna of House Hawk; she needed no one. Sabat's death proved to all that she could fight her own battles.

Yet the day she discovered her pregnancy, she'd turned to Denber for help. He'd come up with the audacious plan to hide her child from the Night Guild. He'd convinced Master Hawk to grant permission to work a job in Voramis—a job that would keep her out of the city for the months when her pregnancy grew too noticeable to hide.

But he hadn't stopped at that. He'd borne the burden of her debts to the Guild when she couldn't steal. While she lay in bed recovering from childbirth, he'd run himself ragged stealing enough to cover for her. Despite his protests, she had repaid him twice over—Journeyman Bryden held a small fortune in Denber's name. But she could never repay him for keeping her secret. Especially now.

For four years, she'd kept him at arm's length. The knowledge of her debt to him stood like an insurmountable barrier. She'd feared he would use her secret against her and had never been comfortable around him since.

She'd also resented his efforts to protect her from the Night Guild; he saw her as weak, so he tried to shield her. Sabat had proven that belief correct. She *had* been weak. Yet her vengeance on the Bloodbear had shown her the truth: she could be strong and self-sufficient. She didn't need protection and she'd damn well make sure everyone knew it, even if that meant pushing away the only person she could truly consider a "friend" in the Guild. The wall she'd built between them kept them apart. She would never have a chance to tear down that wall now. She would never have her friend back.

So she drank. She understood her father now. The liquor didn't erase the pain but numbed it, made it easier to forget. Forget the horrible, choking, gagging sound, the spike of fear driven into her gut at the sight of Denber's corpse twisting in the wind.

A *click* sounded behind her. She whirled, drawing her dagger. The room spun and she staggered.

"Ilanna!"

She caught herself on the stone wall. "I'm fine," she growled.

Concern furrowed Allon's brow. "I can see that." He wrinkled his nose at the liquor bottle. "Smell of that stuff makes it perfectly clear how 'fine' you are." His eyes darted to her dagger. "Want to put that thing away?"

Ilanna slipped the blade into its sheath on the third try. She collapsed onto the bed, not even feeling the *thunk* of her head hitting the wall. "What d'you want?" She glared at him. "S'not really a good time for me right now."

Allon sat on the bed beside her. "I didn't come for *that*." He gripped her hand. "I came to check on you. It's not easy to lose friends."

Ilanna sneered. "I don't need friends!" The liquor made her head whirl, her movements clumsy. The last thing she wanted was for anyone—especially Allon—to see her in her current state. "Leave me alone."

"I'm not leaving, Ilanna." He pried the bottle from her fingers. "Not while you're trying to drown your pain in drink."

"What do you care?" She pushed him away. "You're a *Hound*! They meant nothing to you."

"Fair." He shrugged. "But my House lost a Journeyman today, too. And he's not the first one we've lost. Duke Phonnis has increased his efforts to suppress the Night Guild ever since the Black Spire." He didn't meet her eyes.

The Duke's words swam through her drink-benumbed mind. *"You know who you are. You know what you have done. You will not escape me. You will not escape justice. I will find you."*

Duke Phonnis knew the Night Guild had breached the Black Spire and *this* was his response. He'd have his vengeance—if not on her, the thief who had humiliated him, he would make her friends suffer. If only he knew how close the blow had struck.

Worst of all, she could do nothing to stop it. He disguised retribution as carrying out the law. The Chief Justiciar of Praamis, highest authority after King Ohilmos, retaliated by killing her friends before her eyes. The Field of Mercy made a mockery of the "Watcher's justice", as he called it. No one had ever survived the crossing.

The Duke had declared war on the Night Guild, declared war on *her* when he took her friends. She would not let it stand.

"You've got that look, Ilanna." Allon's eyebrows drew together. "The one where someone dies."

Ilanna balled a fist. "You're damned right. I'm going to make him pay. I'm going to kill the Duke."

Allon shook his head. "You can't."

"Can't?" Ilanna whirled on him, heat flaring in her chest. "You think I'm not—"

"No!" Allon held up his hands. "What I mean is you can't go after the Duke, not directly."

She bared her teeth. "Why not? He'll die just as easily as…" She caught herself before she spoke Sabat's name. "…anyone else."

"Yes, but remember, he's the King's brother. Kill him, and you'll start a war."

"Good!"

"Not good." He spoke in a measured tone. "Think about it first. King Ohilmos has the Praamian Guard. There're more of them than there are of us.

33

Even if every Guild member stood against the Praamian Guard, we'd lose. We can't wage war on the King. Which means you can't harm the Duke."

Ilanna threw herself to her feet. "Don't presume to tell me what I can and can't do, Allon!" She thrust a finger at the door. "If I want the Duke dead, I'll bloody well put the dagger in him myself."

"I'm not telling you what to do. I'm just trying to stop you from ending up like Den—"

Her fist drove into his face, snapping his head back. "Don't do that, you *bastard*. Denber wasn't a fool. He didn't get sloppy or make a mistake. So don't use his name to try to scare me."

Allon stiffened. "You're right. I shouldn't have said that." He worked his jaw muscles. "Not today. Not so soon after, and not with you like this."

He stood and strode toward the door but stopped. "Let's pretend this never happened. I didn't come to insult you. I wanted to check on you. Crazy thing is, I actually care that you're hurting. But I can see you need to be alone to process things your way." He paused with a hand on the door latch. "I can't tell you what to do, but I can say this: you can't take his life without starting a war, but there has to be something else you can take from him. Think about that. You know where to find me."

Ilanna said nothing as the door closed. She was beyond caring. *How dare he come here and try to give me instructions? He may be Master Hawk's nephew, but he has no right!*

Yet his words made sense. The rational part of her mind, the part not clouded by alcohol and rage, knew she couldn't murder the Duke. The Night Guild wouldn't survive an all-out war with the Crown. She had to do something. *But what?*

Her thoughts refused to coalesce. She could think of nothing but sorrow at her loss, anger at the Duke, and helplessness as she watched her friend hang. Right now, she wanted just one thing.

She slipped into her dark cloak and fled the room. She leapt onto the Perch, sped her way up the ladders, walkways, and ropes. The silence of the Aerie rang in her ears. Once, shouts and laughter had filled the vaulted room. Denber, Prynn, Bert, Willem, and Werrin had chased each other through the tangled maze. Only she and Willem remained.

The chill night air of the Praamis rooftops drove back the liquor's haze. She took a deep breath, welcomed the bite of cold. She ran until her arms, legs, and lungs burned from the exertion. She pushed her body to its limits. Anything to push away the memories of her friend's death.

It seemed an eternity before she dropped into the silent streets of Old Town Market, leapt the wall, and stole into her house. She made no sound as she crept up the stairs and slipped into bed beside Kodyn. The child murmured in his sleep but Ria didn't move. Ilanna didn't have the heart to kick the girl from the bed. Ria needed Kodyn's presence as much as she did.

For tonight, the three of them would share the bed. Ilanna closed her eyes and wrapped her arms around Kodyn. She needed the boy's warmth against her flesh, needed to feel his soft hands in hers.

She'd always dreamed of the day she could introduce her son to "Uncle Denber". That day would never come now. But Kodyn's existence remained a secret thanks to Denber. In a way, Denber lived on through Kodyn, just as Ethen did. For now, that had to be enough.

Chapter Seven

Ilanna's mouth watered as she added a pinch of Ria's dried rosemary to the skillet. A chunk of bread sizzled in the butter and she flipped it to brown the other side. Behind her, Kodyn chattered happily from the comfort of his chair, filling the air with tales of the previous day's exploration of Old Town Market.

Ria sat with Kodyn, trying to scoop the occasional spoonful of thick porridge into his mouth whenever he ran out of breath. The mess running down his face and clothing illustrated her limited success.

Ilanna lifted the bread from the skillet and onto a wooden plate. Using a knife from her bracer, she sliced a chunk of cheese from the wedge sitting on the shelf.

A smile tugged at Ria's lips as Ilanna placed the steaming food before her. The smile slipped as her eyes darted to Ilanna's knife.

"Oh, sorry." Ilanna wiped the blade on a wet cloth and replaced it in her bracer.

Ria shook her head and bit into the bread. Kodyn laughed and pointed at the melted cheese dripping down the girl's chin. Ria responded by filling his mouth with porridge.

Ilanna smiled as she turned back to the skillet atop the wood stove. She had so few moments to relax like this. But after yesterday, she needed them.

Thoughts of the previous day brought back the gloom and her shoulders drooped. She forced herself to take a bite of the bread Ria had brought home from the market. The flavor of herbs and garlic couldn't drown the bitterness filling her mouth. The pang of sorrow twisted her stomach, killed her appetite.

She took a seat and leaned back in her chair. She studied the dark-haired, food-stained boy beside her and, as always, her gaze drifted to Ria.

Ria's dark skin intrigued Ilanna. Her own Praamian copper-colored skin was darker than the paler Voramians, but Ria's ebony coloring stood out among even the few dusky Al Hani traders who visited Praamis. Ria had a longer nose, plumper, darker lips, and black hair with far more kinks and curls than Ilanna's arrow-straight locks. She also stood half a hand taller, with a willowy grace

Ilanna envied. Thieving would be much simpler without curving hips and breasts to stop her from slipping through small spaces.

Ilanna had no idea where Ria came from. She'd hesitated to ask. Since the night Ilanna found her in that brothel—an unsanctioned establishment she'd stumbled upon while fleeing from the Duke's Arbitors—Ria hadn't spoken of her past. Hadn't spoken much about anything, for that matter.

"Mama?" Kodyn's voice interrupted her musings.

"Yes, my love?" She turned her attention to the porridge-covered child.

"All done. Can I go play now?"

Ilanna turned to Ria. "He eat enough?"

Ria looked down at Kodyn's bowl and shrugged.

"Very well." Ilanna lifted Kodyn from his chair and pulled him into her lap. "But first, you have to give Mama a kiss."

Kodyn pressed his lips to her cheek. "There."

"Hmm. I think Mama needs more." She held up three fingers. "This many more."

"Mama!" Kodyn tried to squirm out of her grip.

She held him fast, and he squealed as she tickled him. Finally, he relented and gave her the requisite kisses.

"Now I go?"

She placed him on the floor, her eyes following his dash toward the garden. Her sorrow at Denber's death hadn't faded but her son's presence made things better.

Ria stood and followed Kodyn. She no longer shuffled, head down. Instead, she moved with a lithe agility Ilanna found better suited to a warrior than a doxy.

Serving in the brothel hadn't been Ria's choice. Her pimps—slavers, really—had forced upon her daily doses of opiates. They'd beaten and tortured her, kept her chained in a lightless room with more than a dozen other girls. None older than two decades, some barely into their womanhood. All virtually mindless husks unable to protest as scum paraded through the blanket-walled abomination that passed for a bordello.

Ilanna knew that feeling of helplessness. She'd brought Ria to the only place she knew was truly safe. The girl had spent almost a year in Ilanna's home, caring for Kodyn, recovering from the Watcher knew how many years of abuse. She hadn't left the house for six months. In a way, Kodyn cared for her as much as she cared for him. Her first words had been to Kodyn. She'd shown the first hint of happiness when playing with the boy in the garden. It was why Ilanna had brought the girl here in the first place.

38

She'd come within a heartbeat of terminating her pregnancy. More than once, she wrestled with her choice to keep the child. All indecision had fled the moment she saw the little bundle in her arms. When she was with Kodyn, everything else faded. He saw her for *her*, with no pretense, no need to guard herself. The child had pulled her from the shell into which she'd withdrawn after Ethen's death. She had hoped Kodyn would do the same for Ria. Every day, the child's bright spirit drew her out a little more. The half-smile was the most visible reaction she'd shown. Ria had a long way to go, but Ilanna held hope the girl could recover. For now, Ilanna would provide the two things she needed most: a safe haven and Kodyn.

She glanced at the noonday sun and sighed. *If only I had more time.* Slipping into her cloak, she strode into the garden.

"Mama, you're leaving?" Sadness filled Kodyn's honey-colored eyes.

She nodded. "I'll be back as soon as I can." She bent to kiss his forehead. "Be good for Ria."

"I will, Mama." He threw his muddy arms around her leg and clung tight. "Bring me a black birdie this time?"

"Of course, my little hawk."

Regret panged in her stomach as she leapt the garden wall. She hated to leave Kodyn, but she had no choice. The more time she spent here, the higher the risk someone would come looking for her and discover her secret. With Denber gone, only one person knew of Kodyn: the midwife who'd delivered the boy. Better to keep it that way.

Thoughts of Denber darkened her mood. Images of the torments she'd visit upon the Duke filled her mind. He would suffer for what he'd done.

Allon's words pushed the gruesome visions away. *"You can't take his life without starting a war, but there has to be something else you can take from him."*

Her body went through the motions of climbing to the Hawk's Highway, but the problem of the Duke occupied her mind. She would have vengeance for Denber and Werrin. But how? If she couldn't kill him, what else could she do?

Her eyes fixed on the obsidian structure towering over Praamis, and the city flew beneath her as she raced the distance to the Ward of Refuge. She settled onto the flat roof of the Coin Counters' Temple, home of Garridos the Apprentice, god of ventures. She'd spent hours sitting with Denber, Werrin, Willem, Prynn, and Bert, studying the Black Spire and drinking in the colorful sunset over the Stannar River.

Her chest tightened at the memory. A wave of sorrow washed over her, mingling with loneliness. She was alone in the Night Guild. She could trust no one, not Allon, Master Hawk, and certainly not Master Gold.

No, alone is better. She compressed her emotions into a ball that she pushed deep, deep down. *Alone, there is no one to fail me. No one to lose.*

Her eyes roamed the cityscape, taking in the sun-baked roofs, walls washed white with limestone, and colorful awnings of the stalls bordering the Path of Penitence, the broad thoroughfare that cut through the Ward of Refuge and led to the opulent mansions of Old Praamis.

The city had sprung up around the Black Spire—the handiwork of the Serenii, the ancient race lost to time, some said. The old, wealthy families of Praamis owned the fertile land bordering the Stannar River. Opulent mansions dominated the west bank. The shanty towns south of Praamis housed the serfs who worked the pastures, fields of crops, and vineyards that sprawled from the east riverbank and disappeared over the horizon.

Once, Ilanna had gaped at the enormous structures of Old Praamis. Buildings of marble, stone older than the city itself, glass windows that stretched from floor to ceiling, and lawns, gardens, and thickets of old-growth trees. Old Praamis occupied a quarter of the modern city of Praamis. A staggering amount of the city's wealth—that not controlled by the Night Guild or the Crown—passed through the fingers of the three-score nobles who called Old Praamis home.

The mansions had lost their grandeur. Ilanna saw only the arrogance and blinding greed of the petty lords and ladies of Praamis. The secrets hidden behind those façades of stone and perfection made House Bloodbear's predations and the assassinations of House Serpent and House Scorpion seem philanthropic by comparison.

Amidst it all, Duke Elodon Phonnis made his home in the Black Spire, the obsidian dagger thrust into the belly of the sky. He'd boasted that the Black Spire was the most secure building in the city. Dozens of thieves had tried to prove him wrong and died for their efforts. Every failed attempt bolstered the Duke's reputation. Nobles unwilling to turn to the Crown for protection from the Night Guild had sought out the Duke. His private army provided security to dozens of the wealthiest nobles of Praamis. He employed a legion of architects, engineers, and master metalsmiths to design and construct thief-proof security systems. The Night Guild had lost more than a few Journeymen and apprentices to the Duke's clever traps and his private force of blue-robed Arbitors.

She'd tarnished his reputation by breaking into the Black Spire. The Night Guild had whispered into a few ears and spread word of her success among the nobility of Praamis. Many of the Duke's prospective customers had turned to the Crown for protection.

That explains his personal vendetta. In the last five years, the Duke had augmented his efforts to combat thievery. He claimed it was to bring law and order to Praamis, but Ilanna knew better. He needed to repair the damage she'd done when she broke into the Black Spire.

That's it! She couldn't take his life, but she could ruin him.

She leapt to her feet and darted off across the rooftops. Running always helped her to think. Ideas trickled into her mind, but she discarded them as fast as they came. She needed time to formulate a plan of how to take down the Duke.

She could hit any number of homes around Old Praamis, those guarded by the Duke's guards and thief-traps. But which?

It has to be bigger than the Black Spire. Something monumental.

The Duke struck a painful, personal blow when he executed Denber. She would return the favor.

Chapter Eight

Ilanna snorted as she studied the interior of Count Chatham's villa from atop a nearby roof. *If he doesn't want us to steal his wealth, he ought to improve his security.*

Two guards stood at the gate, with another pair stationed at the front door. The four guards wouldn't have dissuaded a mouse from entering the mansion; one guard actually yawned and leaned on his spear. A few lanterns hung from the pillars around the first floor, but they wouldn't illuminate the upper levels after nightfall.

An open third-floor window drew her eye. *That should make things easier.* Even an apprentice could anchor a rope to the chimney and slip into the house that way. Her gaze traced the contours of the rooftop to where it drew within leaping distance of the neighboring house. She wouldn't even need Jarl and the Pathfinders to make a way for her to reach his mansion. She could be in and out within an hour.

Well, that's one task taken care of. She'd return to the Guild tunnels, gather her supplies, and return after dark. If all went well, she'd be home with Kodyn before midnight.

Count Chatham's villa stood in The Gardens, an affluent district built in the shadow of Old Praamis. Close enough that the poorer nobles and wealthier merchants could delude themselves into believing they lived among the upper crust, but far enough that the true aristocracy didn't have to mingle with their lessers.

Where the mansions of Old Praamis sprawled across vast estates, the dwellings in The Gardens were more pragmatic. They resembled strongholds built in a time when war ravaged Einan. The fortress-like manors rose five or six stories high, reaching for the sky instead of occupying valuable real estate. Their owners desired opulence, but not at the cost of protection.

The bulk of Duke Phonnis' clients lived in The Gardens. The old-money nobles of Old Praamis relied on their house guards, while the merchants and landed gentry preferred to pay the Duke's fees rather than hire their own armed watchmen. The blue-clad guards in silver breastplates, black trousers, and spiked helms were a common sight among The Gardens.

Count Chatham, however, appeared to trust his own security. Once Ilanna showed him the foolishness of that belief, he would have two choices: throw himself on the Crown's mercy or swallow the cost of hiring Duke Phonnis' Arbitors.

With a final examination of her intended route, Ilanna slipped away from Count Chatham's villa. The path through The Gardens was a challenge for even a skilled Hawk. The Arbitors dismantled the Hawk's Highway—a network of ropes, wooden footbridges, and ladders interlacing every building in Praamis— wherever they encountered it. More than a few Pathfinders, the Hawk Journeymen who built the Highway, had bemoaned the challenge of finding clever ways to conceal the crossings from the Duke's guards.

The late afternoon sun bathed The Gardens in a brilliant glow, transforming the mansions around Ilanna into something from a master painter's canvas. The marble and granite buildings sparkled in the golden light.

If only more people knew what lay beneath the perfect façades.

It was in one of those mansions she'd found Ria. The Duke's Arbitors had discovered Ilanna leaving the home of a particularly wealthy merchant-noble. She'd eluded them by slipping into the open upper-story window of a house she knew to be empty—the owner had fled the city the previous year on charges of fraud and embezzlement. To her horror, she'd found it home to dozens of hollow-eyed girls living in filth, serving as back-bedders. Slaves in service to sadists masquerading as their pimps. It had taken every shred of willpower for Ilanna to remain hidden when she ached to chop the bastards to pieces as she had Sabat.

When the Night Guild raided the illicit brothel, she'd entered through the window and caught a group of pimps by surprise before the Bloodbears brought down the front door. Blood soaked, a furious snarl twisting her lips, she'd hunted down every one of the flesh-peddlers. Only those who threw themselves on the Bloodbears' mercy escaped her wrath.

In their drug-induced stupor, the girls had stared at her with lifeless eyes and gaunt faces. Yet when the Bloodbears and Serpents came to cart them away, one girl threw her arms around Ilanna's waist and refused to release her. The opiates and abuse hadn't snuffed the fire in her eyes. Master Gold had promised he'd find a place for the victims but, in that moment, Ilanna had known she couldn't let this dark-skinned girl be carted off with the others. She'd gambled that Kodyn's presence would help the girl as he'd helped her. Thus, Ria had entered her life.

That night had taught Ilanna a lesson: she could use others, else be used like those dull-eyed girls.

Looks like I've got to make it up to Allon for last night.

She felt no guilt for lashing out at him, but a man with wounded pride always proved harder to manipulate. She needed him compliant. He'd proven himself useful before—he'd been the one to verify her story, helped her persuade Master Hawk to bring down the Night Guild's wrath on the brothel operating outside the Guild's permission.

His words from last night had set her on the path to exacting vengeance on the Duke. For what she had in mind, she'd need his help. Which meant she had to find a way to make amends, even if every word of her apology was a lie.

Adrenaline surged within her at the thought of her plans for taking down Duke Phonnis. It was a gamble, and an undertaking that far surpassed her conquest of the Black Spire. But if she could pull it off, she would have everything she'd need to be free of the Night Guild.

First, she had a date with a sword.

* * *

The clack of wooden practice blades echoed in the Aerie. Ilanna ducked beneath Errik's slash and followed up with a thrust that he knocked aside. His waster slapped against her shoulder.

"Dead."

Ilanna growled. "Damn it!" Her knuckles whitened on the grip of her sword. "How do you keep doing that? Reading my attacks before I even know what I'm doing."

Errik grounded the tip of his blade and leaned on it. "You can tell one type of padlock from another, or spot a fat purse in a mark's cloak, right?" Ilanna nodded. "It's what you do. Me, I watch people fight and learn how to kill them before they can kill me." He rubbed the pencil moustache sprouting beneath his crooked nose. "Part of being a Serpent."

"You'd think after three years of this, I should be able to hit you at least once."

He shrugged. "You're good, Ilanna. Damned good, for that matter. Better than most in the Guild." He twirled the sword in strong hands. "But you're no Serpent."

She gritted her teeth. "Still, I—"

"No." He shook his head. "Being a killer isn't easy. It's not just about knowing how to wield a sword. It's about being able to put it into someone even when you have no reason to want them dead." He met her gaze and steel flashed in his eyes. "Be who you are."

Ilanna clenched her jaw but said nothing. She wouldn't call Errik a friend, not like Denber, but he came close. He alone knew the secret of what had happened to Sabat. What she'd *done* to Sabat.

45

"Again." She raised her waster to the guard position Journeyman Ullard had taught her so many years ago.

"You sure?" He quirked an eyebrow. "Your ribs are already going to be bloody sore tomorrow. I tried to pull that blow but—"

She waved his words away. "Cost of learning, Errik. Besides, you hit like a Grubber."

"A Grubber, is it?" He mock-scowled at the insult. "Guess I'll have to stop going easy on you."

She grinned. "I'd hope so. Unless you're afraid I'll take you down, Serpent."

With a grin, Errik attacked. He fought with grace, all lean, hard muscles and economic movements. House Serpent trained killers, not warriors or heroes. No fancy flourishes or courtly rules of fencing etiquette, only brutal, quick death.

Twenty seconds later, Ilanna rubbed her stinging cheek and walked to pick up her sword. "You'll have to teach me that disarming move sometime."

Errik folded his arms. "House secret. Can't have just *anyone* learning all our tricks."

"I'll make it worth your while." She produced a pouch from her robes and tossed it to him. "Your saffron, as promised."

He opened the bag and sighed at the rich scent. "For a Hawk, you certainly know how to drive a bargain." The leather pouch disappeared into a pocket. "Fair enough, but it'll have to be next time. I've got places to be."

With a nod, she flipped the wooden waster and handed him the hilt. As he stepped closer, she dropped her voice. "If I need a Serpent for a job, would you be game?" The Aerie was empty, but she wouldn't risk anyone overhearing her plans. Not yet.

"What d'you need a Serpent for?"

"You in?"

He thought a moment and nodded.

"Good. You'll hear from me when I'm ready."

"So be it." He stepped back, spoke in a louder voice. "Same time next week?"

A smile teased her lips. "Only if you're ready for your first defeat."

He raised an eyebrow. "Optimistic, even after losing for three years straight. It's what makes you a good student." He patted his pocket. "And the perfect source for hard-to-procure goods."

The Aerie door boomed shut behind him, and Ilanna set off through the tunnels toward her rooms. As always, her eyes flashed down the corridor that led to the apprentices' chambers. With Denber and Werrin gone, House Hawk grew ever smaller.

She pushed Denber from her mind and focused on her myriad aches and pains. Despite his protests, Errik didn't go easy on her. She'd come within a finger's breadth of catching him on more than one occasion. He couldn't afford to hold back, and her ribs, arms, legs, head, and chest bore the reminders of her mistakes.

Closing the door to her chamber, she slipped off her sweat-soaked shirt with a groan and hurled it into her laundry pile. A quick bath, and she'd have time to—

Ice froze in her veins and every muscle in her body grew rigid. A small fragment of parchment sat on her table. Beside it lay a viola, a single drop of crimson staining the yellow petals. She whirled and scanned the room, drawing a dagger from her bracer. Nothing leapt out at her; everything remained as she'd left it the previous night. There was nothing to indicate anyone else had entered the room.

She dashed to the door and yanked it open. The hallway was empty. She ran a critical eye over the lock. No sign someone had picked or forced it. As always.

Heart hammering, blood pulsing in her ears, Ilanna closed the door and stepped to the table. She reached for the folded paper with trembling hands, opened it.

Alamastri manor, it read, in the neat, familiar handwriting.

She jumped as someone pounded on her door. Crumpling the paper, she stuffed it into a pocket and whirled.

"Ilanna?" Grillan, one of Bryden's Hawks, stepped into the room. "Master Hawk sent me to—" The gaunt, wiry man stopped, wide-eyed.

Ilanna made no attempt to hide her exposed chest. "What?" she snapped.

Grillan swallowed and struggled to lift his gaze. "It's nameday. We're called to assemble in the Menagerie."

"I'll be there."

Grillan's feet seemed as rooted to the floor as his eyes to her chest.

"Is there something else, Grillan?" She took a step toward him and raised her arm.

With one final glance, he fled a heartbeat before Ilanna's dagger *thunked* into the wooden door where his head had been.

Chapter Nine

Keeper damn these stuffy cloaks! Ilanna took a deep breath and fought back the urge to rip off the ceremonial Guild robes. *As if the air of the Menagerie wasn't bad enough.* She shifted, trying to open some space. The touch of the men around her sent a shiver down her spine.

Hundreds of Journeymen and apprentices filled the cavernous underground chamber. They stood still and silent, an eerie assembly of hooded faces surrounding a torchlit clearing at the heart of the room. The banners of the seven Houses provided the only color amidst the dull earthen walls and black robes of the Night Guild.

At the front, Master Gold and the House Masters sat upon ornate chairs. At a gesture from the Guild Master, a figure slipped down an adjoining tunnel. The tyros had been summoned.

Even after fifteen years, nervous tension coiled in Ilanna's stomach. She'd stood before the Night Guild for judgment, undergone the tests of the tyros and almost failed. The memory of the night Master Hawk had chosen her set her heart thudding.

She clenched her jaw as the first tyro shuffled from the tunnel. The boy's hair hung lank, his face pale, cheeks sunken. His eyelids drooped, exhaustion showing clearly. He didn't lift his gaze when he took his place before the House Masters.

Master Velvet walked beside him. His hair had turned to grey, his jowls hung lower, and a grizzled beard flowed down to his shabby namesake waistcoat. He moved more slowly, a hunch in his right shoulder.

Hard to believe the old bastard's still alive.

Her eyes returned to the child. *Eight years old and barely more than a walking corpse. That was me once.*

A sour taste filled Ilanna's mouth. Since Kodyn, she'd come to hate nameday. She saw her son in those fatigue-clouded eyes and cheeks hollowed by malnutrition. She wouldn't let him suffer the same fate as these children.

Master Gold stood and spoke, but Ilanna couldn't keep her mind on the ritual words he repeated every nameday. She fingered the parchment stuffed into her pocket.

Alamastri manor, it said. Why in the bloody hell do they want me to go there? I thought they were under the Crown's protection.

The first note had come after she killed Sabat. It had threatened to expose her secret, subject her to Guild law. *"What would you do to keep the truth buried?"* it read.

The second note appeared more than a year later. Its instructions were simple: *"Your mark is Lord Erriell. Tell no one."* She'd refused. For days, she hid in her room to catch whoever left the notes. She waited in vain. No retribution came. Hours later, when she returned to her chambers, she discovered a note that read, *"Let this be a lesson."* Beside it lay a blood-spattered viola and the dagger used to kill Sabat. The dagger she'd buried with Sabat's body, then hurled into the river after it appeared in her room beside the first note.

The notes had appeared five more times since that day, each time singling out a new mark for her to visit. No one claimed ownership or requested proof of obedience. They didn't need to. She'd carried out the thefts without hesitation.

She believed she recognized the handwriting but would remain silent until she knew for certain.

The "how" of the notes still sent a shiver of fear down her spine. She had no idea how the messenger entered her room. The lock she'd installed last month engaged automatically when she closed the door. The only key hung around her neck and even *she* had trouble picking the eight-pin fixture.

She crumpled the note in her fist. *If someone can get into my room, it means they're watching for when I'm out.* Icy feet danced down her back. *Does that mean they're watching me* outside *the Guild, too? Do they know where I go?*

The walls of the Menagerie pressed in around her. If her movements were watched, she couldn't risk anyone discovering Kodyn. She had to stay away for her child's safety. She couldn't go back until she discovered the source of the notes.

Her eyes focused on the emaciated child standing before the House Masters. Starved, beaten, worked to exhaustion, tormented by Master Velvet and the other tyros. So weak, helpless, just as she'd been all those years ago.

If the Night Guild learned of Kodyn's existence, she had no doubt they'd ensure he followed in her footsteps on his eighth nameday. Kodyn wouldn't be the first child forced to join. Many of the younger Journeymen and apprentices had followed their fathers and mothers into the Guild. Compliant or not.

Master Gold's words drew her back to the present. "Give praise to the Watcher that you have been chosen. From this day on, you are no longer tyros. You are now apprentices to the Night Guild."

The House Masters rose and gathered their apprentices. Before they could leave, Master Gold raised his hands.

"Let them stay." His clean-shaven face bore a somber, sorrowful expression. "It is never too early to learn the rule of law."

He turned to the assembled Guild members. "My brothers and sisters, Journeymen, apprentices of the Night Guild. I come to you in the name of the Watcher in the Dark, god of justice and vengeance."

Clasping his hands behind his back, he strode around the torch-ringed clearing where the tyros had stood a moment earlier.

"Though the world outside these walls sees us as criminals, we know the truth. We are a brotherhood, striving toward a common goal. And what is that goal?" He whirled on the crowd, eyes alight. "Profit, the great pursuit that drives every man and woman. It is through profit that we obtain power, and through power we bring peace."

He thrust a finger at Master Hound. "Master Hound, your Journeymen are charged with bringing to justice the law-breakers and criminals who flee the Praamian Guard, are they not?"

The House Master nodded. "They are."

"And how many have you delivered to the King's justice? Hundreds? Thousands."

Master Hound shrugged and inclined his head.

"And you, Master Fox." Master Gold strode toward a heavy-set man with a walrus moustache. "Do your brothers and sisters not relieve the wealthy of their excess and share it among those with greater need?"

Master Fox pounded a fist on the arm of his chair. "That they do!"

Ilanna stifled a snort. *How altruistic.*

Master Gold returned his attention to the crowd. "We are all governed by the laws of the Night Guild, written out by the Journeymen and Masters who came before us. And we are sworn to uphold those laws, are we not?"

As one, the Night Guild bellowed, *"We are!"*

Master Gold's face hardened. "As we are generous in our rewards of those who obey, so too must we be harsh when meting out justice to those who break our laws."

He snapped his fingers. Two Journeymen in the crimson robes of House Bloodbear dragged a third man between them. Mud spattered his orange-trimmed clothing and a mass of bruises covered his face. Blood caked his nose and split lips. When the Bloodbears released him, he slumped to the hard-packed earth.

Master Gold halted before the man. "Journeyman Adarus of House Fox, you stand accused of larceny and murder."

Ilanna's shoulders tightened at the pronouncement. Around her, the crowd muttered and shifted.

At Master Gold's nod, the Bloodbears pulled the Fox Journeyman to his feet. "These are serious accusations, Adarus. What have you to say in your defense?"

Adarus, a small man with a skull-like face and teeth darker than the mud staining his clothing, said nothing.

"The Night Guild does not mete out punishment without proof. Who can provide evidence of this man's innocence or guilt?"

"I can." A Journeyman in the orange-trimmed robes of House Fox strode into the clearing.

"Journeyman Isseck, what testimony do you bring?"

Isseck opened the leather-bound ledger of House Fox. "I bring the records of my House, which prove beyond doubt that Adarus embezzled the sum of five hundred imperials from the coffers of the Night Guild."

Master Gold beckoned and a wiry, bespectacled man rushed from the crowd. This man wore the gold-trimmed robes proclaiming him the Guild Master's personal aide. He carried on a whispered conversation with Isseck as they studied the ledger. After a few minutes, he turned to Master Gold. "He speaks the truth. The ledger shows the sum of five hundred imperials missing."

"Thank you, Journeyman Entar." He motioned to Isseck. "And what proof have you that it was Adarus who absconded with those funds?"

"I am the proof." Another Fox stepped forward. "I witnessed Adarus steal into House Fox's strongroom. The next day, Journeyman Isseck reported the missing funds." He pointed to the crowd. "Two of my fellow Journeymen saw the same."

Master Gold turned to Adarus. "As is your right, you may dispute the claims brought forth by your fellow Foxes. Is that your wish? Do you doubt the proof brought forth?"

Adarus shook his head.

"What say you, Masters of the Night Guild? Do you find Adarus guilty or innocent?"

As one, the seven House Masters spoke. "Guilty."

"The Masters have spoken." Master Gold bowed to the seated men. "To the charges of murder, who brings proof of Adarus' guilt?"

Ilanna recognized the man who stepped forward. Garrill had helped her break into the Black Spire.

Master Gold folded his arms over his chest. "What evidence do you bring?"

"My testimony and word as a Journeyman of House Hound." Garrill stood straight, head held high. "When Journeyman Isseck reported the theft to Master Fox, it was discovered that Adarus had fled the Night Guild. After three days of searching, the Foxes failed to locate their missing comrade. They contracted House Hound to bring him to justice. I was sent after Adarus, along with Journeyman Sular."

Garrill pushed aside his long, dark hair to reveal two black eyes. "We caught up to Adarus on the Windy Plains, a day's ride from Voramis. When we attempted to reason with him, he attacked us and killed Sular." He gestured, and an apprentice wearing the white robes of House Hound rushed toward him. He took the cloak from the youth and held it up. A crimson stain spread from the hole in the robe's breast.

"Do you have the dagger?"

Garrill nodded and produced the blade, still covered in blood.

"And you alone were witness to the murder?"

"I was." Garrill met Master Gold's eyes. "But I swear by the Watcher himself that we made no move to harm Adarus until he attacked us."

"What's a man to do?" The quiet moan came from the slumped Adarus. "If he can't even feed himself, how's he s'posed to live?"

Master Gold opened his mouth but Adarus hadn't finished. "Yes, I took the money, and yes, I killed the damned Hound, but what choice did I have? You take everything from a man, you back him into a corner like an animal and you're surprised when you get bit!" He stepped forward, eyes burning. "You say the Night Guild is a brotherhood. Pah!" He spat at Master Gold's feet. "This is no brotherhood! There's no honor in what we do. We're just a pack of thieves, thugs, and killers. Me, I can't live with that. The rest of you, well, that's between you and the Watcher."

He rounded on Master Gold. "You carry out this pretense of fairness, but it's no more justice than Duke Phonnis sending men across the Field of Mercy." Adarus straightened and his voice rang out in the Menagerie. "I stole from my House, I killed a man, aye. But when you're so hungry and tired you can't think straight, when you're so cold you'd set yourself on fire just to feel warmth, that's when you've had enough. I did what I had to to get out of this Keeper-damned place. At least I'll die knowing I tried."

Adarus seemed to deflate, the defiance melting from his eyes.

After a tense moment of silence, Master Gold turned to the House Masters. "You have heard the testimony of Journeyman Garrill, and the accused has condemned himself out of his own mouth. What is your verdict, Masters of the Guild?"

The seven spoke in unison, albeit in quieter voices. "Guilty."

Master Gold folded his arms over his chest and bowed. "Journeyman Adarus of House Fox, you are convicted of the crimes of larceny and murder. Alone, each carries a heavy sentence. But together, we are left with no choice." He drew himself up to his full height. "By the laws of the Night Guild, I sentence you to the Sanction."

A gasp rose from the crowd and Adarus collapsed.

Two Bloodbears entered the room, pushing a man-sized, wooden wagon wheel between them. A third carried a wooden club, steel spikes, a mallet, and an axe.

The wheel was laid flat on the floor and Adarus' body draped over it. The four Bloodbears held his wrists and feet against the rim of the wheel.

Master Gold took the mallet and spikes. "Upon completion of your Undertaking, you swore solemn oaths—oaths you have broken." He raised the three spikes. "One for House Fox. One for the Night Guild. One for the Watcher in the Dark."

He stood over Adarus' prone form. The Fox struggled against his captors but his wiry, malnourished body had no hope of breaking free of the hulking Bloodbears.

"As you broke your vows of service to the Guild, so, too, your bones shall be broken. As you severed your ties with your brothers by dishonoring their trust, so, too, your hands and feet shall be severed. With your eyes, you coveted your House's riches. With your tongue, you swore a false oath before the Watcher. Let the offending parts be removed, so you may stand before the Long Keeper cleansed of your shame."

He passed the spikes and mallet to one of the Bloodbears, folded his arms over his chest, and gave a deep bow. "Let justice be served."

Ilanna clenched her fists as the screaming began.

Chapter Ten

Ilanna shivered, but it had little to do with the chill wind shrieking across the quiet rooftops. Adarus' screams still rang in her ears hours after the man had died.

She'd attended two executions since becoming a Journeyman. One, a Scorpion convicted of poisoning a rival in House Serpent, died at the end of ten Serpent blades. The other, a Grubber caught falsifying his earnings, met the justice of his House: a live burial. Those deaths paled in comparison to the brutality of the Sanction.

The images refused to leave her head. Broken bones, a mass of shredded flesh, and the quiet screams of Adarus as he begged for death. The severing of his hands and feet had finally granted him an escape from the torment.

Her fingers clutched the crumpled parchment in her pocket. The Guild had convicted Adarus of murder and larceny. She, too, was guilty of those crimes.

For years, she'd lied about her earnings to Bryden. A risky gamble but she had no choice. She only had a few more years to take Kodyn—and herself—away from Praamis. For that, she needed money.

She'd hacked Sabat to pieces, buried his body in her garden. The Night Guild had suspected her from the moment Sabat disappeared but could not convict her without proof. Whoever left the notes had also brought the bloodstained dagger she'd interred with the apprentice's corpse. They knew the truth of Sabat, and used that knowledge to compel her obedience. She couldn't risk evidence being brought forward against her.

Which was why she crouched on the roof overlooking the Alamastri mansion, studying the movement of the guards below. She risked the Guild's wrath by obeying the note. After all, the Alamastris paid the Crown for protection.

But this wouldn't be her first time slipping into this particular mansion. Since the first time with her fellow Hawk apprentices, more than a decade earlier, she had paid the Alamastris at least a dozen visits. She only took small items worth a few imperials—enough to feed Kodyn for a few weeks, but not enough for the Alamastris to miss—and left no sign of her presence.

She reached for the thin rope that spanned the gap to the distant rooftop. She'd crossed that same line fifteen years ago; the Alamastri house guards hadn't spotted it, hadn't taken it down. With a smile, she draped her body over the rope and began the slow crawl across.

The familiar activity brought back the memories of her friends. Prynn, Werrin, Willem, Bert, Denber: all had joined her the first night she'd made the crossing. Only Willem remained alive.

Enough. She pushed away the pang of sorrow. *I've no time for mourning. I've only an hour to get in and out, then I'm off to finish the Count Chatham job.*

* * *

With a grin, Ilanna slipped from the open third-floor window of Count Chatham's villa and hauled herself up the rope. *If his security is any indication, he really* does *need the Crown's protection. It took longer to get here from the Alamastri's than to finish this job.*

The skull-head dagger embedded in his bedside table would send the Guild's message clearly. *Another ten imperials a month, in the pocket.*

She calculated sums in her mind as she stole across the rooftops, her grey clothes hidden in shadow. With what she had in Bryden's ledgers and the money hidden in her house—plus what she'd stolen from the Alamastris and Count Chatham—she could scrape together close to thirteen thousand imperials. By the year's end, that number would be closer to fifteen thousand.

Not enough to live like a King, but enough to get by. It's a start. She'd figure out how to explain the existence of the extra gold to the Guild Council later. Better if they never learned about it, but she'd talked her way out of bigger problems.

The nameday choosing ceremony and Adarus' execution had reinforced her desire to be free of the Night Guild. No, she thought as her hand stole to the hawk figurine in her purse, her *need*.

She wouldn't stop stealing to feed her son. She couldn't disobey the notes for fear of being exposed, and her attempts to discover their source had proven fruitless. She had to be free of the Guild before whoever sent the notes decided they no longer needed her.

The Night Guild had made it clear: they saw her as an investment. They had expended time and resources turning a child into a capable thief. She had to repay their investment by earning her keep. But if she could put together enough money, perhaps she could *buy* her way free. Master Gold claimed the Guild cared most about profit. She would prove it more profitable to let her buy her freedom than keeping her enslaved.

Since Kodyn's birth, she'd sought the largest scores possible, risk or no. Her fellow Hawks wanted quick money and less risk. The months spent preparing for her Undertaking had taught her an important lesson: repetition reduced risk.

She had entered Duke Phonnis' gardens nearly twenty times before her final attempt. She'd spent hours scaling walls, training her muscles in preparation for the Black Spire. All those hours had enabled her to succeed where others had failed.

She approached each job with the same attitude. Instead of seeking out new marks, she broke into the same homes every time. Her familiarity with the layout of the houses made it easier for her to navigate to her target and obscure any signs of her presence. Her marks never knew she entered, so they took no measures to keep her out. She had boiled it down to a formula, a science of burglary none of the other Hawks—not even Master Hawk—could rival.

Her fellow Hawks passed the time relaxing, spending their earnings, and lounging around the tunnels. She used every hour of the day in training and casing potential new marks. She watched new mansions being erected in The Gardens or old ones torn down. She studied the city architecture to learn new, more efficient ways to travel the Hawk's Highway. She worked with Jarl and the Pathfinders to establish quicker routes.

Other thieves used the rooftops to reach their destination; she made the Hawk's Highway work for her. Praamis was a giant maze. Instead of being confined to the two dimensions of roads and alleyways, Ilanna used the dimension of height to be a more effective thief. Her path led across, over, through, around, and between—the path of least resistance and shortest trajectory. New buildings simply meant one more stepping stone.

Leaving The Gardens, she turned toward the ancient Praamian Wall. Her path cut through a section of Praamis belonging to more affluent merchants. Their homes lacked the fortifications of The Gardens; they stored their wealth in the vaults of the Coin Counters, priests of the Apprentice. She dropped from an overhang onto a rooftop terrace, darted across the tiled floor, and leapt up the low wall on the far side.

Balconies, chimneys, drainpipes, ledges, ladders, and pillars were more than simple architectural fixtures; they gave her access to the secrets of Praamis. Architecture offered the comforting illusion of safety, as if four walls with windows and doors and ceilings with skylights could magically keep out those like Ilanna who wanted to get in.

No matter how complex the security system, she *would* get in. The Duke's Arbitors made her job more difficult, increased the risk, but they couldn't stop her. Anything the Duke could dream up to keep her out, she could find a way in.

His traps had nearly caught her in the Black Spire. Because of the Duke and his guards, the Night Guild had lost dozens of Journeymen to the hangman's noose. But he'd made a mistake when he hanged Denber and sent

Werrin through the Field of Mercy. He'd executed people that mattered to her. He had turned her into his enemy.

She couldn't kill him—King Ohilmos would wage war on the Guild in retribution for his brother's death—but she could ruin him. And in doing so, she would earn her freedom.

A weight lifted from her chest as she leapt atop the crumbling remains of the Praamian Wall. In the days when war ravaged Einan, the city wall had once risen forty paces into the sky. Long centuries had passed since battle visited the cities of the south. The walls of Praamis had fallen into disrepair, the stone carted off for construction. Only a few sections of wall remained—a reminder of the past.

The wall marked the southern boundary of the sprawling shanty towns, warehouses, and markets of the Praamis metropolis. The wooden buildings beyond the wall lacked the sturdy permanence of the multi-story stone and granite constructions within.

Ilanna loved to study the city from the one short stretch of wall that hadn't been torn down. From her vantage point, she could see the concentric rings of wealth that grew narrower and grander the closer one drew to the Royal Palace. Nearer the wall, whitewash peeled from crumbling stone and clay roofs lost their luster.

Leaning back against the cool stone, she drew out the fistful of coins she'd taken from the Alamastri mansion. Gold shone in the early morning light. She smiled. *A few more imperials to add to my collection.*

Bryden wouldn't hear of these. *He'll just have to be happy with what I've taken from Count Chatham's.*

She hadn't found coins lying around—*how inconsiderate of him*—but Lady Chatham would never notice the gold necklace missing from her jewelry box. The Guild fence, a shifty man by the name of Filch, would give her a receipt to deliver to Bryden.

And, of course, he'll give me that suspicious look of his. Damned fool doesn't trust anyone! Not that she'd given him reason to trust her. Her fellow Hawk had no way to confirm his suspicions, but that didn't stop him doubting her.

Not for the first time, she wrestled with the problem of the money she had hidden. If the Guild accepted her offer to buy her freedom, how would she explain where the eight thousand imperials had come from?

If my plan for the Duke goes off right, it won't matter. The money I'll earn from that heist will more than make up for it.

But first, she needed the Guild Council's approval to go after the Duke. There was the chance the Guild Council would find her plan too risky. After all, it would set her not just against the Chief Justiciar, brother to the King, but she would be desecrating a temple. Not something to take lightly, even for a thief.

I have to try. The Guild could turn her down, but that wouldn't stop her. She would do what she must for her son. If that meant going up against the Night Guild and Duke Phonnis both, so be it. She wouldn't let the Guild sink their claws into Kodyn. Her son wouldn't grow up without a mother.

Dawn brightened the horizon. The sun would be up soon, and the Guild Council would convene. But she didn't have to rush off yet. She could bask in the pre-sunrise coolness and forget—if only for a minute—she would soon face the greatest challenge of her life.

Chapter Eleven

"Journeyman Ilanna of House Hawk."

Ilanna looked up as Journeyman Entar called her name. Master Gold's aide ushered a shabby-looking Grubber out of the Council Room and beckoned her. "The Council will see you now."

With a nod, Ilanna stood and followed Entar into the chamber.

The sparseness of the room took her by surprise. She'd half-expected plush rugs, lavish furniture, and bright, ornate decorations to adorn the room. Bare earthen walls and floors met her eyes.

Thirteen men and two women sat behind the red oak table that stretched the length of the chamber. The Masters of the seven Houses with their seconds-in-command, and Master Gold at the center. They waited in silence as Entar led her to the heart of the room.

"Stand here."

Ilanna did as instructed. The aide scurried around the table and slipped into the empty chair beside Master Gold.

The Guild Master steepled his fingers and leaned forward. "What brings you before the Guild Council, Journeyman Ilanna of House Hawk?"

Ilanna resisted the urge to draw a breath to calm the fluttering in her stomach. These fifteen people held her life in their hands. She bowed and tightened her grip on the little hawk figurine she'd purchased on her way back from Count Chatham's mansion. "Master Gold, House Masters, esteemed members of the Guild Council. I come before you with an…unusual request."

Master Hawk's eyes narrowed. She hadn't said anything to him, a fact he clearly disliked.

She turned to Bryden. "Tell me, Journeyman Bryden, you are the bookkeeper for House Hawk, are you not?"

Bryden stiffened. "I am. What of it?"

"Do you have record of my total earnings since becoming a full Journeyman?"

He gave a jerky nod. "I do."

When he offered no further answer, she inclined her head. "Could you read out the sum total for the entire Council?"

Bryden's face reddened and Master Hawk's jaw muscles worked. The House records weren't strictly secret, but each House preferred to keep their income private. Only Master Gold saw all the accounts—and Entar, the Guild bookkeeper, of course.

Master Hawk gave a slight nod of his grizzled head and Bryden cleared his throat. "To date, Journeyman Ilanna of House Hawk has earned the sum of ninety-eight thousand, four hundred and ten imperials."

Master Grubber and Master Fox gasped, and the color drained from Master Bloodbear's ruddy face. Ilanna knew from her time spent among the Foxes that these three Houses were fortunate to earn that in a year. The Masters of the remaining three Houses gave no response, but their aides had less self-control. Journeyman Erys, the bookkeeper of House Serpent, peered down at her ledger. Anorria's slim, scarred hands tightened around the black leather tome holding House Scorpion's finances, and Eburgen of House Hound fixed his eyes firmly on the table before him.

Ilanna fought back a smile. "And what, Journeyman Bryden, is the amount I am owed by House Hawk?"

Bryden squinted down at the ledger. "After expenses—food, board, Guild fees, the cost of equipment, and such—Ilanna of House Hawk is owed four thousand, six hundred and fifty imperials."

She let the number hang in the air. The House Masters exchanged glances with their aides. Their personal fortunes far surpassed hers, but they had saved up for decades. They didn't need an abacus to calculate how long it would take her to eclipse them.

"I fail to see the relevance in all this, Journeyman Ilanna," Bryden snapped. "If you insist on wasting the Council's time—"

Master Gold's glare silenced the Hawk. The Guild Master leaned back in his chair, eyes fixed intently on her. "I, too, find myself curious as to the direction of your thoughts. You say you have a question. Ask it."

Ilanna drew herself up to her full height. "I wish to buy my freedom from the Guild."

A stunned silence filled the room. The Masters of House Fox, Grubber, Scorpion, and Bloodbear stared at her with uncomprehending eyes. A smile tickled at Master Serpent's lips. Master Hawk's face could have been carved from stone, but his dark eyes held the chill of disapproval.

Master Gold tapped his thumbs together. "Intriguing." He turned to the others seated beside him. "An unusual request, indeed."

Ilanna spoke before he could deny her. "But not unheard of." She stepped forward. "Precedent has been set, has it not?"

Entar whispered into Master Gold's ear and the Guild Master nodded. "You speak the truth. The previous Master Gold did permit a Journeyman to purchase his freedom. Journeyman Mallen of House Serpent."

Ilanna straightened. "I only ask for the same chance Journeyman Mallen was given." She pointed to Bryden. "As my House Master and fellow Journeymen will attest, there is none in House Hawk to match or surpass my earnings." She turned to the Masters of House Serpent, Scorpion, and Hound. "Perhaps there are a few in *your* Houses who can claim the same profits I have delivered to the Night Guild, but not in the time that I have." The way their eyes slid away from hers increased her confidence.

Master Gold fingered an ornamental brooch pinned to his vest. "None here can dispute your claims, Journeyman Ilanna. Indeed, the success of your Undertaking has increased the reputation of the Night Guild not only within Praamis, but even as far as Voramis." He picked at a fingernail. "But that begs the question: why would the Night Guild want to pass up such a valuable resource? After all, we would be fools to relinquish our claim to your future earnings."

Ilanna's shoulders tightened. "I have one answer for that." She'd expected the question. "Because it is in your best interest to do so."

Bryden's eyes narrowed, but it was Master Hound who spoke. "Explain your reasoning." His voice, rich and deep, held a note of contempt.

"I hold no illusions that my freedom can be purchased with a mere four thousand imperials." She held Master Gold's gaze. "The Guild has never hesitated to remind me of its investment in me. To purchase my freedom, I must repay that investment." She held up a hand as Entar opened his mouth. "And," she hurried on, "I will make it more worthwhile to *release* me than to hold me to my Journeyman's oath."

Master Gold quirked an eyebrow. "Oh?"

Ilanna gestured to the sixteen figures seated behind the table. "Can any of you calculate what I will owe to the Guild for the next, say, twenty years? Say I was to barely earn the minimum required to cover my room, board, and Guild fees."

The aides scribbled on their papers furiously, and Journeyman Isseck, the bookkeeper for House Fox drew out an abacus.

"I have it!" Bryden shouted. The other aides shot him glares but he met their spite with haughty disdain. "You will owe the Guild a sum total of one hundred and fifty-six thousand imperials."

"Fifty-six thousand, four hundred and thirty," Anorria added.

"Thank you." Bryden nodded to the Scorpion bookkeeper, an acidic edge to his words.

Ilanna's stomach tightened. *That's a bloody lot of money!* She steeled her expression. "One hundred and fifty thousand imperials. Not a paltry sum." With what she had in mind, she could pay that off with ease. "Enough to buy my freedom?"

Master Gold and Journeyman Entar carried out a whispered conversation. After a minute, Master Gold turned to the House Masters. "How many of you were present when Journeyman Mallen stood before the Guild Council with the same request?"

Only Master Hound spoke. "I."

Master Gold folded his hands over the paunchy remnants of what had once been solid chest muscle. "Many of you remember my predecessor. He was not a cruel man, simply a pragmatic one. He knew the value of Journeyman Mallen's services. In all of Praamis, none could match Mallen with a blade. His services commanded prices to rival the Hunter of Voramis himself. Do you know how much Mallen paid to secure his freedom?" He paused for effect, then spoke in a measured tone. "One million imperials."

Ilanna's stomach bottomed out. *Bloody fucking hell!*

Master Gold drew out the words. "One. Million. Imperials." He held Ilanna's gaze. "It took Journeyman Mallen ten years to buy his freedom. But you are younger than he and, as you say, you outearn any other in the Night Guild." He turned to Master Hawk. "What say you, House Master? Is that a fair price?"

Tension lined Master Hawk's face, but he nodded. "It is."

"And you are all in agreement?"

Ilanna studied the Council. The Masters of House Fox and Grubber seemed in shock, as if they couldn't comprehend such vast sums. Master Serpent's finger traced the scar across his forehead, nose, and cheek.

Master Bloodbear leered, delight staining his huge, red face. Since she humiliated Sabat all those years ago, the hairy master of House Bloodbear had hated her. She looked away, stomach churning. His ugly, brutish face reminded her too much of Sabat.

Bryden's expression held a combination of disdain and mockery. The corners of his lips tugged upward, as if he struggled to hide a smile. Master Scorpion's eyes held a hint of pity. A mix of surprise, resignation, and scorn showed on the other faces.

Master Scorpion nodded to Master Gold. "I believe I speak for the other Houses. We are in agreement." His dark eyes fell on Ilanna. "One million imperials, Journeyman."

Though Ilanna's fists clenched behind her back, she forced a smile. The solid feeling of the ebony figurine in her hand brought her comfort. "Done."

More than a few eyes widened. Anorria gave a half-smile and a slight nod.

Master Gold leaned back in his chair and fiddled with the gaudy brooch. "You have the Council's verdict. If that is all—"

"It is not." Ilanna's voice, a bit harsher than she intended, cut through the Guild Master's words. Master Gold's expression froze. Ilanna pressed on. "I have another request to present the Council."

"Another?" Master Serpent fiddled with the hilt of a belt dagger.

Ilanna nodded. "I request permission to target Duke Elodon Phonnis."

All of the eyes in the room went wide. They stared at her, speechless.

"As you know, the Duke has increased his efforts to apprehend and execute us."

The House Masters scowled. More than a few Journeymen had fallen into the Duke's clutches.

"The Night Guild has suffered because of him. Some more than others." She swallowed the lump in her throat. "But I believe the time has come to end the Duke's reign over the city. To that end, I request the Guild's permission to act against him."

Master Gold gave a dismissive wave. "I understand that the loss of your fellow Hawks is a hard one, Journeyman, but surely you can see the folly of attacking the Duke himself."

"I have no desire to face the Crown's retribution. I'm certain you share my opinion." She held up a hand. "What I propose is altogether different. But I believe that, if I succeed, the Duke will be ruined and his vendetta against the Guild will come to an end."

Master Hawk leaned forward, interest in his eyes. "And how, pray tell, do you intend to do that."

"I cannot say."

Bryden stood, knocking over his chair. "Such disrespect to your Guild and House Masters?"

Ilanna lifted her chin. "I cannot say before the Guild Council. I request to speak to Master Hawk and Master Gold. Alone."

More than a few expressions darkened. Curiosity burned in the eyes of all in the room. Master Hawk traded glances with Master Gold. "Why?"

"As I say, the Duke's attempts to bring down the Guild have increased. I would not risk my plan reaching his ears."

Outrage showed on Bryden's face. "You accuse us of treachery? Of betraying our brotherhood to the Duke?"

"No." The Hawk's fury broke against Ilanna's cold calm. "But I will take no chances, not with this." She locked gazes with Master Gold. "I will say this: my success benefits the entire Guild. You know my abilities and my record speaks for itself. If the Guild Council is willing to trust me, we will all reap the rewards."

The Council remained silent, expressions thoughtful. Master Gold glanced over at Master Hawk, who nodded. "So be it, Journeyman Ilanna. Your House Master and I will hear what you have to say in private. And, if we deem her proposal worthy, are we all agreed that she may proceed?"

Most of the men and women around the table nodded. Master Bloodbear and his aide remained stubbornly silent. Bryden's mouth hung open in outrage.

"So be it." Master Gold motioned to Ilanna. "We will speak in my chambers in one hour."

With a bow, Ilanna strode from the room.

* * *

"What in the frozen hell were you thinking?" Master Hawk's eyes blazed and a snarl twisted his lips. "You should have come to me with this!"

Ilanna had never seen Master Hawk so angry, but she wouldn't cower.

"I am your House Master," the hook-nosed man raged. "I could have figured another way to—"

"Jagar." Master Gold spoke in a voice of icy composure. "She was right to bring it to the Guild Council. They are the only ones who can make the decision."

Master Hawk turned his glare on Master Gold but the Guild Master placed a hand on his shoulder. "It's done." He fixed her with a piercing stare. "Before you speak, Ilanna, you would do well to listen."

She stiffened.

"I've made no secret of my personal feelings for you. I told you once you reminded me of myself. I like your bold, brash confidence." His nostrils flared. "But not everyone is as fond of you as I am. The way you spoke in the Council showed your lack of respect for the House Masters. For myself, even." He placed his closed fists on the desk and loomed over her. "Learn respect, Journeyman. Else someone will teach it to you and I will not be able to stop them."

Ilanna wanted to hurl the words into his face. She *had* no respect for the House Masters or their seconds. Those fifteen men and women hadn't lifted a finger to punish Sabat for what he'd done to her, to Ethen. They had claimed "insufficient evidence". They were cowards hiding behind Guild law.

But she kept her feelings hidden and plastered humility over her disdain. "Apologies, Master Gold. It will not happen again."

The Guild Master's expression relaxed. "Good. Now tell me what is so secret you cannot speak in front of the Council."

Ilanna drew in a breath. "What do you know of Lord Auslan?" She smiled as both jaws dropped.

* * *

"Fiery hell!" Master Hawk whistled and leaned back on the couch. "I'll give you this, Ilanna: you've got balls to match your confidence."

Master Gold shook his head as if to clear away his surprise. "And you're sure you can make it work? Alone?"

"No." Ilanna turned to Master Hawk. "Much as I dislike Bryden, I can't say his methods aren't effective. I'll be gathering a crew for the two jobs."

Master Hawk scratched his stubbled chin. "I'm not sure there are many Hawks with the skills you'll need."

"Which is why I'll be recruiting from the other Houses. Paying them, of course."

Master Gold nodded. "Good. Better not to offer them shares in the final score unless absolutely necessary."

"More for me that way." She met his eyes. "It should be enough."

Master Hawk snorted. "I'd say." He climbed to his feet. "I'm not going to lie, I'm bloody tickled to watch you pull this off. You've got House Hawk behind you. Whatever you need." His words held genuine warmth.

Heat suffused her cheeks. "Thank you, Master Hawk."

"If you don't mind, I'll keep Ilanna for a few moments, Jagar." No one but Master Gold called Master Hawk by his name. "Just a few more questions I'd like answered."

"I'll leave you to it. I've got places to be." He inclined his head to Master Gold. "When you're done here, you come find me, Ilanna. We'll talk about a secure room in House Hawk to set you up in."

"I will."

When the door clicked shut, Master Gold turned to Ilanna. "And our arrangement?" He spoke in a low voice, and his eyes darted around the room. "When will you have more?"

"Now." She placed the purse in the Guild Master's hand. "Your share of the take. Fifty percent."

Master Gold eyed the coins within. "Good." He slipped it into a pocket. "I assume this will be all for now?"

She shrugged. "I can try to sneak out occasionally, but I'll be focused on the Duke Phonnis job."

Master Gold sighed. "I need as much as you can give me. This gold is all that's keeping certain…parties in line."

"I understand. I'll do what I can. Some of that came from the Alamastris."

She studied his reaction. Master Gold knew of her unsanctioned visits to the houses on the Crown-protected list. Indeed, he'd suggested them in the first place.

"Excellent." He rubbed his hands together. "Well, I'll let you get on with your business." He sat behind the wooden desk occupying one corner of the room and shuffled papers. "I've got my own worries."

He'd approached her shortly after her acceptance as a full Journeyman, laying out the truth about politics in the Guild. His position as Master Gold was anything but secure. Other House Masters and Journeymen—he never told her who—vied for power within the Night Guild. If he didn't keep enough of the senior Guild members on his side, he would lose his position. Only gold kept his allies loyal.

Ilanna glanced down at one of the papers. She couldn't be certain, but the handwriting bore a strong resemblance to the notes that appeared in her room.

I still don't understand why he doesn't just tell me where he wants me to hit. If he knows, why would he send the notes? Why the veiled threats? She'd puzzled over the question in vain for hours. *I guess it's part of the game he has to play with the other House Masters.*

She paid him half her take to provide him with funding to continue buying support—in secret, of course. In return, he offered his protection. His tacit support had tipped the scales to her benefit on many occasions. Everyone in the Guild knew Master Gold favored Ilanna; only she knew the real reason why.

Master Gold toyed with the brooch on his vest. Up close, Ilanna could make out the details: a silver falcon clutching a dagger in its talons. A single diamond sparkled in the bird's eye. A beautiful piece, albeit too gaudy for her taste. *He certainly loves his ornaments. Lives up to his name, doesn't he?*

Ilanna nodded at the jewelry. "It's exquisite." She smiled at the thought of the glistening brooch in Kodyn's muddy hands. He'd love the ornate hawk but have no idea of its true value.

He gave her an odd expression. "Thank you." It came out almost as a question. He glanced at the piece, then back at her, as if it held some significance.

Not understanding, she gave a short bow. "If that's all, I'll be off. The Duke's not going to rob himself." The words dredged up a memory of the last time she'd spoken to Denber. She swallowed the pain, pushed it to the back of her mind.

"Of course. Let me know if you need anything."

With a nod, Ilanna strode from the room. Before she closed the door, she caught one last glimpse of Master Gold's odd stare.

Chapter Twelve

Ilanna winced at the creaking hinges. Allon's hand darted to his belt dagger but dropped away when he saw her. Surprise flashed across his face. "Ilanna? What are you doing here?" Allon folded his arms. "You've never come to my room before. Why now?" His words held an icy chill.

"You're upset about the other night."

His eyes slid from hers. "Of course not," he said in an unconvincing tone.

"You were hurting."

"That doesn't make up for it." She stepped closer, placed a hand on his cheek. Her skin crawled at the contact, but she held it, turned his face toward her. "I was hurting, but you were only trying to help. It was unfair of me to lash out."

Under normal circumstances, Ilanna would have faced the Duke's justice before apologizing. Remorse and guilt were weaknesses she refused to permit. She'd have chosen confrontation before making amends with someone she considered her equal. But she wanted Allon's help—no, *needed* it—to make her plan work. If that meant she had to suck down a generous helping of mock contrition, she would do it.

"If you were someone else, I'd ask you to forget about it, put it behind you. But we both know that's not going to happen. You can't forget anything. Ever."

He gave her a weak smile. "A curse, sometimes." He tapped his forehead. "There are a lot of things I wish I didn't have to remember. Like the look you gave me that night."

Allon's memory was one of the things that had drawn her to him in the first place. He had a preternatural gift for remembering everything. He could tell her what he'd eaten twenty years earlier or how many coins he'd lifted from his first mark. His mind clung to every detail no matter how insignificant.

"I know. Which is why I'm here."

She was acutely aware of his masculine scent, a mixture of leather, soap, and the scented oil he used to hold his hair in a tight tail. A light beard covered his jaw, and his features—a sharp nose and eyes as dark as her own—turned heads on the rare occasions he slipped into formal wear. He was considered handsome yet she felt only a passing attraction. Just the thought of his hands on her body turned her stomach. It wasn't him as much as *her*; she hated being touched by anyone but Kodyn. Even the slightest contact brought back the memory of Sabat.

Her face showed none of her thoughts as she stood on tiptoes to plant a kiss on his lips.

"I'm here to make it up to you." She bit her lip; a gesture he loved, one that helped her swallow her rising gorge. "But I'm also here because I want that mind of yours."

"For your job?"

Ilanna's jaw tightened. "What do you know if it?"

Allon grinned. "Nothing, but House Hound is abuzz with rumors."

"And what do those rumors say?"

"What *don't* they say?" Allon chuckled. "Some say you're going to murder the Duke in his sleep, or that you're going to break into the Royal Treasury and carry out every gold piece King Ohilmos has squirreled away."

Ilanna rolled her eyes. "As usual, the fools flapping their tongues loudest have the least idea of the truth."

He crossed his arms over his chest and met her gaze. "So does this mean you're going to tell me what you're doing?"

"You mean you won't blindly agree to help me without knowing what's going on?" She stuck out her lip in a pout. "Have my charms truly dimmed that much?"

Allon's gaze dropped below chin level, then darted back up to her eyes. "Oh, not in the least." He gave her a sly grin. "And didn't you say you came here to 'make it up to me'? I'm sure I can think of something you can—"

Ilanna gave him a stern frown. "You men! Only one thing on your minds. And here I thought you wanted to hear about my big job."

Allon laughed. "Of course I do. Doesn't mean I can't think about other things, too." He held up a pair of fingers. "I can have *two* things on my mind. Like a steel trap, remember?"

"Fair enough." Ilanna stepped closer, brushing against him. His muscles tensed as she pressed her chest against his. But before he could embrace her, she smoothly moved past him to hover over the small desk beside his bed.

Upon the desk lay a dozen sketches in various states of completion. More than a few depicted her; she found it odd to see her full lips, round nose, and high cheekbones staring up at her from a piece of parchment.

She tapped the paper with one of the graphite sticks. "You got the eyes wrong. You made them hard, angry." She turned to him with a teasing grin. "Is that how you see me?"

His face colored. "N-No, of course not." He flipped the drawing over to hide it from her. "You weren't supposed to see that. I-It's not finished."

Perfect. She'd thrown him off-balance.

She met his eyes. "It's beautiful, Allon." She spoke in a lower register, with just a hint of smoke. "You're very talented."

His embarrassment turned to pride. Few in the Guild knew of his artistic inclinations, but Ilanna had encouraged his interest. Such a little thing, yet it made a difference in his perception of her, made him believe she cared. All without the need for intimacy.

"That's the second reason I want you for my job."

His eyebrows shot up. "What? Why?"

She smiled. *Too damned easy.*

"Because I need you to draw, from memory, an entire building."

His eyebrows nearly flew off his head. "What building?"

"I'll tell you, but only if you agree to do the job." She placed a finger to his lips to silence his questions and whispered into his ear. "Yes, it *will* be worth your while." Her finger traced the outline of his mouth. She pushed him against the wall and pressed her body against his. He stirred in response. "I take it that's a yes?"

Allon groaned. "Keeper take you, woman! How could any sane man say no to that?"

"Good." Ilanna stepped back with a grin. "Then meet me in the Aerie in half an hour." Her eyes dropped to his breeches. "You look like you'll need a few minutes." With a saucy smile, she strode from the room before he could say more.

The moment the door shut behind her, Ilanna shuddered. She resisted the urge to scrub her skin to rid it of the memory of his body against hers. The fact that she initiated the contact made it bearable, never enjoyable.

Thankfully, that was a lot easier than I expected. She'd come fully prepared to do whatever it took to get him to join her. No matter how distasteful.

A smile of satisfaction tugged at her lips. *All those hours spent with Croquembouche proved* very *useful.* The courtesan had taught her the tricks of her trade. A little touch, a hint of desire, a few words spoken in just the right sultry tone of voice, and men melted like snow in a Praamian summer. Manipulation grew easier when men believed they were needed and wanted.

A good start. Now let's see what it takes to convince the rest of them.

* * *

"No doubt you've heard the rumors flying around the Guild." Ilanna gave a dismissive wave. "They're all rot."

She smiled at the eager curiosity burning in the five sets of eyes fixed on her. The still air of the Hawk apprentices' chamber lent an air of mystery to their meeting, enhanced by the dim lamplight and the hush of Ilanna's voice. Master Hawk had replaced the beds with a handful of chairs and a table. Ilanna would upgrade the lock after the meeting ended. She could take no chances with this plan.

"Three people know the truth." She held up the corresponding number of fingers. "With you, that's eight. Eight people in the entire Night Guild privy to my plan. Master Hawk, Master Gold, and myself I can trust. As for the rest of you…"

"Dramatic, Ilanna." Errik reclined in his chair, grinning. "Now are you going to tell us the plan?"

"We're going to bring down Duke Phonnis."

The words hung in the air, and five sets of eyes went wide.

"What?" Errik nearly fell off his chair. "Twisted hell, Ilanna, I knew you were crazy, but this is something else!"

Ilanna didn't smile. "This is no joke. I'm going to make sure the Duke regrets executing Denber and Werrin." She met the eyes of each person in turn. "Before I tell you anything, I expect your oaths of secrecy." She drew a dagger from her bracer and held it out, hilt-first. "Swear before the Watcher in the Dark that nothing I say here will pass your lips. Not with your House Master, your comrades, no one."

Allon stood first. "I swear it." He dragged the blade across his palm. Blood welled and dropped into the golden platter sitting on the table.

Errik came next. "I swear it."

Darreth, a compact, bespectacled man wearing the black-trimmed robes of House Scorpion hesitated a moment. Wincing, he carved a shallow slice in his palm. "I swear it."

Veslund and Joost, Journeymen of House Fox, repeated the oath. She'd selected them on Errik's recommendation that they knew their business and could keep their mouths shut.

Ilanna added her blood to the plate without flinching. "We are sworn." She slammed the crimson-edged dagger into the table. "Watcher help you if you speak a word of this outside this room."

Shadows hung thick in the room, lending the perfect ambience for the nature of the meeting. She made a mental note to install more alchemical lamps—they'd need more light once they had the blueprints.

"No doubt you're wondering how I intend to bring down the Duke." All nodded. "I can't kill him, but I'm going to do the next best thing. I'm going to ruin him."

Errik, Allon, and the two Foxes leaned closer.

"Unlike the rest of the nobles of Praamis, the Duke derives his fortune from two sources." She held up a finger. "One, from the debts owed him by the Royal Treasury. According to Entar, the interest alone is enough for a comfortable living." She held up the other finger. "But it's his other source of income that we're going to destroy. His business."

A smile played on Darreth's face and Errik's eyebrow danced toward his hairline.

"For decades, the Duke has enjoyed a reputation as Praamis' primary deterrence against crime. The nobles unwilling to pay King Ohilmos for protection from the Guild turned to the Duke. His Arbitors catch ten criminals for every one caught by the Praamian Guard. But it's his security systems that are the true foundation of his reputation."

Ilanna smiled. "As you know, the Black Spire was once believed to be the most secure building in Praamis. Impossible to break in to." Her grin turned sardonic. "Thankfully, someone showed him the truth, but that hasn't stopped the nobles of Praamis from paying him to keep our hands well away from their valuables. He's designed vaults, strong-rooms, and lock-boxes, all impenetrable. His traps and snares have sent many of our fellow Journeymen to an early grave."

Five heads nodded.

"That is how I—how *we*—are going to bring him down." She met the eyes of each person in the room. "We're going to prove that no clever traps or locked rooms can keep out the Night Guild. We're going to shatter his reputation by breaking into the places he believes most secure. Just as with the Black Spire."

Ilanna could see their minds working. They didn't need to know her ultimate target yet. She doubted any of them would betray her—she'd chosen them for their reliability—but wouldn't take the risk.

"You're each here because you have something to offer. Errik." The Serpent straightened. "I need someone who can slip in and out of a building undetected."

Allon bristled, but Ilanna held up a hand. "You have another task, Allon. I need your sharp memory and your artistic skill. I'll need you to get into a specific building and memorize the layout."

The Hound nodded, mollified.

She turned to the Scorpion. "Darreth, there are none in House Scorpion as adept at sums and calculations as you."

"That is true." Darreth was an odd fellow. He embodied the word "slim", all bones with no muscle. His long-fingered hands seemed eternally in motion. He spoke in a grating voice that stopped just short of irritating. He never made eye contact, but his gaze hovered just over her shoulder. Yet the mind behind his wide-set eyes was as sharp as his chin and nose.

She jerked a thumb at the Hound. "You'll work with Allon to draft architectural blueprints of the building. We'll need them to study and figure out the best way to reach our target."

"You two." She indicated the two Foxes with a nod of her head. "I'll need your skills on the streets, finding the quickest escape routes and running errands. Nothing glamorous, but you'll get paid fair just the same."

Veslund, a slant-eyed man with a shock of wild hair, scratched his scraggly beard. "Ye'll be paying us, then? No fair share of the take?"

"Day rates for now." Ilanna met the Fox's eyes. "This is a two-part job, but the first part has no payoff. If I want your Houses' cooperation, I've got to pay you the standard fees." Each House had their fees for intra-Guild work. Not surprisingly, House Serpent and Scorpion charged the highest rates, while House Grubber's costs bordered on pittance.

"S'fair enough, I guess." Joost shrugged and stretched out his too-long legs. "Better'n liftin' purses, says I." His sallow, clean-shaven face contrasted with his fellow Fox's scruffiness.

Ilanna turned to Allon and Errik. "Any problem with that?"

Errik shook his head. Allon looked like he wanted to protest but shrugged.

"Good. To business then." She rubbed her hands together. "As I said, this plan comes in two parts. We can't move directly against the Duke just yet. First, we need to get our hands on as many blueprints as we can find. You know what that means?"

Darreth had no reaction, but Errik whistled quietly. The two Foxes looked lost.

Allon's face turned a shade paler. "You can't be serious, Ilanna! It's impossible, not to mention profane."

"As impossible as the Black Spire?" She spoke in a strong, confident voice. "Keeper-damned difficult, sure. But just because no one's done it doesn't mean it can't be done." She plowed on before the Hound could speak. "Gentlemen, we're going to break into the Coin Counters' Temple."

Chapter Thirteen

"You sure about this, Ilanna? This doesn't just walk the line of sacrilege—it bloody well dances over it!"

Ilanna glanced sidelong at her companion. "I never took you for the superstitious type, Allon."

Grimacing, the Hound adjusted the black vest beneath his deep blue waistcoat. "Not superstitious. Just not the sort to tempt the gods' wrath." He inclined his head in the direction of the squat, grey building. "It's a *temple*, for the Maiden's sake."

Ilanna snorted. "You really think the gods are going to look down from the heavens and strike you with a bolt of lightning or open the ground beneath your feet? They're far too busy with their own 'god things' to take notice of us." She straightened her cloth cap. "Besides, we're not actually stealing from the gods. Just...taking a little jaunt through their temple, is all."

"Still don't like it." Allon scowled. "This doesn't feel right."

Ilanna rolled her eyes. "Keeper's bony knees, Allon! Had I known there'd be so much whining, I'd have—"

"Not whining." Allon's jaw muscles tightened. "Just trying to keep your soul from damnation."

She looked up at the Hound. "Sentiment noted. Now, can you sack up or should I find someone else to take your place?"

Allon's fists tightened but he nodded. "Let's go." He dropped his voice to a whisper. "But if the Apprentice sends you to some frozen hell for what we're about to do, make sure to let him know I was forced against my will."

Ilanna's harsh laughter turned more than a few heads. She ducked, dropping her eyes to the street. Her job was to *avoid* drawing attention to herself. Her hair hung in a tight scholar's braid and she wore the clothes of a page: a brown tweed jacket over a rough shirt and grey trousers. The satchel slung over her shoulder completed the façade.

Beside her, Allon looked prim and proper in his crushed velvet coat, stiff black trousers, and boots that glistened with a fresh coat of polish. He'd applied enough hair oil to light every candle in the Night Guild. The scent of aftershave hung in a thick cloud around him. Chin lifted, his strides long and confident, he moved with every shred of self-importance his disguise conveyed.

She hunched her shoulders, hung her head, and trotted after Allon. The cloth cap gave her cover to study the market around them.

Joost lounged in the shade of a cloth-seller's stall, slicing into an apple with a belt knife. He whistled a tune without looking up, a signal that he had a watch on the street. She didn't expect anything to go wrong, not at this early stage, but she wouldn't take chances.

A steady flow of people moved along the Path of Penitence, the broad, tree-lined avenue that cut through the Ward of Refuge. Many wore the colorful, tailored garments of Praamian nobles and merchants coming to pay respects to their favorite deity. Scores of olive-clad Praamian Guards stood at attention along the avenue, keeping a close eye on the passersby. Even skilled Foxes knew to avoid the Ward of Refuge. The temples didn't take kindly to thieves stealing coins intended for their coffers.

Her gaze slid over steepled towers, elegant marble columns, and statues of the heroes of Einan. She had no need for the gods or their temples. She had eyes only for the squat, grey building that stood at the far side of the plaza.

Coin Counters' Temple was home to the servants of Garridos the Apprentice, god of enterprise. The fortress-like building rose three stories— paltry compared to the towering heights of the Master's Temple or the Monument to the Swordsman, but its length and width surpassed its neighbors.

The dull brick façade belied the true grandeur of its interior. Allon's high-heeled boots clacked on the marble floor and echoed off the ceramic-tiled walls. The Hound led her into a pillared gallery, down a broad staircase, and through the entrance to the temple itself. The walls narrowed to a single door flanked by a pair of olive-clad Praamian Guards.

One held up a hand as they approached. "Name and business?"

Allon drew himself up. "Alten Trestleworth, private clerk to Lord Gileon Beritane." He jerked his head at Ilanna. "Carrying records of *great* importance to House Beritane."

Unimpressed, the guard studied the Hound. "Never seen you before."

"And I've never seen *you*," Allon sniffed, "yet you don't hear me questioning your right to be here."

The guard opened his mouth.

"What's your name, fellow?" Allon drew out a stylus and wax tablet. "It will come in handy when I'm explaining to Lord Gileon why I was late for his meeting with Grand Reckoner Edmynd."

The guard glanced at his companion, who shrugged. "Right." He gave Allon an indifferent wave. "Know how to get where you're going?"

Allon sniffed again and strode past. Ilanna bowed and shuffled after him.

Suppressed mirth crinkled the corners of Allon's eyes. *He's having far too much fun with this.* "The point is to *avoid* drawing attention."

"Just playing the part," he said. "Now, I believe it's a page's job to be silent unless spoken to." His voice held the hauteur of a bureaucrat, the tone that grated on her ears every time Bryden spoke.

The chamber they entered could have garrisoned a hundred soldiers—horses, gear, and all—with room to spare. A grand chandelier hung from a gilded chain, conveying an air of supreme importance and solemnity enhanced by the marble tiles on the walls and floor. Two Praamian Guards stood against the far wall, eyes wary, hands hovering near their clubs. A long, dark marble counter ran the length of the temple interior. Priests in the formal grey robes of Reckoners stood behind the counter, attending the people that formed a long line. Every so often, one of the priests would turn from the counter, carrying away purses, chests, and satchels and returning with slips of paper.

That's where all the money goes. Her eyes fell on a smaller entrance set into a corner of the hall. *So records storage is behind that door.*

A balding, paunchy priest hustled toward them. He took one look at Allon's clothes and bowed. "Welcome, good sir. I am Reckoner Helmor. May I ask what brings you to the Apprentice's temple today?"

"Private business for my Lord Gileon Beritane."

"Lord Gileon is a valued patron of the temple, but I must admit your face is unfamiliar."

"As it should be." Allon gave a dismissive wave. "My time is best spent balancing the finances of House Beritane, not running errands. Alas, my lord insisted that I make this delivery in person." He drew out a signet ring and a letter bearing an official seal. "I trust that this will convey my Lord's desires in sufficient clarity."

After a moment of study, the priest cracked the seal and opened the letter. His eyebrows did a little dance as he read the contents. "All is in order." He handed the parchment back to Allon. "I thank you for understanding our need to be certain."

"Of course. There are records of inestimable value held here, more than a few of which belong to my Lord Gileon. He values your thoroughness, as do I."

"I will admit," Helmor said, hesitation in his voice, "that some of your master's requests are somewhat…irregular." He fingered the silver chain hanging from his neck. "It is uncommon for us to allow any outsiders into the records room. For security reasons, you understand."

"Irregular, but not unheard of." Allon held the priest's gaze. "Lord Gileon was very clear that *I* must store the records with my own hands." He lifted the satchel from Ilanna's shoulders. "They are not to leave my sight."

"Surely you cannot believe that we would allow your records to come to any harm." Helmor's displeasure leaked through his fawning. "The Reckoners treat the safekeeping of all documents with the utmost solemnity." His voice rose in pitch and volume and his face reddened. "For centuries, these very halls have served as haven for the most vital and sensitive records in the city. Even through the Great Strife itself!"

Allon held up a hand. "I intended no disrespect, good Reckoner. Indeed, my Lord has the utmost faith in your reverence for his personal records. Yet you read the letter. I must obey my master's will. Perhaps there is some way to convince your superiors to allow me to carry out my Lord's wishes." He drew a purse from his robes. "House Beritane is ever aware of the Reckoners' attentiveness to their duties."

Helmor took the purse from Allon. "A donation to the Temple is always welcomed." He stroked the fine hairs on his round chin. "Let me speak to the Chief Reckoner. As you say, your request is not unheard of. He may be convinced to allow you to carry out your Lord's command."

The rotund priest strode off, leaving them standing in the middle of the grand floor.

Ilanna spoke in a whisper. "Think he'll bite?"

"Course he will. Lord Gileon's letter and signet ring were all we needed, but a few imperials always go a long way with priests."

"I'll take your word for it."

Unlike the persona of Alten Trestleworth, Lord Gileon Beritane actually existed. He counted among the wealthier nobles of Praamis, in name only. Few in the city knew that Lord Hunnan Beritane had squandered away the family fortune before his untimely death at the ripe age of thirty-two. Before sending a Serpent to do away with the foolish noble, the previous Master Gold had formed an alliance with his heir. The Night Guild provided finances to sustain the nobleman's lavish lifestyle, and the young Lord Beritane gave the Guild legitimacy. The signet ring in Allon's hand truly belonged to House Beritane. Gileon himself had penned and sealed the note. His services had proved invaluable on many occasions, worth every imperial the Guild spent.

Reckoner Helmor shuffled toward them, a newcomer wearing a golden chain in tow. "Chief Reckoner Passitter, I have the honor of presenting Alten Trestleworth, private clerk to Lord Gileon Beritane."

Allon gave a short bow. "The honor is mine."

Chief Reckoner Passitter, a tall, lean man with a neat goatee, held out a hand. "The ring and note." Allon complied. The upper priest squinted at the note, drew out a pince-nez, and settled it on the bridge of his nose. "All appears to be in order." Returning the items, he turned to Helmor. "Deposit Lord Gileon's donation in the coffers. I will escort Master Trestleworth personally."

Helmor rushed off without a backward glance.

Passitter extended a long-fingered hand toward a nearby doorway. "Through here, good sir." He glanced at Ilanna and raised an eyebrow.

"She stays, of course. No need to stretch propriety any more than necessary."

The priest pointed at a wooden bench along a nearby wall. "She can wait for you there."

Allon turned to Ilanna. "Try not to wander off like last time, girl." He poured a concentrated dose of scorn into his voice. "Unless you want the lash again."

"Yessir," Ilanna mumbled and ducked her head. Shoulders hunched, eyes downcast, she scurried to the bench and sat.

Allon muttered something about "useless scoundrel" and "wool-headed twit" as Chief Reckoner Passitter led him away. The priest tapped on the door, which swung open with the groan of hinges straining beneath an immense weight of metal. The *clang* as it closed reminded Ilanna of an anvil dropped from a second-story window.

Bloody thing has to weigh as much as ten men, and is at least a hand thick. No way we're getting in through there. She could only hope Errik found a better entrance.

As she settled to a comfortable position on the bench, a half-dozen Reckoners rushed past her, scurrying toward a pasty man wearing expensive clothing cut in the ridiculous lacy, frilly style the nobles of Old Praamis found so appealing.

The foremost priest bowed. "My Lord Munder, it is an honor."

"Yes, of course." Lord Munder's voice dripped impatience. "Now show me to the Grand Reckoner's office at once. I've a meeting with the King to get to, but not before I deposit a few items."

"Right this way, my lord." The fawning man backed toward a third entrance, one Ilanna hadn't noticed. Four men stood guard, hands on their sword hilts, faces hard. "Grand Reckoner Edmynd awaits you in his office."

The rotund nobleman sniffed at the stairs but lifted his cloak and began the ascent. A servant bearing an oversized scroll tube hurried up behind him, the Reckoners in their wake.

Time crawled by as Ilanna waited for Allon to return. She occupied herself studying the enormous chamber. A few dozen people milled around the temple. Merchants and noblemen spoke with grey-clad Reckoners, handing off heavy purses, chests, and satchels for safekeeping in the vaults of the Coin Counters' Temple.

The wealth stored within these walls rivaled that of the Royal Treasury. Merchants, nobles, and those unwilling to invest in a private vault entrusted their earnings to the Reckoners. The priests of the Apprentice kept meticulous records of every copper bit that flowed through their fingers.

To hear the Reckoners tell it, they had never lost, misplaced, or miscounted a single coin. Anyone without a valid reason to enter the temple found themselves detained and subjected to ferocious, often violent questioning. The Praamian Guards at every entrance and exit discouraged even the most brazen pickpocket from theft.

Yet the Reckoners' greatest deterrent came from the fact that they served in the house of Garridos. Few would dare to risk the wrath of the gods for the sake of a few imperials. After all, the Reckoners taught, a man's soul was worth more than all the gold in Praamis. To steal from the temple would bring down the Apprentice's swift justice.

Ilanna gave a quiet snort. *Like that's going to happen! The gods can't hear us.* She'd cried out to the Bright Lady, goddess of healing, when her mother lay dying. And again when Sabat beat her, broke her bones, and brutalized her. The goddess hadn't listened; the gods cared nothing for the suffering of their people.

Ilanna's gaze fell on a tall man taking his place in the line that led to the Reckoners' coin counting table, a small purse clutched in weather-beaten hands. He winked and gave her a snaggle-toothed smile.

She rolled her eyes. *Someone else is having too much fun playing dress-up.*

A commotion to her left drew her attention. The pack of priests appeared from the doorway a heartbeat before a huffing, puffing Lord Munder heaved his bulk down the last stair. He waved away the Reckoners, barked at his servant, and waddled toward the exit.

Odd. Her eye fell on the servant. *He doesn't have the scroll tube with him.* Perhaps the secretary had left it in the Grand Reckoner's office. *Maybe—*

Just then, the heavy metal door swung open and Allon strode into the vaulted chamber. Passitter hovered at his heels.

"I trust your master will be satisfied?"

"He will." Allon inclined his head to the Reckoner. "I will ensure House Beritane's contribution to the Apprentice is more than satisfactory next quarter."

Passitter gave a deep bow. "May the god bless your master's endeavors."

"And yours." Allon strode toward Ilanna, barking. "Up, girl! We've business to be about, and no time for your dozing."

Ilanna dipped her head. "Yessir. Sorry, sir."

With a nod to Passitter, he strode from the temple. Ilanna trotted to keep up.

"You got it?"

Allon tapped his head. "All in here. Or as much as I could manage with that busybody Passitter breathing down my neck."

"Will it be enough?"

"It had better be. I doubt we're going to get a second chance at it. Any sign of Errik?"

Ilanna waited until they passed the guards before replying. "He's there. Let's just hope he can find a way in. Security's tight."

"Even tighter, once you get into the records room."

"I want to hear all about it, but first you need to head back to the Guild and get Darreth to help you map the place. I'm going to hang around a while longer, see if Errik leaves and find out what he's learned."

A passing merchant gave them an odd look as he tipped his hat to her. "You got it, boss." With a grin, he strode down the street.

Excitement set Ilanna's heart racing. *It begins.*

Despite her lack of faith in the gods' concern for mere mortals, Ilanna found herself praying silently for the Watcher in the Dark's aid. Her quest had begun and she'd take all the help she could get.

Chapter Fourteen

"How accurate is this?" Ilanna leaned over the table and studied Darreth's blueprints.

"If the Hound's memory is correct—"

"It is," Allon cut him off, glaring.

Ilanna nodded. "It's why he was the one to deliver Lord Gileon's documents."

Darreth inclined his head. "Then it's as accurate as if the original architect himself had drawn it."

Ilanna smoothed the parchment. Rough lines marked the boundaries of the I-shaped Coin Counters' Temple, with notations of distances between the various sections. Smaller squares and rectangles indicated the presence of shelves, racks, and cabinets.

"Describe the temple layout to me, Allon."

Allon lifted the graphite stick from the table. "Right here," he said, tapping a small rectangular chamber on the southeastern side of the building, "is the temple lobby where you waited."

Blueprint:

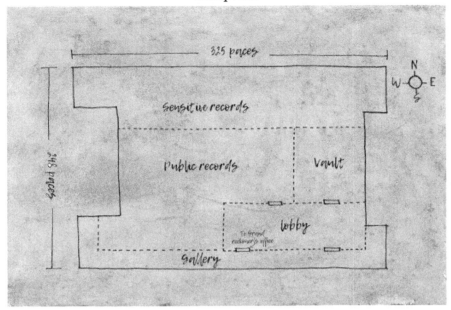

Ilanna's eyes grew wide. "*That?* It looked a lot bigger when I was there."

The Hound nodded. "That's how enormous the temple really is. That huge room occupies a fraction of the building." He returned his attention to the blueprints. "Here, on the northern wall of that chamber, there are two doors. I'm guessing the eastern door leads to the vault where the Reckoners store the gold, silver, and copper that flows into the temple. Just beyond the western door, the one I went through, is public records storage. Mortgages, deeds, contracts, and the like."

Ilanna gave a dismissive wave. "None of which matters to us for this job."

"Most of the building is for public records, but this section here—" he tapped the chamber at the far north of the temple—"is for more sensitive documents." He gave a mocking grin. "Reckoner Passitter didn't take too kindly to my questioning the safety of Lord Gileon's records, and he made sure I saw how secure it was." He held up two fingers. "Two keys, each carried by a different Reckoner."

Ilanna stroked her chin. "Did you get a good look at the locks or the keys?"

"I tried, but the Reckoners concealed the keys with their bodies. I did get a clear view of the locks. Looked a bit above my pay grade, if you know what I mean."

Ilanna chuckled. "Guess I'll need to take a closer look. Did you see anything that could help Errik find a way in—not just for himself, but for me as well?"

Allon's brows furrowed. "Not really. The doors were bloody thick and the noise they made as they opened could rouse a sleeping Bloodbear." He ran fingernails through his beard. "Alchemical lamps only, no windows that I saw."

Ilanna cursed and leaned over the blueprints again. "Problem is, this is just the first floor. If the Duke's records aren't stored in that back room…"

"I saw a few staircases in the public records rooms. Maybe they'll get us to the upper floors?"

"Won't know until we get in. That leaves us stuck waiting for Errik." She ran a hand over the blueprint.

"Don't touch!" Darreth's tone turned scolding.

Ilanna raised an eyebrow, but Allon interjected. "Graphite smudges easy. Comes off easy, too." He gave her a wry grin.

Ilanna raised her hands. "Don't want to ruin the plans." She worried at her lip. "I think we're best starting off our search in that back section. The Duke seems the sort to keep his records under lock and key."

"You sure you don't want me with you? I've got a pretty clear picture of that area in my mind. I'd come in handy with the search, too."

Ilanna shook her head. "No. The more people that go in, the higher the chance one of us makes a stupid mistake. I won't risk us *all* getting caught."

Allon looked unconvinced, but he nodded. "You're the boss, boss."

She grinned. *And don't you forget it!*

"Keep working with Darreth and see if you can add anything more to these blueprints. The more detail I have, the better I'll be able to get around in there." She held up a hand to forestall his protest. "I'm not doubting your memory. But even the slightest thing—the placement of a desk, whether a door opens in or out, even the color of the furniture—can make a difference."

"Color of the furniture?" Allon tilted his head, incredulity written plain across his face.

She gave him a condescending sigh. "Some colors reflect lamplight better than others. Color also indicates the finish of the material, or even the material itself. Metal shelves hold more weight than wooden. Need I go on?"

He held up his hands. "I defer to your wisdom, oh great and wise Hawk."

"Damned right you do!"

Joost's laconic drawl echoed from a nearby armchair. "If the two of yous are quite done with your flirtin', maybe you can tell us what we're meant t'be doin'?"

Ilanna stiffened. In her study of the temple layout, she'd forgotten about the two Foxes. "I need the two of you to keep an eye on the place tonight."

"Anything partic'lar ye'll be wanting us to look for?" Veslund scratched his bushy beard, adding to the pile of flakes on his lap.

"Everything. Guard patterns in and around the temple, comings and goings of the Reckoners, light in the windows. The more I know about the place, the better."

"Got it." Joost uncurled his lanky frame from the armchair and stood, towering a full head and a half over her. "Better get a warm jacket, Ves. Looks like it'll be a cold one."

Grunting, the bearded Fox followed his companion from the room.

Darreth stood from his wooden stool and gathered his graphite sticks, rulers, compasses, and other odd paraphernalia. "If it's all the same to you, I'll take my leave. House business. Back in the morning." His eyes never met hers as he nodded and slipped from the room.

Ilanna gave the blueprints one last look before rolling them up and slipping them into an oversized scroll tube. The tube went under the loose floorboard beneath Joost's armchair. No one but she, Allon, and Darreth knew the hiding place.

She turned and collided with Allon's chest. She stiffened as his arms snaked about her.

"Errik won't be back for a few hours." His whispered words felt hot on her neck, and he nuzzled against her ear. "Seems like we've got time to slip off and—"

She extricated herself from his embrace. "Not now."

The Hound wouldn't be so easily dissuaded. "Why not?" He pushed the door closed with his foot. "We won't find a more *private* place in the Guild than here."

"I…" Ilanna cast about for an excuse.

He stepped closer. "You know that what we're doing isn't wrong, right? There are no rules against…fraternization. Fiery hell, if you knew how many times Master Hound and Journeyman Serah have…"

"I know, Allon." She hid her revulsion behind a saccharine smile. "But don't you want someone who's actually *present*? My mind's all full up with worries about the job." She spoke in a breathy voice, tracing a finger down his chest. "I'd rather save it for when we're done and we can focus on what really matters." Her hand slipped to his trousers and she applied more pressure.

His breathing quickened, and he stirred against her grip. "Sweet gods, Ilanna!" He pressed against her.

She slipped away. "After, I promise. See you tomorrow, Allon." With a cherubic grin, she gestured to the door, resisting the urge to scrub her hand on her clothes.

"That's plain unfair." Groaning, he shuffled out the door, half-crouching to hide his body's reaction.

She pulled the door shut, and the lock engaged with a *click*. Lifting the key from around her neck, she inserted it, twisted, and shot the deadbolt home.

Satisfied, she strode down the tunnel toward the Aerie. There, she caught a glimpse of the snaggle-toothed man from the temple.

"What'd you find?"

Errik tugged the false teeth from his mouth. "A Watcher-damned lot of security, that's for sure."

She shrugged. "Priests love their gold."

"Oh, I could've found my way into that vault my first month in House Serpent. But the record room's buttoned up tighter than Conn's bunghole."

Ilanna's laugh turned into a snort. "That bad, huh?"

Errik nodded, his grin fading. "I'll need a couple more days to figure out the best way in."

"We've got time. Our way in and out has to leave no tracks, even if it takes longer to figure out."

"It's your coin." He pulled off his wig and shrugged out of the merchant's cloak. "I'll go back in tomorrow. But first I've gotta get around a proper meal."

"Good." She gripped his arm. "Find that way in, Errik. Everything's riding on you."

"I know." He met her gaze. "For Denber."

Swallowing the lump in her throat, Ilanna nodded. She watched him go, only turning away once the doors of House Hawk boomed shut behind him.

She glanced down. She had to get out of the page's robes and into her regular work clothes. She would pay the Coin Counters' Temple a visit once night fell. She'd spent hours sitting atop the flat-roofed temple with her fellow Hawks. *Maybe there's a way in from up there.*

She strode through the silent tunnels of House Hawk. After Denber and Werrin's deaths, the mood in the House had grown more subdued. The passages seemed emptier, gloomier. No one passed her in the halls; no words of greeting or peals of the twins' exuberant laughter echoed around her.

She glanced down the passage to the room Willem had shared with Werrin. The door stood open. Guilt surged through her. She hadn't spoken to Lem since Denber's death. Taking a deep breath, she knocked on the door.

"Lem?" Clearing her throat, she spoke louder. "Lem, you in here?"

No answer came. She poked her head into the room.

Willem sat on his bed, hands folded in his lap, expression vacant. The rise and fall of his chest were the only indications he still lived.

She stepped closer. "Lem, can you hear me?" He gave no indication he had. "It's me, Ilanna."

He didn't move as she sat on the edge of his bed.

"Bloody hell, Lem! You look awful." She pressed a cup to his cracked lips. "Drink."

His mouth opened and he swallowed, but his eyes remained fixed on empty air.

"Come on, Lem. You've got to snap out of it."

She recognized his condition. Her grief over Ethen's death and horror at Sabat's brutality had rendered her immobile. She'd lain in her bed for days, unthinking, uncaring, willing herself to die. A desire for vengeance had pulled her back from the brink of despair. It had to work for Willem, too.

"Willem." Her hand cracked across his face.

His eyes widened a fraction, and he turned to stare numbly at her.

"So Werrin dies and *this* is what you do? Starve yourself to death?"

Willem winced as he swallowed. "Go...away...'Lanna."

"No." She folded her arms. "Not until you eat something." Her nose wrinkled. "And take a shower. I haven't smelled something this bad since the first time I cleaned Werrin's bed."

Willem's mouth twitched.

"Remember how he used to hide his clothes under his mattress? They'd pile up, but he'd wear 'em again and again until they reeked." She chuckled. "I swear there had to be something wrong with his nose!"

"Filthy...bastard." His words came out in a quiet rasp. He didn't meet her eyes. "Hated...bathing."

"Almost as much as someone else." She dug an elbow into ribs that had grown far too prominent. "What d'you think he'd say if he saw you now?"

"Doesn't matter." His shoulders slumped.

"Yes it does! Do you think he'd want you to waste away like this? Or do you think he'd want you to figure out how to get back at the bastard responsible?"

For the first time, life flickered in Willem's eyes. "The Duke?"

"That's right." Ilanna squeezed his hand. "I've got the Guild's permission to take down the Duke and I need your help."

Confusion cracked the mask of numbness. "My help?"

"Something only you can do. You're the only one I can trust." She searched his eyes. "But I need to know you can do it. For Werrin."

His hands tightened around hers. "For Werrin." The spark of vitality flared to life, and a trace of the old Willem shone through. "Tell me what you need me to do."

Chapter Fifteen

Cloaked in grey, Ilanna blended with the moonless night. Torchlight illuminated the courtyard below but failed to reach the upper level of the Coin Counters' Temple. She'd have plenty of time to examine the flat rooftop.

A quick sweep confirmed what she already knew. *I'm not getting in this way.*

She'd spent hours up here with Denber and the other Hawks, relaxing, sharing meals, studying the Black Spire. The roof had no access hatches, not even a glass skylight or a chimney protruding from the featureless space.

Damn it! She hated waiting for Errik to find a way in. *No upper-story access, so now what?* She drew out her miniature quickfire globes—each barely larger than a man's knuckle—and held them close to the rooftop. Pulling a dagger from her bracers, she scratched at the masonry. Chunks of mortar came loose with minimal effort.

With an anchored rope, she could slide down the walls, away from the guards, and into an upper-floor window.

Wouldn't take much to pound an anchor into the stone. Bloody noisy, though.

In the distance, twelve peals echoed across Praamis; the Lady's Bells tolled midnight.

That'll do. The bells should cover any noise. But it would take her more than twelve strikes to anchor a spike securely enough that she would trust her weight on it. *Better call Jarl in to get it set up.* The Pathfinder's enormous arms would make short work of the job.

She trusted Errik to find a way in but she needed a back-up plan just in case. No such thing as overplanning, Denber had told her.

She peered over the edge of the roof. The guards had retreated from the chill evening breeze and huddled in the meager shelter of the gallery. The torches and alchemical lamps rendered them night-blind. No way they'd see her leaping the gap to the neighboring Temple of Derelana. From there, she could slip through the maze of spires and dart across the slim plank bridge that connected the Lady of Vengeance's temple to a nearby warehouse. The Hawk's Highway traversed the length and breadth of the city, a network invisible to all below. The Pathfinders, the Journeymen of House Hawk responsible for maintaining and expanding the Highway, knew their work well.

She stopped as she came to an intersection. One way led back to the Aerie and the Guild, the other to Old Town Market, her home, and her child. Longing twisted in her chest. She ached to wrap her arms around her son, see his eyes and face light up the way they did whenever he saw her. But she couldn't. Not yet. She'd carried out the orders in her note, but there was a chance that *someone,* whoever it was, had an eye on her. If they could slip into her room unnoticed, they had skills to match her own.

In a way, that narrowed the potential suspects. House Bloodbear hadn't three intelligent thoughts between them, much less the stealth to sneak through House Hawk. They relied on brute strength and intimidation. A Bloodbear wouldn't have the foresight to use her secret against her.

She'd discarded House Grubber as well. A few Grubbers had some skill at sneaking, but *very* few. She snorted. *That only leaves House Hound, Serpent, Scorpion, and Fox. Narrows it right the hell down! Just three hundred-odd people to suspect.*

Much as she wanted, she couldn't rule out her own House. Bryden was the only one to make his dislike for her public but more than a few Hawks resented her success, hated the fact she'd risen so quickly. She trusted Jarl, Werrin, and Master Hawk as much as she dared. She could only truly trust one person: herself.

And Ria. The fire in Ria's eyes told Ilanna she would die before she allowed anything to happen to Kodyn. In a way, it was as if Ria's fierce protectiveness made up for the fact no one had protected her. *Is that why I took her home with me? Am I doing the same?*

She pushed the thought aside and stepped onto the bridge that would lead her back to the Guild. If she hurried, she'd have time for a few hours of rest. She needed a clear head for the next step in the job.

* * *

Nursing a steaming cup of tea, Ilanna listened to Joost and Veslund's report.

"…guards stayed put the night through. Four squads of three: here, here, and here."

Darreth slapped Veslund's grimy finger away from the temple blueprints, as if completely unaware that the Fox stood almost a full head taller and far broader in the shoulders.

Scowling, Veslund continued. "As I was saying, they got all ways in covered. A patrol goes 'round the outside 'bout once every hour."

"Forty-five minutes, by my count," Joost drawled.

Veslund flushed and opened his mouth to retort, but Ilanna held up a hand. "Close enough. Anything else?"

Veslund dug his fingers into his bushy beard, scratching his cheek. "Nothing I can be thinking of."

Joost scratched the hair on his head, dropping flakes onto the map. "Maybe this helps, but I saw lights come on up here." Under Darreth's glare, his pointing finger stopped just short of touching the map. "Northwest corner, lookin' out over the plaza, there are windows on the third floor."

"Any idea what's up there?"

Joost shook his head.

"Speaking of..." Veslund's forehead scrunched. "Right about midnight, the temple got a visitor. Hood, cloak, the works. When he came out, I coulda sworn he was Lord Vorrel."

Joost snorted. "And how in the frozen hell d'you know what a nobleman looks like?"

"I seen 'im around town. Ye know, I may not have yer poncy skill with numbers, but I've got a good head for faces. I don't—"

Ilanna snapped her fingers. "Joost. What time did the lights go on in that window?"

"Right 'bout midnight, says I."

"Interesting." Ilanna leaned over the blueprints. "Right here, northwest corner?"

Joost nodded.

"Lord Vorrel pays a late night visit to the Coin Counters. I'd wager the lights came on *after* he showed up. Means he, like Lord Munder, probably went up to see the Grand Reckoner."

Darreth finished her thought. "The Grand Reckoner's office, you think?"

"Makes sense. The temple's built like a fortress, yet there's a bloody great window on one corner? Seems reasonable the Grand Reckoner's got the pull to claim that for his office."

She tensed at a knock. The tightness faded at the familiar voice. "It's Errik."

At Ilanna's nod, Veslund pulled the door open. Errik's expressionless face revealed nothing but his eyes sparkled.

"You've found a way in!" Excitement set Ilanna's heart thumping.

"I did. And a way to get you in, too."

Triumphant laughter burst from Ilanna's throat. "Excellent!" She smacked the Serpent's back. "How do we do this?"

Errik shouldered his way up to the table and stabbed a finger at the northeastern wall. "There's a second-floor window, right about here. Two hours before midnight, I'll open it for you. Be ready."

"I'll be there." She'd have Jarl set up the anchor under cover of the midday bells. Tight, but it would work. "How're you getting in?"

He gave her a sly grin. "Serpent's secret."

Ilanna wanted to pry but knew better. Every House had secrets of tradecraft they guarded with fierce zeal. She respected Errik enough to restrain her questions.

"Joost, Veslund, be outside the temple before sunset. I'll want you close at hand in case of trouble."

The bearded Fox nodded. "Gotcha."

"Darreth, you got as many details from Allon as you could?"

The Scorpion nodded. "It won't get any more complete."

"Good. Then you're done for now. But don't get busy. If all goes well, I'll be back with the blueprints tonight. We're going to need you for the second job, too."

"As you say."

Ilanna rubbed her hands together, excitement setting her pulse racing. "Gentlemen, tonight is the night!"

* * *

Ilanna crouched at the edge of the Coin Counters' Temple's roof, peering down at the small window set into the northernmost section of the temple's east wall. Her neck ached from the awkward position but she refused to move. She had to be ready for Errik's signal.

The window opened outward and an arm protruded from within. *Time to move.*

She dropped the silken cord over the side of the building, checked her harness one last time, and slid down the rope. They'd chosen a perfect night. A sliver of moon hung among the twinkling stars and a gentle breeze carried away what little noise her soft-soled boots made as she walked down the wall. She'd studied the pattern of the patrol with care; she should have two or three more minutes before they showed. She could drop the few paces to the window in a matter of—

Light appeared around the corner of the temple, accompanied by the clatter of hobnailed boots. The second-floor window closed.

Ilanna cursed. *Damn them! Bloody bastards are early.*

Heart thundering, she flattened herself against the wall. The guards' conversation grew louder as they approached. Sweat beaded on her forehead despite the night's chill. She clung to the rope, not daring to move, to breathe. Even the slightest sound or flutter of cloth could attract the guards' attention.

The guards moved at a steady pace. But to Ilanna, the patrol seemed slow as snails. Her forearms and fingers burned from the effort of gripping the rope. Moisture softened her leather gloves and she felt her hold slipping. She couldn't adjust her position but if she didn't do something, she would fall. Every shred of strength went into clinging to the rope.

She imagined she could feel the heat of the torches drifting up to singe her legs as the guards passed. Their boots clicked on the cobblestone street, and one actually took up a whistled tune. Ilanna willed them to move faster; her grip would give out at any moment.

After long, agonizing seconds, she couldn't bear it any longer. Burying her head in her cloak, she reached for the rope with her free hand and let her breath out in a gasp. Fire thrummed through her hands, turned her aching fingers to claws. For a few pounding heartbeats, she clung to the wall.

Below her, the window opened, and Errik's beckoning hand appeared again. Biting back a grunt at the pain in her arms, Ilanna slid the last distance. Errik gripped her legs and pulled her into the room. Her boots landed without a sound on a rolled-up carpet. Faint starlight revealed a pile of dusty furniture.

"What took so long?" she mouthed to Errik.

He shrugged.

Her nose wrinkled at the smell wafting from his clothing. She was glad she had no idea how he'd gotten in; it clearly involved the privies.

Errik poked his head out the open door. "This way," he whispered.

Ilanna followed him into a carpeted corridor. No furniture decorated the hallway and the walls stood bare of tapestries, paintings, or art. The plain, utilitarian interior of the temple was a far cry from the high-vaulted ceilings, marble pillars and floors, and expansive luxury of the main chamber.

Errik thrust her through a doorway as light washed down the corridor. A grey-robed Reckoner strode into the hall, an alchemical lantern in his hand. The beam of light drew closer with every heartbeat.

Ilanna's fingers sought a dagger from her bracer but Errik gave a barely perceptible shake of his head. She gripped the blade anyway. The familiar metal calmed her racing heart, stopped her hands from trembling with nervous excitement. The thrill of the job always set her on edge at first. Her mind would regain control of her body within a minute or two.

The Reckoner stopped at an entrance less than fifteen paces away, knocked, and entered. The light disappeared as the door closed behind him.

"Let's go."

Errik led her past the occupied room and down a corridor that turned left. A short distance away, a set of stairs descended to the first floor. The Serpent crouched at the bottom of the stairs and, holding up a hand, peered around the corner. Ilanna counted ten rapid heartbeats before he moved on.

He slipped from shelf to shelf with a stealthy grace Ilanna couldn't help envying. It seemed to come natural to him, moving without a sound.

She counted out every pace in her mind. Darreth had drawn the plans according to Allon's stride, then calculated she would need three steps to match his two. If her mental map was accurate, they were in the far rear of the public records room. *We should be close to the locked room Allon mentioned.*

The sound of footsteps sent Ilanna diving behind a shelf. Her dark grey cloak blended with the shadows but she would take no chances. The beam of an alchemical lamp tracked across thousands of scrolls, papers, binders, notebooks, and leather-bound tomes burdening the wooden shelves around her. The heavy breathing of a night watchman echoed in the silent chamber. After a minute that seemed like an eternity, the guard moved on.

Errik jerked his head to the right and Ilanna followed. Less than ten paces away stood an enormous metal door, nearly twice Ilanna's height and three steps across. She drew out her quickfire globes and held them up to study the door.

Keeper take these priests! Four cylinder locks held the door secure. At a glance, she guessed each had four pins, perhaps even six.

Ilanna tapped a fingernail against the door to draw Errik's attention. "Know how to deal with these?"

He shook his head. Serpents only learned to pick rudimentary locks.

"Gonna take me a few minutes."

He nodded. "I'll keep watch."

Storing her quickfire globes, Ilanna thumbed a ball pick and snake rake from her bracer. She set to work on the lock and cursed as she felt not six pins, but eight. *Bastards think you're so clever, eh?* It would take her longer than expected, but she'd cracked eight-pin locks before.

She smiled at the satisfying *click* of the first lock.

Errik hissed at her. "Too loud."

"Nothing I can do about it."

The second lock opened a minute later and she moved on to the third. These pins had a much higher tension, so she switched to a slant hook and triple rake. The lodestone in her bracer kept the picks not in use close at hand.

Sweat trickled down her back and she clenched her cramped fingers into fists.

"This is taking too long." Errik hissed in her ear. The warmth of his breath made her shudder, and she nearly dropped a pick.

"Keep watch!" The third lock *clicked* open. "Just one more."

She slid the pins of the final lock into place like a bard strumming a lute. Four pins. Three. Two.

Just as she set to work on the last pin, a beam of light splashed across the shelves to her left. She had a moment to decide. If she released the pick, the pins would re-set, but she couldn't risk being spotted.

She froze. Her heart stopped and she held her breath.

The light slipped over her head, across the door, and along the row of shelves. The guard's whistling grew fainter as he continued his patrol.

Ilanna gave a half-sigh, half-gasp and twisted the pick. The final lock snapped into place. The door swung open.

"We're in."

Errik slipped past her with a grin. "Never doubted you."

Closing and locking the door behind her, she turned to examine the thousands of scrolls filling shelves, cabinets, and drawers. *This is going to be a long damned night.*

Chapter Sixteen

Muttering a curse, Ilanna shoved the scroll back onto the shelf. *Two hours of this and not a Keeper-damned thing to show for it!* At Errik's hiss, she ducked behind a desk. *Things'd go a lot easier if that bloody Reckoner didn't pass every ten minutes.* The broad beam of his lantern shone through the metal grate separating the secure storage room from the public records. If he saw them, they'd have no way out.

Her eyes ached from studying plans by the light of her miniature quickfire globes. Not for the first time, she considered sending Errik to dispatch the guard. At least they'd have an hour or two to search the enormous records storage room with a proper lamp. She shoved the thought away. Better to remain undetected for as long as possible, even if that meant straining to see in the dim light.

The guard finally moved on and, with a sigh, Ilanna rummaged through another cabinet. The room stretched fifty paces long and close to three hundred wide. Scrolls, boxed records, books, and stacks of parchments lined the walls from floor to ceiling, not to mention the four rows of free-standing shelving in the middle of the room.

Thankfully, she didn't have to read each piece of paper. The Duke's engineers used a special paper stock: larger and thicker than clerical parchment, made of compressed cotton rather than vellum or wood pulp. Cotton better held the graphite lines used for diagrams, sketches, blueprints, and architectural designs.

How Master Gold knew what Duke Phonnis' blueprints looked like, she'd never know. The Night Guild cultivated contacts everywhere—was it so hard to believe someone was willing to sell information on the Duke? She wouldn't complain; it made her job easier. She could feel her way along the shelves, though the absolute darkness of the enclosed records room made her skin crawl. The faint glimmer of the quickfire globes kept her from bumping into obstacles.

Errik had his own globes but she moved far faster than he. He kept an eye out for the guard, freeing her to focus on the search.

Not that we're getting anywhere. She'd found a few dozen blueprints stored among the property of other nobles. Nothing belonging to the Duke.

"How much longer?" They had to leave before sunrise.

Errik shook his head. "An hour, maybe two."

With a low growl, Ilanna bent her attention to the laborious search. A nagging in the pit of her stomach told her they'd have to come back tomorrow night.

* * *

"What?" Ilanna clung to the rope, her body half-out the open window. "You're not coming with me?"

Errik shook his head. "Easier if I stay. Means I can get you in earlier tomorrow night. More time to search." He motioned to the dusty furniture piled around him. "No one'll find me in here."

Ilanna wanted to protest but his resolute expression dissuaded her. He knew his business.

"Until tomorrow night."

"Be on the roof before sundown. I'll get you in the second hour after dark. Most Reckoners are in their rooms by nightfall."

Ilanna nodded. "So be it."

"And bring food."

"You got it. Stale bread and moldy cheese."

He gave a rueful grin. "My favorite."

Returning his smile, Ilanna slipped out the open window. The guards had passed scarcely five minutes before; she had plenty of time to climb the short distance to the roof. She left the rope in a tight coil around Jarl's anchor.

A quick glance at the sky told her she had another hour before sunrise. The thrill of breaking into the temple hadn't worn off; the way her heart pounded its excitement, she'd never get to sleep. Her desire to see Kodyn warred with her fear of getting caught. Prudence won.

At least I'll have time for a bath and a meal before the House meeting today. Another confrontation with Bryden would leave her wishing for a bath *after* the meeting as well.

* * *

Where is everyone? Ilanna looked around the empty chamber where House Hawk held its weekly meetings. The Aerie had been empty when she entered, the tunnels deserted. She'd thought nothing of it. The Hawks should all be in here. *So where in the Maiden's name are they?*

Halfway down the corridor, she spotted Eustyss, one of Bryden's crew. "Oi, Eustyss, where is everyone?"

The Hawk spun. "There you are!" Annoyance flashed across his face. "Been searchin' every bleedin' corner of this place for you. Master Hawk says to get yer arse over to the Menagerie an hour ago."

The Menagerie? The Guild only used the enormous chamber when choosing apprentices, swearing in new Journeyman, or discussing matters that affected every House, matters the House Masters deemed important for all to know. Apprehension settled like a stone in her gut.

"What for?"

Eustyss shrugged. "My name ain't Master bleedin' Hawk, is it? Now you gonna keep askin' useless questions, or are we goin' to get gettin' so we don't miss whatever's so important a man's roused from bed before sunrise?"

Stifling a rejoinder, Ilanna strode past him and out the enormous doors of House Hawk.

* * *

"Brothers and sisters, fellow Journeymen, for twenty-three years, I have served as Guild Master." Master Gold's voice boomed through the Menagerie. "For twenty-three years, I have borne the burden of making difficult choices. Together with your House Masters"—his gesture included the seven figures seated at the front of the crowd—"I have strived to ensure that each and every one of you has a chance to prosper in service to the Night Guild. Many of our choices were made behind closed doors, with only a few voices to lend counsel."

The Guild Master wore no ceremonial robes, no jewelry. He stood clad in simple clothing of muted colors cut in a style common among the tradesmen of Praamis. The modesty somehow underscored the solemnity of the occasion. The knot in Ilanna's stomach grew.

"But today, I bring to you a matter that cannot be decided only by your House Masters. What you are about to hear affects us all, and it is a choice you each must make. Listen well, for now you, too, will share the burden of difficult decisions." He bowed and stepped aside.

The man who took his place stood almost a head taller than the Guild Master, and the breadth of his shoulders rivaled even Master Bloodbear's. His rich garments, the precision of his neat goatee accented the confidence in his eyes as he stared out over the sea of Journeymen.

"Honored members of the Night Guild, my name is Blinton, but I am simply the mouthpiece sent by my master to deliver a message. I bring you a message of hope, a promise for a better future for every one of you. I greet you in the name of Saldinar, First of the Bloody Hand."

Ilanna stiffened. The Journeymen around her muttered, a nervous tension thickening the air.

"My master has a question for you." A fiery intensity blazed in the man's eyes. "He asks you: who is the ultimate power in Praamis?"

No one answered.

"Does the Night Guild rule supreme? Duke Phonnis? King Ohilmos?" He turned his palms up as if balancing a scale. "There is an equilibrium, one that must be maintained for the sake of order. You answer to the King and he turns a blind eye to your activities. After all, a unified Guild is in the interests of all. Duke Phonnis and his Praamian Guard protect the citizens of this city, but they will only act insofar as the King permits." He nodded. "It is the way things are and have been for decades. All in the name of a peaceful city."

His face grew stony. "But in Voramis, there is one true power. King Gavian may sit the throne but he is naught but a figurehead. He dares not send his Heresiarchs against the Bloody Hand for fear of retribution. The Bloody Hand rules supreme in Voramis."

He spread his arms wide. "*That* is what I offer: true power, control over the city of Praamis."

"An intriguing offer." Master Serpent leaned forward in his chairs. "Only a fool would turn it down."

A smile spread across the Voramian's face.

"But," Master Serpent held up a hand, and the man's confident grin slipped a fraction, "I've learned that an outstretched hand often distracts from a hidden dagger. Show us the dagger, man of Voramis."

"A fair point, Master of House Serpent." The man's jaw muscles worked. "My master's offer is simple: join us. Unite the power of the Night Guild with the Bloody Hand. In Voramis, every Justiciar, every Heresiarch commander, every nobleman either serves the Bloody Hand or knows what will happen if they interfere in our business. Our rule over Voramis is complete. We offer you the chance to do the same in Praamis."

Master Scorpion spoke. "And what's in it for the Bloody Hand? Why would your master extend such generosity and help us take control of *our* city?"

"For a small share of your profits." The Voramian gave a dismissive wave. "Just as your Journeymen turn over a percentage of their earnings to you in exchange for the protection of the Guild, the Guild will do the same to the Bloody Hand. In return, we offer the total domination of Praamis, just as in Voramis."

The crowd shifted and murmured. More than a few of the Journeymen around Ilanna sounded intrigued at the idea.

"What of our tyros?" This voice belonged to Master Velvet. "How will they be trained?"

Master Bloodbear spoke up. "Who would rule the streets and keep order? Is the Bloody Hand thinking to replace House Bloodbear?"

"Would the Bloody Hand conform to our Guild structure?" Master Hawk chimed in. "Or would we be expected to admit any hoodlums and thugs that seek acceptance?"

Ilanna pushed through the crowd. "And what of our independence? Are you expecting us to take orders from your ilk?"

"What percentage of our profits?" Anorria, the Scorpion bookkeeper, moved to stand beside Ilanna. "How much will our 'alliance' with the Bloody Hand cost?" Her words held a generous helping of scorn.

The barrage of questions seemed to catch Blinton off guard. He stammered, flustered.

Master Gold stepped forward and, raising a hand for silence, turned to the Voramian. "We have heard your master's offer. As you can see, there are a lot of questions that must be answered."

Blinton blinked, recovering his composure only with great effort. "My master would be happy to answer all your questions. All are good questions. The Bloody Hand will negotiate the answers to your, and our, satisfaction. I simply bring his message, and would be happy to return to him with yours."

"Of course." Master Gold nodded. "Allow us time to discuss amongst ourselves. You will have our answer before nightfall."

"As you say." Bowing to Master Gold, Blinton addressed the gathered Journeymen. "Your Guild Master called you brothers and sisters, comrades. It is my fervent wish that I, too, will soon call you my brothers and sisters." With that, the Voramian strode from the Menagerie. A surreptitious gesture from Master Gold sent two Serpents in his wake.

The Guild Master gestured at the crowd. "You have heard the Bloody Hand's offer. You've all heard the tales from Voramis and you know the reputation of the First and his organization. I will not taint your thoughts with my own opinions. It is up to each of you to choose for yourselves what we will do. Go to your Houses, discuss our course of action, and put it to the vote. Your Masters and I have sworn to abide by your decisions. The fate of the Night Guild rests in your hands, my brothers and sisters."

* * *

"There's not a Keeper-damned chance we're going to accept their offer! If even half of the stories about those bastards are true, they make the Bloodbears look like the bleedin' Sisters of Mercy."

Ilanna had never seen the quiet, grey-haired Sayk so animated. The man paced around the Hawk Council Chamber, red-faced, arms waving for emphasis.

"The fact that we have to discuss it shows that some of you are too stupid to find your own arses with a map and a search party."

Master Hawk held up a hand. "Your sentiments are noted, Sayk. But all must have a chance to speak."

Sayk took a seat, his expression a tapestry of indignant rage.

The House Master motioned to the room. "Anyone else have aught to say?"

More than a few brows remained furrowed in thought.

How in the frozen hell can they consider this? Ilanna would rather be planning the Duke's job, but she had to attend to this very serious problem.

The Bloody Hand had appeared in Voramis before she was born. Once, nothing more than a pack of thugs, thieves, and assassins, they had staked their claim to the Blackfall District in Lower Voramis. They'd turned the Blackfall into a place where the citizens of Voramis—first the commoners, then the nobility—could indulge in every vice and pleasure of the flesh. Their power had grown slowly at first, then at a terrifying speed as they expanded their hold on the city.

For years, war had consumed Voramis. The rival gangs refused to relinquish their territory but the Bloody Hand would not be stopped. They used whatever means necessary to eliminate the competition.

Master Hawk had told her stories of the headless corpses left hanging from the city gates. Hundreds of Voramians had simply vanished, hundreds more killed in violent altercations between gangs. In vain, the Heresiarchs had attempted to stem the tide of bloodshed and brutality.

Then came the day when the Bloody Hand had either eliminated their rivals or convinced them to join. The First had turned his attention to the nobility. The commoners of Voramis had hidden in their homes as bands of thugs swept through Upper Voramis, dragging noblemen and women from their mansions to execute them in public. On the First's orders, an entire section of Upper Voramis had been set to the torch to send a message: noble blood could not protect against the Bloody Hand. The nobility responded by acceding to the demands for gold, and the violence ceased.

The King at the time, Darayn, had ordered his Heresiarchs to bring the Bloody Hand to justice. Two days later, his chancellor found the King and Queen in bed, throats slit, royal blood staining silks and bedding worth a fortune. King Gavian hadn't repeated his father's mistake. The young King preferred to ride his horses, train with his blademaster, and bed the gaggle of aristocratic daughters eager for the honor.

For almost a decade, the Bloody Hand had reigned supreme in Voramis through cruelty and savagery. They controlled the populace by providing what they most desired: fair wages, cheap alcohol, and carnal pleasures. The city had adapted to the Bloody Hand's presence but still they remembered the horrors endured.

And now the Bloody Hand wanted to bring that to Praamis.

"I'm with Sayk." She stood, hands on her hips. "If we agree to their offer, we all know what'll happen to our city. Praamis might not be paradise but I can't let it become another Voramis."

Bryden rose to his feet. "On the other hand, their offer does have merit." He met her gaze, scorn sparkling in his eyes.

Ilanna glared. *Damn you, Bryden.* The Hawk would insist the sun set in the south, if only to contradict her.

"After what happened to *your* friends"—he struggled to hide a gleeful grin at the jab—"I think you, of all people, would want to do whatever it took to prevent more deaths. If the Bloody Hand's offer of power is good, we could run Praamis however we wanted to." He turned to Master Hawk. "No more contracts for the King, no more limits on which houses we can and can't hit. We would be masters of the city!"

"At what cost, Bryden?" Ilanna's voice rose to a shout. "You want thousands of people to die so, what, you can earn a few more imperials? Can your greed truly eclipse your intelligence?"

Bryden scowled. "I—"

"Enough!" Master Hawk's voice cracked like a whip. "If you can't restrain yourselves from bickering when lives hang in the balance, shut your Watcher-damned mouths and sit down."

Bryden opened his mouth to speak.

"NOW!" The roar set the walls rattling.

The Hawk dropped into his seat and Ilanna followed suit.

"Does anyone else have something *useful* to add to the discussion?" His piercing gaze scanned the room. "No? Then let us put it to a vote."

"All in favor of accepting the Bloody Hand's offer?"

A knot of fear formed in Ilanna's gut as she waited. Two hands rose. Bryden's wasn't one of them.

"All opposed?"

Close to twenty hands shot into the air with no hesitation.

"So be it." Master Hawk nodded, his face growing somber. "House Hawk stands against the Bloody Hand."

For better or worse, Ilanna thought. *Gods help us all.*

Chapter Seventeen

Ilanna's boots wore a groove into the packed-earth floor as she waited for the Guild Council to reach a decision.

I can't understand why this is even a debate. How could anyone actually want *the Bloody Hand running loose in Praamis? Are any of the other Houses that stupid?*

She couldn't deny the allure of the power they offered. If the Guild controlled Praamis, Denber wouldn't have died.

It's still not worth it. Inviting the Bloody Hand to Praamis would spell the end of the Guild's way of life. The Voramians would bring only chaos, turmoil, and bloodshed.

Her gut tightened at the *click* of the Council door opening. A red-faced Master Bloodbear stomped down the tunnel. Master Hound gave her a curt nod, and Master Fox's moustache bristled as he strode from the room.

Ilanna darted forward. "So?"

Master Hawk shook his head. "The Guild declines the Bloody Hand's offer."

Relief drained the tension from Ilanna's shoulders. "Thank the gods."

"It was a close thing." Master Hawk's lips pressed into a thin line. "Too close."

"What do you mean? Who voted in favor of the Bloody Hand?"

"The Bloodbears, of course."

Ilanna snorted. "Not surprising. They only think with their fists and purses."

"House Fox and House Hound voted as well."

Ilanna's eyes widened. "What?"

The Foxes had little enough, so she could understand their desire for the wealth and prosperity offered by the Bloody Hand. But House Hound? Their earnings might not match House Hawk or House Serpent, but surely they enjoyed a degree of luxury. It didn't make sense that they would accept the Bloody Hand's offer.

"House Scorpion and House Serpent were as quick to shoot down the offer as we were, but Master Grubber said the vote almost went the other way. If it had…"

Ilanna shuddered. *Keeper forbid!*

"This was the closest it's ever been."

"Ever been?" Ilanna's spine stiffened. "This has happened before?"

"The Bloody Hand has been trying for *years* to get their claws into Praamis. The first offer came before I became Master Hawk."

"That was more than twenty years ago!"

Master Hawk nodded. "And still they try. Their persistence grows with their increasing hold over Voramis." He sighed and, for the first time, Ilanna noticed how old he looked. The lines on his weathered face had deepened. Grey hairs outnumbered the black on his head and beard, and his shoulders drooped as if beneath an immense weight.

"Prepare yourself, Ilanna. The Voramians will bring their trouble upon us. Perhaps not today or tomorrow, but sooner than we'd like." He rubbed his eyes. "And when that day comes, may the gods have mercy on us all." Leaving ominous words hanging in the air, Master Hawk strode toward the Aerie.

Muscles tightened at the base of her spine. She'd believed Master Hawk unflappable, yet even a blind man couldn't miss the fear lurking behind his eyes.

Raising a hand, she knocked on Master Gold's door.

"Enter."

Masters Grubber, Serpent, and Scorpion stood around the Guild Master. Their conversation died as she strode into the room.

"Ah, Journeyman Ilanna." Master Gold beckoned. "Thank you for coming so quickly. I feared you would be too busy to heed my summons."

Ilanna bowed. "I am here, as requested. But if you are occupied, I can return another—"

"No, no." The Guild Master gave a dismissive wave. "The good Masters and I were simply reminiscing on better times." He gave his three companions a meaningful look. "But I'm sure they have their own duties to be about."

"Of course." Master Serpent uncurled from his chair and stood in one smooth motion. "I believe all of our Houses expect to hear the outcome of the vote."

Master Scorpion bowed to Master Gold, nodded to Ilanna, and followed Master Serpent out. Ilanna tried hard not to wrinkle her nose as the odorous Master Grubber scurried after them. She didn't miss his surreptitious attempt to slip a purse into his pocket.

Ilanna raised an eyebrow. "You didn't send for me."

"We must maintain appearances. For any other Journeyman to speak to me, he must make an appointment through Entar or wait until they are summoned. If you simply walked into my chambers to speak to me and I was seen to encourage it, it would raise suspicions."

"Amongst who?" She crossed her arms and held his gaze.

"Anyone who wants something to use against me. My position as Master Gold is not as secure as you might think."

The words Master Gold had spoken to her on the night she became a full Journeyman echoed in her mind. "*It will be good to know I have one such as yourself to watch my back. There are ever more daggers in the dark.*"

She studied the Guild Master. He reclined in his chair, for all appearances at perfect ease. Ilanna saw through the façade. His calm demeanor failed to hide the worry in his eyes and the tightness around his mouth.

"Master Hawk said it was close, but we won."

Master Gold's lips pressed into a thin line. "We didn't."

Ilanna sucked in a breath. "But Master Hawk told me—"

"Master Grubber said his house voted against the Bloody Hand's offer. He lied."

Ilanna's eyebrows shot up. "Is that why you paid him?"

It was Master Gold's turn to show surprise. "What?"

Ilanna gave him a hard, cold smile. "Master Grubber isn't as quick-fingered as he thinks. That purse he pocketed could only have come from you. Unless he's gotten in the habit of lifting your belongings?"

The Guild Master's shoulders tightened. "Well…" He met her eyes, but had nothing more to say.

"Is that why you said you needed more coin? To pay off the House Masters?"

"Not just the Masters. Many Journeymen are willing to be bought." He turned his palms upward. "Every man and woman has a price, some higher than others."

"Master Grubber I can understand but Master Serpent, Master Scorpion?" She hesitated, a bitter taste in her mouth. "Master Hawk?"

"Master Hawk and I don't agree on everything, but there are few I trust more to keep the wellbeing of the Guild ahead of his personal desires. Masters Serpent and Scorpion need a bit of…encouragement, as do many of the Journeymen." He sighed. "Unfortunately, gold is the primary method of motivating recalcitrant Journeymen to make the right decision. And the gold I have is simply not enough. Which is where you come in."

"And what about the other Masters?"

"Master Bloodbear couldn't come up with an original idea if it punched him in the face. Master Fox is willing to bend over for anyone with enough coin. He insists it's for the sake of his Journeymen and apprentices, but I suspect more than his share of imperials wind up in his pocket."

"And Master Hound?"

"Bernard has his own beliefs about how the Guild should be run. We were friends once, many years ago. We were as fiercely competitive as brothers, yet it was a rivalry built on a mutual desire to succeed. Until our Undertaking."

"What happened?"

"My triumph cast a shadow over his. I rose in the ranks of House Hawk faster than he did in House Hound. When the seat of Guild Master became vacant, he failed to drum up the support needed. He came to me for help, but I told him I, too, intended to become the next Master Gold. He's resented my election for twenty-three years."

"And *that's* enough to have him join the Bloody Hand?"

"It seems petty, but Master Hound truly believes the Bloody Hand's offer is for the good of the Guild. A painful transition, to be sure, but ultimately beneficial to all. For over twenty years, since the first offer was extended, he's been its most vocal supporter. Until this latest vote, I had no idea just how much influence he has over the Journeymen. If I don't step up my efforts to undermine that support, I fear what will happen the next time the Bloody Hand comes calling.

"Wait, they've been asking for over twenty years?" Ilanna gave an angry snort. "And you're just telling us now?"

Master Gold shrugged. "Until now, the Council was mostly in agreement to refuse the Bloody Hand's offer. Yet Bernard has gathered enough support to bring the Council to a deadlock. We had no choice but to present it to the Guild body."

Ilanna struggled to digest the information. Master Gold's cryptic words had begun to make sense. Both he and Master Hound sought whatever tools they could use to sway Guild support in their favor. She was a tool in the Guild Master's political battle against Master Hound's faction.

"How many Journeymen support him?"

"Too many, if this last vote is any indication." He counted on his fingers. "If the majority of the Hounds, Foxes, Bloodbears, *and* Grubbers support him, he can call for a vote and have me removed as Guild Master. That is his ultimate goal and he will use the Bloody Hand's offer as leverage to sway as many as he can to his side. We must respond with gold, else we stand to lose everything." His brows furrowed. "How soon do you anticipate success with the Duke's job? That influx of gold could do wonders to buy the goodwill of all but Bernard's most fervent supporters."

Ilanna shook her head. "We're still a long way off. We haven't even found the blueprints yet, much less figured out the way in. The job will take time."

"Time is not on our side." He pinched his nose. "The Bloody Hand's offer will soon turn to demands. When that happens, if I don't have the majority of the Guild to stand against them, I fear for our survival."

The words hung heavy in the silence. Master Gold's fingers toyed with the silver falcon brooch, and his eyes stared into emptiness. Ilanna didn't need to wonder what he pictured; she, too, had no trouble imagining what would happen if Master Hound accepted the Bloody Hand's offer.

"If all goes well, the job should be done tonight."

Master Gold's eyes snapped to her. "But you said—"

Ilanna shook her head. "The first part only. Thanks to your information, Errik and I have a chance of finding those blueprints. Once we have them, it will take weeks to set everything else into motion. I'll have no problem finding the time to slip out unseen."

The Guild Master nodded. "I will do what I can to conjure up more gold on my end." He gave her a wry grin. "Not for the first time, I find myself missing the freedom of roaming the rooftops of Praamis and sneaking into homes. Far easier than being Guild Master."

This surprised Ilanna. Master Gold always seemed so confident, so content in his authority over the Guild. Yet the burden had to weigh heavy on him. With what he'd told her about Master Hound…

"And Ilanna," the Guild Master's voice snapped her back to reality, "I'd appreciate it if you could do some quiet research about Master Hound's supporters. From what I understand, you're close with a high-ranked Journeyman in his House."

Ilanna blushed. What could she say? She'd thought it a secret but if Master Gold knew, there was no use denying it.

"Don't worry." He gave her a reassuring smile. "It's not public knowledge. Jagar told me. Seemed quite happy about it, for that matter. Something about seeing his favorite nephew happy with a good woman."

Ilanna suppressed the urge to cringe. She'd encouraged Allon's developing feelings for her; it made him easier to use. When the Hound no longer served a purpose, she'd discard him without a second thought. But the idea that it would hurt Master Hawk sat uneasy in her gut.

Master Gold's grin grew hard. "Use it, Ilanna. Use *him*. Whatever it takes to keep the Bloody Hand out of Praamis. I'd rather kiss the Duke's arse a thousand times than allow even one of those vicious bastards to step foot in my city."

Ilanna gave him a sharp smile as cold as icicles. "Whatever it takes, Master Gold."

Chapter Eighteen

"What'd you bring me?"

Errik's eyes gleamed as Ilanna drew the bundle from beneath her cloak. He devoured the thick slice of bread stuffed with soft goat cheese, cured meat, and herbs.

"Nice to see you, too." Ilanna pulled the window shut behind her.

The disheveled, dust-covered Serpent muttered something around a mouthful of watered wine.

"Any bright ideas on a faster way to find those blueprints?"

Errik shook his head.

"All those hours spent hiding, wasted!" Ilanna snorted. "Guess we'd better get to it."

Gulping the last of the wine, Errik stoppered the skin, tucked it into his cloak, and opened the door a crack. At his wave, Ilanna slipped into the corridor after him. Unless they got lucky, they had a long night ahead.

* * *

Ilanna leaned against the shelf, arms folded, eyes narrowed. *There has to be a better way to do this.*

The Lady's Bells had rung midnight at least an hour earlier. After four hours of searching, they hadn't found a shred of parchment with the duke's name on it. Everything belonged to minor nobles or merchants.

So where do the truly wealthy store their belongings?

More than a few had private vaults, safes, and strongboxes built into their mansions, used primarily for physical wealth: gold, silver, and other precious metals and gemstones. For legal documents—records, patents of nobility, contracts, and proprietary designs—Coin Counters' Temple guaranteed security. Though the relationship between Duke Phonnis and Grand Reckoner Edmynd bordered on hostility, the Duke availed himself of the Reckoners' services.

No way the Duke would keep his important documents in the same place as a merchant. He's way too aristocratic to mingle with the lowborn.

She pictured Duke Phonnis striding into the Coin Counters' Temple and demanding the respect owed the King's brother, Chief Justiciar of Praamis, and one of the city's wealthiest nobles. Just as Lord Munder had.

She sucked in a breath. *Idiot!*

The watchman's lantern swept the room. She ducked behind a shelf, mind racing.

Lord Munder had insisted he be escorted to the Grand Reckoner's office with all the haughty disdain that marked residents of Old Praamis. He would insist on exclusive treatment.

So if he's storing documents in the temple, it makes sense that he'd deliver them to the Grand Reckoner—the only one "on par" with his noble status.

The nobleman's servant had climbed the stairs carrying an oversized scroll tube and come down empty-handed.

"Errik," she hissed. When he turned, she beckoned him.

"What?"

"What's on the third floor?"

Errik scratched the stubble sprouting on his cheeks. "Second floor's living quarters for most of the Reckoners. Grand Reckoner's office is on the third floor, maybe his private rooms as well. Probably a lot of offices for the upper priests. Why?"

"We're not going to find what we're looking for here." She explained her theory to him.

He nodded. "Makes sense."

"We've got to get into that office."

Errik jerked a thumb over his shoulder. "The staircase on the northeastern wall bypasses the second floor."

"Lead on."

They slithered through the rows of shelves, silent as shadows. The locks on the enormous steel door engaged with a *click* that made Ilanna wince. Her irritation flared as the watchman's passage forced them to hide. They'd wasted too much time searching the secure records room; they'd have two hours to get into the Grand Reckoner's office, locate the Duke's blueprints, and get out.

That's cutting it bloody close!

She swallowed her annoyance and forced herself to match Errik's measured pace. Even on the dark stairs, he moved in total silence, without a rustle of cloth or an audible breath. *Whatever they teach Serpents, it's worth learning.*

He paused at the top of the stairs and whispered in her ear. "Wait here." Crouching motionless for several seconds, he peered around the corner then slipped out of sight. He reappeared a minute later, holding up five fingers. "Guards."

Keeper's teeth! Not surprising, but no less frustrating.

"No way around?"

Errik shook his head.

"Let me see."

A few paces from the staircase, the plush-carpeted corridor ended in an intersection. Light streamed from the passage on the right. Ilanna dropped onto her belly and inched forward to peek around the corner. At the end of the hall, a pair of olive-clad men flanked an ornate bloodwood door. The Praamian Guards stood rigid, eyes on the hallway, hands on their weapons. Two more sat at a table, playing cards and drinking from steaming mugs. The fifth, who wore the black armband of a captain, paced before the doorway.

Not taking any chances, are they?

Cursing the guards for their competence, Ilanna beckoned for Errik to follow her down a floor and around a bend in the stairs. "Can't get in that way."

"Now what?"

She sat, mind racing.

The guards' presence indicated she'd had the right idea. Grand Reckoner Edmynd's office had to be the place. *But if that's the only way in, we're in trouble.* They couldn't fight the guards; the success of her plan hinged on getting in and out undetected. Perhaps she could get in through the office's windows. *That'll just make it even more difficult. There's no way to easily replace a whole bloody wall of glass.*

Hobnailed boots clacked on the stone stairs and lamplight flooded the stairway above her.

Ilanna leapt to her feet and ran down, Errik a heartbeat behind. She peered into the records room, froze. The watchman's whistled tune grew louder, as did the clink of the descending guard's armor. The staircase brightened with every thundering heartbeat.

Ilanna muttered a silent stream of curses. In seconds, the guard would round the bend in the stairs and spot them. But they couldn't advance until the watchman below moved on.

Come on, come on! Her fists clenched and relaxed, and she resisted the urge to reach for a dagger. *Don't make me do this, you bastards.*

The watchman's lamp slid past the mouth of the stairway, moving to the rest of the shelves. Without hesitation, Ilanna darted across the room and ducked behind a bookshelf. Light flooded the stairwell a second after Errik slipped in beside her. The Praamian Guard stopped at the bottom of the stairs, hung his alchemical lamp in its sconce, and took up position.

Bloody hell! Her hands trembled and her heart tried to hammer its way free of her chest. Beside her, Errik let out a slow, quiet breath.

They crept through the rows of shelves at a much slower pace. Ilanna hardly dared to breathe until they reached the stairs that led to the second floor. She pressed her lips to Errik's ear. "Let's get out now. We have to figure another way into that office."

Errik nodded and slipped up the stairs ahead of her. After a glance at the empty corridor, he darted toward the storeroom. Ilanna followed, boots silent on the carpeted floor.

Three steps from safety, Ilanna's heart lurched as a door clicked open behind her. The light of a lantern streamed into the hallway. She leapt the remaining distance and threw herself into the room. Errik pressed the door closed without a sound.

"Did he see you?"

Anxiety burned in her gut, but she shook her head. "I don't think so." She placed her ear against the door and listened. No cry of alarm came. "I think we're good."

Errik strode toward the window. "Get out of here. I'll poke around a bit more, see if I can find another way in."

"No. You don't—"

The latch *clicked*. Ilanna had a heartbeat to slip behind the door before it opened. A grey-robed Reckoner stepped into the room and lamplight shone full on Errik's face.

"Wha—"

Ilanna slammed the pommel of her dagger into the back of the man's head and he collapsed. Errik dove to catch the alchemical lamp before it shattered on the stone floor.

Keeper take it! Closing the door, Ilanna stared down at the unconscious Reckoner. *What the hell am I going to do with him?*

Errik drew a dagger but Ilanna stopped him with a gesture. "We can't leave a body."

The Serpent shrugged. "No one comes here. It's why I chose the place."

"Can't take the risk."

"Then what? The minute he wakes up, he'll raise—"

"We take him with us."

Errik's eyebrows shot up. "Take him…with us?"

Ilanna nodded. An inkling of a plan formed in her mind. "Look." She pointed at the man's golden chain. "He's a Chief Reckoner. He may have the information we need."

Errik's forehead wrinkled but he nodded. "Fair point. But how in the frozen hell are you going to get him out of here?"

The Reckoner personified the word "rotund". His belly strained against the leather belt cinching his ample waist. Ilanna grunted as she tried to roll him onto his back; he matched her height, but one of his legs weighed as much as she did.

Ilanna scowled. "You're right. There's no way I'm getting him out of here without help."

"That rope won't hold him either."

"Tie and gag him." Ilanna produced a glass vial. "But first, give him a drop of this." She eyed the corpulent Reckoner. "Make that three drops. Should be enough to keep him from waking for a few hours." She cinched the rope to her harness and slid the window open. "When I yank, pull this in."

"What are you going to do?"

"Go for help."

"Better make it quick." He glanced at the night sky. "Sunrise ain't far off."

Ilanna leapt out the window and slid down the rope. Seconds later, she unclipped her harness and dashed toward the alley where she'd posted Joost.

"Joost," she hissed. The Fox ducked out of his shadowy hiding place, eyes wide. "Get to House Hawk now, and tell Jarl to meet me on top of Coin Counters' Temple an hour ago. And tell him to bring Gorin and a heavier rope. Got it?"

Joost's eyebrows rose, but he nodded. "Jarl. Coin Counters' Temple. Gorin and a heavier rope."

"Go!"

* * *

Gorin groaned as he and Jarl dropped their burden. "Next time you need someone to lug your dreck halfway across Praamis, find someone else, eh?"

Ilanna gave the sweat-soaked Hawk a dismissive wave. "It's what you Pathfinders do, right? Haul heavy things?"

Jarl gave an amused grunt, but Gorin scowled. "I'll be charging you double for hauling this."

Ilanna gave Gorin a syrupy smile. "Load this size, I'd have paid triple."

The Pathfinder strode away muttering, hands pressed to his lower back.

The Reckoner weighed more than she expected. Errik had had to help Gorin and Jarl haul the priest out the window and onto the roof. The journey across Praamis had taken hours; they'd been forced to hide their unconscious captive beneath a bale of hay and cart him to an abandoned warehouse near the river. Jarl and Gorin earned every imperial of their fees dragging the canvas-wrapped bundle into a secluded storage container at the heart of the building.

Ilanna laid a hand on Jarl's enormous arm. "Thank you, Jarl. I'll speak to Bryden about your fees, with a little extra thrown in. Next drink's on me."

He grunted in acknowledgement and followed his fellow Hawk, sans theatrics.

Ilanna turned to Joost. "Bloody good work, Joost. You earned double today."

The Fox gave a lazy salute without lowering his mug of wine.

"Keep an eye on him, will you? I should be back before the draught I gave him wears off, and Errik's knots should hold."

Veslund spoke from his seat beside Joost. "What if he gets all antsy and shouty?"

She shrugged. "We need him alive and talking."

The bearded Fox cracked his knuckles. "I can be working with that."

Ilanna narrowed her eyes. "Only to keep him manageable and to help him understand the situation. If he's afraid of what's to come, he'll be easier to break." She clenched her fist. "And break him we shall!"

Chapter Nineteen

Ilanna strode through the Aerie, her pace unhurried but determined. She had at least another hour before she had to return to the warehouse. Plenty of time to gather a few important items.

Locking her bedroom door, she shrugged out of her dark grey Hawk's robes and into the ugly brown outfit she'd bought off a Grubber. She knelt and reached under her bed for a small purse hanging from the ropes supporting her mattress. Its contents—a stoppered glass vial the size of her index finger, filled with a colorless liquid—went into a pocket.

A knock sounded at her door.

"Who is it?"

"Allon."

She opened the door. "Can it wait? I've got someplace I need to be."

Allon shook his head. "You're going to want to hear about this *now*."

With a sigh, Ilanna moved aside to let him enter.

"No, not here." He spoke with confidence, though his eyes darted toward her bed. "In the work room."

She followed Allon down the tunnel to the chamber where Darreth hovered over the table, squinting at the blueprints.

"I'm here. Tell me what I need to know."

Darreth's furrowed forehead smoothed as he looked up. "I-I think we've found something."

Ilanna cocked an eyebrow as he tapped a finger on the northwest corner of the Coin Counters' Temple. Whatever he'd discovered, it had him worried—or excited—enough he'd forgotten his injunction against touching the blueprints.

Allon stepped up to the table beside her. "So we were going over the layout of the temple one more time, and something struck Darreth as odd." His shoulder grazed hers, but he didn't move away.

Hiding a shudder, Ilanna slipped around the table to study the northwestern section of the blueprints. "Darreth?"

Darreth fiddled with the graphite stick and his notepad. "According to the original temple blueprints, the building is precisely three-hundred forty paces wide and two-hundred sixty long. This morning, Allon and I were looking at the blueprints again and he thinks that the rooms inside are actually smaller."

Ilanna fought her impatience. "Go on."

Allon spoke up. "Nothing in the records room stood out as odd when I went in, but Darreth and I've been going over it." He drew in a deep breath. "I can't be totally certain, but the room looked closer to two-hundred sixty paces wide."

Darreth studied the notations in his book. "If he's correct, the figures don't add up. There's something missing."

Ilanna narrowed her eyes. "You're sure?"

The Scorpion shook his head. "It's a theory at the moment."

"A tough one to confirm, too." Allon gave her a wry grin. "Unless you can bring me into the temple with—"

"No!" Ilanna cut him off with a chop of her hand. When Allon's face hardened, she spoke in a gentler tone. "More people in the temple means a greater chance of getting caught. I won't risk it, not when we're so close."

She turned to the Scorpion. "What if *I* take the measurements?"

Darreth's brow wrinkled, the corners of his mouth pressing together. "Let me see..." After a few moments of furious contemplation, he looked up. "Adjusting for the length of your stride, that comes out to just over four hundred paces."

"Good. I'll pace it tonight." *Though the damned night watchman's going to make that difficult.*

Allon looked ready to protest but Ilanna didn't give him a chance. "I'm not going to risk you, Allon." She poured feigned sincerity into her words. "If anything happened to you..."

The Hound's eyebrows rose slightly, and he looked taken aback. "I...uh..."

She squeezed his shoulder. "I can do it."

Allon swallowed, nodded. "I know you can." He reached for her hand. "I just—"

"Wanted to help." She gave him a disarming smile and slipped her hand away before he touched it. "You've already done more than you know." She inclined her head to Darreth. "The both of you. When I return, I'll have what we need to finish this job once and for all." She strode toward the door, paused on the threshold with a wink for Allon. "Until tonight."

Outside the room, she wiped her hand on her pants. She didn't have to enjoy the things she did to keep Allon pliable to her desires. She would keep doing them until they no longer worked, or until she couldn't use him any longer.

Pushing aside her revulsion, she strode toward the Perch. *Time to see a man about a temple.*

* * *

Errik waited for her just inside the warehouse door, slouched against the wall, arms folded, his face a mask of stony passivity. "He's awake."

"Good. In one piece?"

Errik nodded. "Won't be pretty for a few days, but I made sure Veslund didn't break anything."

"Thank you." The rigidity of his posture and the tension in his face spoke volumes. "Whatever you want to say, spit it out already."

Errik met her gaze with eyes of ice. "You don't have to do this, you know."

"We need answers; he has them."

"Not like that." He thrust his chin at the bundle in her hands.

She quirked an eyebrow. "This, from a Serpent? Of anyone, I thought you'd understand."

"I'm not saying we don't need to get the information from him. But do *you* need to do it?"

Ilanna tensed, jaw muscles tightening. She pressed her lips together to hold back her snarl.

"Torturing a man doesn't just inflict pain on the victim." He met her gaze, the fire in his eyes unyielding against her icy fury. "It takes something out of you, too."

She spoke in a flat, cold voice. "Thank you, Errik." The words came out clipped. She held his gaze for long seconds. He was trying to help, to spare her from suffering, and Ilanna despised him for it. It meant he saw her as weak, unable to do what needed to be done. She could take care of herself. "Anything else?"

He shook his head.

"Good, then let's get this over with."

She strode past him and into the inner room. Depositing her armload on the table, she came to stand before the Reckoner. "Good morning, Priest."

The bald head darted up. "You insolent little bitch! Do you have any idea what you've—"

She punched him hard, snapping his head to the side. He reeled in the chair and would've fallen if not for the ropes holding him fast.

Ilanna kept her expression calm. "Want to try that again?"

The Reckoner glared up at her. "You stupid cu—"

Her second punch left a bruise on the other side of his jaw. Judging by the cuts over his right eyebrow and the blood trickling from his nose, Veslund hadn't appreciated the priest's poor manners.

"I can keep doing this all day. You're going nowhere, and I've got plenty of food and wine for when I get tired of beating you."

The priest's eyes flicked over to the table where she'd deposited the two cloth-bound bundles and the clay jar of wine she'd brought.

"Oh, foolish me. You must be thirsty. Tell me your name and maybe I can spare a drop or two."

The priest set his jaw and leaned back, defiance written in his eyes.

Ilanna gave a theatrical sigh. "So be it. Don't say I didn't try to be friendly."

She strode to the table, removed the stopper from the wine jug, and took a long pull. She gave an apologetic shrug. "Not the finest Nyslian red I've had, but you won't find better for the price." She held it out to him. "Sure you don't want any?"

Eyes fixed straight ahead, the priest said nothing.

Shrugging, Ilanna placed the jug on the table. "See this?" She untied the knots holding one cloth-bound bundle closed and rolled it open. "Conversation starters, my friends call them."

The priest refused to look at her.

She picked up the bundle and placed it on the floor before the corpulent Reckoner. The priest's eyes widened a fraction as he stared at the knives, chisels, hammers, pincers, pliers, and other crude implements. Crouching, Ilanna reached for a hammer and gave a few experimental swings that came far too close to his kneecaps.

"Now, if it was up to me, I'd really rather not use these. Messy's not my style." She dropped the hammer on his slippered foot. "Oh, clumsy me."

He winced but kept his jaw clamped tight.

She gripped his flabby chin and forced him to look at her. "Don't make this harder than it has to be, Priest. I'd rather we all go home with our fingers, toes, and kneecaps intact. You're the only one that will make that happen. Let's start out with your name."

The priest returned her gaze with a glare.

"Not even for a sip of that wine? Surely that's a fair trade."

She held the Reckoner's expression without wavering. After a long minute, he unclenched his jaw. "Tyren."

"Chief Reckoner Tyren. No doubt you're thinking we're not going to harm you because you're Garridos' chosen servant." She dropped her voice to a menacing whisper. "Your god isn't going to save you. There's only one way you walk out of here in one piece: tell me what I want to know."

Fear darkened the Reckoner's eyes, though he tried to keep his expression neutral.

"But, as promised, a drink of wine." At Ilanna's gesture, Joost brought the jug over and poured a trickle down the priest's throat. "There. I've kept up my end of the deal. How about we make another?" She pointed at the tools on the floor. "Tell me what I want to know and I won't use those on you. Fair?"

She didn't wait for a reply. "The good news, Chief Reckoner Tyren, is that I only need an answer to one question."

"Only one?" He failed to hide his eagerness.

Ilanna nodded and held up a finger. "Shouldn't be too hard, right? You're not going to want to give it to me, but remember our deal." She crouched and picked up a dagger. The silver blade glinted in the sunlight, flashing as she twisted it. "There's no need for you to suffer. It's a simple answer. No one will ever know it came from you."

His eyes followed the motion of the blade in her hands. She hid a grin.

"My question is this: how do I get into the Grand Reckoner's office unseen?"

Surprise widened the priest's eyes. "What?"

"Oh, you thought I was going to ask about the gold in the vaults." She gave a dismissive wave. "I can get in there any time I want. But those guards on the Grand Reckoner's office are a bit more complicated than a handful of locks. So I want you to tell me how I can get in."

"No." The priest's expression grew hard, stubborn. "I will not have you desecrate the sanctity of the temple."

"You sure?" Ilanna stood, dagger in hand. "You're going to break our deal so soon?"

"A deal with faithless scum like you means n—"

Ilanna's arm whipped back and forward. The dagger embedded into the wooden chair between the priest's flabby legs with a *thunk*.

"Think again, Priest." She reached for another blade from the pile.

The priest licked his lips, eyes fixed on the dagger. "I will not," he said, but his voice had lost much of its conviction. "I swore an oath to my god. You cannot—"

125

The second knife joined the first, and the priest squealed as it clipped his fat thigh.

"There's no use resisting. Tell me what I want to know."

Sweat stood out on the Reckoner's forehead but he pressed his fleshy lips into a thin, tight line.

"Here's the thing, Priest." Ilanna shoved the bundle of tools away. "That was just my little bit of fun. I don't need to use any of those on you. In fact, I don't have to lift a finger. I can just wait until you tell me what I want to know. By my calculations, you have about three minutes until the poison works."

Tyren's eyes widened. "P-Poison?"

Ilanna shrugged. "A little something I learned from a friend of mine. He called it cyanide. Me, I don't care what it's called—I just want it to work."

Perspiration streamed down the priest's face.

"Heavy sweating's one of the signs the cyanide's working. That, with a touch of nausea, dizziness, and fatigue thrown in. But that's just for the warm-up."

Tyren's face tightened and his jaw clenched.

"Headaches kicking in? Feel like you need to vomit. Good. That means we're getting to the good stuff. Soon, you'll start gasping for breath and your heart's going to speed up until it feels like your chest's ready to explode. Then it gets bad real fast. That's when the poison's in your blood. When you hit that stage, you've only got a minute before you're off to the Long Keeper."

She drew out a glass bottle filled with a pale yellow liquid. "Unless you get the antidote, of course. You'll be in bed for a few weeks, but at least it'll stop the poison from killing you."

The priest gasped, cried out, and vomited.

"Three minutes left, Priest. How do I get into the Grand Reckoner's office? He's got something stored there I want."

"He doesn't store anything there!" Tyren cried out. "There's nothing of importance to anyone but him in his office."

"So tell me where he keeps the really important things." She leaned over him. "Things like Duke Phonnis' private documents."

The priest's eyes went wide. "I-I can't!" His breath came in wheezing gasps. "The Reckoner's...oath."

"Better a living oathbreaker than a dead fool." She shook the glass bottle. "Time's running out."

The priest coughed, vomited again, and groaned. "Please!"

"Choice is yours. I'd give you a minute to decide but you don't have that. Tell me before it's too late."

"Damn…you!" He struggled for each breath, and pain twisted his features. "Hidden…lift carriage. Door…in his…office."

Ilanna narrowed her eyebrows. "How can I be sure you're telling the truth? Not just saying what I want to hear so I'll give you the antidote?"

"Swear…by… Apprentice!" His voice came out in a weak gasp as his strength faded. "Told…truth."

"Good." She stepped back.

Tyren's face took on a terrible pallor. "An…ti…dote!" He strained toward the bottle in her hands.

"Oh, this?" She shook her head, opened the lid, and poured a few drops down the priest's throat. "This is just a little drink I brought along. This sort of thing always makes me so thirsty." She emptied the rest of the fruity white wine into her mouth. "Hits the spot."

Tyren shrieked, a weak, pathetic sound like a dying animal. His body twitched as the poison set in, and he thrashed against his bonds. His wheezing faded to a quiet gasp, a harsh rattle, and silence.

Ilanna turned away from the corpse. Both of the Foxes remained in their seats. Shock and horror filled Joost's eyes and Veslund had gone pale. She ignored them, facing Errik instead.

"Can you dispose of him?"

The Serpent stared at her, his face hard, eyes flat and dead as his House's namesake.

"We had to." Ilanna met his gaze without flinching. "We kidnapped a high-ranking priest from *inside* the temple. I couldn't take the risk he'd talk. The Reckoners wouldn't have stopped coming until they had their vengeance."

Errik gave her a stiff nod.

"Get rid of the body and everything else in here. He can't be found. Ever."

Chapter Twenty

Not for the first time tonight, Ilanna cursed the watchman. *One hundred ten paces,* she repeated in her mind. *Not even halfway there.*

She drew a deep breath and waited for the guard to move on.

After far too long, the light faded around a row of shelves and Ilanna resumed counting. She struggled to keep her pace measured when she wanted to race through the darkened records room. She'd learned to get in and out quickly, not hang around waiting to get caught. But if Darreth and Allon's suspicions proved true, she'd have found what she sought.

If only this didn't take so damn long!

Forced to duck out of sight every time the guard passed, she'd lost her count twice. Much longer and she'd miss her deadline. She had to return to the storage room before the Lady's Bells tolled the third hour before midnight.

Let's hope Errik has better luck with his task.

The Serpent hadn't said two words since he returned from disposing of the Reckoner's corpse. His dead-eyed stare and the tightness of his face spoke volumes.

I did what I had to. She'd had no desire to slip the cyanide into the wine pitcher while all eyes focused on her tools of torture. But what choice did she have? *I can't risk anyone finding out what we're doing.*

Errik might not approve but she knew he understood. If he needed time to accept it, she'd give it to him. Just as soon as they completed this job.

Her excitement mounted as she reached three-hundred fifty steps and the western wall drew closer. She half-ran the last dozen paces. *Yes!* Three-hundred and ninety six. The secure records room ended, but the public storage section continued for another fifty or sixty paces. She didn't bother trying to do the figures in her head—Darreth would do the sums and tell her how much space was missing. She only cared that the Hound and Scorpion had been correct.

She called a picture of Allon's map to her mind and made the mental annotations to include the missing space.

Updated Blueprint:

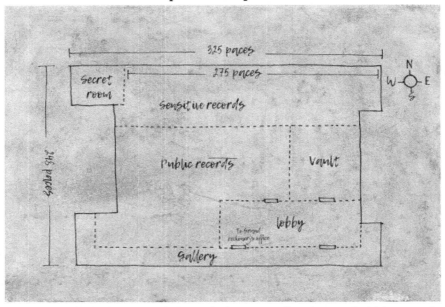

Heart pounding, she slipped through the rows of shelves and cabinets and up the stairs toward the second floor. Every shred of self-control went into keeping her steps quiet and measured. When the door to the storage room finally closed behind her, she turned to Errik with an elated grin. "Yes!" She pumped her fist in the air. "What did you find?"

Pressing a finger to his lips, he motioned for her to follow. They slithered down the lightless corridor, ears attuned for even the slightest sound. Sweat trickled down her back and moistened her palms. Errik half-flung her down a corridor as the tread of booted feet filled the passageway. She pressed herself flat against the wall, pulling her dark grey cloak over her face. She had no desire to deal with another Reckoner.

The minutes dragged by as they slithered down the hallway. After what seemed an eternity, Errik pulled her into another unlit room piled high with furniture. He thrust a finger at the room's northern wall. "This is it."

Ilanna drew her quickfire globes and held them up. Simple, unadorned stone met her gaze. The section of wall resembled every other part of the temple.

"You're sure?"

Errik nodded. "Room's right up against the western wall, as far north as I can find. Has to be it."

Ilanna opened her mouth to speak, but the tolling of the Lady's Bells cut her off. The second peal had already faded before she realized. Heart lurching, she fumbled in the bags at her feet. She seized a stonemason's hammer and pounded at the stone wall. One strike for each peal of the bells. Too late, Errik rushed to join her.

The ninth ring echoed across the city and fell silent. With a curse, Ilanna flung the hammer onto a stuffed armchair. She raised the quickfire globes. Her rushed strikes had scratched the stones and chipped a small crack in the masonry.

"Damn it!" Pacing off the temple had taken longer than she'd anticipated. They'd arrived in the room too late.

"Easy." Errik placed his hammer on the floor beside the wall. "We've got until midnight."

Ilanna ground her teeth. "That's cutting it too close." The twelve peals of the Lady's Bells would cover the sound of the hammers striking stone, but if they didn't get through with twelve strikes—a feat even a skilled mason would find challenging—they'd have to wait until the third hour. There was a very real chance they wouldn't make it through tonight.

And the wall was only the first obstacle. If the Chief Reckoner had spoken the truth, they would find an elevator shaft beyond. The Grand Reckoner's office sat on the top floor; he'd *descend* to the hidden chamber. How far down the shaft went, she had no idea. In addition to mason's tools, she'd brought enough rope for a four-story drop. She had to hope they had enough and the shaft didn't drop below the ground floor.

Errik settled into a comfortable chair and closed his eyes. Ilanna couldn't bring herself to relax. She paced, gaze fixed on the wall, fists clenching and unclenching. *What am I supposed to do for three gods-damned hours?*

She held the quickfire globes up and ran her hands over the wall. Her fingertips traced the scratches and chips left by her hammer. She'd done little more than score the masonry. One blow, however, had gouged away a section of mortar the depth of her little fingernail. She could work with that.

Crouching, she fumbled in the bag of tools and drew out a slim chisel. She inserted the diamond-point tool into the narrow hole and scratched at the mortar. Dust peppered the ground as she worked at the crack. Slowly, the hole grew wide enough for her to insert a broad-headed chisel.

Her hands ached from the effort but she refused to stop. She had three hours to weaken as much of the wall as she could. Hope surged within her. They could make it!

The *scratch, scratch* of steel on stone echoed loud in the room. She couldn't take chances anyone outside would hear.

She hissed at Errik, "Go keep watch."

Errik positioned himself by the door and nodded for her to resume.

She sucked in a breath as the rough steel chisel tore her gloves and sliced her flesh. The crack widened at an agonizing pace. Once she'd scraped away the mortar around the first stone, she moved to the next. She couldn't drive the chisel deeper without a hammer but she could broaden the seam in the wall. Perhaps, she could weaken it enough to break through under the cover of the Lady's Bells.

Sweat trickled down her forehead and mixed with the dust covering her face. Her breath came in loud gasps. Pain stabbed her lacerated fingers.

Errik's hand gripped her shoulder. "Take a break."

Ilanna didn't resist. She leaned against the wall, lungs burning. She didn't dare open the door for fear of discovery but she had to keep watch.

A glimmer of light showed in the corridor. She hissed at Errik and the rasp of chisel on stone fell silent. Ilanna's heart pounded a nervous tattoo against her ribs. The passageway brightened, the sound of slippered feet on carpet growing louder. She half-drew a dagger from her bracer. She wouldn't hesitate to use it, not so close to success.

The light and footsteps faded. Pressing the door closed, Ilanna nodded at Errik to continue. She replaced him when he grew tired, and he in turn relieved her when her forearms ached from the effort. The minutes seemed to crawl as they worked at the seam in the masonry.

"How long d'you think it's been?"

Errik shrugged. "Should be midnight soon. No way to tell, though."

Ilanna stooped and retrieved two hammers, passing him one. "Be ready for when the bells ring."

She'd just raised her chisel to continue working at the mortar when the Lady's Bells sounded. She pounded the weakened stone and felt it give. Passing the tool to her right hand, she held it poised for the next peal.

With each chime of the bells, Ilanna and Errik drove their hammers against the wall. Ilanna's heart leapt as the loosened mortar crumbled. They chipped away, careful not to knock the stones into the shaft beyond but, instead, pull them into the room. By the time the Lady's Bells fell silent, they'd opened a gap wide enough for her head to slip through. She reached into the void and met only air.

She grinned at Errik. "You keep working at the stone. I'll anchor the ropes."

He returned the smile, all traces of tension gone from his face, and set to work expanding the hole. Ilanna searched for something she could use as an anchor. A solid wooden desk at the bottom of a pile of furniture caught her eye. She wrapped the rope around the table legs and gave a few experimental tugs. The pile shifted but held.

She tied the anchor knots with deft fingers and ran a length of rope around a heavy armchair in a nearby stack of furniture. Removing the harnesses from her bag, she slipped into one and passed the other to a sweaty, dust-covered Errik.

"Ready to do this?"

"If I have to." Wincing and shifting his breeches, he eyed the harness with distaste. He hadn't enjoyed the drop from the temple rooftop to the window.

Ilanna considered leaving him behind. She could make the descent faster alone. But with no idea what she'd find below, she preferred to have the Serpent close at hand.

She slung the wooden scroll tube she'd brought over her shoulder. "Let's go." Clipping her harness onto the rope, she shoved her head through the hole. Her slim shoulders fit without difficulty, though she had to wriggle her hips hard. Once again, she envied Ria's willowy build. *It would make this so much easier!*

She held up the quickfire globes to survey her surroundings. She hung in a shaft perhaps three paces across in both directions. Darkness hung above and below the radius of her lamplight. She knew only ten or fifteen paces separated her from the temple ceiling, but she couldn't guess how far down the shaft went.

Only one way to find out.

Leaning back in her harness, she walked her feet down the wall. Errik grunted as he squeezed through the gap. The lean Serpent was far broader in the shoulders than she, though his hips and buttocks lacked her roundness. She'd chosen him for his slim build. That, and the fact she could trust him. After all, he'd kept the secret of Sabat for five years. He, alone, knew she had summoned the Bloodbear to a secret rendezvous, the one from which Sabat had never returned. He'd never tried to use the secret against her. That earned as much of her trust as she dared give.

The Serpent groaned and shifted in the harness, trying to adjust the ropes around his upper thighs.

"Deep breaths, Errik."

He coughed. "Bet you're bloody glad you're a woman right now."

She held the globes near her face to illuminate her gloating smile. "Always." She gave an evil chuckle. "Now grow a pair of balls and get moving."

They descended at a slow, steady pace. The quickfire globes did little to illuminate the shaft.

She listened for Errik's periodic grunts and groans. He hung a few paces above her—a safe distance, given his limited experience with the ropes and harness.

A sudden curse echoed overhead, followed by the sound of metal grinding on rope. Ilanna had a heartbeat to reach out her free hand—dropping her quickfire globes—and seize Errik's arm as he fell. She bit back a cry as his weight wrenched her shoulder but she refused to release him. They dangled there, her left hand clasped around his wrist, her right gripping the rope with white knuckles.

"You good?" Ilanna gasped.

"Yes." Errik sounded shaken.

Ilanna spoke through gritted teeth. "Grab the rope *below* the harness and pull it tight. It will support you."

"Got it!"

With a groan, Ilanna released the Serpent. She tested her shoulder; it twinged, but she hadn't torn or dislocated anything.

"Sorry. My hand cramped and slipped." Embarrassment tinged Errik's words. "You hurt?"

"No. You?"

"Just a bit of crushing in the wrong places."

Ilanna chuckled. "Lost the quickfire globes." For the first time, she realized she hadn't heard them land. How far down did this shaft go?

"Take mine." Faint red and blue light shone on Errik's face, a shade paler than usual and covered in a sheen of sweat.

Ilanna dropped to Errik's level and took the quickfire globes. The limited radius of illumination revealed solid stone walls and darkness all around.

"Good to continue?"

Errik nodded. "Let's get this over with."

Chuckling, Ilanna continued her descent. But after just a few moments, the quickfire globes flickered, the light fading. Ilanna cursed. They had perhaps another five seconds of light. If they didn't find the vault soon, they'd—

She spied the outline of a wooden doorframe. *Could that be it?*

Stuffing the globes into her pouch, she slid down the rope and jumped across the shaft. Her feet struck the far wall, then slipped on the lintel. She gripped the rope to halt her descent. For a terrifying moment, she swung wildly from one side of the elevator shaft to the other. A twist of the rope around the harness locked it securely in place before she leapt toward the door.

Solid wood met her questing fingers and she gripped tight. Her toes clung to the lower edge of the door's frame. Heart thundering, she flattened her body against the door. She wavered and caught her balance.

"Errik," she whispered. "Stay where you are."

He answered with a pained grunt. "Make it quick. Don't want to hang here much longer. This is squeezing things I'd rather not have squeezed."

Chuckling, Ilanna ran her fingers across the cold, steel door. The absence of locks and keyholes came as little surprise. Thievery in Praamis remained predominantly the realm of pickpockets and muggers. The city's nobles invested in armed guards to stand watch over their valuables, not traps or locks to keep clever thieves out. Grand Reckoner Edmynd clearly believed his vault to be as secure as the Royal Vaults. No thief could slip past the armored Praamian Guards stationed in the temple halls. Nothing short of an invading army would gain access to his private office. No doubt, he'd invested a small fortune in stonework to hide the door to the elevator. It would be impossible for anyone who didn't know its secrets to find.

But he hadn't reckoned on Ilanna.

The doors slid smoothly open. Alchemical lamps flickered to life, bathing the shelves, cabinets, and drawers with bright light.

Ilanna's laughter reverberated off the steel-lined walls. She had found the Reckoners' secret.

Chapter Twenty-One

The sheer enormity of the hidden storage room surprised Ilanna. Row after row of book-filled and scroll-laden shelves filled the middle of the chamber and lined the walls. The contents looked innocuous but were worth more than all the gold in the Reckoners' vaults.

She seized Errik's flailing arm and dragged him into the room.

"Thank you!" The Serpent groaned as the pressure on his legs and groin diminished. He hunched and took deep breaths. "Just give me a minute."

Ilanna strode among the shelves, keeping a wary eye open for traps. She doubted she'd find any. Grand Reckoner Edmynd wouldn't risk the wellbeing of the wealthy nobles who came here. She laughed at the mental image of the rotund Lord Vorrel caught up in a rope snare or the haughty Duke Phonnis furious over robes shredded by a trip wire.

She opened boxes and notebooks, unrolled scrolls, and flipped through portfolios at random, moving from section to section quickly. Midnight had just passed—they had less than five hours before sunrise. She and Errik needed to be long gone by the time the Reckoners awoke.

Her quick search turned up an invaluable store of information on the inhabitants of Old Praamis—the secrets of manufacture held by Lord Riddian, private business arrangements between Lords Kannassas and Illiran, and letters incriminating enough to send their owners to the Royal Dungeons. But the Duke's documents eluded her.

Think like the Duke, she told herself. *The most powerful man in the city brings his private records here, but where would he store them?* The metal shelves and cabinets, iron-bound chests, and wooden crates that held the other nobles' documents wouldn't suffice for the King's brother. *No, he'd demand someplace* extra *special for his belongings.*

"Errik, look for something that stands out from the rest."

The Serpent cocked an eyebrow.

"A fancy chest, an especially gaudy cabinet, an ornate shelf—anything that would make you think you were getting special treatment."

Ilanna had preyed on the nobles' arrogance for years. Their reputations mattered above all else. They never reported missing money, wouldn't admit losses to their fellows. It made them perfect targets—that and their seemingly endless wealth. She depended on the nobles' unending rivalry, with Duke Phonnis leading the way.

"We're standing in a secret room accessible only by an elevator from the Grand Reckoner's private office. How much more *special* does it get?"

"Just look!" Ilanna pointed to the opposite end of the room. "The Duke would insist on preferential treatment."

An ornate bloodwood cabinet stood at the end of a row of shelves. Ilanna marveled at the exquisite details of the intricate symbols etched into the scarlet wood. Bloodwood came from one place on Einan: the Crimson Forest, a small grove thousands of leagues northeast of Praamis. The clay-rich soil gave the wood its color, made it harder and denser than oak, teak, or even the black ironwood of the Twelve Kingdoms even farther northwest. Old-growth bloodwood was worth far more than gold and jewels, among the rarest materials in the world. Felling even a single tree required weeks of hard labor. Craftsmen labored for years to shape the material. The cabinet—two arm's lengths wide and a head taller than Ilanna—cost more than all the mansions in The Gardens combined. Its platinum locking mechanism seemed a pittance by comparison.

Ilanna ran her fingers over the lock. She couldn't simply force the cylinder, not with the metallic guard set flush against the cabinet door. There was only one way in: she'd have to pick the lock. Knowing the Duke, it wouldn't be easy.

She drew out a rake and tension wrench and set to work. One deft stroke of the rake over the pins and she cursed. She'd never encountered a ten-pin lock before. *This is going to take a while.*

The minutes ticked by at an agonizing pace as she maneuvered the pins into place. Her hands cramped from holding the tension wrench. More than once, she had to stop to wipe sweat from her face.

Something about the lock plate seemed off. She couldn't explain it, but even the slightest pressure of her fingers set it twitching.

Realization struck her and she froze. Slowly, she withdrew the tension wrench, stuck it to the lodestone on her bracer, and reached for a wrench with an extra-long handle. When the lock *clicked* open a moment later, the lock plate gave way and a tiny needle stabbed out of the locking mechanism. Had she not switched wrenches, the sliver of metal would have pierced her finger.

Bloody twisted hell! A ten pin lock and a poison trap? This is definitely what I'm looking for.

She gave the door a gentle tug and inserted a dagger into the crack. The blade hit no trip wires or back-up snares. With a sigh of relief, Ilanna opened the cabinet.

"Errik!" Excitement set her heart racing. "I found it!"

The Serpent slipped through the rows of shelves toward her. "About bloody time." Ilanna glared at him, and he held up his hands. "No indictment of your skill, Ilanna. Just figured three days is a lot of time to spend at this."

"I thought they taught you Serpents patience." She gave him a hard look. "I don't suppose they taught you to read?"

He shrugged. "A bit. You won't find me reading Modan's *Principles of Probability,* but I'm no Bloodbear."

She pointed at the mountain of scrolls on the bottom shelf. "Then take these and start reading."

"Aren't we looking for blueprints?" He pointed at the papers stacked on the top shelf.

"*I'm* looking for blueprints. *You're* going to see if you can find anything useful on the Arbitors in there. Training instructions, guidebooks, manuals, guard rosters, client list, anything! The more we know, the easier it'll be to avoid them."

Groaning, Errik drew a scroll and unrolled it.

"And make sure to put them back *exactly* the way you found them. On the same page, knot tied the same, everything."

Errik muttered under his breath. "Trying to tell me how to do my job."

Ilanna turned back to the cabinet. The pile of oversized, over-thick papers had to belong to the Duke. She could barely reach the documents stacked on the top shelf, much less examine their contents. Sighing, she dragged out a handful and spread them on the shelf beside Errik.

She shoved the topmost blueprints aside after a cursory examination, her lips twisting into a wry grin. She'd already broken into the Black Spire once—she had no need to learn the locations of the traps and snares installed in the tower chamber.

The blueprints beneath required more attention; the complex images and notations made her head swim. She found herself wishing she'd brought Darreth. His skill with numbers and letters would make him the perfect partner to help her find what she sought. The image of the lithe-fingered Scorpion clinging to a rope high above the ground made her chuckle.

"I hope you're having better luck," Errik grumbled. "I'm not finding a damned thing about the Duke."

Ilanna stood and eyed the documents. "What've you got?"

He pointed to a stack of papers. "This looks like the Grand Reckoner's private correspondence." His finger indicated the scrolls she'd handed him. "These might be ledgers of business deals, though I can't make sense of them."

She elbowed him aside. "Let me take a look."

The columns of names, numbers, dates, and what seemed to be amounts intrigued her. She recognized more than a few of the people on the list. Whatever the Grand Reckoner was doing, it involved enormous sums of money. The fact that he felt the need to store them in the most secure place in the most secure part of the temple spoke volumes. If only she could understand the notations.

Her interest waned after perusing a few more scrolls. "We're not here for the Grand Reckoner. Put these back where they belong—*exactly* how you found them—and start working on those up there." Her finger indicated the scrolls sitting on the shelf beneath the blueprints. "They ought to be the Duke's documents." The Duke would keep all his records together, even if he had to share the storage space with Grand Reckoner Edmynd.

"Makes sense."

Ilanna returned to poring over the blueprints. Her excitement mounted with every new schematic and diagram she studied. The Duke provided security to fully a third of the nobility and wealthier merchants of Praamis. Given time to study them, these papers would reveal every secret, every flaw, every vulnerability in the security systems.

But she didn't have the time—or desire—to study them now. She'd come for just one.

She examined the notations, markings, diagrams, and labels on each parchment with care. The sheer volume of information overwhelmed her, numbing her mind. The light strained her eyes, set her head aching, yet she forced herself to continue. She wouldn't leave until she found—

Her heart stopped mid-beat. She licked her lips, her mouth suddenly dry, and leaned closer. She read the name on the blueprint three times before her mind registered. *Lord Auslan.*

Fingers trembling, she tugged the blueprint free of the pile. Adrenaline surged in her veins and she held it up to Errik with a grin.

His questioning glance turned into a broad smile at her expression. "You did it!"

She punched his arm, excitement lending force to the blow. "*We* did it."

Errik rubbed his arm but his grin didn't waver. "Now replace it and let's get out of here."

Ilanna unscrewed the top from the scroll tube and drew out a sheet of the Duke's special blueprint paper. Master Gold had obtained it for her—at great cost, he'd made clear—in anticipation of her success. The parchment lacked the notations and diagrams of the authentic blueprint, but she'd had Darreth illustrate a layout of an imaginary vault. If the Duke happened to count his blueprints, he wouldn't find any missing. Only close scrutiny would reveal the imitation. A one in a million chance—she liked her odds.

She rolled up and slipped the Duke's blueprints into the tube, sliding the forgery into the stack, which she replaced on the shelf. Errik had already returned the Grand Reckoner's documents to their place. Holding her breath, Ilanna set the spring on the needle trap, careful not to touch its poisonous coating. She studied the room, searching for any sign of their presence. The steel-lined walls kept out moisture and dust so they didn't have to worry about leaving footprints. She had only to straighten a few items on her way to the door.

She clipped her harness to the rope, slung the scroll tube strap over her shoulder, and stepped onto the ledge. Muttering curses, Errik climbed into his harness.

"If it makes you feel better, I can bring Allon next time."

The Serpent scowled. "If it involves these bloody harnesses, I hope you do. Damned Hound can have his bollocks pressed in a vise."

She smacked his head. "Get up there, you whining lout."

Errik swung across the shaft and began the ascent.

The light in the vault dimmed and faded as she pulled the doors shut. She reached for her lockpicks, then remembered the outer door had no locks. *Good thing they'll never know I was here. Can't have them upgrading their security.*

Above her, Errik grunted with the effort of hauling himself up the rope. Ilanna followed with a dexterity earned through more than a decade of daily training. The scroll tube rested comfortably against her back. They had what they came for.

On to the next—

Something *clanked* overhead. Ilanna froze, heart hammering. An odd whirring sound filled the shaft and she bit back a shout as something hard scraped across her back. Horror sent icy feet dancing down her back.

The elevator!

"Climb, Errik!"

She hauled herself up the rope at a pace even a sailor would envy, breathless and fighting a stab of panic. Errik's body blocked out the light as he slipped through the hole in the wall.

A part of her mind shrieked in time with her furiously beating heart. *What the hell is the Grand Reckoner doing visiting the vault at this time of night?* She couldn't stop to ponder.

The opening hung ten paces above her head, then five. The air around her grew heavy, as if an immense weight descended. She didn't know how fast the elevator car moved; she only knew she had mere seconds to reach the hole in the wall. The frantic effort set every muscle in her body screaming. Her hands burned, her legs and arms ached, and her back cried out.

She couldn't stop.

Three paces. Two. One. She threw herself through the hole. Stone tore at the skin of her shoulders, back, and hips. A heartbeat later, air puffed from the gap as the elevator cart descended.

"Ilanna?" Errik's voice held a mixture of horror and anxiety.

She lay on her back, gasping for air, feeling every twinge and pain. Terror blended with exhilaration, and laughter bubbled up from her chest. "I'm here." A giggle garbled her words. She fought to control the mirth borne of the narrow escape. "I made it out."

He blew out a long breath. "Bloody hell, Hawkling. Don't scare me like that!"

Ilanna drew in a long, shuddering breath and reached for the scroll tube. "We got it, Errik. By the Watcher, we've bloody well got it!"

Chapter Twenty-Two

"Gentlemen, we did it! Best of all, no one knows we were ever there." She and Errik had waited until the elevator returned to the third floor before replacing the stones, shoving the debris and dust under a pile of furniture, and dragging a shelf to cover the hole.

Joost and Veslund stared at the tube wide-eyed. The twitching of Darreth's fingers sped up, as if he ached to unscrew the lid and discover the mysteries within.

"Well?" Allon reached for the tube. "Aren't you going to show us what we worked so hard for?"

Ilanna slapped his hand with a grin. "Tomorrow."

His interest turned to disappointment. "Now that's not fair, Ilanna! Surely we deserve at least a glimpse of—"

"Tomorrow." The *clink* of a purse on the table cut Allon's words mid-sentence. "Tonight, you get a full night of sleep. After a few dozen drinks. On me, of course."

She dropped a pair of imperials into Joost and Veslund's hands and the Foxes rushed out the door. Darreth and Errik reacted with more decorum, inclining their heads. "I owe you one, Hawkling. Until tomorrow," Errik said and followed Darreth.

Ilanna turned to Allon. His crestfallen face proclaimed his displeasure. "Don't give me that look, Hound. You know how I like to keep my little secrets." She ran a finger along his jawline. "From what I recall, you're quite happy with one of my secrets."

His dissatisfaction transformed to interest in a heartbeat. "Are you saying what I think you're saying?"

She pressed her body against his. "A promise is a promise, isn't it?" Stomach churning, she stood on her tiptoes to kiss him. She suppressed a shudder as his arms slid around her waist and pulled her closer. "Perhaps we should take this someplace else?"

Allon followed her through the tunnels of House Hawk with an eagerness his trousers failed to hide. Thankfully, Ilanna knew the House would be mostly empty at this time of the night. Those Hawks not in their beds would be occupied by jobs. The thin sliver of moon gave just enough light to see on the Hawk's Highway, but plenty of darkness for third-story work.

Allon radiated impatience as she inserted the key into her lock. He half-dragged her over to the bed before she'd fully closed the door.

With a sly smile, she pressed him onto the bed and stepped back. She dropped her belt and pouches to a heap on the floor, tossed her cloak atop the pile. Her fingers danced over the buckles and snaps of her leather jerkin. Eager desire shone in Allon's eyes and his gaze followed the upward motion of her thin undertunic. When she finally removed her trousers and stood fully naked before him, he all but ripped his clothes off.

He stood, reaching for her, but she placed a hand on his chest and pushed him onto his back. "You've done good work, Hound." Her voice held an imperious, commanding edge. His breath came fast and blood rushed in his face. Ilanna climbed atop him, a saucy smile on her face. "Your reward, as promised."

He groaned as she guided him inside her. His hands reached up to the soft roundness of her breasts, but she seized his wrists and leaned forward to trap them against the bed. He buried his face in her chest, his tongue dancing across her flesh. She gave the obligatory moans and cries of pleasure, and his body moved faster in time with his increasing arousal. Her grip on his wrists tightened, her nails digging into his flesh.

She stared down at the man on her bed as if from across a vast gulf. It seemed as if someone else controlled the sensuous undulations of her body, produced her sighs of feigned delight. She felt only disgust at his touch, the reek of his sweat, the hardness pressing against her.

Much as she hated this part, she had to do it. She needed him for what came next.

* * *

"Sweet Mistress!" Sweat stood out on Allon's forehead. His breath came in gasps. "Just when I think I know everything about you, you surprise me. How d'you keep getting better at this?"

"What can I say?" Her syrupy smile hid her true feelings. "I'm just that damned good." She arched her back in a stretch she knew would hold his gaze.

"No arguments from me." Allon's eyes slid down her body.

Ilanna reclined against the footboard. "You know, in everything that's been going on, we haven't had the time to talk much."

The Hound cocked an eyebrow. "You? Talk?" He gave a sardonic chuckle. "Will wonders never cease?"

She dug an elbow into his ribs. "What's that supposed to mean?"

Allon clutched his side with a theatrical groan. "Let's just say our interactions don't extend beyond the job and the bed." He raised his hands in a defensive gesture. "Not that I'm complaining, mind you. You're damned good at both. But we've never done much in the way of talking."

"Well, I'm giving it a try now. So shut up and talk."

He laughed. "Of all the women in the world, Ilanna, I had to take up with the most complicated, incomprehensible, stubborn, independent thief ever to walk Einan." He twirled a lock of her hair. "Most beautiful and sensual as well."

"Flatterer!"

A part of Ilanna knew she should cherish his compliments. The way he looked at her spoke volumes about his true feelings. Yet she couldn't muster anything beyond grudging acceptance. She allowed him in her bed because she needed him. He was her mark, her body simply another tool to use for a job; intimacy always made him more pliable.

He grinned. "So what d'you want to talk about?"

"Well…" She twisted the blanket in her hands. She had to play this just right to get the information Master Gold wanted without arousing his suspicions. "I found myself thinking about the Bloody Hand's offer."

His face fell. "That's what was going through your mind as we—?"

She smacked his thigh. "Before that, you fool." She shook her head. "I know House Hound voted to accept, but what did *you* think of their offer?"

He cocked an eyebrow. "The vote was taken in confidence, remember?"

"So?" She gestured around. "It's not like we're in public. Seems like this is as *private* as it gets. No one to hear but us." She leaned forward, giving him an eyeful of her curves, and rested her chin against his upper thigh. "Or don't you trust me?"

"Now that's not fair." His face took on a wounded expression. "Not when you're so close to my vulnerabilities."

She slid a hand up his muscular leg. "If you don't want me to use it against you, start talking."

His leg tensed and his hips pressed forward.

Her hand stopped mid-thigh. "Better yet, if you want me to continue, start talking."

"So not fair!" He sighed and ran a hand through his hair. "I'm not going to lie—the Bloody Hand's offer definitely had House Hound divided. On the one hand, none of us could deny just how appealing the power they promised was." His eyes sparkled. "Think about it: no more Field of Mercy, no more hangings or executions. You've heard the stories about Voramis, of how the Bloody Hand can do whatever the fiery hell they want with impunity." The brightness in his eyes turned hard, cold. "I've lost too many friends to the Justiciars. You have, too. We *had* to consider it."

She wanted to scream at him. How could he be so blind by the allure of power? The Bloody Hand's offer was like poisoned wine: a moment of pleasure before torment and death.

"On the other hand," he continued, as if unaware of the tension in her shoulders and the tightness around her mouth, "none of us wanted to concede power to the Bloody Hand. Praamis is *our* city, after all." He met her gaze then. "It was a close decision but in the end, more Hounds wanted to accept than refuse."

"And you?" She studied his eyes for any hint of his thoughts.

"Me?" Lines appeared at the corners of his mouth and his face grew carefully neutral. "I abstained."

"What?" Ilanna sat upright. "On such an important decision?"

He shrugged. "I couldn't decide which to vote for. I wrestled with the decision for as long as I could, but couldn't figure out which was the lesser of two evils."

Ilanna stifled a derisive snort. She had no doubts which option would be worse. But Master Gold didn't care about *her* opinions. He wanted to know which Hounds favored the decision. "Was it even close?"

Allon's eyes slid away and he shook his head. "Master Hound's speech convinced a lot of the undecided. In the end, more than two thirds voted in favor."

Two thirds of House Hound. She couldn't ask Allon for names but he'd given her more than enough information. Master Gold wouldn't be pleased.

"I take it you voted against?"

She nodded without hesitation. "I've been to Voramis, remember? I've seen what they can do."

"I remember. You don't talk about the job much, but I know you well enough to know that it wasn't one you enjoyed."

She gave a dramatic shudder. She hadn't actually spent more than a few days in Voramis. Denber had cooked up the story about a job that required a good deal of time and planning as cover for when she could no longer hide her pregnancy. She'd visited the city to show her face to the Guild contacts in Voramis, then slipped back into Praamis without letting anyone know. After recovering from Kodyn's birth, she'd made her official "return" to the city. The loot she'd turned over to Bryden had come from Denber.

"Walk the streets of the Beggar's Quarter and you'll see what I'm talking about. Not even The Tenement can compare."

Allon's eyes went wide. Beggars, lepers, and the poorest of the city had turned the ten-block area known as The Tenement into Praamis' hidden shame. Only the Beggar Priests and the Weeping Sisters entered the slums willingly. The nobility had submitted scores of petitions beseeching King Ohilmos to erect a wall around The Tenement.

"That bad?"

"Worse." She pulled her knees to her chest. "I won't have that for Praamis."

"So be it." He sat up and took her hand. "Let me talk to the other Hounds, see if I can sway them."

She cocked an eyebrow. "Why? I thought you said you were undecided."

"Because it matters to you." His expression grew earnest. "You've never lied to me, so if you say it's that bad, I believe you. I can't promise I'll get results, but I can try."

Her reaction to his words surprised her. She'd gone into their relationship knowing full well she intended to use him. She'd encouraged his desire for her, gone out of her way to say and do things to help him develop genuine feelings. Yet she'd always maintained a distance in her mind. She saw him as a tool to be used and discarded at will. So why did her smile feel so real? She didn't need to pretend gratitude, couldn't fake the warmth spreading through her at the sincerity in his eyes. She almost felt...something.

"Thank you."

He leaned forward and kissed her. The warmth faded, replaced by the icy chill that accompanied his touch. In another life, one without Sabat, there might have been something between them. But after what the Bloodbear had done to her, she couldn't allow herself the weakness of feelings. Ethen's death had torn out her heart, made her vulnerable when Sabat came for her. Allon's gentle touch only served as a reminder of Sabat's groping, pawing hands, his breath hot on her ear, the violence of his actions. She would never truly be comfortable in Allon's presence—she'd learned firsthand what men were capable of.

She broke off the kiss and smiled to cover her revulsion. "Much as I'd love for you to stay, I've got a few errands to run in preparation for tomorrow."

Disappointment flashed through his eyes. "And here I thought we were making such good progress."

Leaning over, she placed a kiss on his lips. "We were. Don't think I'll forget what you've promised to do for me." She stood slowly, giving him a chance to admire her form before wrapping a sheet around herself. "But if I don't go now, I'm going to fall asleep." She gave him a wink. "I've had a pretty adventurous evening."

Allon rolled from the bed with a grin. "Fair enough." He shrugged into his clothing. "I'll take full responsibility for that."

She held the door open for him. "See you tomorrow?"

He winked at her. "Can't wait to see what you've got in store for us next." With a grin, he slipped out of her room.

Ilanna pressed the door shut and, shuddering, turned to the wash basin. She had to be rid of his smell before she went home.

Chapter Twenty-Three

Ilanna cast a glance over her shoulder for the hundredth time in the last hour. She'd detoured halfway across the city, doubled back on her path thrice, and descended to the streets half a dozen times. She hadn't spotted anyone following her across the Hawk's Highway or through the busy avenues she'd chosen specifically to shake pursuit.

The discovery of the latest note had shaken her. She hadn't wanted to risk Kodyn or Ria by visiting the house without taking proper precautions, but she couldn't stay away any longer. She needed to see her son, to take him into her arms and hold him close. The next phase of her plan to bring down Duke Phonnis would occupy all her time. This could be her last chance to see Kodyn for a few weeks. She refused to allow herself to ponder what would happen if the job failed.

Tugging the hood farther forward to hide her face, Ilanna dropped into the alleyway near Old Town Market. There was always the chance a Fox or Bloodbear would spot her, but she had to risk it.

A brightly painted wooden soldier caught her eye as she slipped through the crowded marketplace. She laughed at the sum the merchant quoted and, after a minute of bargaining, walked away with the toy for a quarter of the initial price.

Ducking into an alleyway beyond Old Town Market, Ilanna crouched in the shadows and studied the bustling square. For half an hour she remained there, hidden by a stack of pallets, watching the street with a wary eye.

A part of her insisted she was just being paranoid. No one could possibly know where she was. Only two or three Journeymen had the skill to follow her convoluted path across the rooftops. A Serpent or Hound could track her through the streets, but she'd taken a route so circuitous she'd have lost any but the cleverest of Hawks.

The minutes dragged by. Her house stood just a few short paces away, but she couldn't go, not yet. She had to be certain she wasn't followed. She wouldn't take chances. A nagging in the back of her mind knew she had to be cautious. Those notes hadn't simply appeared in her room by magic. If someone could slip into House Hawk and bypass her locks, they had to have the skill to track her.

After an hour of watching, she'd had enough. She'd spotted a few of the White Fox apprentices and a pair of Bloodbear Fifth Claws, but no one else. Pulling the cloak over her face, she shuffled across the street, ducked around the corner, slipped the key into the lock on her front gate. She backed in, casting one final glance up and down the street before closing the gate.

The door to her house flew open and a willowy figure appeared. The noonday sun glinted off bared steel.

"Easy, Ria." She drew back her hood. "It's just me."

The tension in Ria's face smoothed, and she sheathed the knife.

"Mama?" A childish voice sounded from within the house. A moment later, Kodyn hurtled from the door and sped toward her. "Mama!"

Ilanna's worries melted away as she scooped her child into her arms and held him tight. Kodyn's arms gripped her neck. She drew in a deep breath, reveling in the scent of his long, dark hair.

"You're home, Mama."

"Yes, baby, I'm home."

Kodyn squirmed in her arms, frowning. "I'm not a baby, Mama."

"You'll always be *my* baby, even when you're as old as Mama." She set him down and took a long look at him. "What have you been doing?"

The boy gave her an excited smile and held up one sticky, brown-stained hand. "Ria's teaching me to make cacao cake!" He licked a finger. "It's delicious."

"Cacao cake?" Ilanna glanced up at the dark-skinned girl, who lounged in the shadows of the porch.

Ria smiled. "A special treat."

"Want to see, Mama?" Kodyn shoved a batter-covered hand in hers and tugged her toward the house.

Ilanna allowed herself to be dragged. Her eyes widened as she entered the kitchen. "What happened here?" A heavy dusting of flour covered the chairs, table, and floor.

Kodyn giggled. "We're having fun!"

"I can see that." She lifted him before he stepped in a pile of spilled flour. "A bit too much fun, perhaps?"

"Ria says we're almost done, then we get to put it in the oven!" Kodyn thrust a chubby finger at their small brick oven.

Ilanna turned to Ria. "Want me to build the fire while you finish…" She looked at the chaos in the kitchen. "…whatever this is?"

Ria laughed. "Yes, thank you."

Ilanna struggled to hide her surprise. She'd never heard Ria laugh. The sound was bright and melodic, like the Lady's Bells on festival day, and held genuine mirth. For a moment, the shadows had retreated from Ria's eyes and the girl she'd once been peered through. Ilanna caught a glimpse of the same happy, carefree spirit she'd once possessed, before the Night Guild.

She busied herself with starting a fire, only half-listening to Kodyn's chatter as he helped Ria mix the ingredients. The young girl didn't seem to mind that Kodyn spilled half the bowl's contents. With gentle hands, she helped the boy stir the mixture and pour the batter into the baking pan.

Ilanna cleaned while Ria and Kodyn waited for the cake to cook. The boy sat perched in his high chair, alternating between licking the wooden mixing spoon clean and waving it like an imperious monarch. Ilanna couldn't help laughing at the sight of his stained face and hands.

Finally, after Kodyn had asked "Is it ready yet?" for the tenth time, the cake came out of the oven. Ilanna's eyebrows shot up as the smooth, rich flavor of the cake filled her mouth. "Sweet Mistress!" She dug her spoon into the cake for another bite. "This is amazing!"

Ria's smile returned. "My mother's recipe, and my baby sister's favorite." A shadow passed over her eyes and she dropped her gaze to the table.

"It's the most delicious cake I've ever tasted. What's in it?"

Ria lifted a cloth-wrapped packet from the table and passed it to Ilanna. "Cacao nibs, straight from Ghandia." The girl spoke with an exotic, almost musical accent Ilanna found intriguing.

"How have I never heard of this *cah-cah-oh* before?" The nib's bittersweetness tantalized her taste buds, yet had a soothing, luxurious flavor she found almost sensual.

"Ghandian secret." Ria gave her a sly smile. "Very hard to find in Praamis."

Ilanna took another bite of cake to mask her surprise. Ria had spoken more words in the last minute than in the last month. She seized the opportunity to draw the girl out more. "So where did you get it?" She studied the nibs. "Where can I find more?"

Ria shook her head. "You cannot. Ghandians will only sell it to another Ghandian."

"Is that where you are from?" Ilanna had longed to ask Ria about life before the slavers, but the girl had never seemed willing to speak about it. Until now. "Tell me about Ghandia."

Ria's eyes took on a faraway look. "Ghandia is not like Praamis. No big city, no houses all packed together. No wicked men to tie you up and drag you away from home."

Ilanna held her breath, not daring to speak for fear Ria would clam up again. But when Ria didn't continue, she prodded, "What was the land like?"

Ria spoke in a quiet voice. "Plains and grasslands, as far as the horizon. Trees and bushes with fruits, berries, and cacao fruit."

Ilanna held up a cacao nib. "This comes from a fruit?"

Ria nodded. "The fruit is good for eating, but the best part is the beans. Cacao, they are called. 'Gift of the gods' in the ancient tongue of the Serenii, my mother told me."

Kodyn tugged on her sleeve. "Mama, I get down?"

Ilanna helped Kodyn from his seat without taking her eyes from Ria. Now that she had the girl talking, she had to encourage her to continue. "And your mother, she taught you to make this?" She lifted a spoonful of cake to her lips.

"She did. Much more besides. Hunting and dressing the kill. Foraging for food in the barren grasslands. Digging to find the earth's bounty. Weaving rushes to make beds, roofs, and shields for the warriors. Wielding the *assegai* and *makrigga* spear, and dancing the *Kim'ware* war dance."

Ilanna felt a stab of envy. She had lost her mother at seven years old—for all Ria had endured, in many ways, she'd had a better life. But she quickly shoved the emotion aside. She finally had Ria talking.

A child's cry pushed all other thoughts from her mind. Her head whipped around.

"Kodyn!" Her mind registered the scene in a terrified heartbeat. Kodyn had fallen and tried to catch himself by seizing the oven, still hot from the cake. The child stared down at his hand with wide eyes and a shrill of pain.

Keeper, no! Ilanna leapt up, Ria a heartbeat behind. She scooped Kodyn into her arms and rushed over to the bucket of water used to wash dishes. As she plunged Kodyn's hand into the water, she turned to Ria. "Get me lavender oil."

"No." Ria shook her head and darted from the room. Ilanna watched her go, mouth hanging open. Had Ria just told her no? She pulled Kodyn tighter, rocking him in an effort to calm his wailing.

"Easy, Kodyn. Everything will be okay."

The boy's crying grew more strident.

Ilanna clutched her son to her chest, rocking him and whispering soothing words. "Shh, be brave my little hawk. Mama will make it all better."

Ria returned a moment later with a fleshy, serrated leaf. "Aloe. To soothe the burn and ease the pain."

Ilanna held out a hand.

"Not yet." Ria set down the aloe and darted into the kitchen for a bucket. "Water first, to cool and stop the swelling."

Ilanna couldn't hide her surprise at the change that had come over Ria. The girl's hesitance disappeared, replaced by confidence and a tone of command. She knelt and plunged Kodyn's hand into the bucket, all the while stroking the boy's hair and murmuring something in an unfamiliar language. The singsong tone calmed the boy, and his crying quieted to a pained snuffle. After fifteen minutes, she applied the sticky goo of the aloe leaf to the burn, moving with deft confidence.

Ilanna wrestled with her envy once more. Ria had such a natural way with Kodyn, and the boy responded to her.

But she couldn't fault either Ria or Kodyn. The three of them needed each other and, though the arrangement was less than ideal, it was all they had. For now.

"Look, my little hawk." She produced the ebony hawk figurine from her pouch. "Look what Mama brought you."

Kodyn took the bird with his uninjured hand and cradled it to his chest.

"Do you want Mama to read you a story?" She had nowhere to be until the sun set.

Kodyn's tear-stained face popped up, and he gave her a bright smile. "The one about Agarre the Giantslayer?"

Ilanna grinned. "If you want." She carried Kodyn to the stuffed armchair in the sitting room—the one where her mother had spent hours teaching her to sew—and settled into a comfortable position. A book sat on the table next to the chair. She flipped to the first page of Agarre's story. "Once upon a time, there was a young girl who lived in a small village. Agarre was her name. She learned to sew, to milk the cows, to cook and clean, and to gather wheat with her father, mother, and five older brothers."

The story of Agarre the Giantslayer had been one of her favorites when she was younger. She'd dreamed of being the heroine who killed the giants of the Empty Mountains. That was all before the Night Guild. Reading the story brought back memories of a happier time, sitting in the cozy stuffed armchair with her mother.

Kodyn snuggled into her chest as she read, pointing at the illustrations on the pages and playing with the carved hawk figurine. From the corner of her eye, Ilanna caught Ria sitting on the stairs. The dark-skinned girl occupied herself with the repair of one of Kodyn's shirts, but she couldn't hide her interest in the story.

Ilanna hid a smile. She and Ria shared more than just their love of Kodyn. They had both lost a great deal, endured horrors that should have crushed their spirits. Ilanna's suffering had hardened her, but Ria's eyes held a glint of wide-eyed wonder. Ilanna hadn't felt that since the day her father sold her to the Night Guild. The slavers had taken Ria's childhood, but the dark-skinned Ghandian girl remained unbroken.

Kodyn's breathing grew rhythmic and heavy as she read. When she finally reached the end of the story, he murmured. "Ria, sing the song?"

"Of course, little one." Ria set aside her sewing and came to sit by Kodyn. With a shy smile for Ilanna, she began to sing.

Though Ilanna didn't understand the words, the haunting melody stirred something within her. The song spoke to her of home, of family, of sorrow, and love. Memories of her mother, Ethen, and Denber drifted through her mind, brought a lump to her throat. She closed her eyes to suppress the tears. The warmth of Kodyn's body melded with hers, and she allowed herself to be carried along on the tune. Slowly, gently, she slipped into a peaceful rest.

* * *

The *crack* of a burning log tugged Ilanna from her sleep. The smell of wood smoke and the glimmering light of fire filled her senses. She cracked an eyelid. Ria sat beside the fire, the book of stories open in her hands, running a gentle finger over the illustrations.

The girl looked up as she stirred. "Nightfall is two hours past."

Ilanna glanced at the child in her arms. Ria had draped a blanket over them. "I must go."

"You looked like you needed sleep." Ria stood and lifted Kodyn's sleeping form. The boy murmured and wrapped his arms around her neck, and she rocked him.

Ilanna stretched. Her neck ached from the awkward position but she felt more rested than she had since beginning the Duke's job. "See if you can find some gokulah unguent for his burns."

"I will."

"Thank you." Ilanna met the girl's gaze. "I…" She swallowed. "I won't be coming around for a while. A few weeks at least. There's a job…"

Ria nodded. "I understand." She stroked Kodyn's hair. "He misses you, you know. Asks where you are."

Ilanna drew in a deep breath. "I know. And it kills me every time I leave him."

"Telling you to stay would be to waste my words. You do what you must for him."

"But not for much longer." She bent to retrieve the figurine that had fallen from Kodyn's hand, setting it on the mantelpiece beside the rest. Ten sets of avian eyes stared at her with silent recrimination. "After this job, things will be different."

An earnest intensity burned in Ria's dark eyes. "I hope so. For his sake, and yours."

Ilanna turned away. "Goodnight, Ria." She tugged on her cloak and strode to the door. "I will return as soon as I can, but I rest easy knowing he has you to care for him." With a heavy heart, she slipped into the darkness of the Praamian night.

Chapter Twenty-Four

Ilanna froze at the door to her room, eyes fixed on the scrap of parchment sitting on her table. Ignoring the viola beside it, she opened the folded paper. *Lord Ulimar,* it read.

Mind racing, she stuffed the paper into her pocket and rummaged through her equipment chest. She'd just delivered the skull-headed dagger to the Ulimar mansion a few weeks before. *Why would Master Gold want me to go back?* It didn't make sense.

Perhaps Lord Ulimar hadn't paid for the Crown's protection, and the Guild Master sent her back to…convince him. *If so, where's the threat?* No dagger lay beside the note.

She slipped into her dark grey clothing, cloak, and the baldric that held her blades and the pouches for her lockpicks and other gear. She'd planned to visit a few houses anyway; it wouldn't be too difficult to add Lord Ulimar's mansion to her targets for the night.

But it didn't sit right with her. Master Gold had told her he needed money to pay the other House Masters and their Journeymen. Had his patience run out? Was the note his way of prodding her to move quickly? It rankled that he would resort to blackmail. Hadn't she proven herself to him often enough?

Sighing, she slipped her daggers into place, locked the chest, and replaced it under the bed. She strode down the hall toward Master Hawk's chambers and office. The heavy oak door stood open, and the House Master sat at his desk.

"Master Hawk?"

Master Hawk looked up and groaned. "What is it, Ilanna?" He lifted a mug filled with frothing beer. "It's not often I get to enjoy a meal undisturbed."

"Just a second of your time, I promise."

With a pained expression, the House Master pushed the tankard away. "How can I help you, Journeyman?"

Ilanna ignored the chill in his voice. "Lord Ulimar."

"What of him?" The House Master leaned back in his chair.

"I visited him a few weeks ago, left him the Guild's message. Has he requested the Crown's protection yet?"

Master Hawk produced a key from a pocket, inserted it into his desk drawer, and *clicked* the lock open. He unrolled the scroll and ran his finger down the list of names. "As far as I can see, he...hasn't?" Furrows appeared in his forehead.

"What is it?"

Master Hawk's frown deepened. "I could've sworn I saw his name." He ran an absent-minded finger over his scar.

"You're sure?" Age hadn't dimmed Master Hawk's mind; he didn't forget little details. The House Master gestured at the list.

"It's Bryden's handwriting, no doubt about it." Updating the list counted among one of the Journeyman's duties. "Everything looks right. I'll run it by Bryden, just to be certain."

Ilanna nodded. "So Lord Ulimar is *not* on the list?"

Master Hawk shook his head. "Fair game. Make sure he gets the message this time, eh?"

"Thank you, Master Hawk."

The House Master inclined his head. "By the way, Bryden was looking for you earlier. Seemed less than his usual chipper self."

Ilanna gave a puckish grin. "I'll just go and find him straightaway, won't I?"

Master Hawk snorted. "Just don't wait too long to talk to him. Else he'll bring all his whinging to me."

"Of course, Master." Ilanna swept an exaggerated bow. "I'll leave you to your beer."

The House Master waved her away, reaching for his beer with his other hand.

Ilanna shut the door behind her. Her fingers curled around one of her belt daggers. *Time to ensure Lord Ulimar is* very *clear on where he stands with the Guild.*

* * *

"Oi, Filch, open up!" Ilanna pounded on the door of the ramshackle warehouse.

Ilanna wiped her hands on her cloak and wished to be anywhere else. The stink of Fishmonger's Row turned her stomach, and the wooden buildings around her looked one strong breeze from collapsing. But she had goods to fence.

"Whoozit?" A slot opened at eye level, and a tired voice drifted through the decrepit door. "Oh, 'Lanna, it's you."

Ilanna fought down her impatience. "Yes, it's me. Now open up. Stinks almost as bad out here as in there."

Filch mumbled under his breath, and a series of *clicks* and *thunks* sounded as he shot the bolts and locks. The door swung open and Filch poked his head out the door. With a quick glance up and down the street, he motioned for her to enter.

Ilanna followed him inside and waited for him to re-lock the door. The light of an oil lantern outlined the unkempt man. On the wrong side of fifty, with half as many teeth as he should have, Filch wore a nightshirt that had seen better days before Ilanna was born. Calling his beard and moustache ratty was an insult to rats, and the man's belly seemed over-large on his twig-like frame.

Door secured, Filch turned to Ilanna, rubbing his three-fingered hands together. "What'cha bringin' me? Something val-*yoo*-ble, I trust?"

She snorted. "Have I ever wasted your time?"

Filch inclined his head. "Step into my office, if'n you please."

Ilanna walked a few paces behind to avoid his reek of unwashed flesh and whatever food stained his nightshirt. Her stomach protested at the thought of being enclosed in his office, but that was the price she paid to deal with the Guild fence.

As she followed Filch around a haphazard stack of pallets and boxes, the dilapidated, chaotic appearance of the warehouse gave way to precise organization. Trinkets of gold, silver, steel, iron, and other metals mundane and precious sat in crates on shelves. Filch's appearance screamed "gutter scum", but no one in Praamis could match his skills at fencing stolen property. Those skills explained why he bore the responsibility of selling off the loot packed into the warehouse.

The fence led her through the rows of shelves and into a small office. Alchemical lamps filled the room with ample illumination. Binders and notebooks sat stacked on a cabinet behind the ornate desk that occupied far too much of the cramped space. Slipping into his usual chair, he motioned for her to take the opposite seat. "Now, what brings Ilanna of House Hawk to my humble warehouse at this ungodly hour?"

Ilanna drew out a necklace and slid it across the table without a word.

"Intriguin'." Filch's eyebrows rose and his hand shot out to snatch the jewelry. "Masterful work, this piece. Crimson ruby channel-set in white gold." He turned it over and hefted it with a thoughtful expression. "Solid weight, so the gold's not too heavily alloyed."

Ilanna swallowed her impatience. Every visit served as a reminder of why she despised dealing with Filch.

The fence looked up. "Sorry, girlie, it ain't worth all that much."

Ilanna's fingers twitched toward her belt dagger, only to remember she'd left it in Lord Ulimar's mansion. That, and the ominous note—"*In four days, you stand before the Long Keeper*" it had read—should convey the Guild's message with sufficient clarity. Good thing she had more blades to use to correct Filch's coarseness.

"It's not *girlie*." Filch flinched as she drew the dagger and set to work cleaning her nails. "Suppose you tell me what makes *that* worthless?"

"Not worthless. Just can't be sold whole." Filch licked his lips and held up the necklace, bottom side up. "See this?" He tapped the smooth gold surface with a fingernail. "Some sort of inscription." He settled a jeweler's loupe on his right eye and squinted down at the piece. "*To the keeper of my heart, yours forever, Adann Ulimar.* Touchin', innit?"

Ilanna cursed. She'd lifted the piece from Lady Ulimar's jewelry box at random. The inscription meant the necklace had been custom-made and, therefore, recognizable if Filch tried to pawn it off.

"Still," Filch said, shrugging, "gold's good enough to melt down, and that ruby's value ought to make it worth your time."

"How much?"

Filch sat back, eyes fixed on the necklace, and scratched his filthy face. "Couple hundred imperials, easy. If you're really nice," he gave her a leering grin that showed far too many gaps in his teeth, "might be I'll give you a full three hundred. The stone'll be hard to make disappear, but I c'n manage."

Three hundred imperials. Ilanna fought down her frustration. She'd hoped to come away from the night's efforts with a lot more. The next phase of the Duke Phonnis job would occupy all her time and attention. She didn't know when she'd have a chance to steal more. *At least it's something.* Master Gold had sent her to Lord Ulimar's, so he'd have to be happy with the results.

Filch leaned forward. "Got any more?"

Ilanna shook her head. "That's it for now. You know me, I like to steal coins. Harder to trace."

Filch shrugged. "Not worth as much." He held up the necklace. "Little'un like you couldn't carry this weight of gold or silver across Praamis. Might be you think about that next time, eh?"

Ilanna scowled. "You let me worry about the thieving, and I won't tell you how to repulse every skirt in Praamis. Seems like the both of us are doing our jobs just fine, Filch."

Filch laughed. "Y'always know how to make business a pleasure, 'Lanna." He reached for a notebook. "Let me give you a stub. Bryden likes his books nice and tidy, he does."

Ilanna folded her arms and watched Filch fumble with the pen and paper. He gripped the quill between thumb and forefinger, with his middle finger to steady it. The Guild took their money seriously. More than a few fences had found themselves staring down a Serpent's blade after mistaking the severity of sneaking off with gold that belonged to the Night Guild. Filch held the record for longest-surviving Guild fence. His career hadn't been without mistakes. The Night Guild had taken the last two fingers on his left hand the first time he'd tried to cheat them, and the two fingers on his right the second time. A third, and he'd be short a neck.

"There you are. Payment stub for three hundred imperials for one inscribed necklace from Lord Ulimar." He slipped the paper across the table and replaced the quill. "If'n that's all, I've a warm bed to get back to." He gave her a leering grin. "Can't tempt you to join me, eh?"

Ilanna's dagger pierced the table a hair's breadth from what remained of his right hand.

Filch flinched and half-squeaked. He gave a shaky laugh. "Seems that's a no."

Scowling, Ilanna stood, wrenched the dagger free, and strode from the room.

"You didn't have to ruin th' table!" Filch's wail followed her through the warehouse. A smile split her face as she threw open the locks and bolts and slipped out into the night.

Three hundred imperials for the pretty trinket. She patted the purses in her pocket. *With the rest, that's a decent take.*

She muttered a silent curse. *Of all the necklaces in the box, I had to grab that one!* The inscription meant it held value to Lord Ulimar—or Lady Ulimar. There was a chance he'd raise a fuss when he discovered it stolen. It didn't matter that she'd been in a hurry. She should have taken the time to study the jewelry to ensure it bore no identifying marks. She preferred no one found out about the houses she hit, the only way to keep her extra looting a secret.

At least Master Gold will be pleased. With the imperials in her pocket and the information she'd extracted from Allon, perhaps the Guild Master would stop trying to coerce her with the notes. He had to see that their mutual interests aligned. At least, until the day she purchased her freedom.

And with the next phase of the Duke Phonnis job, that day is not far off!

Chapter Twenty-Five

Ilanna studied the men standing around the table. "So, are you ready to find out how we're going to take down the most powerful man in Praamis?"

"'Bout bloody time," Veslund growled.

Joost grinned at his fellow Fox's impatience. Darreth's fingers twitched faster than usual. Even Errik's cool façade couldn't quite mask his interest.

Allon laughed. "You've had us dying to know for days, Ilanna. Enough with the dramatics and get to it."

Ilanna's smile came easy. "Fair enough." She produced the blueprints she'd stolen from the Coin Counters' Temple and unrolled them on the table. "Here's everything you need to know."

Everyone leaned forward, craning their necks to see. Long seconds passed as they studied the depiction. Veslund was the first to look up. "What in the frozen hell is it?"

Ilanna chuckled. "It's the plans for a vault door. The most secure vault in the city."

"Watcher's teeth!" Allon's eyebrows rose. "And here I thought you were crazy going after the Reckoners' vaults. Now you're telling me—?"

Ilanna met his gaze with confidence. "Damned right I am." She bared her teeth in a snarl. "We're breaking into Lord Auslan's crypt."

Errik whistled, and Darreth's eyes went wide.

"Now wait a bloody minute!" Veslund held up his hands. "Ye're not talking about *that* Lord Auslan, are ye?"

Ilanna nodded. "The one and only."

Joost scratched his head. "Am I missin' somethin'? What's so special about 'im?"

"Sweet Mistress!" Veslund gave a derisive snort. "And ye always tell people ye're the *smart* one."

Joost scowled.

"Lord Auslan," she interjected before the Fox retorted, "is counted among the five wealthiest men in the south of Einan. His wagon teams carry goods all over the world. If someone wants to move anything larger than a crate of tomatoes from one city to another, they're almost guaranteed to hire Lord Auslan's teams—or any of the hundreds he owns around Einan."

Allon nodded. "Calling him wealthy would be an understatement. He could spend a hundred imperials a day for a thousand years and not make a dent in his fortune."

Joost whistled, and even Veslund looked impressed. "So we're just going to help ourselves to some of his gold? If he's as rich as ye say, he won't miss a few score thousand imperials." He grinned and clapped a hand on Joost's shoulder. "We'll be rich!"

Ilanna held up a hand. "There's no doubt you'll walk away from this job the wealthiest men in your House, but we're not going to touch a single copper bit of Lord Auslan's money."

Allon turned a curious expression on her. Errik leaned forward, and Darreth's gaze ceased its wandering.

Joost narrowed his eyes. "So how we gonna get paid?"

"We're going to steal Lady Auslan."

Allon choked on his ale. "Twisted hell!"

Errik's cool demeanor cracked, and he stood. "How the hell do you plan to do that?"

"Hold on!" Joost slammed his palms on the table. "I'm all for thievin', but kidnappin's a different matter." His face fell as Ilanna laughed. "What?"

"Lady Auslan has been dead for more than two decades, Joost." She fought back her mirth, but her laughter refused to subside.

"So we're kidnappin' a bleedin' corpse?" Disgust twisted Joost's face. "That ain't the sort of thing we signed on for."

"Not a corpse," Darreth said in his grating voice. "We're stealing Lady Auslan's golden sarcophagus."

"Sar-what-now?"

"Sarcophagus." The Scorpion's mouth twitched. "A fancy coffin, made of stone or metal, usually adorned."

"In the case of Lady Auslan," Allon added, "it's made of solid gold and crusted with gemstones." He turned to Ilanna. "Worth hundreds of thousands of imperials, from what I hear."

Ilanna shook her head. "Not hundreds of thousands." She dropped her voice. "*Millions.*"

The word hung in the air, and none of the men in the room could hide their shock.

"Death is the one thing money can't fix. When Lady Auslan fell ill, Lord Auslan spent a fortune on physickers and healers from around Einan. Didn't do a damned thing. After her death, Auslan did what he could to make her live forever: had her embalmed and stored in a golden sarcophagus. Spent millions of imperials on the purest gold, the brightest diamonds and gemstones. All to make his lady love a final resting place worthy of her memory."

"How romantic." Errik's voice held a sardonic edge.

Ilanna shrugged. "Serves our needs perfectly."

Veslund scratched his beard. "Seems to me the man who'd make a golden sarcophagus would be the sort to make it impossible to get at."

"And you'd be right, Ves." Ilanna tapped the blueprint spread out on the table. "This is Duke Phonnis' greatest invention. A vault door designed to be impenetrable."

The heavy bearded Fox gave a defeated shake of his head. "As I said, impossible."

Ilanna gave him a cold, hard smile. "Which is precisely why we're going to do it."

Allon studied the blueprints through narrowed eyes. "And that's what this is?"

"The way in." Ilanna tapped the drawings. "The Duke's original plans for the vault door. Dimensions, metals used, design of the locking mechanisms, fail-safes—everything we could need to get in." She leaned forward with an eager grin. "*This* is how we bring down the Duke."

Joost and Veslund looked confused. Darreth spoke up. "Prove the Duke's most secure vault is a failure, and his reputation and business fail."

"Damned straight." Excitement brightened Allon's face. "With this, we can figure out a way to get through that door and get at the treasure stored within. Millions of imperials' worth!"

"So we've got the blueprints to the door, a good first step." Errik crossed his arms. "But that's just the beginning. We've got to figure out how to get into the house—no easy task, mind you—get in and find the vault. Of course, pretending we can do all that, there's the little matter of moving the sarcophagus itself. Not exactly sized to fit in your pocket."

Darreth drummed his fingers on the table. "By my calculations, we're talking the weight of four or five men. *Big* men, like him." His finger indicated Jarl, who sat quietly in the corner.

"And that's exactly why I've brought him in on this." At Ilanna's nod, the huge Hawk came to stand at the table.

All eyes turned to the Pathfinder. Jarl met their scrutiny with calm, a hint of a smile on his face.

"Now, don't get me wrong," Veslund spoke with hesitation, "I'm all for the big fella doing the heavy lifting, but won't we need a few more of him?"

Ilanna grinned. "No." More than a few eyebrows shot up. "Jarl's not going to be carrying the bloody thing. He's going to figure out how to get it—and us—out of Lord Auslan's mansion." Ilanna placed a hand on Jarl's shoulder. "Plus, he's going to build the vault door for us to figure out how to break in. Unless any of you all have any smithing experience to speak of?"

The assorted Guild members shook their heads. "No?"

"And you're sure you can trust him?" Joost asked in his laconic drawl.

Ilanna's lip curled upward.

The Fox held up his hands in a defense gesture. "Hey, I have to ask. You made us all swear an oath—"

Jarl's voice, rarely heard, sounded like rumbling thunder. "I, too, have sworn." He met Joost's gaze, as if daring him to speak.

Swallowing, Joost held out a hand. "Welcome to the team, big guy."

Jarl didn't drop his eyes or grasp Joost's hand.

"I trust Jarl." Ilanna allowed a note of steel into her voice. "That is enough for all of you."

No one seemed inclined to argue, either with Ilanna or the hulking Pathfinder.

"Now, with that settled, it's time to move on to the assignments." She turned to the Foxes. "Joost, Veslund, I need you to find out everything you can about Lord Auslan. His travel habits, the establishments he frequents, the food he likes to eat, and more. Hell, find out how many times he pisses in his chamber pot. Any tidbit of information, no matter how useless it seems, is important."

The two men nodded, but made no move to leave. Ilanna raised an eyebrow.

"Well," Veslund said, eyes darting around the room, "seems like we're going to be doing a share of the works. Seems only fair to me we gets a share of yer haul."

Ilanna pursed her lips. "Day wages aren't enough for you?"

Joost cringed behind Veslund, but the bearded Fox continued. "Don't get me wrong, ye've been nothing but fair. But we're talking *millions* of imperials here."

Ilanna nodded. She'd expected this. "I'll offer you one percent of the take. Each."

Veslund's eyebrows knitted, and Joost frowned in concentration.

"Tens of thousands of imperials each." Exasperation tinged Darreth's voice.

Both Foxes went wide-eyed. "Done!" They rushed from the room before Ilanna changed her mind.

"Errik, for now, I need you to do the same. Find out everything you can about Lord Auslan."

The Serpent inclined his head.

"And," Ilanna held up a finger, "scout the property." She jerked a thumb at the door. "Those two'll stick out in Old Praamis like a Bloodbear in petticoats."

Errik grinned. "Got it."

"Three percent's the best I can do."

Errik pondered for a moment. "Five."

"Done." Ilanna shook his hand. Considering the total value of the haul, five percent was absolutely fair—and the amount she'd intended to give him from the beginning.

She turned to Darreth as Errik strode from the room. "Darreth, your task is to interpret this blueprint. Somewhere among all these numbers are the dimensions of the vault door. Figure them out, and give me the details." She placed a hand on Jarl's shoulder. "Jarl here is going to build the door with your help. Your job is to figure out the materials he'll need. When the time comes to put the door together, you're going to make sure it's built *exactly* as it's shown here."

Darreth gave a little twitch of his fingers. "I'm not much of an architect."

"I know. But you've got a head for numbers. Between you and Jarl, I trust you can figure it out."

Darreth frowned as he studied the blueprint. "I may have to bring in some outside help on this."

Ilanna shook her head. "Only if absolutely necessary. I chose you because you're among the smartest of the Scorpions."

"Yes, but this," he tapped the parchment with a slim finger, "looks like some kind of code."

Ilanna bent over the parchment. Indecipherable symbols and markings occupied the upper right corner of the blueprint. "Damn, so it does." She looked up. "Think you can crack it?"

Darreth shrugged. "I'll give it a try. Might know a few people I can ask." He spoke before she could protest. "I'll copy a few of the symbols on a separate parchment to show around."

"Good. The fewer people who know what we're doing, the better."

"So be it." Darreth fumbled in his satchel and produced a graphite stick and parchment. Bending over the blueprints, he began muttering to himself and scratching notes on his paper.

Ilanna turned to Allon. "I'll want you doing some digging on Lord Auslan, too, but not just yet."

Allon quirked an eyebrow. "Got something else in mind for me?"

Ilanna nodded. "You, me, and Jarl are going to do a different sort of digging first."

* * *

"I thought you said digging, not wading through shite!"

Ilanna laughed as the Hound wiped sewage from his clothing. "Pleasant environment, isn't it? Besides, don't you Hounds love the hidden ways?"

Allon gave an annoyed sniff and winced at the aromatic cocktail of human ordure, offal, and assorted rubbish filling the sewer system. "We use it; doesn't mean we have to love it."

Jarl grunted, the closest he'd get to complaining about the stench.

The Praamian sewer system was a maze of tunnels, pipes, channels, and canals designed to funnel the city's refuse toward the Stannar River— sufficiently downstream from Old Praamis, of course. The sewers predated most of the city. Storm drains around Praamis fed into the sewer system and kept the streets largely free of detritus. Many of the nobles and wealthier merchants ran pipes from their bathing rooms and commodes directly into the sewers.

Ilanna turned the beam of her alchemical lamp on the sewer walls. The stone bore the same esoteric symbols carved into the tunnels of the Night Guild. *Makes you wonder how old these tunnels really are.*

Age had worn away at the walls and ceiling. Wooden beams and supports dotted the tunnels where the Foxes and Hounds had shored up collapsed portions. The Foxes utilized the sewer system as a quick way to get around, but only House Hound knew the true extent of the underground maze that ran through the entire city—a mirror image to the Hawk's Highway. Just as Ilanna and her fellow Hawks ran free across the rooftops, the Hounds dedicated themselves to committing every twist and turn of the sewers to memory. No one knew the sewers better than Allon.

That didn't mean he enjoyed being down here. He'd grumbled the entire journey. His memory of the labyrinthine sewer system was perfect, so he avoided the underground maze whenever possible. Ilanna hadn't given him a choice.

"This way." He led them down the left-handed tunnel of an intersection without hesitation. "Careful here." He picked his way along a crumbling section of floor, hugging the slime-covered wall to avoid plummeting into the river of sewage dozens of paces below. "Current gets stronger the closer we get to the Stannar River."

"How far are we?"

"Not far." Allon pointed at the intersection behind them. "A few hundred paces that way and you'll hit The Gardens. We're beneath Old Praamis now."

"Good." They'd trudged through the sewers for at least two hours.

Not for the first time on their trek, she considered abandoning this part of her plan. Jarl had the near-impossible task of dragging the sarcophagus upstream through the sewers and back to the Night Guild. Crumbling sections of floor, collapsed walls, and caved-in roofs had forced them to backtrack time and again. More than a few tunnels had been dangerously close to giving way.

She turned to the Pathfinder. "What do you think, Jarl? Can you do it?"

Jarl scratched his bearded chin, then realized his hand was covered in slime and grimaced. "Conditions aren't ideal. Gonna be a bastard nut to crack." He shrugged. "I'll need time to sit down with the others."

Ilanna nodded. "Of course." Jarl was a Pathfinder, one of the Journeymen of House Hawk responsible for maintaining and expanding the Hawk's Highway—the system of ropes, ladders, bridges, and arches that connected the city's rooftops. He would have to adjust his mindset to build an identical network underground, but if anyone could do it, he could.

"No promises," he rumbled.

Ilanna grinned. "Perfect."

Allon paused at the end of a tunnel, where a wooden plank spanned a gap five paces across. "This is the iffy part. Drop's three or four man-heights, but the rocks at the bottom'll make for a rough landing."

Ilanna shone her light into the chasm. The powerful beam failed to reach the water she could hear rushing at the bottom.

Allon darted across the plank. "Easy does it."

Hiding her amusement, Ilanna made the crossing without so much as a wobble. The Hound clearly had no idea how precarious the Hawk's Highway could be.

The plank creaked under Jarl's weight. He crossed the distance with a single powerful bound.

"First task'll be to shore up that bridge, eh?"

Jarl nodded.

The Pathfinder had a monumental job on his hands. In addition to transporting the sarcophagus, he'd design and build their escape route. It would have to be sturdy enough for her to traverse easily, but they'd need to collapse it behind them in case of pursuit. No easy task, even for him.

"This is it." Allon pointed to a wall.

"You sure?" The section of stone resembled every other wall in the tunnel.

Allon nodded and tapped his forehead. "Got the map in here, remember?"

Ilanna nodded. "Good. Now it's time for the two of you to figure out how we're going to tunnel up under Lord Auslan's safe room."

Chapter Twenty-Six

"Ilanna!"

Ilanna winced at Bryden's call. With all the things requiring her attention, she had no desire to deal with him.

"Journeyman Ilanna!"

Sighing, Ilanna stopped. *Better get this over with.* She forced a pleasant smile and turned. "Ah, Bryden, I was just on my way to see you."

Bryden gave her his best "you're lying through your teeth" look. "Clearly." He jerked a thumb over his shoulder. "My office is this way." He spun on his heel and limped down the passageway, clearly expecting her to follow.

When he reached his office, he waved for her to close the door as he shuffled around his desk. "I take it your encounter with Filch was as unpleasant as usual. He alerted me you might be paying a visit."

Ilanna crossed her arms. "Spying on me?"

"Of course not." Bryden gave a dismissive wave. "Oh, don't think I haven't tried it. But while Eustyss and Grillan may be capable thieves, they're terrible trackers. They lost you before you stepped off the Perch." He quirked an eyebrow. "Almost like you were trying to shake them."

Ilanna snorted. "Some things never change. I value my privacy, and you do your damnedest to invade it."

"Just one of my duties as Master Hawk's second-in-command." He sat in his plush chair and reached for his ledger. "Someone has to keep you honest."

Ilanna gave a harsh laugh. "Honest?"

"Honest as a thief can be." He held out a hand. "The stub."

Ilanna drew the paper from her pocket and handed it over.

Bryden scratched his chin as he studied the stub. "Three hundred imperials. A tidy sum for a night's work." His eyebrows furrowed and he glanced up at her. "From Lord Ulimar's?"

"He's not on the list."

Disbelief flashed across Bryden's face. "How would *you* know?"

"I asked Master Hawk."

"That'll be a first." Bryden cocked his head. "You've always been the sort who does whatever the frozen hell she pleases, consequences be damned."

"Is that so?" Ilanna fingered the handle of her bracer dagger. "If that were the case, this office would be a lot...bloodier." She bared her teeth in a feral grin.

Bryden didn't so much as flinch. "Charming as ever, Journeyman." He tapped the quill feather against his lips. "I trust your latest job is proceeding well?"

Ilanna stiffened. How much did he know? She doubted he'd thwart her plans, but...

"Oh, relax." Bryden gave a dismissive wave. "Master Hawk hasn't told me anything more than I learned in the Council meeting. I simply ask because your House dues are just around the corner." He tapped Filch's stub. "Most of this gold will go toward covering the day wages for your crew. Add to that the cost of the equipment you've used for the job, and you'll come up short for the month."

Heat radiated through Ilanna's chest. *I'm taking on the most powerful man in Praamis, and he's worried about my House dues?*

Her jaw tightened. "I received permission from the Guild Council to—"

"To engage in whatever harebrained scheme entered your mind." Bryden slammed the book shut. "You received permission for that, but *not* to avoid paying what is owed."

Ilanna's fists clenched. "I'm not avoiding anything. I'm simply focused on the job, Bryden. Ask Master Hawk."

"I have, and he said nothing about your asking permission to delay payment of House dues." His smile turned icy. "Now, I suggest you find a way to come up with the coin before the week's end, or..." He trailed off and spread his hands in a gesture of helplessness. "Rules are rules, Ilanna."

Ilanna fought back the urge to leap across the desk and throttle the Hawk bookkeeper. *You'd better be glad I left my sword in my room, you preening ass.* An overwhelming temptation to hack the smug expression from his face seized her.

"How...much?" she growled between clenched teeth.

"What's that?"

Ilanna drew in a deep breath. Bryden was enjoying himself far too much. "How much are the House dues?"

He made a show of studying the ledger. "Twenty imperials."

Ilanna couldn't believe her ears. *So much fuss over such a paltry sum?* But with Bryden, nothing was too small. He would use any excuse to lord his power—limited as it may be—over her.

"Shouldn't be too hard for someone like you to come up with that." His smile turned caustic. "Of course, if that's beyond your reach, perhaps you'd rather be in another House? Might I suggest House Grubber?"

You'd love nothing more, wouldn't you? He'd never done or said anything overt, but hadn't kept his disdain for her secret either.

"Tell you what," Ilanna said, her voice slow and her words acerbic, "take it from my balance. I'm sure there's enough there to cover such a princely sum." Her lip curled into a sneer. "Some of us are able to earn our own way, rather than depending on incompetents and fools to do our legwork for us."

Bryden flinched at that, his face hardening.

"If that's all, Journeyman Bryden." Ilanna gave him a mocking bow and turned to leave.

"One more thing, Ilanna."

Ilanna whirled, teeth bared. "What?"

"I'll be sure to ask Master Hawk to see the list. Perhaps Lord Ulimar's name really isn't on it, after all."

"Anything else?" She held out her arms. "Do you need to keep track of every tavern I visit, every pot I piss into?"

"If I expected it to reveal the truth, I would." Bryden stood, his expression darkening. "Since the moment you joined House Hawk, you've brought nothing but turmoil and misery. From your run-ins with the Bloodbears to the death of your fellow apprentice to the matter of the dead Scorpion, you've cost this House. You're a disease, Ilanna. You may have Master Hawk and Master Gold fooled, but not me. I see you for what you really are: a canker. As far as I'm concerned, the day you buy your freedom can't come too soon."

"On that," Ilanna said, her voice growing dangerous, "we agree."

Before Bryden could say another word and earn himself a dagger in the gut, Ilanna strode from the room. She didn't bother closing the door.

* * *

"I'm afraid Master Gold is occupied at the moment." Entar didn't bother to look up from his ledgers. "You'll have to come back at another time."

The long trek through the Guild tunnels hadn't cooled Ilanna's fury. Unlike Bryden, Master Gold's aide had no personal reason to thwart her. That didn't make it any easier for her to deal with stubborn adherence to protocol. Not when she had more important things to do.

In her mind, she called down a thousand curses on petty bureaucrats, but fought to keep her tone measured. "Please, Entar. If you could tell him it's—"

"Life or death?" Entar looked up now. "Please tell me you weren't going to use *that* nonsense."

Ilanna ground her teeth. "I was going to say 'important'."

"Let me guess, you've half a hundred things to do for your secret job."

Ilanna nodded.

"Well, take that number and multiply it by ten, and that's how much the Master of the Night Guild has on his plate every single day."

Ilanna stifled a growl. "I respect your desire to protect your master's time, but I have to see Master Gold today."

Entar waved at the hard, wooden chair across from the Guild Master's office door. "Like I said, Journeyman. Have a seat, and if—*if*—Master Gold has a minute in his day, I will usher you in."

Anger churning in her gut, Ilanna sat. The tight folding of Entar's hands and the set of his jaw spoke of the tenacity of a loyal underling. She'd have better luck enticing a smile from Bryden and a kiss from Master Bloodbear. Entar would no sooner budge than the earthen wall behind him.

After what seemed an infuriating eternity, Master Gold's door opened. Master Serpent glided from the office and strode away with a nod for Ilanna.

Master Gold poked his head out of the office. "Entar, what's next on the docket?"

Entar cleared his throat. "You have five minutes until your meeting with Journeyman A—"

"Journeyman Ilanna?" Master Gold's words interrupted Entar. "What brings you here?"

"A matter of some importance," Ilanna said, shooting a glare at the seated aide.

"Well, come on in." The Guild Master stepped aside.

Entar's expression soured. "But Master Gold, you have—"

"Will this take long, Ilanna?"

Ilanna shook her head. "No, Master Gold. Two or three minutes of your time, I promise."

Master Gold held up a hand to stifle Entar's protest. "Thank you, Entar. I am aware of my next engagement. The Journeyman and I will be quite quick, I promise."

The aide made a decidedly miffed sound and turned back to his ledger.

Ilanna hid her grin as she entered Master Gold's office.

"He means well." A hint of annoyance crept into the Guild Master's voice. "Loyal as a guard dog, and at least twice as bright."

Ilanna grinned. "I doubt the Long Keeper himself could get past Entar without scheduling a month in advance."

Master Gold chuckled. "How can I help you, Ilanna?"

"Two things. First, this." She drew three purses from within her cloak and set them on the desk. "Two hundred imperials each."

Eagerness sparkled in Master Gold's eyes. "Wonderful!" He made the purses disappear into a desk drawer with the skill of a street illusionist. "Dare I ask where they come from?"

"Lord Illidan, Lord Cairus, and Lord Ulimar." She studied the Guild Master's expression at the last name. His eyelids didn't so much as flicker.

Does he know that I know he's the one sending the notes? If so, he's damned good at hiding it.

"Excellent." He stroked the head of the falcon brooch pinned to his jacket. "That should be enough for now."

"For now? How much more do you need?"

"Honestly? I have no idea." He jerked a thumb at the desk. "That six hundred won't go half as far as I need it to." He held up a placating hand. "It should buy enough Journeymen to keep the Bloody Hand's offer off the table, but I know Bernard. He's doing exactly the same thing, and I doubt he has to keep it a secret. If he has enough of his Hounds behind him…"

"Two-thirds, according to Allon."

Master Gold cursed. "Too many. He can operate with impunity, using his Hounds to put out feelers, deliver bribes, and find him the gold for those bribes. All I have is you."

"What of Masters Hawk, Serpent, and Scorpion? Can't they help you?"

Master Gold tilted his head. "Master Hawk does what he does out of a desire to care for his House, but Masters Scorpion and Serpent are more swayed by gold. I can't ask them to earn the coins I'll use to pay them. No, Ilanna, we're alone in this. Which is why I need you to finish the Duke's job as quickly as possible. With the gold we'll earn from that, I should have more than enough to keep the Journeymen happy."

"I understand your need, Master Gold, but I trust you can understand the importance of doing this job right. I'm facing off against not just the Duke's most secure creation, but against his Arbitors as well. One wrong move, a single misstep, and it'll be me dancing at the end of a hangman's noose." She gave a bitter chuckle. "If I live that long."

"I do not take your task lightly, Ilanna, but the Bloody Hand will not wait long before asking again. Perhaps they will stop *asking* entirely. I need as much as you can bring me."

"Then I need something from you."

Master Gold quirked an eyebrow.

"Waive my Guild dues for as long as it takes me to complete this job."

The Guild Master's eyes widened. "What?"

Ilanna sneered. "It seems I forgot to ask the Guild Council permission to delay paying my dues. Bryden came to me demanding it—a pathetic twenty imperials."

"So why not pay it?"

"Because," Ilanna growled, "if I'm to complete this job, I need as much independence as possible. This is the greatest challenge the Night Guild has ever undertaken, and I can't have some fool breathing down my neck over something as ridiculous as House dues."

Master Gold stroked his chin.

"Think of the endgame, Master Gold." Ilanna leaned forward. "That sarcophagus is worth more than the entire Guild earns in five years. If I succeed..." She didn't need to complete the thought.

"Done." Master Gold nodded. "I'll have Entar draw up the waiver immediately."

"Thank you." Ilanna inclined her head. "I will do what I can to bring you more, but I cannot guarantee anything. I must be completely focused on this job if I am to succeed."

Master Gold's face grew earnest. "And we *need* you to succeed, Ilanna. We have to keep the Bloody Hand at bay, whatever the cost. If you can do this, you may save not just the Night Guild, but the entire city of Praamis."

Chapter Twenty-Seven

Jarl and Darreth looked up from the blueprint table as Ilanna strode into the room. "This had better be good."

Jarl's jaw tightened. "We've got a problem."

Ilanna raised her eyebrow.

Darreth squinted in her direction. "Your ever-eloquent comrade excels in understatement. We're dealing with *problems*."

Ilanna clenched her teeth and tried to push down her frustration. Two days of studying Lord Auslan's mansion and she still hadn't found an unguarded entrance. "Let's hear it."

Darreth's fingers twitched. "The Hawk and I have spent every spare minute he has poring over these plans. I'm afraid our results aren't promising."

"Why?"

The Scorpion sighed and rubbed his eyes. "I'm ashamed to admit, but a good deal of it is far beyond my understanding. Don't get me wrong, I deciphered the mathematics easily enough, but the complexity of the design is a tad beyond my abilities."

"Understood. Which is why I had you work with Jarl to…" She trailed off as Jarl shook his head. "You, too?"

Jarl counted among the Pathfinders' most skilled metal-workers. He'd spent two years of his apprenticeship working with metalsmiths and carpenters. His additions to the Hawk's Highway had significantly improved its stability and opened dozens of new avenues and shortcuts around the city. If the vault door was beyond his skill, no one in the Night Guild could solve the problem.

"You want to bring in someone else."

Jarl nodded.

"Who?"

"Master Lorilain. She's good."

"You apprenticed under her, didn't you?"

Jarl replied with a nod.

"Can she be trusted?"

Jarl's nod came more slowly. "Guild pays her well."

Master Lorilain was one of the craftsmen in Praamis who catered to the Night Guild. In return for handsome fees that bordered on the exorbitant, she provided the Guild with metal-wrought tools and equipment. The extra gold bought her silence, but Ilanna couldn't be certain the smith wouldn't inform on them should the Duke provide proper motivation—financial or otherwise.

"We can't do it without her?"

Jarl shook his head. "Handful of smiths in Praamis can do the job. She's among 'em."

Ilanna hesitated. She couldn't risk the Duke finding out about her plan ahead of time, but she needed someone who could recreate the blueprints. "I need to meet her first."

Jarl shrugged.

She turned to Darreth. "You said problems. Multiple. What else?"

Darreth tapped his graphite stick on the symbols that filled the upper right corner of the Duke's blueprint. "I've spent the last two days working on these, tried every cipher and code I know. I showed it to half of House Scorpion. Nothing."

"Damn it!" Ilanna pressed her fists into the table. She'd had pored over those symbols for hours and come no closer to understanding them. She'd hoped Darreth could figure it out.

Darreth's eyes slid away. "I've a few more people I can show it to, but after that…"

After he failed, what else could she do? Perhaps Master Hawk or Master Gold could help her. But she wouldn't turn to the House or Guild Master until she had no other choice.

"Keep at it, Darreth. We need to figure out what they mean."

"Well, I have a theory." Uncertainty filled Darreth's voice and wrinkled his forehead. "But I'm loathe to say anything until—"

"Spit it out." Ilanna's voice cracked like a whip. "We've got nothing to go on, so even crazy notions could give us a lead."

Darreth drew in a deep breath. "Mind you, I can't make sense of the symbols, but something tells me they're related to whatever mechanism is used to trigger the lock."

Ilanna leaned forward, eager. "What makes you say that?"

Darreth's finger tapped an empty space in the middle of the illustrated vault door. "If I was designing this door, I'd put the lock here. Chest height, close to the handle. And there certainly wouldn't be a gaping hole in the middle of the door."

Ilanna narrowed her eyes. The blueprints depicted a circular door that, according to Darreth's calculations, was close to three paces across and high, with a thickness matching the length of her forearm. She didn't understand the rest of the illustration, but couldn't dispute Darreth's logic.

"So you think these symbols"—she motioned at the markings—"are somehow related to the locking mechanism?"

"That's the best I can come up with."

"It bears thinking. Keep at it. See if you can crack it."

Darreth gave her a crooked smile, and his eyes met hers for an instant. "Anything else?"

Jarl nodded. "Need more hands."

"For the escape route?"

Jarl shook his head. "Vault tunnel."

Ilanna gave a dismissive wave. "I'm sure House Grubber has a few able bodies who'd be interested in a few weeks away from the street." She snorted. "For most of them, it'll be a pleasant respite. Get as many as you need, Jarl. But only those who can keep their mouths shut. They'll earn double their day rate for discretion."

Jarl nodded.

"How goes the escape route?"

"Got it figured, I think."

"Good. Will you need help to rig it, or can you handle it alone?"

Jarl scratched his shaggy chin. "Gorin'll do."

"Only if you have to." Ilanna's face hardened. "The fewer people that know, the less chance of mistakes. Did Allon get you that map of the sewer system I asked him to draw up?"

Jarl nodded.

"Good. Any more problems that need handling?"

Darreth and Jarl exchanged glances and shook their heads.

"So be it. Darreth, keep at these symbols until you figure them out. Jarl, you and me are going to pay a visit to that smith of yours."

* * *

Ilanna tried hard not to gape at Master Lorilain. The woman stood well over six feet tall, but it was her girth that so impressed Ilanna. Beside the smith, the hulking Jarl seemed frail and petite. Master Lorilain had small hands but forearms thicker than Ilanna's calves. The muscles in her shoulders and arms bunched with every movement. Jarl grunted as the smith pounded him on the back.

"Who's this now?" The smith gave Ilanna a once-over with eyes as dark as her ash-stained forge and pushed a lock of curling brown hair out of her dusty face. "You didn't tell me you had a girlfriend, Jarl."

Jarl reddened. "Master Lorilain," he mumbled, "meet Journeyman Ilanna. Ilanna, Master Lorilain."

"Ilanna, eh?" The smith crossed her arms and tapped her hammer against the meat of her shoulder. "You treatin' the big lug good?"

Ilanna returned the gaze with icy calm. "Good as he deserves." She had no need to disabuse Master Lorilain of her notions, and if it encouraged the smith to help, all the better.

After a moment, Master Lorilain's face split into a grin. "I like this one, Jarl. You could've done far worse."

Ilanna couldn't help returning the grin as Jarl turned the color of a fresh-picked tomato.

Master Lorilain set down her hammer. "What can I do for the Guild? I assume you're here on business, not paying your old master a social call."

Jarl produced the copy of the blueprint Allon had sketched out. He'd insisted he needed more time for a truly accurate duplicate, but this would suffice to give the smith an idea of what they expected. Better to present Master Lorilain a half-completed replica than take the risk she'd recognize the original and flat-out refuse the job.

The smith shoved aside a mess of tools and scrap metal and laid the blueprint atop a soot-covered table. "Let's see what you've got here." She studied the illustration for long minutes, then looked up at them. "You're wanting me to build this?"

Jarl nodded.

"Not sure you know what you're asking here." She tapped the drawings with a dirty forefinger. "What you've got here is a room with walls, floor, and ceiling made entirely out of cast steel sheets. With each sheet being roughly two paces long and one across, you're talking a great Swordsman-damned lot of metal to build it. These dimensions correct?"

Jarl nodded again.

"So a room that's five paces long and wide, with a ceiling just above the average man's head. I don't need to do the sums to tell you that you're talking a few tons of cast steel." She looked at Ilanna and smirked. "By your girlie's expression, I can see I'll have to keep things simple."

Ilanna stiffened at the use of *girlie* and the insult, but she kept her mouth shut.

"Most smiths work with forged metal—steel that's heated red-hot and hammered into shape. But for a room of this size, it'd take a dozen master smiths months to complete this job using forged metal. Judging by these markings, I can see they went with cast metal—steel that's melted down and poured into a mold. It'll then be rolled out to the correct texture."

"Now, cast steel ain't as tough and flexible as forged steel, so the sheets'd need to be mounted on a frame. Iron'd do best for the bones, as it's tough and can handle all that weight of steel. But a frame wouldn't be enough. There'd have to be a solid bed of stone beneath. I'm no stonemason, but I'd say granite or slate. Should support the weight of the metal and give you a solid foundation for the steel—plus whatever's going to be stored inside this room."

Ilanna shrugged. "So what's the problem?"

Master Lorilain rolled her eyes. "Where to start?" She counted off the items on her fingers. "First, it's expensive. Like 'buy yourself a patent of nobility' expensive. Second, you're talking a team of stonemasons working for weeks to build the foundation, and again as much time to build the iron frame and weld the steel plates together. Third, you're not going to get your hands on the material you need before the end of the year."

Ilanna's eyebrows shot up. "What?"

The smith nodded. "You heard." She tapped the blueprints. "Only one place in the world makes steel like this: Odaron."

Jarl sucked in a breath, but the name meant nothing to Ilanna. "Odaron?"

"City of Steel, some call it. A few decades ago, metalsmiths got together with the Secret Keepers to figure out a more efficient way to do things. Combined, the Secret Keepers' alchemy and the smiths' metallurgical knowledge produced some scary results. Metals stronger and harder than steel, yet lighter than copper. Metals that can catch fire but don't burn your hand." Master Lorilain shook her head. "Some say they discovered the secrets of the ancient Serenii. Whatever happened, they found a way to increase their production of better-quality steel than the rest of Einan."

"So why not use that?"

"Sure, if you've got a few hundred thousand imperials to spare." Master Lorilain gave a harsh laugh. "They figured out how to produce more of the better-quality steel, but that doesn't mean they'll just give it away. You'll pay more for those steel plates than you will for gold or silver. Odarian steel's harder to get your hands on, too. Only sold to those with a 'Lord' stuck to their name. Even if you used all the Night Guild's connections"—her eyes grew as hard and sharp as the axes hanging on the wall—"you'd only get a score of sheets here before the end of the year. Odarians are bloody stingy with their resources."

Ilanna's heart sank. "So you're telling me it's impossible."

"Not quite, but the next closest thing." The smith turned back to the blueprints. "The fact that these plans call for Odarian steel means you're dealing with something big—something I prob'ly want no part of. The last thing I want is to call attention to myself by doing anything of this nature."

Ilanna opened her mouth to speak, but the smith didn't stop.

"That being said, I'm pretty sure I know why you brought this to me." She pointed at Jarl. "This one's not sure he's got the chops to build this monster of a vault door. That about right?"

Jarl nodded.

Master Lorilain drummed her fingers on the table. "Here's what the Night Guild's gold'll get you." She held up two fingers. "I'll build your vault door. Judging by these plans, it's a much simpler task, though one that'll take me a good few weeks of work. We can make it out of high-carbon Voramian steel. Not a whole lot cheaper than Odarian steel—we'll just need a whole lot less of it."

Ilanna thrust her chin at the second finger. "And?"

"And I'll give some thought as to your predicament of getting in or out of that vault room." The smith gave her a calculating grin. "Assuming you'd be interested in that sort of thing."

Ilanna nodded. "Could be your help would prove useful. I'd certainly pay well for information."

"Good." Master Lorilain held out a hand to Jarl. "Be good to work with you again."

Ilanna gripped the smith's hand before Jarl could. "You'll be working with *me*. And I'm *not* his 'girlie'."

Master Lorilain's grip tightened, but Ilanna kept her face impassive. The muscles in her forearms, hardened from years of climbing ropes and stone walls, bunched as she returned the crushing force. For long moments, neither spoke but simply held the posture and the unyielding stare.

The smith broke eye contact and the grip first. "So be it." She gave a slight grin and turned to Jarl. "Prob'ly for the best she's not your girl, Jarl. She's a good deal more than you c'n handle."

Jarl muttered under his breath. "More than you know."

Chapter Twenty-Eight

Ilanna slid into a stuffed armchair with a weary huff. She'd spent the last week surveying Lord Auslan's mansion from every conceivable angle. The lack of sleep and results had her on edge.

The door opened and the sound of four booted feet echoed in the room.

Ilanna didn't bother opening her eyes. "I hope you've something useful to tell me."

When no reply came, she stood and walked over to the table. Veslund shook his shaggy head. "Not a lot of information on Lord Auslan."

"Aye," Joost added. "From what we've seen, there's three types of people enterin' his estate: fellow noblemen, his servants, and scores of the Duke's Arbitors."

Ilanna chewed her lip. "No tradesmen, merchants, or carts of foodstuffs? Surely even an Old Praamian has to eat."

Joost shook his head. "Auslan's servants do all the haulin'. They have their own wagon for bringin' in goods." He gave a frustrated growl. "Place is buttoned up tighter than a miser's pocket."

Ilanna nodded. She'd come to the same conclusion over the last week. The blue-clad, spike-helmed Arbitors came and went as they pleased, but Lord Auslan's servants only left the mansion once a week. The Arbitors subjected them to a thorough search before being allowed in or out.

"Any unguarded entrances into the mansion complex?"

Veslund shrugged. "None we've found yet. Problem is, there are sections of the mansion wall we can't get at. Damned Arbitors are too sharp."

Ilanna stifled her annoyance. The rooftops of Lord Auslan's neighbors gave her an unobstructed view into the property, and what she saw hadn't encouraged her.

The estate stood at the end of the cul-de-sac that was Old Praamis. Twenty of the Duke's Arbitors held the mansion complex's two entrances: the main gate, where the fancy carriages of Lord Auslan's guests entered; and the postern gate for the servants. The wall around Lord Auslan's mansion rose at least four or five man-heights, with a team of sentries walking the parapets day and night.

If they somehow managed to get over, under, or through the wall, Lord Auslan's estate would prove a far greater challenge. A broad, tree-lined avenue connected the main entrance to the mansion itself. Even after dark, torches provided clear lines of sight in all directions.

Thick hedges of blackthorn cordoned off the main avenue and hid Lord Auslan's private gardens from his visitors. The thorns served as a secondary wall, running around the interior of the property like a twisted, torturous maze. If she somehow managed to cut through, she still had to contend with the five groups of four guards that patrolled the expansive gardens and Lord Auslan's private quay on the Stannar River. A broad lawn surrounded the house, a wide-open, torchlit space she had little hope of crossing unseen.

And that was *before* she reached the mansion itself. The construction stood four stories high and spread out hundreds of paces along the river's edge. She had no clue where she would find Lord Auslan's vault.

One problem at a time.

"What do you think of the northeast?"

The northeastern side of Lord Auslan's estate was the one area she hadn't been able to study. The Duke's Arbitors rarely ventured in that direction—they had no need. The wall abutted the Field of Mercy, in plain view of the Praamian Guards who stood in Watcher's Square.

Joost cringed. "Not a grubbin' chance we're going near that." Veslund's emphatic nod set his shock of hair bobbing.

The thought of going near Watcher's Square and the Field of Mercy twisted Ilanna's stomach in knots. She had no desire to see the place where her friends had faced the Duke's justice. But she had to consider *all* possible avenues of entrance, no matter how unpleasant.

"I've been thinking," Veslund said, scratching his beard, "and I ain't sure I understand how ye plan to pull all this off. Say we manage, by the Mistress' own luck, to get inside that mansion. Ye figure out that great big vault door, and we get our hands on that golden coffin. Then what? How in Derelana's tits do we get it out of there?"

Ilanna met the Fox's gaze. "I have a plan for that."

When she offered no more, Veslund growled. "Well, what is it?"

She shook her head. "I can't tell you. The fewer who know, the less likely the wrong person'll find out."

Veslund bristled. "Ye saying I can't be trusted?" He loomed over her, eyes flashing.

Ilanna didn't back down. "You're still here, aren't you?"

"But ye won't tell us the plan." Spittle flew with Veslund's words. "Like ye expect we can't keep it to ourselves."

"Tell me, Veslund, have you ever had too much to drink?"

Joost snorted beside her.

Veslund colored. "What's that got to do with anything?"

"Ever found yourself boasting about some great feat of skill or strength?"

Veslund hesitated, but nodded.

Ilanna stepped toward him. "Now, let's say you find yourself trying to match a fellow drink for drink, exploit for exploit. He's one-upped you, and you're looking for a way to even the score. What's to stop you from hinting at the greatest heist in the history of the Night Guild?"

"Well, if that ain't a—"

Joost cut him off. "She's got you there, Ves. Don't think I haven't heard you tradin' tales with the Third Claw Bloodbears or those fellas from Grey Fox."

Ilanna looked up into the bearded Fox's eyes. "It's not that I don't trust *you*, Ves. I don't trust anyone. The fewer who know the plan, the less risk someone'll say it in the wrong place at the wrong time."

Veslund's mouth hung open, but his anger deflated. "Pah!"

"Come on, Ves." Joost wrapped his arm around his fellow Fox's broad shoulders. "Let's put you to the test and see if'n you can hold your tongue after a few mugs of ale."

Veslund perked up at the mention of ale and allowed himself to be drawn away.

"Just don't have too many," Ilanna called after them. "You've work to do."

Joost's voice floated back to her. "Lord Auslan's mansion will still be there tomorrow." The door swung shut before she could retort.

Stifling her frustration—at the two Foxes and the lack of results—Ilanna bent over the rough outline of Lord Auslan's estate she'd helped Allon sketch out. Veslund and Joost provided her with the street-level view of the complex, but their understanding was as limited as their attention span.

They understood things in length and width, only perceived as far as their feet could walk or their eyes could see. She saw Praamis in a way none of the others did or could. Allon and his fellow Hounds understood the advantages. They moved around beneath the city, where the confines of walls and houses meant little. Deep underground, they had to rely on their sense of direction.

But from the rooftops, Ilanna could see in every direction. What others saw as obstacles, she used as stepping stones to cross Praamis far faster than anyone on the streets below. The higher the building, the greater the vantage point it provided. The height of Lord Auslan's walls meant little to her when she sat atop the six-story mansion beside it.

Fatigue turned the world to a blur. She rubbed her eyes. Exhaustion threatened to dull her mind; she needed sleep to keep a clear head, but she couldn't shake the sense of foreboding that nagged in the back of her mind. The look on Master Hawk's face at the last House meeting told her something was wrong. Judging by Master Gold's drawn expression, it had something to do with the Bloody Hand. The Guild Master had said the Voramians would return, demanding instead of requesting. She couldn't shake the feeling that she had to carry out the Duke's job as soon as possible—they'd reach "too late" before long.

She half-jumped as the door opened.

Allon's smile faltered as he strode up to the table. "Bloody hell, Ilanna, you look awful."

"Thanks." She gave him a scathing look.

"When was the last time you slept?"

She waved her hand in a dismissive gesture. "Too many things to do."

"Don't make me haul you off to your room. I can, you know." He took a step toward her.

Instinct kicked in and Ilanna's hand flashed to her dagger. At the sight of his half-grin, she stopped herself from baring steel. She forced her face to mirror his expression. "Just you try, Hound."

Allon held up his hands. "At least promise me you'll grab an hour or two of sleep before you head back out there."

Ilanna wanted to protest, but a wave of exhaustion set her wobbling. She waved away Allon's steadying hand. "Fine, you win." She straightened. "Tell me you have some good news."

Allon winced. "You're not going to like it."

"Let me hear it anyway."

Allon took a deep breath. "I've talked to half of my contacts and come away with little more than we already knew. The one thing everyone tells me is that they can't remember the last time Lord Auslan stepped foot outside his mansion. The man is a total recluse. The only parties he attends are the ones he hosts. He runs his business using private couriers." He shook his head. "Don't bother thinking about using them as a cover to get in. They're all in service to the Duke, just like the Arbitors."

Ilanna bit back a frustrated curse. "What else?"

"From what little I can gather, his mansion is like a maze. Lord Beritane said he got lost walking from the front door to the ballroom." He snorted. "Of course, when you're on your eighth bottle of wine, you tend to forget a lot of things."

"Don't worry about the interior of the house."

Allon cocked his head. "Why not?"

Ilanna gave him a sly smile. "Let's just say I know a man."

The Hound waited for her to add more, but she gave him nothing. He shrugged. "I'll keep digging for any tidbits I can find out about Lord Auslan. Don't hold your breath, though."

Ilanna nodded. "Between you and Errik, I'm sure we'll come up with what we need to know. I can try to talk to Master Gold, too." Now she had the excuse she needed to speak with the Guild Master. "Whatever it costs, Allon, I'll pay. We have to find out everything about Lord Auslan."

"Your will, my lady." Grinning, he swept a bow. He turned to leave, but paused at the door. "How's Jarl getting along with that map?"

"Like a miser in a pool of gold."

Allon grinned. "I'll pop down and see if he needs help. I remembered a few things that might help him set up our escape route."

"Our?" Ilanna cocked an eyebrow.

"You know what I mean."

Ilanna bit back the sharp words that sprang to her mind. "I do. Just don't take too long down there. I need information more than I need a filthy, sewage-covered Hound."

Allon grimaced. "Don't remind me. Now, before I go, promise me you'll get some rest. You look like the Long Keeper's paler cousin."

Ilanna growled. "That how you talk to a lady?"

"When she looks like she's been sleeping on her feet for a week and refuses to listen to wisdom, sure." His expression grew somber. "I mean it, Ilanna. You can't let the burden of this job get to you. You have to take care of yourself. We're all depending on you."

Ilanna wanted to argue, but she lacked the strength. "Fine. I'll rest."

"That's all I wanted to hear." With a wink, he strode from the room.

Ilanna had said the words with no intention of following through, but the idea of rest had suddenly grown more appealing than Lord Auslan's gold. She needed at least a few hours' sleep.

Stowing the blueprints and sketches, Ilanna locked the door and shambled yawning through the tunnels toward her room. She didn't bother lighting a lamp or removing her clothes, but slipped straight into her bed. A groan escaped her lips at the comforting warmth of the blankets. Reaching under her pillow, she drew out a threadbare, wool-stuffed cloth hawk. She'd made the toy for her infant son, but Kodyn had outgrown the toy a year earlier. She hadn't. Traces of his smell lingered on the fabric.

Exhaustion played tricks with her mind. Thoughts of Lord Auslan's mansion blurred with images of her entry into the Coin Counters' Temple. Grey-clad Reckoners in silver breastplates chased her through twisting corridors and into a hedge of thornbushes that tore at her flesh.

Then she stood in a garden. Kodyn ran toward her with outstretched arms and her heart soared at the sight of her child. She raced toward him, scooped him into an embrace. A tall, swarthy girl in long-sleeved robes of a brilliant blue to match the sky smiled at her. Warmth flooded Ilanna, and sleep claimed her.

Chapter Twenty-Nine

Ilanna awoke in darkness. For a moment, she was trapped inside the Treasure Room, desperate for air. The inky blackness pressed in on her. Panic dug painful fingers into her mind and set her heart racing.

Her dreams faded and reality asserted itself. She fumbled for the lever to turn on the alchemical lamp sitting on her bedside table. Her questing fingers felt parchment, and icy feet danced down her spine. She leapt from the bed and drew a dagger in one smooth motion. Panting, her eyes darted about, seeking an enemy.

Was the note there before I fell asleep, or after? Had someone slipped into her room while she slept, stood over her? She shivered and wrapped her arms around herself. She'd been so vulnerable.

Not releasing her dagger, she found and lit the lamp. Her hands trembled as she opened the note and read the written words. *Lord Ralston.*

Her sleep-numbed mind took a moment to recognize the name. She'd delivered the skull-headed dagger to the mansion in Old Praamis over a year ago, had received her monthly payoff from the Crown.

Why is Master Gold sending me there? Surely there are better people to visit.

Lord Ralston was descended from one of the oldest families in the city, but had little wealth outside his vast real estate investments in Nysl. She'd be lucky to come away with a hundred imperials in coin.

She buckled on a brace of daggers, threw on her cloak, and rushed to the Aerie. If Master Gold needed the money urgently enough to send such a clear message, she had to deliver. The shadows in his eyes at their last meeting had hinted at ill-concealed anxieties. If the Bloody Hand had returned, she was running out of time.

* * *

Ilanna lowered her body over the lip of the roof and dropped onto the veranda without a sound. Lord Ralston's security hadn't improved much since her last visit. The nobleman trusted the Crown to keep its word.

If only Lord Auslan was as foolish and trusting. Between the guarded exterior wall, the blackthorn hedges, and the scores of Arbitors patrolling his grounds, Lord Auslan had made her job close to impossible. Yet, as she'd proven with the Black Spire, impossible didn't exist.

Case in point, she thought as she crouched beside the servant's entrance and used her picks to tease open the lock. *Every building, no matter how secure, has vulnerabilities of some sort.*

Noblemen and women needed clothing laundered, food prepared, and their every pampered whim met. Servants had to come and go without being seen by their betters. That meant every mansion had entrances and exits often left unguarded, and lower levels and exterior buildings where the servants lived.

But these were not the only ways to get in and out. Every wealthy merchant and nobleman built grand houses with picture windows and balconies that offered spectacular views of the city. Household guards maintained tight security on the lower levels, but were forbidden from entering the bedchambers and private upper floors. Only the Duke's Arbitors seemed to understand the vulnerability of a badly-placed window, the shadows of an overhanging roof, or an unguarded servant's passage. Ilanna left no trace of her entrance, and none of the pompous lords and ladies she visited seemed to understand that the threat came from above instead of below.

Praamis was a Hawk's paradise. Except for the sprawling estates of Old Praamis, the buildings were packed close together. Instead of being forced to traverse narrow alleys, Ilanna could simply leap from roof to roof. Like everyone in the Night Guild, she learned her way around Praamis, but she saw it from the view of a bird instead of being forced to walk the streets.

Her vantage point had made it clear she'd never leave Lord Auslan's mansion with the enormous sarcophagus in tow. Even if she somehow got it out of the vault and onto a wagon without alerting suspicion, the guards at Lord Auslan's front gate wouldn't allow her to pass without a search. Old Praamis lacked the broad avenues of The Gardens. A laden wagon could never navigate the twisting road. The Arbitors would catch them before they could escape.

So she had only one option: to go under. Jarl, with the help of Allon's map and Darreth's skill at charting distances, would dig an escape route for her and her loot. But first she had to find a way into the mansion.

Her mind worked on the problem of Lord Auslan as her body went through the motions of locating Lord Ralston's poorly hidden stash of gold. She'd visited the Ralston manor enough times to find and open the cache behind the hideous painting of Lady Ralston in the office.

Lord Auslan's mansion would prove a challenge on par with the Black Spire. She would have to find a weakness in his outer layers of security. That meant getting over the wall, through the thorny hedges, and around the guards. No easy task.

Over the wall, she mused. *Or under it?*

Excitement set her heart racing and brought a smile. *What if there's to be a way to get in through the sewer system?* The underground network of tunnels and drains had service entrances all around the city. *Surely Allon knows of one that opens onto Lord Auslan's grounds.*

In her eagerness to return to the Night Guild, Ilanna almost missed the sound of footsteps in the hall. She barely had time to slip into the shadow of a bookshelf before the door opened. The light of an alchemical lamp slithered toward her as the tall, lean figure of Lord Ralston entered the office. Fighting the urge to hold her breath, Ilanna forced herself to take slow, silent breaths.

The yawning nobleman set the lamp down on his desk and lowered himself into a plush chair. With a furtive glance at the door, he slid open a drawer. "And the battle-axe has the gall to tell me what I can and can't do! In my own house?" He drew out a silver pipe, and his slim fingers packed the bowl with brown tabacc leaf. "Those idiot physickers have no idea what they're talking about. Tabacc, harmful?"

Producing a firestriker, he lit the bowl, sat back in his chair, and puffed at the pipe. Ilanna grimaced as the noxious odor of burning tabacc filled the office. Pipe in one hand, Lord Ralston shuffled a stack of papers, muttering about "hatchet-faced harpies" and "addle-pated, pitiful excuses for physickers".

Ilanna pressed against the bookshelf, mind racing. She couldn't get past Lord Ralston unseen, and his office had only one door. She had no desire to leave a corpse behind. *Better to wait him out.*

Lord Ralston seemed disinclined to leave. He drew out a snifter and popped the cork on a dust-covered bottle. The scent of brandy drifted up from the glass as he leaned back in his chair with a sigh.

"Dynnis?" A shrill voice echoed from the hallway.

Lord Ralston went from relaxed to panicking in a heartbeat. He gulped down the brandy, dropped the still-smoking pipe into a drawer, rushed to extinguish the alchemical lamp, and ducked under the desk. His heavy breathing filled the office.

Candlelight flickered in the doorway, shining on a face that somehow seemed sharper and more angular than the hatchet-faced woman in the painting. "Dynnis, don't think for a moment I don't know you're in here!"

The huddled Lord Ralston gave no response.

"I can smell that damned tabacc smoke, you fool." The carpet bunched under Lady Ralston's angry strides. "You know what the physickers said about your humors." She stood behind the desk, hands on hips, staring down at her husband with an expression somewhere between a pucker and a sneer. "Hiding, are we? And here's me thinking you couldn't look any more like the idiot you are."

"Er…not hiding dear. Just…er…retrieving a fallen coin." He held up a copper bit. "See?"

"No doubt you'll tell me you came in here to do some late night work, I suppose?"

Lord Ralston's mouth snapped shut.

"Come, Dynnis." The woman motioned and a chagrined Lord Ralston fell into step behind her. "No more of this sneaking around. You know what'll happen if you keep smoking that infernal…" The shrill voice trailed off as Lady Ralston closed the door.

The laugh Ilanna had held for the last few minutes burst free. For a moment, she almost pitied Lord Ralston. *I'd have murdered Lady Ralston long ago.*

On a whim, she reached into the desk drawer for the silver pipe. In his hurry, Lord Ralston had upended the smoldering tabacc leaf onto a sheaf of papers. Ilanna extinguished the embers with a breath and pocketed the pipe. Lord Ralston would suspect his wife had gotten rid of it, and Lady Ralston wouldn't question its disappearance. The silver would bring her a few imperials if she decided to sell it for scrap metal. If not, she knew a few Journeymen who would happily trade a favor for such a beautiful pipe. No one would question its provenance.

With a grin, she slipped out of the office. The halls were deserted as she slinked down the hall and through the servants' entrance onto the veranda. A few moments later, she reached the roof and raced into the darkness of the Praamian night.

* * *

Ilanna was surprised to find Entar's desk vacant and the door to Master Gold's office open. She strode in without knocking.

The Guild Master lay on a couch, fingers pressing the bridge of his nose. He opened one eye as she entered. "Ilanna? What brings you at this ungodly hour?"

Ilanna dropped the purse onto the table. "Another hundred imperials. That ought to be enough for now."

Master Gold bolted upright, his gaze darting toward the door.

Ilanna shook her head. "There's no one there."

Master Gold pushed the door closed, shot the bolt home, and turned to her with a grim expression. "You never know who's listening."

"Like you said, it's an ungodly hour. Anyone without the sense to be in bed is either out on the streets or too tired or drunk to care."

"Still, now is the time for circumspection. With things the way they are…" His expression darkened.

"That bad?"

Master Gold grimaced. "The Bloody Hand has sent a message." He waved at the box on the table with one hand while making the purse disappear with the other.

Ilanna peered into the box and recoiled with horror. "They sent *that?*" Blood stained the fingers and palm of the severed hand within. Five claw-tipped fingers had been burned into the flesh.

"Who else?" Master Gold's face hardened. "They didn't exactly send a note, but they couldn't be more explicit. The Bloody Hand, indeed."

Ilanna studied the unadorned box and its grisly trophy. "We're running out of time, aren't we?"

"We are. I've already spent most of what you brought me, but it's not going to be enough. Not even with this additional hundred imperials. If I'm right, Master Hound is spreading around a small fortune in gold—gold that no doubt comes straight from Voramis. There's no way I can hope to keep up with him. I've heard whispers that he's going to call for a vote at the next Guild Council. If you don't pull off the Duke's job soon, we're going to lose."

"How much time do I have?"

Master Gold sighed and collapsed into his chair. "With the Labethian Tournament just four weeks away, all the Houses will be busy. The Guild Council won't be able to meet until then."

"So be it." She had four weeks to pull off the Lord Auslan job. A tight deadline, but she had no other choice. "But if I'm to succeed, I need to know everything you can tell me about Lord Auslan."

"I've already told you everything I know."

"Then use your contacts to find out more!" Ilanna growled. "If anyone can get me what I need to know, it will be the Master of the Night Guild."

Master Gold narrowed his eyes. "Anything in particular?"

"The man's a recluse. I need to find something that will get him out of the way so I can do the job without leaving corpses."

"Then I'll see what I can do."

"Thank you, Master Gold."

The Guild Master nodded and returned to his couch. As she left, Ilanna couldn't help casting a final glance at the Bloody Hand's message.

Chapter Thirty

The cacophony of hammers on steel set Ilanna's head ringing. The reek of scorched flesh and metal filled the warehouse she'd claimed for her project, and her lungs burned from the shavings in the air. A wave of heat from the improvised forges washed over her.

A sweating Master Lorilain paced before an enormous steel door, gesticulating wildly and yelling orders at her apprentices. In the far corner of the warehouse, Jarl and Darreth hovered over a table.

Ilanna had to shout. "How goes it?"

Master Lorilain shook her head and tapped her ears. The clangor drowned out her response. Face darkening, the smith put her fingers to her lips and gave a piercing whistle. The pounding hammers fell silent.

"Much better!" Master Lorilain waved at the door. "Break time, lads. The lady here and I need to talk."

Ilanna raised an eyebrow. "So it's 'lady' now?"

Master Lorilain's shoulders bunched as she shrugged. "You said to drop the 'girlie'. Now, d'you come here to see your door or gripe about names?"

Ilanna grinned. No fancy words or small talk with the smith. She could get used to that. "How much progress have you made?"

The smith tapped her lips with a filthy finger. "We're most of the way done, truth be told. With the help of your fellow over there," she motioned to Darreth, "we've come as close to the original as you could ask for."

Ilanna studied the vault door. "Not quite completed yet, is it?"

"I figured I'd give you a chance to see the inner workings for yourself. Seeing as you plan to break into it, and all." The smith gestured at the unfinished construction. "As you can see, the locking mechanism isn't all that complicated. The wheel on the door's outer face turns a helical threaded shaft. Turn it to the right, and the shaft extends the locking bolts into the jamb."

She tapped a bolt extended from the left edge of the door. "The plans call for eight of these—two per side. Steel bars as thick as two fingers sliding deep into the door jamb. If these are engaged, not a bloody chance you're getting the door open. But spin the wheel to the left, and the shaft retracts the locking bolts. Once the bolts are retracted, it's a simple matter of pulling on the door to open it."

Ilanna pointed to a thin steel bar hanging above the wheel shaft. "What's that for?"

"Keen eye you've got. See that notch at the end there? When the lock is engaged, this bar slides down like so." Master Lorilain pulled the bar down, and the notched end slid onto the shaft.

"Sort of like a wrench biting down on the head of a bolt."

The smith nodded. "Right you are. Exceptin' this stops the shaft from turning."

"And if the shaft doesn't turn, we can't retract the locking bolts."

"Precisely. But truth is, this thing is heavier than clever. If you can find a way to get through the outer face of the door, you'll be able to cut your way through this locking bar and turn the shaft. Problem is, you're talking about going through solid steel. And not just any steel—we're talking Odarian steel, which is tougher'n regular. You'll need two or three days to drill your way in."

Ilanna shook her head. "That won't work." She doubted she could spend more than a few hours working on the vault door. Less if someone screwed up and alerted the Arbitors. "We need to find a way to get through it quickly."

Master Lorilain shrugged. "'Fraid I can't help you there. If this was plain steel, might be you could melt your way through. But this is Odarian steel. That means it can handle higher temperatures without melting." Her brow furrowed. "Unless…"

"Unless?"

The smith rubbed her soot-stained face. "Well, I've given the matter of the vault room a great deal of thought. I think the answer to the room itself could be the solution for your door."

Ilanna's heart leapt. "Explain."

"It all comes down to the practicality of building that room. If I was building a strongbox out of steel, I'd do what's called pattern welding. Basically, heating the edges of two steel plates and hammering them together. When the metal cools, the welded pieces are almost as strong as a single piece. Plus, there's less chance of air and moisture seeping through—something those blueprints place a lot of emphasis on. But pattern welding takes a bloody lot of heat. It's bad enough when you're in the open air of a forge; imagine what it would be like in the confines of a room. Especially one lined with metal."

"You'd look a lot like a roasted chicken."

"Aye." Master Lorilain nodded. "If it was me, I'd use brass. Doesn't require as much heat and it's easier to work. But the plans say steel, so I've been racking my brains as to how that vault room of yours was built."

"And?"

The smith raised a defensive hand. "I'm not much for rumors, but when it affects my line of work…"

Ilanna stifled her impatience. "Rumors often hold more truth than you'd expect."

"Rightly said." Master Lorilain scrubbed sweat from her forehead and drew in a deep breath. "Well, I've heard whispers of a special alchemical concoction brewed up by the Secret Keepers. Something that gets the steel hot as a forge ever could, all in the space of a few seconds. If it's true and such a thing exists, it would make it possible to build your underground room." She scratched her chin. "Come to think of it, you might be able to melt a hole in that door and lock. You'd have your way in. But, like I said, it's nothing but whispers."

Ilanna's heart sank. If the rumors were true, she was no closer to finding a solution. The Secret Keepers, servants of the Mistress, goddess of trysts and whispered truths, guarded their alchemical secrets with ruthless ferocity. They wouldn't simply *give* her what she needed, and everyone knew what happened to those who stole from the Temple of Whispers. Only corpses, twisted and burned beyond recognition, remained of the last thieves who'd dared.

Maybe Darreth knows someone who could brew something. House Scorpion had more than a few back-alley alchemists. They couldn't come close to the Secret Keepers' skill or knowledge, but Ilanna had to try.

"When will the door be finished? I'll need to do a few trial runs."

Master Lorilain's forehead scrunched. "I'll need another few days. A week maybe."

"*Another* week?"

"Listen up, little Journeyman." Master Lorilain loomed over Ilanna, her forearms bunching as she flexed her hands. "You came to *me* because you wanted a job done. What I've done in this last week would take any other Praamian smith twice as long. You're asking for a miracle. Miracles take time."

Ilanna met the smith's ferocity with a calm shrug. "So be it." She could use the week to think of a way to get through the door that didn't involve stealing from the Secret Keepers. "But the sooner you can do it, the bigger your bonus."

"Good," Master Lorilain grumped. "Now, if you'll excuse me, I've a handful of lazybones to round up." With that, the smith strode from the warehouse, shouting for her apprentices.

Ilanna gave the vault door one final examination. *Just when I thought we were getting somewhere.*

Sighing, she strode over to Jarl and Darreth. "Did you hear all that?"

Jarl nodded.

Darreth spoke without looking up from the blueprints. "I can ask around House Scorpion, see what I find out."

"Good." She drew in a deep breath, fighting back her frustration. "Now tell me you two have better news for me."

Jarl's impassive face revealed nothing, but Darreth winced.

"Seriously? Nothing?" Ilanna slammed her fist on the table. "I need that lock built so I can figure out how the fiery hell I'm going to pick it."

Darreth looked up. "I'm trying," he said simply. "No one in House Scorpion can crack it either. I've done everything I can think of to—"

"Ilanna!"

She whirled at the sound of Allon's voice. The Hound rushed toward her. "I think I have something." He bent over the table, red-faced and panting, and stabbed a finger at the blueprints. "The codes. They're Illusionist Cleric script!"

Darreth's eyes went wide. "What?"

Allon gave an emphatic nod. "Heard stories…Duke Phonnis—"

"Easy, Allon." Ilanna poured him a cup of watered wine. "Catch your breath."

Allon gulped down the drink and wiped his mouth. When his frantic breathing slowed, he spoke in an excited voice. "I was attending one of Lord Beritane's luncheons—in disguise, of course—and I got a few of the younger lords talking about Lord Auslan." He shook his head. "It's amazing how much the nobles of The Gardens *hate* those Old Praamians."

"Allon!" Ilanna snapped her fingers. "The stories?"

The Hound nodded. "So Count Chatham and Lord Dorris start going on about how ridiculous Lord Auslan was to entomb his wife in gold, and that foolish underground room of his. And Lord Dorris starts going on about how Lord Auslan could have bought a whole team of gladiators with the money he spent hiring the Illusionist Clerics to design an impossible lock for him."

Ilanna's mind raced. More than once, she'd fought back nausea after staring at the mind-boggling patterns on the Temple of Prosperity's façade. The Illusionist was the god of coin, success, and madness; his clerics' reputation for insanity was rivaled only by their understanding of the human mind and their ingenuity in designing intricate puzzles, trick boxes, and toys. It made sense that Duke Phonnis would bring in the Illusionist Clerics to create an impossible lock for his impenetrable vault door.

She turned to Darreth. "It has to be, right?"

198

The Scorpion's brow furrowed as he stared down at the indecipherable markings. "Can't say for sure. I've never seen Illusionist Cleric script."

"Do you know anyone who has?"

Darreth scratched his chin.

A memory of Reckoner Tyren, the priest she'd abducted from the Coin Counters' Temple, flashed through Ilanna's mind. Perhaps she could do the same with an Illusionist Cleric. She discarded the idea immediately. She had no desire to leave more corpses in her wake.

"Come on, people! Think." Ilanna pounded her fists on the table. "Surely one of us knows someone who's had experience with an Illusionist Cleric."

Allon gave her a blank look, and Jarl shrugged his huge shoulders.

She returned her gaze to the Scorpion. "Darreth?"

Darreth winced. "I have an idea. But you're not going to like it."

"Spit it out, man! I'll do it, no matter what it costs."

The Scorpion grimaced. "We need to pay a visit to Master Velvet."

* * *

Ilanna stifled a shudder as she stared across the table at Master Velvet. Even now, fifteen years later, memories of the time spent in the Menagerie set her hands trembling. She clenched her fists and forced herself to meet his gaze.

"Well, well, if it isn't little Seven." Master Velvet gave her a leering grin— the same toothless expression that still woke her screaming in the night. "I hear it's *Ilanna* now."

Ilanna swallowed. "That's correct." Her jaw creaked with the effort of holding back the acid surging to her throat.

Master Velvet leaned back in his chair. "Kind of you to visit your old master after all these years." He rubbed a grimy hand over his stubbled cheek. "Though something tells me you're not here to share a glass of agor." He didn't offer her a cup, but emptied the foul-smelling liquor down his throat and belched.

Ilanna's eyes dropped to his namesake vest. Was it just her imagination, or had the number of bloodstains multiplied? Her fingers twitched toward her bracer as her eyes sought the pulsing vein in his throat. It would be so easy to slice the bastard from crotch to gullet. It would be no less than he deserved for the torment he'd inflicted upon her—that he inflicted upon every new batch of tyros delivered into his care.

"What brings the great Journeyman Ilanna to my door?" Master Velvet picked at his nose, flicked away his findings.

"This." She slid a piece of parchment across the table.

Master Velvet's eyebrows shot up as he studied it. "Now that's something I haven't seen in an age and a half." He settled a pair of cracked spectacles onto his red, pitted nose. "The script of the Illusionist himself."

Excitement warred with Ilanna's revulsion. "You can read it?" No one knew what brought Master Velvet to the Guild, but it was whispered he once served in the Temple of Prosperity. The fact that he understood the Illusionist Cleric script proved the rumors true.

Master Velvet nodded. "Some."

"Can you tell me what they mean?"

Master Velvet stroked his scruffy cheeks, winced as a scab on his nose bled. "It'll take me time, but I think I can manage." He reached into a drawer and drew out a tabacc pipe. He spoke without looking away from stuffing the bowl. "But, as fond as I am of my former tyros, I'm not the sort to—" He cursed as the clay bowl broke off the pipe stem, fell, and shattered.

"Will this provide sufficient motivation?" Ilanna produced Lord Ralston's pipe.

Greed sparkled in Master Velvet's eyes, stretched his face into a wide grin. "Oh yes, indeed. That should do nicely." As he took the pipe, his hand brushed against hers. He let the contact linger.

Ilanna snatched her hand back. "How long will it take?"

Master Velvet raised the pipe to his lips with a sigh. "For this, you'll have the translation in the morning."

Ilanna didn't bid Master Velvet farewell, didn't even look back as she strode from the room. She had to get away from him and the chilling memories of her past before she added his blood to the stains on his vest.

Chapter Thirty-One

"Gah!" Ilanna's throwing dagger *thunked* into a wooden beam, followed by two more. She wished she had one of Master Velvet's straw dummies to chop into pieces. Or the man himself.

"That bad?"

Ilanna whirled. Allon stood at the entrance to the work room, a worried expression on his face.

"Worse!" She stalked over to the beam and tugged her daggers free. "Yet another bloody cold night spent studying Lord Auslan's mansion and nothing to show for it." She pointed to the map of the estate he'd drawn. "The walls are maintained and guarded too well. The only section of the grounds we'd have any hope of slipping into unnoticed is the northeastern side."

The Hound grimaced. "By the Field of Mercy." He shut the door behind him.

Ilanna nodded. "There are a few crumbling sections of wall that we could slip over. If only we could reach it."

"Crossing forty paces of quicksand."

"Exactly. Now, let's say we somehow manage to do what has never been done and get across the field. There's still one small problem."

"Watcher's Square."

"Between the Praamian Guards and the steady stream of traffic in and out of the Palace, we'd be spotted before we took three steps." She buried another throwing dagger into the beam. "We're better off trying to fly into the mansion."

"You're not wrong there."

Ilanna gritted her teeth. "I take it you've got more good news for me?"

Allon's expression turned grim. "I found a way to exit the sewers into Lord Auslan's property."

She sensed a "but" in his voice. "Don't tell me: the Duke's men have sealed it."

Allon nodded. "Welded the damned thing shut. No way we're getting through there without some serious effort." He stroked his chin, his mouth pulling into a tight line. "Problem is, if we try to go at the grate, we're going to raise some serious ruckus. If we were talking Praamian Guards, there might be a chance. But no Arbitor's going to miss the sound of a hacksaw."

"Damn it!" Ilanna's fists clenched and relaxed. She'd known this job would be difficult, but it had begun to look impossible. How could they succeed if they couldn't even get into the same estate as the vault? Then there was the little matter of getting through a door made of Odarian steel—according to Master Lorilain, an impossible task given their time frame. Unless, of course, they stole from the Secret Keepers, an act commensurate to committing suicide in the most painful manner possible.

"It gets worse."

Ilanna quirked an eyebrow. "Let me guess: the Apprentice himself has descended from the heavens to punish me."

Allon gave a mirthless chuckle. "Perhaps not that bad, but not much better. I ran into Jarl down in the sewers and he asked me to pass on a message. He says he needs more Grubbers. They've hit bedrock. It means they're getting close to the river—where the mansion is. But if he doesn't have more hands, they're not going to make it through."

Ilanna gave a curt wave. "He can hire all of House Grubber if it gets the job done in time." If he didn't, they'd have no escape route, no way to get the immense golden sarcophagus out of the vault.

"He also said he needs to know *where* he's digging. Something about being sure what part of the house to aim for."

Ilanna rolled her shoulders. "I should get that information any day now." The last three visits to her dead drop had found it empty. She'd have to try again tonight.

A knock sounded at the door. Allon glanced at her and, at her nod, opened it.

"Message from Master Velvet for Journeyman Ilanna." An apprentice in the white-trimmed robes of a Hound entered.

Ilanna leapt across the room and snatched the envelope from his hand. She ripped it open, spilling sheets of parchment over the table, and bent to study the contents. Excitement swelled in her chest.

"Yes!" She beckoned Allon over. "Take a look at this."

Allon slid in beside her, his shoulders rubbing up against her. His eyes went wide as he scanned the writing. "Incredible!"

Ilanna glanced up as a cough sounded behind them.

The Hound apprentice held out a hand. "Master Velvet said you'd cover the fee."

Using the distraction as an excuse to avoid Allon's contact, Ilanna flipped a half-drake at the boy. "Shut the door behind you." She didn't wait to hear the *click* of the latch before returning her attention to the parchment. "Bloody hell, that's complex!"

Master Velvet's deplorable handwriting proved difficult to read, and the Illusionist Clerics' words made little more sense than their script. The translation spoke of twenty-four interlocking rings, one for each of the noble Houses in Old Praamis. The first page had a plethora of details on the mechanisms for connecting the rings to the lock's various cylinders and springs.

She looked up at Allon's breathy exclamation. "What do you think?"

Allon shook his head. Bewilderment etched deep lines in his face. "I'm willing to say I understand even less than you do."

Ilanna nodded. She'd spent a year of her apprenticeship studying under the best locksmiths in Praamis. The Illusionist Clerics' design left her head spinning. "I think we need to take this to Master Quorin, see if he can build it."

Master Quorin counted among the merchants and artisans beholden to the Night Guild. The locksmith had borrowed from the Guild to repay gambling debts. When he inevitably defaulted on his loan, Master Hawk had convinced House Bloodbear to let the locksmith work off what he owed. The Guild called on Master Quorin infrequently, but he never turned them down. If anyone could recreate the lock, he could.

"I'll take it to him." Allon held out a hand. "I'll be heading back into the sewers to see if I can find another way in and to deliver the message to Jarl. I just had to stop by the Guild for a pair of galoshes and workman's clothing." He wrinkled his nose at the green-and-brown splotches on his clothes. "I'd almost forgotten how filthy it is down there."

Ilanna gave him two sheets of paper. "Tell him I'll be stopping by tomorrow night to see his progress. Double his usual fees if he has good news." She half-drew a throwing dagger from her bracer. "He won't like what happens if he gives me more bad news."

Allon snorted. "Always the charmer, Ilanna." He moved toward her.

"Oh, hell no!" Ilanna poked a hand into his chest. "As long as you smell like that, you're staying far away."

"Fair enough. But when I'm clean…"

Ilanna quirked an eyebrow. "You're going to need *a lot* of baths to get rid of that stink."

Allon groaned. "Don't I know it? Until later, little Hawk." With a wink, he left the room.

Ilanna let out a slow breath and the tension in her gut relaxed. His interest in her had increased since they started working together. He always sought excuses to be near, to touch her. She'd have to do something about him. She needed to sever their personal relationship without angering him. She still needed his help to finish the Duke's job.

Let's just hope Master Velvet found more information than just the lock. The envelope had contained three sheets of parchment. Two provided detailed information on the locking mechanism. *So what's this other one about?*

She recognized a few of the words on the parchment: acid, steel, Odaron, and Lord Auslan. But the majority made no sense to her. Phrases like "Derelana's Lance" and "Kharna's Breath" couldn't refer to the gods themselves, could they? The rest looked like the sort of chemical names Ethen had once spouted at her—names she had no way to recognize.

I need to get this to Darreth and see if he recognizes anything. She'd have to pay a visit to the warehouse before she checked her dead drop.

"Ilanna? You in here?" The door swung open, and Errik poked his head in. "Oh, good. I think I've found the solution to our Lord Auslan problem."

Ilanna snorted. "Which *one*? Every day brings some new impossibility."

"The man himself."

Ilanna leaned forward. "I'm intrigued."

"The Labethian Tournament." Errik gave her a meaningful look.

Every twenty years, Praamis held the Labethian Tournament in honor of King Labeth. Legends held that Labeth had led an army that defeated the demons who held the ancient city of Praamis during the War of Gods. Though his soldiers died by the thousands, Labeth had been the first to set foot upon the wall, the first to wet his blade with demonic blood. When the demons threw his men off the parapets, he had battled alone for an hour. At the battle's end, he had slain more than a thousand demons, or so the stories said. Of the hundred thousand men that joined battle with him, only ninety-nine remained to crown him the first King of Praamis.

The Labethian Tournament paid homage to the nobility and honor of Labeth by pitting gladiators in combat to the death. People came from as far as the distant Hrandari Plains, bringing their most skilled warriors and ferocious beasts to compete for the honor of being crowned Labeth's Scion and taking the Royal prize of two hundred thousand imperials. Champions around Einan battled in arenas and beast pits to be one of the sixty-four contestants selected to enter the tournament. Only one left the arena alive.

Visitors from every corner of the world flocked to Praamis for the Labethian Tournament, and even the Labethian Arena's ten thousand seats failed to contain the throngs jostling to see the battles. Trade in and out of the city ground to a halt during the week-long celebrations prior to the tournament.

The Foxes and Grubbers had already begun sharpening their finger-knives in anticipation.

"You think Lord Auslan will be attending the tournament?"

Errik nodded. "From what I hear, he's an avid fan of the games. Rumor has it—"

Another knock sounded, and another Hound apprentice entered. "From Master Gold."

"Thank you." Ilanna handed him a coin, opened the folded parchment, and read aloud. *"Lord Auslan's great-grandfather was Dannis Hundred-Lives."* She looked up at Errik, her brow furrowing. "That mean anything to you?"

The Serpent gave her an eager nod. "It's what I was trying to tell you! Dannis Hundred-Lives was the only Praamian to win the Labethian Tournament in the last two thousand years. The King at the time—Sagede, I think—rewarded him with a patent of nobility. His victory in the Tournament won him the heart and hand of Hildur, Lady of House Auslan."

Ilanna's eyes went wide. "Lord Auslan's great-grandfather was a gladiator?"

"Yes. And every Lord of House Auslan has attended the tournament ever since."

"If that's true..." Excitement set Ilanna's heart pounding. Lord Auslan—and likely most of the Arbitors protecting him—would be at the Labethian Arena in just under four weeks. The estate's guard would be depleted, the mansion vulnerable. "It's the perfect opportunity!"

Errik nodded. "It is." His face scrunched up. "But do we have enough time?"

The question cast a bucket of cold water on the fire of Ilanna's elation. Too many things hung in the air. She had to find a way to crack the Illusionist Clerics' lock and get into the vault. She needed Master Lorilain to figure out how to break through the steel room, Allon to find a way into the Auslan estate unnoticed, and Jarl to complete the escape route in time. If even one failed, her plan wouldn't work.

But what choice did she have? She couldn't complete the job with all of Lord Auslan's guards on the property. She had to take advantage of the tournament if she was to get her hands on the one thing she needed to be free of the Guild. That meant she *had* to have everything ready in time.

She met Errik's eyes. "We're going to do it, no matter what happens." She couldn't fail, not so close. She would do whatever she must to succeed.

Chapter Thirty-Two

Ilanna flew across the rooftops of Praamis, elation lending wings to her feet, the packet from the dead drop nestled in her breast pocket. The contents filled in some of the blanks in her plan. A number of critical elements of the plan remained in their beginning stages, but she had enough to give her crew directions. *It's all coming together!*

She leapt across an open space and tucked into a roll as she landed on a balcony. Slipping over the railing, she closed her fingers around the rope and slid the last few paces to the alley. Night had fallen over Praamis hours earlier. She hurried through the deserted streets toward the riverside warehouse.

"Jarl? Darreth?" Ilanna's voice echoed off the rafters. "You in here?"

Silence met her ears. The light of an alchemical lamp at the far end of the warehouse revealed a deserted table and chairs. Ilanna's hand went to her belt dagger as she slithered through the shadows.

Her gaze darted around. *Where is everyone?* After the clangor that had filled the warehouse just days earlier, the utter absence of sound seemed ominous. The excitement that had sent her hurtling across the city gave way to an uneasy tension.

A gentle rumbling echoed from the small room beyond the work table. Ilanna's heart paused mid-beat before she realized the source of the sound. *Darreth's snoring.*

She slid the dagger into its sheath and cursed herself for a timid fool. The Bloody Hand's message had left her jumping at shadows.

Darreth lay on a ratty couch. His long nose and feet protruded from both ends of a blanket that had passed threadbare a decade earlier. The graphite stains on his hands and forehead spoke of the hours he'd spent toiling over the blueprints. She turned away. *I'll let him sleep for a few hours.* She'd hoped to find Jarl here rather than in the stinking sewage tunnels. *Guess I don't have much choice now.*

She crossed the warehouse floor, pausing to study Master Lorilain's handiwork. The smith had completed the door, installing the outer face and wheel. Only a hole remained where the locking mechanism went. That was in the hands of Master Quorin. She would pay the locksmith a late-night visit to check up on his progress.

The warehouse door opened and she whirled, every muscle tense, dagger half-drawn. She relaxed as she recognized Jarl.

The Pathfinder gave a tired grunt. "'Lanna."

"I have something for you." She reached into her breast pocket and drew out a piece of parchment. "The plans for Lord Auslan's mansion."

Interest warred with the fatigue in Jarl's expression. He took the parchment and studied it. "Rough."

Ilanna shrugged. "The person who drew it isn't much of an artist. Will it suffice?"

The huge Hawk inclined his head. "Should do."

"How close are you?"

"Week. Maybe two. Escape route's proving tricky."

Ilanna nodded. "We have a date. We go in on the day of the Labethian Tournament."

Jarl grunted agreement. "Good choice. City'll be busy."

"And Lord Auslan will be out of the way, with most of his guards, hopefully. You have four weeks to get everything ready."

Jarl's head bobbed.

"Excellent." She jerked a thumb over her shoulder. "The Scorpion's sleeping. If he wakes up, let him know to come find me. I've one more errand to run then I'm off to my bed. Same place you should be, by the look of you."

Sweat, dirt, and other stains Ilanna didn't want to contemplate covered the Pathfinder from head to toe. His usually neat beard had grown wild, and his blond hair lay plastered against his forehead.

"I'll do that." He nodded at the room where Darreth lay sleeping. "Came to talk with the mathematician, but it can wait."

Ilanna placed a hand on his huge bicep. "Rest well."

"Same." With a grunt, Jarl strode toward the small chamber next to Darreth's room. He, like the Scorpion, had slept here most nights since the construction of the door commenced. The warehouse stood a few blocks from the hidden sewer entrance he and Allon used.

Outside, Ilanna pulled up her hood and slipped into a narrow alleyway. At her request, Jarl had constructed a series of ladders and ropes for easier access to the Hawk's Highway. A few minutes of climbing and Ilanna reached the rooftops.

Her eyes turned south, toward Old Town Market. An image flashed through her mind: Ria lay in a warm bed, her arms wrapped around Kodyn's small form. Ilanna hadn't had the chance to slip away for a visit in close to two weeks now. Sorrow panged in her heart. She would make the time in the next few days. She needed to see her son.

With a sigh, she headed east, toward Smith's Street in the heart of the Artisan District. A chill evening wind tugged back her hood, whipped at her hair. She drank in the fresh, clean air of the rooftops, only too glad to get away from the reek of Fishmongers' Row.

The Artisan District stood one street away from Labeth's Highway, the broad avenue that ran east to west through Praamis. Even at this time of night, the main street bustled with laden wagons and pedestrians. Only the most desperate merchants hawked their wares this late.

Labeth's Highway was the only street in Praamis too broad for the Hawk's Highway to span. Descending to the street, Ilanna slipped into the flow of late-night traffic. After a short walk, she turned onto Artisan's Row and sought the sign that proclaimed "*Huridar Quorin, Master Locksmith*".

Instead of knocking on the front door, she turned down a side street and into the narrow alley that cut behind the buildings. After dark, Master Quorin retreated to the workshop at the rear of his establishment.

Ilanna tapped thrice, waited two seconds, and tapped thrice again. A moment later, the door swung open and the locksmith squinted up at her. "Help you?"

"I've come for the lock."

Master Quorin adjusted his jeweler's glasses with a slim-fingered hand. "Course you have. No one comes to me to break a stallion." He waved for her to follow. "This way."

Ilanna entered and shut the door behind her. Two alchemical lanterns filled the workshop with brilliant light, and warmth emanated from a wood stove in the corner. Scraps of metal littered the long tables and benches. *Definitely a locksmith's workshop.*

"So you're the one who sent me this, eh?" Master Quorin flapped the parchment at her.

"Have you managed to finish it?"

"Finish it?" Master Quorin gave her an incredulous look. "Haven't even started the thing. D'you have any idea how complex it is?"

"I do." She thrust a finger at him. "That's why I brought it to *you*."

"Well you've wasted your time." He slid the parchment across the table. "I won't charge you for—"

"Wait a moment! You're telling me you're not going to build it?"

"Can't." The locksmith shook his head. "And if you knew anything about me, you'd know I don't say that lightly." His chest puffed out. "I've built locks for half the nobles in Praamis. King Ohilmos himself commissioned a few of my finest. But *that*"—he jerked his chin at the parchment—"is the closest thing to impossible I've ever found."

Ilanna's eyes widened. Master Quorin, one of the finest locksmiths in the city, unable to recreate the lock?

"What's so impossible about it?"

"Oh, where to start?" Master Quorin gave her a withering glare. "The twenty-four interlocking rings, each of which has to be made just the right size so they fit into a tiny groove. The seventy-seven springs that connect the pieces together, and the perfectly fashioned housing to fit it all. Oh, don't forget the forty-odd wires intertwined in some impossible Illusionist's knot." He tapped his forehead. "Set my head spinning just to think about it. Almost like it was designed by one of those mad bastards at the Temple of Prosperity."

Ilanna gave him a wry grin. *If only you knew the truth.*

"So there's no way you can build it?"

"You'd have better luck hiring a watchmaker to put it together. Of course, it'd cost a bleedin' fortune and take a year or so to build. At least."

Ilanna ground her teeth. "If you can't do it, is there anything you can tell me how to get into it?"

The locksmith snorted. "Get the combination from the owner. Short of that, you're straight out of luck. That lock has close to a million possible combinations. I'd say take a sledgehammer to open it, but I doubt it'll be that easy. Fail-safes and back-ups and all that." He shook his head. "You'd have a better chance getting King Ohilmos himself to kiss your feet."

Frustration added to Ilanna's fatigue, setting her head pounding. The light of Master Quorin's shop pierced her eyes and added to the ache. She pinched her nose to lessen the throbbing in her skull. "Not a damned thing you can tell me, is there?"

Master Quorin gave a dismissive wave. "You want me to blow smoke up your arse, I'm happy to take your gold and tell you I can do the job. But the truth's that I'd build a piss-poor copy of whatever infernal mechanism you're up against. Figure I owe the Guild an honest answer." A wry grin twisted his lips. "It's the only thing keeping those damned Bloodbears from breaking my fingers and toes."

Ilanna growled. "Keeper's teeth!" She wanted to slam her fist on a table, but couldn't find a space free of metallic bits and pieces. She settled for a white-knuckled clench.

Master Quorin settled into his chair and reached for a disassembled lock. "Shut the door on your way out."

Ilanna stalked from the workshop. Her jaw ached from clenching, and annoyance twisted her stomach. She hurled a stream of curses into the night sky. Would *nothing* about this job be easy?

* * *

A run across the Hawk's Highway did little to dim the blazing inferno of Ilanna's anger. Exhaustion augmented her frustration. She knew of only one way to take out her irritation without hurting someone.

Retrieving her sword from her room, she settled into the defensive stance Errik had drilled into her. She moved slowly at first, allowing her body to remember the motions. She'd neglected her practice since beginning the job. Her movements grew faster as the familiar patterns returned, each stroke precise and controlled.

She was breathing hard by the time she completed the sword forms. Sheathing her blade, she strode through the tunnels and into her room. She leaned the sword against the wall and threw her clothing into a heap in the corner. Naked, covered in sweat, she lay on her blankets and stared at the ceiling.

The pressure in her chest mounted with each breath, filling her head with a buzzing. She closed her eyes in a vain attempt to still her racing heart. Kodyn's face floated in her vision. Something squeezed at her heart. She needed to get home, to see her son. Just being with him would make—

A knock came at her door. "Ilanna?"

She leapt from bed and pulled on a fresh change of clothing before opening the door. "Darreth? What are you doing here?"

"Jarl said you came by the warehouse." He rubbed his eyes. "I tried to wait up for you. I think I found the solution."

"Solution? To what?"

"To the vault. To get through that door and the steel room."

Ilanna's eyes went wide. "What? How?"

"I've found someone who can give us information about the Secret Keepers' potions. I know it's a bit late, but we can go now if—"

"Yes!" Ilanna fairly leapt through the doorway and dragged him down the corridor. Hope surged within her. Right now, she would seize any chance, no matter how slim.

Chapter Thirty-Three

Ilanna hurried to keep up with Darreth's long strides. "You sure she'll be up this late?"

The Scorpion nodded. "The Journeyman's a nocturnal creature. Sort of like you." He paused at the door to House Scorpion, a hand on one of the twin arachnid claws that served as the handles. "Fair warning, she's a bit…unusual."

Ilanna raised an eyebrow, but Darreth only shrugged. "One of a kind, she is." He pushed the right claw upward and the left claw downward, and the door lock *clicked*. As the door swung open, Ilanna's eyes traveled upward to the black steel scorpion tail hanging over the entrance. The thing seemed poised to drop and impale anyone walking through the doors.

"Don't take kindly to visitors, do you?"

Darreth shook his head. "House Scorpion's secrets are our own. It took a lot to get permission to bring you here."

Ilanna's jaw dropped as she stared around the Nest, House Scorpion's main room. Dozens of long tables occupied the high-vaulted chamber, each cluttered with an assortment of glass vials, bottles, vases, and other containers she had no name for. Metallic tools of all shapes and sizes sat on shelves beside hundreds of jars, crates, and boxes filled with powders and liquids of every conceivable hue. A furnace blazed at the far end of the Nest. Colorful stains on the earthen floors and walls showed where experiments had gone wrong.

She shook her head. "Science was never my thing, but this…this is impressive."

Darreth's eyes filled with pride. "And this is just the main room. I wish I could show you where the real work takes place, but…" He shrugged. "House rules."

House Scorpion served as the Night Guild's poison-makers. Their concoctions delivered instant death with visible, messy results or killed their target over the course of years, leaving no traces for physickers to find. They offered their services outside the Guild as well.

However, the demand for poisons was limited, even amongst the back-stabbing nobles of Praamis. The Scorpions found other ways to earn money: producing unguents, philters, and draughts for every conceivable purpose. Some, like Journeyman Tyman, used their knowledge of human anatomy to heal as well as harm. More than a few Scorpions dabbled in the alchemical arts, ignoring the Secret Keepers' proscription. The priests of the Mistress, goddess of whispered secrets, couldn't stop the inquisitive minds of House Scorpion from delving into the mysteries of metals and chemicals.

In truth, no one but House Scorpion knew the extent of House Scorpion's interests. Their Journeymen had free rein to research, create, and experiment at will. The House accepted new inventions in lieu of Guild dues.

Darreth pointed down a tunnel. "This way."

Ilanna followed him through the tunnels. The alchemical lamps that illuminated the way bore little resemblance to the lamps the rest of Praamis used. They burned with a blue light that seemed somehow brighter than the warm golden light of normal alchemical lamps. "Are these Scorpion-made?"

Darreth nodded. "Created by Master Scorpion himself more than two decades ago." He ran a hand over the long, slim tubes mounted at intervals along the tunnel. "He's also the one who created quickfire globes."

Ilanna's eyes widened. She brought the little glass globes to House Scorpion to be refilled with the alchemical fuel after every use, but she'd never given much thought to how the Scorpions knew the secrets of the lamps.

"Here." Darreth knocked on a plain wooden door.

A warbling voice called out. "Who's there?"

"It's Darreth, Journeyman Donneh. I've come to talk to you about—"

The door opened, and lamplight shone on the smallest woman Ilanna had ever seen. The top of her grey-haired head barely reached Ilanna's chest. Her eyes—a blue so brilliant they bordered on unnatural—seemed far too large compared to her snub nose and thin, pale lips.

"Get in quick, before Barnabus Timmenson gets out." Something scratched at the door, and the woman stuck her head inside the room. "Back, Barney! Or no treats for you."

A loud primate call responded, and something flew behind the diminutive Scorpion.

"Oh, no you don't!" The door slammed shut but failed to muffle the sounds of clattering glass and metal. "Come back here at once, Barnabus!"

Ilanna exchanged glances with Darreth. The Scorpion shrugged. "I told you."

After a minute, the door re-opened. "Come in, please." Journeyman Donneh beckoned for them to enter.

Ilanna couldn't stop her eyebrows from rising in surprise. The room seemed an endless source of oddities—from the countless apple cores littering the floor to the clutter of glass vials and metal instruments atop the table to what looked like a rope swing hanging from bolts anchored in the roof.

Donneh shot a glare at the little animal sitting on the back of a wooden rocking chair. "Barnabus is always a tad jumpy at this hour of the night. Nocturnal thing, he is, but can't sit still for the life of him!" She turned a frown on the creature. "He's learned his lesson, though, hasn't he?"

Barnabus Timmenson sat atop a shelf, an apple clutched between its long-nailed forepaws. It had the same too-big eyes as the woman, ears far larger, and a pointed snout that ended in a black nose. Light brown fur covered the little primate from its head to the tip of its long, flexible tail.

"What is that thing?"

"Thing?" Journeyman Donneh glared up at Ilanna. "*He* is a nagapie, girl. And he doesn't take kindly to being called a thing, do you Barnabus?"

The nagapie gave a loud call and buried its tiny teeth in the apple.

Ilanna couldn't help watching the tiny creature. After a few bites of the fruit, Barnabus shook his head, flattened his delicate ears, and studied his surroundings with his enormous eyes. Suddenly, his tail curled and he leapt from the shelf. Ilanna gasped as he flew across the room to land on a shelf against the opposite wall.

"Don't you dare!" The tiny Journeyman darted toward the little creature, who had seized and begun to shake an uncorked vial. The dark purple liquid within sprayed over the table. Something sizzled and spat bright sparks, followed by a loud bang. The nagapie screeched and bounded away from Donneh's grasping hands.

"You get down here now, Barnabus Timmenson."

Ilanna cast a wide-eyed glance at Darreth, who sighed.

Barnabus landed on a nearby desk, scattering papers and leaving pawprints across a pristine sheet of parchment. Donneh's screech sounded suspiciously like the nagapie's as she gave chase. The little creature eluded her grasp time and again, every time leaving a mess in his wake. More than a few times, Ilanna flinched as one of the Journeyman's experiments popped, fizzed, or—in the case of one black powder—detonated.

Finally, Barnabus darted to the top of a shelf, well out of Donneh's reach.

"Don't think I won't come up there, Barney!" The Scorpion shook her fist at the animal.

With a shrill cry, he swung down the levels and darted into a small house.

"And say in there!" Journeyman Donneh turned to them. "Sorry about the little bastard." She placed another slice of apple on the shelf. "He's likely to calm down once he's had his dinner. He's a curious little thing, though, so no telling what he'll do."

The nagapie poked his head out, snatched up the apple, and disappeared again. Ilanna could've sworn she saw the same mischievous twinkle that had gleamed in Werrin and Willem's eyes as they planned a fresh prank to pull on Conn.

Journeyman Donneh reached for a firestriker to light an incense burner. "Don't mind me. Barnabus will be doing his late-night business any time. Better to cover up *that* smell, if you know what I mean."

For the first time, Ilanna noticed the unique aroma filling the room: a mixture of sweet incense smoke and wet dog layered over a foundation of acrid urine.

Blowing out the firestriker, Journeyman Donneh pushed aside a pile of blankets and lowered herself into a rocking chair. "So, what can I do for you, Darreth? Master Scorpion didn't give me details, just said you needed advice."

Darreth nodded. "We've run into a bit of a problem."

"That why you brought *her* here?" Journeyman Donneh jerked her head at Ilanna.

"This is Journeyman Ilanna of House Hawk."

"Ilanna, eh? So *you're* the one Ethen always snuck off to see."

Ilanna's breath hitched at the name.

"Shame what happened to him." The woman shook her head. "One of my best, you know."

"You were his teacher?"

"I was." Journeyman Donneh leaned forward and patted Ilanna's hand. "You should've seen the look in his eyes whenever he talked about you. Came alive, he did."

Ilanna pushed down the emotions welling in her chest. Guilt over Ethen's death always followed the happy memories of the time they'd spent together.

"If you're *that* Ilanna, I'll do whatever I can to help. For his sake."

Ilanna met Journeyman Donneh's eyes and found real warmth there. "Thank you."

Darreth handed her the third piece of paper from Master Gold's envelope. "What do you make of this?"

The tiny woman's expression grew grim, and her eyes darted to Ilanna. "Where'd you get this?"

"Doesn't matter. Can you understand it?"

Darreth leaned forward. "I recognize a few of the names there. Antimony, carbon, and a few others. Most, I've never seen before."

216

Journeyman Donneh's fingers drummed an arrhythmic beat on the chair's arms. "I recognize them. Thing is, they're a problem much bigger than whatever you're dealing with."

"What do you mean?"

The rocking chair creaked as Journeyman Donneh reached for a cloth-bound bundle on a nearby table. She unwrapped it with reverence. "This, young Hawk, is the single most dangerous thing in the Night Guild."

Ilanna leaned forward, curiosity burning.

Journeyman Donneh peeled back the layers of cloth to reveal a metal-bound book. "Every word in this book is forbidden knowledge. Stolen from the Secret Keepers decades ago. If they knew I had it, they'd kill me and everyone in House Scorpion. I wouldn't lay odds against them destroying the entire Night Guild. They're not called Secret Keepers for nothing."

She opened the metal-bound cover and flipped through the stiff, yellowed pages. "Many of House Scorpion's greatest creations are thanks to this book. And to think, this is just one among *hundreds* of such volumes. The scientific knowledge of thousands of years, guarded by the priests of the Mistress."

The Scorpion pointed to Ilanna's parchment. "See these names? Derelana's Lance. Kharna's Breath." She held up the book. "This doesn't mention them specifically but it does refer to a few of the chemical names. If they are what I think they are, they're incredibly potent."

She turned a few pages. "These chemicals, the ones for Derelana's Lance, I've worked with many of them before. An old associate told me a story that's stuck with me after all these years. Secret Keepers were transporting these chemicals up the Stannar River, and some idiot struck a spark too near the powder kegs. Next thing the priests knew, fire ate through their wooden barge like it was so much kindling. Never tried it myself—never knew the right amounts of each—but the chemistry is sound."

Ilanna's pulse quickened. "You think it could melt through Odarian steel?"

The Journeyman frowned. "Odarian steel's tougher than Praamian steel, thanks to whatever chemicals the Secret Keepers mix into it. But the base components are the same, so it should work."

"What about Kharna's Breath?"

"That's a curious one." Journeyman Donneh flipped to the back of the book. After a moment of study, she waggled her head. "Looks like some sort of acid, a stronger version of what stonemasons use to smooth out granite and slate." Her eyes widened. "With these chemicals, though, you're looking at something strong enough to eat through steel."

Adrenaline coursed through Ilanna's veins. "Can you make it?"

Journeyman Donneh gave a violent shake of her head. "Not for all the gold in the Reckoners' vaults! That combination of ingredients is as volatile as a drunk Bloodbear. If it comes in contact with even a single drop of moisture, BOOM!"

Confused, Ilanna scrunched up her face. "What?"

Donneh rolled her eyes. "I don't have time to explain the alchemy to you, but suffice it to say that you *do not* want to mix an acid like this with water." She closed the book and fixed Ilanna with a severe expression. "Now, I've given you what you came for. I think it's time you tell me what you need this for."

Ilanna glanced at Darreth, who nodded. Ilanna explained her plan to break into Lord Auslan's vault—leaving out the personal vendetta against Duke Phonnis. Journeymen Donneh frowned at the description of the door and vault construction.

"Seems like you're on the right track," she said after a moment of contemplation. "Problem is, you're never going to get your hands on these chemicals. Half of them don't even exist outside the Temple of Whispers. And there's no way you're stealing from the Secret Keepers. You remember what was left of the last poor fools who tried it?"

Ilanna nodded. "I do. But you managed to get away with that book, so don't tell me it's impossible."

Donneh studied the book in her lap. Silence stretched on for long moments before she met Ilanna's gaze once more. "You sure about this? There are less painful ways to kill yourself."

Ilanna spoke with no hesitation. "Tell me what I need to do."

Chapter Thirty-Four

"*Voramis?*" Allon's eyebrows nearly flew off his forehead. "Are you out of your mind, Ilanna?"

Ilanna folded her arms, face hardening. "Going to try to talk me out of it, aren't you?"

"Damned straight, I am!" Color suffused Allon's face. "I've put up with your more harebrained schemes, but don't expect me to—"

"What?" Ilanna's lip curled and her fists clenched. "You're not *putting up* with anything. I'm telling you what I'm *going* to do because I need you to keep things on track in my absence. Not because I need your permission to do this."

"That came out wrong. I…" Allon sighed. "I just mean I worry that you're going to get hurt, is all." He ran a hand through his hair. "You know how tense things are with the Bloody Hand after the last Guild meeting."

"I know." Ilanna shrugged. "Doesn't mean I have much of a choice." She'd spent the last two days showing the sketch of the Illusionist Cleric's lock to half the locksmiths in Praamis. "We have just over three weeks until the Labethian Tournament. Do you think that's enough time to find someone to build the lock *and* show us how to crack it when the best craftsmen in the city have told me it's impossible?"

Allon hesitated, then shook his head.

"So, unless you have another suggestion, let's pretend I'm capable of making my own decisions and you stop trying to tell me what I can and can't do." She hadn't reached the decision lightly, but now that she had, she wouldn't let anyone dissuade her.

"I'm not trying to tell you what to do, Ilanna." Allon's shoulders slumped. "I'm just trying to help."

"No. You're being a man and trying to protect me." Ilanna's eyes narrowed and her voice hardened. "But I don't need your protection. I need you to tell me that you'll keep things running while I'm gone."

"Take me with you." He reached for her hand, a note of desperation in his voice. "You need someone you can trust to watch your back. At least let me do that."

Ilanna forced herself not to cringe from the contact. "I will have someone. I'm taking Errik."

Allon jerked back as if struck. "What?" His eyes narrowed. "Why him?" The *"why not me?"* went unsaid.

Ilanna spoke in a low voice. "Allon, right now I need you thinking with your head, not any *other* part of your anatomy. You can't let what we have get in the way of your ability to think clearly." She crossed her arms, disgust roiling in her gut. She'd allowed him to grow too attached. Now he believed he could tell her what to do, question her actions. *Just like a man!* "I need my full attention on the job, as do you. Tell me now if you can't keep your emotions out of this."

"I understand." Allon looked as if she'd plunged a knife in his gut, but shook his head. "You're doing what you need to do. I can do that, too."

"Good." She gave him a smile to ease his misery. "I'm taking Errik because he's been there and has contacts that can keep me out of the Bloody Hand's clutches. Unless you know people in Voramis?"

He gave her a strange look, and the silence stretched on for a long moment before he shook his head.

Her words had wounded him—she'd had to put him in his place, for his sake. Now she had to smooth his ruffled feathers. She leaned forward and looked in his eyes. "Once this job is over, we'll have all the money in the world." She squeezed his hand. "We can go anywhere, do anything."

The tightness in his face relaxed and his hurt expression softened. "I'd like that."

She hid a smile. *Too easy.* "But to get that, I *have* to go to Voramis. And that means I won't be here to keep things running. I need someone who can do that for me."

Allon nodded, an eager light in his eyes. "I'll do it, Ilanna. Just tell me what you need."

"Keep Veslund and Joost digging into Lord Auslan and scouting the place. I *need* a way in. If you can't find an entrance in the sewer, I need a realistic plan for getting over the wall unseen."

"And Jarl?"

"He knows his business. He'll keep working at that tunnel. You get him anything he needs. Darreth can work with him to chart the quickest route to Lord Auslan's vault using that map I gave him."

"So be it." Allon placed his hand atop hers. "I'll do it. You can trust me."

Though her skin crawled, Ilanna forced warmth into her smile. "Thank you, Allon. You have no idea how much it means to me." She'd grown better at lying convincingly.

He tilted his head toward her, going for a kiss. She gave a theatrical sigh and stood. "Now for the hard part. Master Gold and Master Hawk are *not* going to like this."

* * *

"Not a Keeper-damned chance, Ilanna!" Master Hawk slammed a fist on Master Gold's ornate office desk. "This is one risk I will *not* allow you to take."

Ilanna winced. Allon had never stood a chance of talking her out of her plan, but Master Hawk could simply refuse her request. She couldn't fault his desire to protect her. Allon looked at her like a frail woman to be sheltered, but Master Hawk's instinct came from genuine concern for her wellbeing. It didn't demean her or insinuate weakness. He simply wanted to spare her from harm, as he did all of the Journeymen under his care.

But she couldn't let that stop her. She had to take a different approach with the Master of House Hawk.

"I'm taking Errik with me. He has contacts in Voramis from his Undertaking, from hunting Malak Short-Hand. And who better to keep me safe than a Serpent?"

Master Hawk's expression didn't soften. "Surely there has to be another way."

Ilanna shook her head. "There isn't."

"You are certain?" Master Gold stroked his head, his brow furrowed in contemplation.

Master Hawk whirled on the Guild Master. "Tell me you aren't considering this, Elliam!" His finger stabbed like a dagger. "*You* are supposed to be the voice of reason here."

Master Gold held up a defensive hand. "And if I had any other option, I'd be the first to tell her not to go. You know as well as I how icy our relationship with Voramis has grown since we refused the Bloody Hand's offer. You think I want to send her anywhere near those Voramian bastards if I had any choice?"

Master Hawk scowled.

"I've tried everything, Master Hawk." Ilanna poured a hint of pleading in her voice. She had to appeal to his desire to help. "I've visited half the locksmiths in Praamis and *none* of them can build it. There's no way I can drill through Odarian steel in the few hours Lord Auslan will be away at the Labethian Tournament. If I had more time, perhaps it would be possible to find another way. If I miss this opportunity, I'd be forced to break into a house patrolled by scores of Arbitors, rather than a handful. It would be suicide!"

That was how she appealed to Master Hawk. He cared about the gold as much as any in the Night Guild, but his resistance to her plan stemmed from his desire to keep her safe. She had to present it as the lesser evil.

"Journeyman Donneh of House Scorpion has told me how to find her contacts among something called the Hidden Circle. Supposedly a group of rogue alchemists defying the Secret Keepers' ban against practicing alchemy."

Master Hawk's face darkened, but Ilanna drove on before he could protest.

"Think about it. If this Hidden Circle has been practicing alchemy without the Secret Keepers finding out, surely they're in the ideal position to help me get what I need."

Master Hawk opened his mouth to speak.

"But why Voramis?" Master Gold preempted the House Master. "There is a Temple of Whispers right here in Praamis."

"I know, but according to Journeyman Donneh, the Secret Keepers brew the specific concoctions I'm looking for in Voramis. The Temple of Whispers there is much larger, and they provide their alchemical potions to Odaron, Malandria, and other cities that don't have the specialized equipment." She turned her palms up. "I don't like it either, but I don't have a choice!"

Master Hawk wouldn't give up. "Surely this lock can't be impossible. There has to be a way in, which means Lord Auslan has the combination. An old man like him would be certain to write it down."

Ilanna nodded. "How do you suggest I get my hands on it? My crew hasn't yet found a way to get into his estate, much less the mansion itself."

She couldn't count on getting lucky and finding the password to the lock. The note she'd found on her last visit to the dead drop had read, "*No luck on combination. Will keep looking, but consider alternatives.*"

"You haven't even found a way in?" Master Hawk's face turned an angry purple. "So why in the Keeper's hairy elbows do you think traipsing off to Voramis to steal from the Watcher-damned Secret Keepers is the smart play here?"

Ilanna didn't back down. "Because I trust my crew to do their jobs while I'm away. I have three people looking for a way in. But that'll take time—time we don't have." She held up three fingers. "Three weeks, Master Hawk. If I don't leave for Voramis now, we're not going to make it."

Voramis lay a week's ride away. Crossing the Windy Plains at this time of year would prove challenging at best. Once in Voramis, she'd have two or three days to get her hands on the Secret Keepers' potions. Even if she rode hard, she would only reach Praamis a few days before the Labethian Tournament. She was cutting it close—too close—but she could think of no other option.

She turned to Master Gold. "I know protocol is to send a messenger to the Bloody Hand and request permission to operate within Voramis. But it would take two weeks just to receive an answer. And do you really want to let the Bloody Hand know we are going to be alone in Voramis, just the two of us? Errik is one of House Serpent's best, but against the entire Bloody Hand..." She let the words hang in the air.

Master Gold's brow furrowed. "You're not exactly doing your case any favors, Ilanna."

Ilanna threw up her hands. "I know, but I can't think of any other way to do this. I need your permission so I can get what I need to complete the job. It's the only way I can get vengeance for Denber and Werrin!"

Her words hit the mark with Master Hawk. Pain flashed in his eyes. He'd felt the loss of the two Journeymen. Ilanna almost hated to use his remorse against him, but she would in order to get what she wanted.

"Please, Master Gold." She turned to the Guild Master. "You said we *need* this to keep the Bloody Hand at bay." His fear exposed him to her manipulation. "If we want the money from Lady Auslan's sarcophagus, this is how we have to do it."

The two men stared at her, hesitation written in their eyes. Yet, as the silence dragged on, she saw the change come over them. Master Gold's face showed reluctant agreement. Master Hawk's expression changed to one of dismayed acceptance.

"So be it." Master Hawk spoke in a gruff tone. "I can see there's no talking you out of this. Be safe, Ilanna." He strode from the room, his gait as stiff as his ramrod-straight spine.

Master Gold sighed. "I wish I could dissuade you from doing this. You're already making an enemy of Duke Phonnis, and the Reckoners if they ever find out what you did. Now to take on both the Bloody Hand *and* the Secret Keepers." He shook his head. "If I didn't know you better, I'd say you had a death wish."

In Ilanna's mind, everything was perfectly clear. She *had* to make enemies of the most powerful people in Voramis and Praamis because it was her only way to live. She couldn't remain in the Guild forever. She would spit in the face of the Long Keeper himself if it meant she'd be free.

"Thank you, Master Gold." She bowed. "This is how we keep the Night Guild safe."

"I know, Ilanna. Doesn't mean I have to like it." He dismissed her with a wave.

Ilanna's hands trembled as she closed the door to Master Gold's office. She had what she'd come for. Allon and Jarl would keep everything moving in her absence. Her plan to break into Lord Auslan's mansion would proceed, and they *would* be ready when she returned. She'd instructed Errik to make the necessary travel arrangements and meet her at nightfall at the city's West Gate.

She had one more person to see before departing for Voramis.

Chapter Thirty-Five

Ilanna's stomach twisted in knots as she slipped in through the front door of her house. She hadn't seen her son for almost two weeks. The thought of wrapping her arms around him brought a smile to her face, but she couldn't help the anxiety roiling in her gut. She'd be hundreds of leagues away, in a city she barely knew, hiding from the Bloody Hand and breaking into the Secret Keepers' temple. Every step away from him led her further into danger. Try as she might, she couldn't convince herself of the certainty of her return.

But she couldn't let him see her worry. Or Ria. For their sakes, she had to pretend all was well.

She forced herself to smile as she pushed open the front door. "Kodyn? Mama's home." Silence met her ears. "Ria? Are you here?"

The stillness felt at once peaceful and eerie. Kodyn's toys lay scattered before the fireplace. Ilanna grimaced as she picked up a half-eaten piece of bread from the stuffed armchair. Evidently Ria hadn't had much luck training away Kodyn's messier habits.

The wooden stairs creaked under her feet. "Ria?"

The upstairs room was empty, the bed made with Ria's trademark precision. Ilanna had never managed to get the corners of the sheets tucked in as tightly as the Ghandian girl. She smiled as she ran a hand over the faded leather cover of the book of fables. Ria couldn't read, but she loved the pictures as much as Kodyn.

Down the stairs and out into the garden she went. Her gut tightened. No sign of Ria or Kodyn. She clenched her fists and pushed the worry from her mind. *They just went out,* she told herself. *They'll be back soon.* Hopefully, before she had to leave to meet Errik at the gate.

A patch of color riveted her attention. Ilanna's breath caught in her throat. She stumbled forward, her mind reeling. Amidst the bare soil of the backyard, life flourished. Purple and yellow violas bloomed beside a small rose bush.

Ilanna fell to her knees before the plants. She ran a finger over the delicate leaves, smelled the sweet scent. She couldn't believe it!

How is this possible?

Once, she had knelt in this garden, tending the plants with her mother. The flowers had suffered from neglect once her mother died. Years later, she'd rediscovered the garden and cared for them with the help of Ethen. Then Sabat had trampled the flowers and killed her friend. She hadn't thought of the flowers—her violas and the rose bush her mother had planted for her little sister—since that day.

But now, to find them like this…

She turned as the door opened and Ria stepped out.

"You did this?"

"I did." Ria's smile held a brightness Ilanna had never seen. "Sometimes, a little care is all it takes to bring dying things back to life."

A lump rose in Ilanna's throat. She couldn't find the words. Kodyn's squeal saved her from having to talk. The little boy rushed across the garden and threw himself into her arms. She clutched him close and squeezed her eyes to hold back the emotions flooding her.

"You came for our lesson, Mama?" Kodyn grinned up at her.

"Lesson?"

His cheeks wobbled as he bobbed his head. "Ria's teaching me to dance!"

Ilanna's eyes widened. "D-Dance?"

Ria's eyes slid to one side. "I-I thought to teach him…" She swallowed. "Teach him a little of my people. The *Kim'ware.*"

"A *war* dance?"

Ria gave a quick nod. "To my people, the *Kim'ware* is not just for times of war. It is also a thing of beauty and grace, a reminder of who we are."

"And Ria's been teaching me!" Kodyn slipped out of her arms and ran over to the dark-skinned girl. "Can we show her, Ria?"

Ria glanced at Ilanna, anxiety mingling with her hesitation. At Ilanna's nod, the lines in her face relaxed. "Wait here." She disappeared into the house. When she returned, she carried a small wooden cylinder with rawhide stretched over one end. She handed it to Ilanna. "Can you play a beat?"

Ilanna took the odd-looking drum. "I…I've never tried."

A smile played on Ria's lips. "It's easy." She crouched beside Ilanna and tapped a simple rhythmic sequence. "Like this."

Ilanna tried the unusual pattern of beats. After a few seconds, Ria nodded.

"Good." The dark-skinned girl glided over to Kodyn. "Stand like this." She helped him adjust his posture. "Ready?"

The boy nodded. At Ria's signal, they began to move. In her surprise, Ilanna nearly missed the beat. Kodyn's movement lacked the grace and precision of Ria's, but his little hands twirled in time with hers and his feet almost kept pace with her steps.

A lump rose in Ilanna's throat. Years ago, she had spent hours in this very garden with her mother, learning to dance. The sight of her son dancing sent warmth coursing through her. Ria's dark eyes sparkled, and Kodyn's grin brightened as laughter bubbled up from her chest.

Ilanna's gaze followed Ria's sinuous movements. A smile played on the Ghandian girl's lips and she closed her eyes. Her lithe frame seemed weightless as she moved in time with the beat, graceful as willow branches on a gentle breeze. She lost herself in the dance, as if she allowed herself to simply exist for the first time in forever.

Kodyn's breathless giggle cut into her thoughts. "Did you see me, Mama?"

"I did!" Ilanna set down the drum and clapped. "You were wonderful!"

The boy laughed and turned to the dark-skinned girl. "Did you hear, Ria?"

Ria ruffled his long hair. "I did. And to think it took me two months to learn, not two *weeks*."

Kodyn beamed. "Will you teach me another one?"

The lump returned to Ilanna's throat. She coughed and swallowed hard.

Ria cast a sidelong glance at Ilanna, hesitation in her eyes. "I think your mama wants to spend time with you."

Ilanna waved. "Oh no, I want to learn to dance, too." She leapt to her feet and came to stand beside her son. "Teach us, Ria."

Ria blushed. "A-Are you sure?"

"Of course." Ilanna gave her a reassuring grin and winked at Kodyn, eliciting a giggle from the boy. "I can't let my son become a better dancer than me."

"As you wish." Ria squeezed Kodyn's shoulder. "Can you help me teach her the *Ris'ale*?"

"The Wind Dance?" Kodyn's head bobbed. "Oh yes!" He took Ilanna's hand. "So, to do the Wind Dance, Ria says you have to stand like this…"

* * *

A log cracked in the still-hot oven. A sweet smoke filled the room, adding to the aromas drifting up from the bowl of stew in front of Ilanna. She took her time to enjoy every bite of the savory dish Ria had prepared using a handful of spices Ilanna had never tasted before.

Ilanna stroked Kodyn's long hair. The boy had fallen asleep in his high chair, his chubby fingers still gripping the carved birchwood hawk she'd brought. She didn't want to be parted from him. The shadows had begun to lengthen, but neither Ria nor Ilanna moved to light the lamps. For a moment, Ilanna was content to bask in the peaceful silence filling the kitchen.

Ria spoke first. "You're leaving again, aren't you? For longer this time."

Ilanna met the girl's eyes. "How did you know?"

Ria gave her a sad smile. "Something about you today reminded me of my mother before she traveled across the grasslands." She inclined her head toward Kodyn. "She wouldn't let go of me or my sister until she had to leave. Almost as if she feared she'd never see us again." Sorrow filled her eyes. "The last time, she was right."

"That won't happen." Steel rang in Ilanna's words. "Nothing's going to stop me from coming back." She bent to kiss Kodyn's head. "Nothing. I'll be in Voramis for—"

Ria stiffened, her breath catching. "Voramis?" Her shoulders hunched and a shadow passed over her face. "No, no, no, no…" She rocked in her chair, head shaking, her gaze unfocused.

"Ria? What's wrong, Ria?"

Ria's gaze snapped to Ilanna, fire burning in her dark eyes. "You must not go there!"

The girl's ferocity shocked her. "What?" Ilanna jerked backward as Ria drew her belt knife in a white-knuckled grip. "Why?"

Ria clenched both fists around the knife. "Bad things happen there." She shuddered and closed her eyes, pain etched in the lines of her face.

"What happened, Ria?" Ilanna's eyes never left the knife. The blade hovered a hand's breadth from Ria's chest. "What happened in Voramis?"

Moisture sparkled in Ria's eyes. "The men who took me…"

Ilanna's breath caught. *Of course.* The men who'd held Ria and the other girls in the warehouse hadn't been Praamians. *I should have known.* The Bloody Hand weren't the only flesh traders to operate through the Port of Voramis.

"Those men, th-they killed my father and brothers, dragged me from my home in chains." Tears streamed down her cheeks now. "My sister…she was too young, too weak to reach the ship. So many others, dead at sea." Her voice dropped to a whisper. "Theirs was the kinder fate."

Horror twisted in Ilanna's gut. What words of comfort could she offer?

"I do not remember much of that city, Voramis. Or this city, either. But what I do remember…" Ria shuddered. "They tried to break us. Beatings first. Starving us. Opiates. Many gave in. I did not."

Ilanna nodded. She'd glimpsed strength in Ria that day in the warehouse brothel.

She pointed to the piercings in her nose and eyebrow. "My captors never took these from me. Said they wanted me to look 'exotic'." She gave Ilanna a savage grin. "That was their mistake. These were my mother's, and her mother's before her. The men saw only pretty jewelry, but these are more than just silver.

They are the mark of a Ghandian *nassor*—a warrior chieftainess, like my mother."

The fire burned in Ria's eyes again. "No matter what they did, these rings reminded me of who I am. I did not let them break me. Until the day I found a way to be free."

Ilanna's eyes widened. Had Ria somehow escaped her captors?

All thoughts faded from her mind as Ria pulled up the long-sleeved shirt she always wore. Two jagged scars ran up the smooth ebony flesh of her forearms. Before she realized, Ilanna reached across the table and ran her fingers along the raised flesh. She was surprised to find Ria didn't flinch at the contact.

Ria's eyes met hers. "You have the strength of a *nassor*, Ilanna. The look in my mother's eyes, I see the same in you when you look at your son. You would do anything for him. Even leave his side, if it means he is safe."

Ilanna nodded. "I do this for him. For us." The words poured from her mouth. "I will not let him suffer the same fate as I."

It was Ria's turn to look surprised. "As you?"

Without a word, Ilanna fumbled at the straps holding her bracer. She slid it off and unwrapped the cloth beneath.

Ria gave a tiny gasp. "What does it mean?" Her dark fingers traced the outline of the numeral "7" tattooed in Ilanna's forearm.

"The people I work for, the Night Guild, they tried to break me just like you. They took my name, gave me this number. That's all I was to them: just one more slave to be molded as they pleased."

Ilanna shivered at Ria's touch. Yet it wasn't out of revulsion; something about the gentleness of Ria's hand on her arm sent sparks coursing through her.

"They branded you like this?"

Ilanna shook her head. "No. I did it to myself. A reminder of who they are." Her free hand gripped Ria's. "And a reminder of who *I* am."

She'd gotten the tattoo the day she discovered her pregnancy. Not even Denber had known about it. It was her way of telling herself she would never again be that weak, scared tyro. She was Ilanna, and nothing in the world would frighten her.

An odd tingling ran through Ilanna's hands. Ria's skin had a musky, spicy scent that seemed suddenly alluring. Ria's hand in hers felt soft, lacking the calloused roughness of Ilanna's. Yet that grip had a strength mirrored in the dark eyes that met hers.

Ilanna found herself drawn into the girl's gaze. In Ria's eyes, she caught a glimpse of the person she could have been. Once, a scared girl desperate for anyone to take her away from the horrors she'd endured; now, someone who had found a sense of purpose, a place of peace. Ilanna had outlived the fear and desperation. Perhaps, one day, she could find peace as Ria had.

But for now, it had to be enough to keep her son—and, by extension, Ria—safe. That meant going to Voramis, taking on the Secret Keepers, and defying Duke Phonnis. No small challenge, but worth it if it meant Ria and Kodyn would be safe.

The ringing of the Lady's Bells shattered the afternoon calm. Kodyn shifted, murmured, and continued sleeping. The moment had passed.

Ria squeezed her hand. "Be careful, Ilanna."

Ilanna nodded. For the first time, she had no desire to break off the contact. The feel of Ria's hand in hers, the strength in the grip, comforted her.

"I will." She returned the squeeze. "I wish there was another way, but…"

"I know." The warmth of Ria's smile reached her eyes. "You're doing what you must. For him."

The lump returned to Ilanna's throat. "When this is over, we're leaving. Kodyn and me. To get away from all these memories, start a life somewhere else." She met Ria's gaze. "Come with us."

Ria's eyebrows rose and her lips parted.

"Kodyn will be miserable without you." Ilanna swallowed as the truth hit her. Ria had brought that "something" she'd been missing since Ethen. Ilanna had told herself she'd kept the girl around for Kodyn's sake, but that had been a lie. Ria, like Kodyn, was "home" to Ilanna. "I want you to come, too."

Tears sparkled in Ria's eyes but her smile lit up the kitchen. "I-I'd like that."

Though every fiber of Ilanna's being protested, she slowly broke contact with Ria's hands. She didn't dare meet the girl's dark eyes for fear she'd never leave. Placing a kiss on Kodyn's head, she slipped toward the door, pausing only long enough to take one of the hawk figurines from the mantelpiece.

"Ilanna."

She turned at Ria's call.

"Come back to us safe."

Ilanna couldn't speak through the pressure mounting in her chest. She could only manage a weak smile before slipping out the door and into the late Praamian afternoon.

Chapter Thirty-Six

"You're doing it again." Errik's sharp tone pierced Ilanna's listless mind.

Confusion wrinkled her brow. "What?"

Errik rolled his eyes. "Grinding your teeth, like you always do when you're worrying about something."

Ilanna narrowed her eyes, but the ache in her jaw and gums told her perhaps he was right. "Sorry," she muttered.

Silence, thick as cheap wool and twice as stifling, hung over the Windy Plains. Flat land surrounded them on all sides. A single broad wagon track cut through the yellowing grass that stretched beyond the horizon. In the last day, they'd seen precisely one tree—a stubby elm barely twice her height. The featureless terrain added to the boredom and exhaustion of their ten-hour days of riding in the wagon. The baking sun and the utter absence of a breeze— *Windy Plains, my foot!*—added to her misery.

She hated every second of inactivity. Her instincts screamed at her to be doing something, anything, to further her plans for breaking into Lord Auslan's mansion. But she could do nothing but sit, drink in the scenery, and—according to Errik's scowl—grind her teeth at the plodding pace set by the tired draft horses.

And think of Ria and her son. The first day out of Praamis had passed in a blur. She'd replayed the last moments spent with Ria over and over. Her fingers had toyed with the ebony hawk figurine as the memory of Ria's dark hand in hers, the feel of soft skin on her forearm, stirred something deep within her. The touch had seemed so innocuous at the time, yet it had grown to mean so much more.

Since Sabat, Ilanna had flinched at even the slightest contact not initiated by her. Only Kodyn had been able to touch her without provoking an instinctive flash of fear. Yet when she touched Ria's hand, there had been no fear. Something about the dark-skinned girl made her feel… safe.

That moment had changed Ilanna. She found herself dreaming again; not the nightmares of being pursued or screaming in Sabat's grip, but about a future filled with possibility. She'd clung to that dream since Kodyn's birth. She'd envisioned herself taking her son away from Praamis to start a new life. Everything she'd done since that day had been to further that goal.

Now, a new face entered those dreams. She stood beside Kodyn *and* Ria, building a new, happy life. Though it left her confused, she wouldn't drive those dreams away. They served as the single bright spot in a life that had, thus far, been filled with misery and suffering. *One day soon,* she told herself, *I'll be done with this.*

But first they had to get across this endless stretch of the most boring landscape on Einan. She wished for a rain cloud, a pack of animals, even an extra-long blade of grass to break the monotony.

"What's got your fuss up?"

She glanced at Errik. He seemed so at ease on the hard wooden bench, as if he'd spent years driving a wagon team. How could he be so calm at a time like this?

"Going over all the things that have to be done, and realizing there's not a damned thing I can do about it." She stabbed a frustrated finger at the draft animals. "Worse, somehow we got stuck with the slowest pack of horses in Praamis!"

Errik chuckled. "And Jarl said you'd never relax."

"How can you?" His mirth irked her. "Aren't you thinking about everything that could go wrong while we're gone?"

The Serpent shrugged. "Sure, but what are you going to do?" He gestured at the barren landscape. "You've made your plan, left the right people with their tasks, now there's nothing more to be done. The more I make this trip, the more I realize worrying doesn't make time pass more quickly."

She raised an eyebrow. "You do this often?"

Errik shook his head. "Not often, but House Hound sometimes gets us in to help if they suspect their fugitives will get violent. Seeing as I learned the ways of Voramis while hunting Malak Short-Hand, I usually get the job."

Ilanna had known of his Undertaking hunting the ruthless Praamian killer-for-hire who had fled the King's justice. But she knew of very little else of his life or work for House Serpent.

"What's it like? Being a Serpent?"

Errik gave her an odd look. "What does that mean?"

Ilanna rolled her eyes. "Back with the Reckoner, Tyren, you said torturing a man takes something out of you. Is that how you feel?"

The Serpent's face hardened to a blank, stony mask. "It's the way of things," he said with forced nonchalance.

"Don't give me that." She scowled. "Look around you. There's no one to overhear, just you and me, Serpent."

For long moments, Errik remained silent, the tension in his expression spreading to his shoulders and back. Finally, he shrugged. "Not a job I thought I'd end up doing, but it could be worse. The way things were before…" He trailed off, his eyes narrowing.

"Before what?" Ilanna pressed.

Errik cocked his head but said nothing.

"Errik, wh—"

"Hush!" he snapped. "Listen."

Ilanna, furious at being cut off, had a retort ready, but something stopped her. A curious whistling reached her ears. "What is it?" Judging by Errik's stiff posture, nothing good.

She glanced around. Nothing seemed out of place on the stark barrenness of the Windy Plains, save for the occasional gust of breeze and that eerie sound.

Errik glanced behind. "Keeper's teeth!"

Ilanna whirled, her eyes going wide. Thick clouds formed a wall that reached down from the sky to blanket the land in dark grey.

She turned to Errik, heart racing. "Can we outrun it?"

"Not a chance!" Errik snapped the reins, and the horses lurched forward into a run. "We've got maybe half an hour to find cover before that windstorm hits us full force." He turned to her, face pale. "Trust me, we do *not* want to be in the open when that happens."

"Where can we go?" She stood, her gaze sweeping the landscape for any shelter from the storm.

"I don't know!" Errik's voice bordered on panicked. "There's nothing around for—"

"There!" She thrust a finger eastward. "There's a dip in the land, with what looks like a rocky hollow."

"How far?"

Ilanna squinted. "I don't know. Half a league, maybe." She glanced back. The cloudwall had closed the distance between them. She had no idea if they could make it, but what choice did they have? "We have to try!"

With a shout for the horses, Errik turned the wagon off the track. The whistling grew louder with every heartbeat, the wind picking up speed. Soon it whipped her hair free of its restraining ties and set her cloak lashing around. Errik snapped the reins over and over, driving the stubborn draft horses to their full speed. Ilanna clung to the bouncing wagon. Her teeth rattled and her back and rear ached from the hard wooden bench, but she made no protest.

She cursed as the first drops splashed down around them. The sky soon poured in earnest. The chilling rain soaked through her cloak and tunic in a matter of seconds. She winced as her knees slammed against the wooden dashboard but dared not move for fear of being thrown. One wrong jolt could send her off the side.

Beside her, Errik squinted into the blinding rain. Dark clouds blotted out the sun, making it near impossible to see more than a few paces in any direction. Ilanna could only hope Errik's sense of direction held true. Without any distinguishing features to guide them, they had *one* chance to find shelter—pitiful as it may be—from the storm.

The ground dipped beneath them, and Ilanna shouted in triumph as the wagon rattled down the hill toward the pile of stones. Errik guided the animals around the stones. Relief flooded Ilanna at the sight of the overhang carved into a mammoth boulder. Seizing their packs, she flung herself from the wagon and into the shelter before Errik drew the wagon to a full halt.

The rocky hollow had a shelf at knee height, far enough off the ground that they could escape the water creeping across the ground. Errik pulled the horses as far into the shelter as possible, removed their traces, and climbed onto the shelf beside her. The animals and wagon blocked the hollow's entrance, keeping out the wind and rain.

Relief flooded Ilanna. She quickly stripped to her thin undertunic and wrapped herself in the blanket from her pack. Errik did the same, hanging their clothing over the wagon's bench. They reclined against the wall, huddled in their blankets, listening to the windstorm pounding the Windy Plains.

Errik spoke first. "Well, that was bloody close!"

Ilanna grinned. "I never doubted you."

The Serpent returned her smile, but his face fell.

"What is it?" Ilanna asked.

Errik frowned. "These storms can last for hours, sometimes days."

Ilanna's gut tightened. "Meaning we might be here a while."

"Aye. And, as you well know, we don't have a lot of time to spare."

Ilanna inclined her head. "Which is why I made sure we had a day or two to spare." They *should* have enough time to make the journey, provided the windstorm abated soon.

He leaned forward and studied the sky. "At this rate, we'd best settle in for a long wait."

"So be it." Ilanna nodded and wriggled to a comfortable position. "But someone once told me 'worrying doesn't make time pass more quickly'."

Errik raised an eyebrow. "A very wise someone, indeed."

"Maybe." A sly smile played on her lips. "But I find myself questioning the wisdom of a man who gets himself stuck dangling two stories above the street."

Errik blushed. "You bring *that* up, now? You swore you'd never speak of it."

One of the conditions for his training her was that she took him up on the Hawk's Highway. His first trip had *not* gone well. She'd had to summon Jarl and Gorin to help him down.

"I'm sure the Pathfinders *never* sit around House Hawk talking and laughing about it, either."

The pink in his cheeks turned to a deep red. He'd grown more adept at the ways of the rooftops since, but the memory still embarrassed him.

"Just remember, Hawkling, I have a long memory." He gave her a mock scowl. "Insult me too often, and you might wake one morning up with a scorpion in your bed."

Ilanna laughed. "Fair enough. I'll never speak of it again."

A companionable silence descended in the hollow. Ilanna found her mind wandering back to Praamis, her son, and Ria. She'd spent hours puzzling over her feelings for the dark-skinned girl. It didn't make sense. She hadn't felt this way about anyone since Ethen.

"Your forehead's gone all wrinkled again." Errik raised an eyebrow. "What's on your mind?"

Ilanna hesitated. She trusted Errik as much as anyone, but he was Guild. She had to protect Kodyn and Ria. "I was thinking about what you said earlier," she deflected. "You say 'the way things were before'. You mean before the Guild?"

Errik went rigid, the expressionless mask descending again, but he nodded.

"Things must have been bad if the Night Guild is the lesser evil." She leaned forward. "Tell me about it."

Errik said nothing.

"Fine, I'll go first."

She told him what she remembered of her childhood: her mother, the time they spent in the garden, learning to dance, and Baby Rose. Her voice went cold as she spoke of her father, of how he'd taken the few coins she earned and wasted them on drink. Finally, of how he'd promised to take her someplace special for her eighth nameday, and how he'd delivered her to Iltair—a Bloodbear Journeyman, she'd learned—in payment of his debts.

Errik nodded. "I always wondered why you were wearing such a bright dress."

Ilanna's eyes widened. "You remember that?"

"Of course." Errik gave her an odd smile. "You were the *one* girl in the crowd. Smaller and weaker than the rest of us, but the only one who never gave up."

A warm glow suffused Ilanna's chest.

"It's why I stood up to him, you know."

"Him?"

"Sabat. Twelve."

The name curdled Ilanna's stomach. It brought back the memory of the Bloodbear apprentice's leering face. During their time in the Menagerie, under Master Velvet, Two had defied the bigger boy, even though it earned him a beating.

"I saw how he tried to shove you around, but you wouldn't cower. Sure, he hit you hard, yet you always got back up. You might have been afraid of him—hell, we *all* were. You didn't let it stop you."

It was Ilanna's turn to blush.

"Life wasn't always good for me." Errik's eyes slid away. "Living on the streets isn't easy, 'specially if you've got no older brothers to keep the bigger boys away. I learned fear from a young age. The Guild offered me a better way, a way where *I* could be the strong one. It's why I was happy to be selected for House Serpent. The things they've taught me, I'll never be weak again."

He met her eyes now. "But it wasn't the Serpents that taught me not to be afraid. You did that. Seeing you struggle on no matter what, I learned the meaning of courage." He gave her a sad smile. "I...I wanted to be like you."

Ilanna's eyes widened. How could he say that? She had been a fearful, weepy creature afraid of what would happen if she failed.

"So I stood up to him, like you did. Sure, he beat me, but I've been pounded worse by my Serpent trainers. I learned that it's better to take a beating than be a coward. You showed me that."

Ilanna blushed. She could find no words.

"Then I saw you survive on the streets, with the Foxes. Even after Sabat broke you, you got right back up. That determination I saw in you got me through some tough times."

He shrugged out of the blanket, and she caught her breath. His bare chest and arms bore dozens of scars.

"Training in House Serpent is neither easy nor kind. They put us through hell to turn us into what we are." He hesitated, drew in a breath. "I nearly put an end to it all, more than once. Just to escape the cruelty, you know?"

His eyes met hers. "But you didn't quit, and I'd be damned if I let a girl like you show me up."

Ilanna smiled, but a maelstrom of emotions seethed within her. She'd always thought of Errik as a comrade, an ally, even. She felt comfortable around him though she never thought to ask why. She'd succeeded in her Undertaking because of his help. But hearing this from him…did he see her differently?

As if he'd read her thoughts, he said, "Don't think I'm saying this expecting anything from you. Watcher knows Allon's already got a big enough bee in his britches."

She relaxed slightly.

"Besides, you're not the *only* girl in the Night Guild." He winked. "Not even the prettiest one, for that matter."

She growled and punched his arm. "Dangerous words, Serpent."

He smiled. "I'm saying this so you understand why I'm here. Not that I mind the fact you're going to make me the richest Serpent since Journeyman Mallen. But I'm in this because I know that if anyone's going to succeed, it'll be you. You never stopped in the Menagerie, and you haven't gotten any less stubborn over time. You're going to do big things, Hawkling. I know it." He turned a mischievous smile on her. "And I'll be damned if I miss out on all the fun along the way."

Chapter Thirty-Seven

Ilanna groaned in relief as Traders' Gate came into view. "About bloody damned time."

Errik grunted in agreement and clicked his tongue to urge the horses up the gentle incline. A small line of carts queued before Voramis' southernmost gate. Ilanna forced herself to take a deep breath and relax. Impatience wouldn't get them into the city any sooner.

The journey to Voramis had taken two days longer than anticipated. The draft horses had suffered the worst of the windstorm. Only Errik's foresight to bring ten days of supplies for the week-long trip had kept them from starving. Over the last few days, they'd settled into a comfortable familiarity. It brought a sense of sorrow; she'd miss the Serpent when she left the Guild behind.

"Papers." A gruff, businesslike voice snapped her from her reverie.

Errik placed his travel documents in the hands of the red-robed Heresiarch, Voramis' city guards and peacekeepers. The man muttered as he scanned the parchments, shrugged, and handed them back.

"Business in Voramis?"

Errik jerked a thumb over his shoulder. "Got a load of raw Praamian wool heading to market." He tapped the wax seal. "Sent by Lord Gileon of House Beritane."

The guard lifted the tarpaulin covering the wagon and prodded the bales. "Any weapons larger than that belt dagger of yours? Sword, perhaps?"

Errik turned his palms up. "Wouldn't know what to do even if I had one."

"Good." The Heresiarch tapped his sword hilt. "Only *we* can carry weapons in Voramis. You get caught with a sword…" He mimicked a noose. "Them's the laws."

"I'll remember that." Errik dipped his head. "If that'll be all, I've a load to deliver before the sun sets."

The guard glanced at the sky. "Better hurry. You know your way through the Merchant's Quarter?"

"Aye, though I'd appreciate a recommendation of a tavern where the missus and I can get a decent meal."

The guard nodded. "The Iron Arms, a short walk from the port. Good ale, and Mistress Gunna makes a wicked lamb stew. Wine's not much better'n piss, though."

"I'll remember that." Tipping his wide-brimmed hat to the guard, Errik flicked the reins and set the horses moving. "After a week on the road, I'd welcome a hot meal."

Ilanna didn't catch the guard's reply as the cart clattered through the gate.

Merchant's Quarter lived up to its name. Stalls and shops lined the cobblestone avenue, vendors cried their wares, and wagons laden and empty clattered past. Farther into the city, the crowds grew thicker. The smell of spices and cooking food blended with the pungent odors of the draft horses and oxen hauling carts. After a week on the open road, the low murmur of the city seemed almost overwhelming.

To the west, squat warehouses stood between the main avenue and the bustling Port of Voramis. To the east rose an enormous cliff, upon which sat the luxurious mansions of Upper Voramis. Errik turned the wagon up a side street and into a spacious wagonyard.

"We're here."

Ilanna stifled a groan as she climbed off the wagon. The wooden bench had done terrible damage to her rear. She doubted she'd ever stand straight after the last few days of travel, but at least they'd made it to Voramis—late, hopefully with enough time.

"Let me deal with this and we'll be off." Errik strode into the warehouse, papers in hand. The load of wool belonged to Lord Beritane. The Guild's pet noble had signed their travel documents. After the expenses of the trip, Lord Beritane stood to make a tidy profit off Ilanna's trip to Voramis.

While she waited, Ilanna slid open the hidden compartment and extracted the satchel that contained their gear and weapons.

Errik returned a few minutes later. "Foreman says he'll have something ready for us to haul back to Praamis by day after tomorrow." His brow furrowed. "Seems a bit tight to me."

Ilanna couldn't help but agree. She had no idea how to *find* the Secret Keepers' temple, much less come up with a way to get in and out unnoticed. She'd hoped to have a few days to learn her way around and get a feel for the city before pulling off the heist. But given the delay—and factoring another potential delay into their return home—she had no more time to work with.

"It'll have to do. Let's just hope Donneh's contact is as good as she says he is."

Errik raised an eyebrow. "And where did she say we'd find him?"

"Lower Voramis. Someplace called The Angry Goblin."

"A bookstore, eh?" Errik scratched his chin. "Makes sense, considering we're looking for an alchemist. Though all those books around some of those alchemical potions." He shook his head. "Seems a mite flammable to me."

Ilanna shrugged. "Not everyone is born gifted with the same common sense you and I have." A grin tugged at her lips. "But if Donneh says a book store, it's off to the book store we go."

Nodding, Errik adjusted his floppy merchant's hat and slung the satchel over his shoulder. "Right then, lady wife." He held out his elbow. "What say we go find you great Voramian literature to read?"

* * *

The bell over the door of The Angry Goblin gave a tinny protest as Errik pushed it open. With a glance over her shoulder, Ilanna stepped inside and shut the door behind her. She let out a long, quiet breath.

Though they'd crossed Lower Voramis in less than an hour, her back ached from the nervous tension tightening her spine. The rational part of her knew the Bloody Hand couldn't know of their presence, but she still half-expected thugs to jump out from every shadow and alleyway. She'd channeled all her self-control into keeping her hands away from the daggers hidden in the bracer she wore under the flowing homespun dress that completed her merchant's wife disguise. She'd squeezed Kodyn's hawk figurine so tight she fancied she could hear the bird screaming. Judging by the lines around Errik's eyes, the Serpent hadn't enjoyed their trek through Voramis either.

A wrinkled face appeared from behind the counter. "Welcome to The Angry Goblin, my young friends. I am Lornys, the proprietor of this humble establishment."

Lornys resembled a male version of Journeyman Donneh—his head barely reached Ilanna's chest, and his spectacles made his green eyes appear far too large for his bald head—but with three times as many wrinkles and no furry pet.

"Tell me," he said, spreading his liver-spotted hands wide, "what sort of book have you come in search of today? Perhaps one of the classics, like *The Journey of Man* by Q'orn Goldentongue. Or are you the sort of man who delights in the philosophical, such as the journals of Master Qi Pe Pe, Divine Teacher of Tian'shen?"

Ilanna stepped forward. "Do you tell fortunes?"

The little man shook his head. "Unfortunately, we do not."

Ilanna pointed a thumb at the sign outside. "Your sign there says—"

"I know what it says!" Lornys waggled a finger. "But it's nothing more than the last remnants of the former owner of this establishment. The fool

241

actually believed he could tell the future—something only the *gods* can do. If my useless nitwit of an assistant wasn't so busy burying his nose in the works of Taivoro, he'd finally get around to taking it down." He rolled his eyes and gave a despairing sigh. "Now, are you certain I can't interest you in anything to read? We've just received some excellent volumes from—"

"We were sent by Journeyman Donneh of House Scorpion."

To Lornys' credit, his eyes only widened a hair's breadth. "I don't know anyone by that name."

Ilanna grinned. "She said you'd say something like that. She also said to tell you, 'It's your turn to wear the baboon's arse, you long-nosed gibbon'."

Lornys spluttered and muttered a string of curses that made Ilanna's ears sting. "She swore she'd never say a thing!"

Ilanna desperately wanted to know the story behind it but had the good sense to say, "And she hasn't. But she knew it would convince you I'm for real."

Lornys studied her up and down. "Look real enough to me." He cocked an eyebrow, his eyes stopping just below the level of her neck.

"Oi!" Ilanna snapped her fingers. "We've come a long way to have our *fortunes told*. Now, can we get on with it or do you need to look a bit more?"

Lornys gave her a lascivious wink. "Never hurts to look." At Ilanna's growl, he threw up his hands. "Easy, girlie. You're far too young for me. Bit too short, for that matter."

Errik failed to stifle his laughter. Ilanna rewarded him with a sharp poke in the ribs, eliciting a grunt.

Lornys' face broadened in a good-natured grin. "This way, you two." His hand disappeared beneath the counter. Ilanna tensed at the *click*, her hand flashing to her dagger, her body preparing to spring from the path of the hidden danger.

"Easy, lass." The shelf behind Lornys swung to one side. The little man disappeared into a back room, and Ilanna and Errik followed.

Dried herbs and spices hung on the walls, and a gruesome collection of skulls, bones, and animal corpses littered the shelves in the back room. Glass bottles filled with liquids and potions of every conceivable hue sat in neat rows in a cabinet. A middle-aged man wearing an ink-stained robe and reading spectacles hunched over a dilapidated table.

"Graeme, you lazy sack of swill, get out to the front room."

Startled, the man jumped, the book falling to the floor. He colored all the way to his receding hairline. "Master Lornys, I-I—"

"I-I..." Lornys mocked his assistant. "If you'd spend less time studying the erotic works of Taivoro and more time reading something *useful*, perhaps you'd be able to string together a coherent sentence. Now off with you. Mind the front while I deal with this matter."

Graeme ducked his head and rushed from the room. Ilanna felt a stab of pity for the assistant.

"Worthless lout." Lornys lifted his eyes heavenward. "If I wasn't so enamored with his mother, I'd throw him out on his ear. Can't brew a gods-damned love potion! Last time he tried, he broke out in pox and lost his memory for three days!" He climbed onto the stool Graeme had fled, removed his glasses, and cleaned them with a corner of his robe. "So, tell me what I can do for Journeyman Donneh."

"She needs you to get me into the Temple of Whispers."

For a moment, the little man just stared at her, his face blank. Then he hopped down from his stool and padded over to the door. "I hope your return to Praamis is a pleasant one. Give my best to Donneh."

Ilanna crossed her arms. "So you're not going to help us?"

He raised a bushy eyebrow. "Break into the Temple of Whispers? Not even if you promised to sit on my lap! Anyone who messes with the Secret Keepers is either a fool or suicidal. Shame that a pretty thing like you is both. Now get the fiery hell out of my shop before I…" His voice trailed up as Ilanna drew an object from her pouch. "Oh, that is not even a little bit fair!"

Ilanna grinned and handed him what could only be the stuffed, bright red posterior of a very furry animal. *What I'd give to find out the story behind this.* Journeyman Donneh hadn't seemed inclined to share and she doubted Lornys would be more forthcoming.

Lornys studied the object with obvious distaste. "Sly little minx. Hasn't lost her touch, after all this time." Sighing, he squinted up at Ilanna. "Why the Secret Keepers?"

"They have something I need."

"Of course they do." Lornys snorted. "Doesn't explain why you're willing to get yourself killed—and me in the process. They've got all sorts of things that could prove valuable in the right hands. Or dangerous in the wrong ones."

Ilanna inclined her head, but said nothing. Donneh had warned her Lornys would prove hesitant to help but provided leverage. "There are two reasons you're going to help me. One, because Donneh says, 'Do this and we're square'."

Lornys nodded. "More than even. But what's the other reason?"

Ilanna gave him a syrupy smile. "Because I'm going to steal you whatever you want from the Temple of Whispers."

243

Lornys leaned against the wall, his finger tugging at the sparse hair above his lip. Ilanna met his scrutiny with calm. She could see the wheels in his head working to figure out how best to take advantage of the situation.

He cocked his head. "Anything?"

Ilanna nodded and hid a grin. She had him.

"So be it." He held out a short-fingered hand. "You've got yourself a bargain."

Chapter Thirty-Eight

Something about the tunnels beneath Voramis sent a shiver down Ilanna's spine. The symbols etched into the walls resembled those of the Guild tunnels in Praamis, but with a decidedly more sinister feel. The alchemical lamp in Graeme's hand did little to drive back the thick shadows that seemed to cling to her. Her grip on her dagger tightened as an eerie wailing echoed through the darkened passageways.

"Always hated the sound of that wind." Graeme adjusted the knob that brightened the alchemical light. "Gets louder the closer we get to the Midden. Almost like it comes from way down deep." He shuddered. "And the smell…"

Ilanna gritted her teeth. "So why make us come down here? I'd prefer the rooftops anyway." The walls and low roof pressed in on her, as if trying to squeeze the breath from her lungs. She'd give anything for open air.

The middle-aged assistant shook his head. "Not safe." He cast a nervous glance around and dropped his voice. "*The Hunter* travels the rooftops. No one in their right mind would risk running into him up there."

Ilanna raised an eyebrow. "The Hunter? I heard he was just a myth, a bogeyman."

Errik shook his head. "He's real."

Graeme looked surprised. "You've seen him?"

"No." Errik's face took on an unusual pallor. "But I saw what was left of one of his victims. The look of horror on that man's face…" The Serpent's eyes darkened.

"They say he devours the very souls of those he kills," Graeme whispered, his gaze darting up and down the tunnels.

"And you believe that?"

Errik said nothing, but Graeme shrugged. "Does it matter? Whether or not the legends are true, it's enough to know that we *don't* want to run into the Hunter. If that means going through these tunnels, so be it." The assistant's face brightened. "Besides, this is the easy way into the Temple of Whispers." He tapped his nose. "Let's just say the Hidden Circle has a few secrets even the Mistress' priests don't know about."

Ilanna gave him an encouraging smile. "If it gets us in and out, I'm all for it."

Just ahead, the tunnel split into three passages. Graeme knelt in the center of the intersection to study something etched into the stone floor. "Not much farther now." He stood and, wiping his hands on his robes, pointed down the middle passage. "We're beneath the Master's Temple."

By Ilanna's calculations, they'd trudged through the underground tunnels for close to two hours. Graeme had led them in a direct line northward, through Lower Voramis to the Temple District. Ilanna wondered how the assistant navigated the maze of passages—something to do with the odd symbols etched into the walls or floor. The Hawk's Highway had no need for signposts or direction markers. High above the city, she had clear lines of sight to any destination.

A few minutes later, Graeme stopped and ran his fingers along the wall. A *clunk* echoed in the tunnels, followed by the rumble of stone grating on stone as a section of wall slid to one side.

Greame stepped into the opening. "This way." The light of the alchemical lamp shone on a set of marble stairs, which culminated at another blank wall. "We go in dark."

He set the alchemical lamp on the floor and pulled the lever that switched it off. Darkness, thick and cloying, swallowed Ilanna. Instinctive fear coursed through her. Images of being locked in a dark room with other tyros flashed before her eyes. She clenched her fists and forced herself to take slow, quiet breaths.

The sound of Graeme's breathing and his fingers scrabbling over stone echoed in the tunnel. Beside her, Errik made not a sound. The Serpent didn't share her instinctive fear of dark, enclosed spaces.

The *clunk* of the hidden mechanism snapped the tension in Ilanna's chest. The door slid open and Graeme poked his head out of the hidden stairwell. After a moment, he stepped out and motioned for them to follow. "Stay close now," he murmured. "This place is a maze."

Ilanna found herself in a featureless, windowless corridor. Knuckle-sized stones set into the wall at intervals leaked a pitiful pale light that grew brighter as Graeme approached.

The balding assistant grinned at her surprise. "Clever things. Respond to body heat." The light dimmed as he stepped back. "They'll stay dim so long as you remain in the middle of the corridor."

Ilanna passed a hand over the stone, and the illumination increased. "Frozen hell!"

"Prepare yourselves." Graeme gave her a wry smile. "This place is filled with wonders that will set your mind awhirl."

"You've been here before?"

Graeme nodded. "Master Lornys may be a clever man, but no way he comes up with all his 'inventions' on his own. We of the Hidden Circle pride ourselves on our ingenuity, even if it means borrowing from the Secret Keepers." His teeth flashed bright in the pale light. "The old man may complain, but he keeps me around because I'm one of the few who know the ways around the Temple of Whispers."

Ilanna followed the balding assistant down a nondescript stone corridor, which led to another, and another, and still more. She saw no indications, no markings to guide them yet Graeme made each turn without hesitation. It appeared he had a memory to rival Allon's.

A soft green light shone at the end of one passage. Ilanna's jaw dropped as she stepped into an enormous, high-ceilinged room ringed with dimmed alchemical lamps. Three massive skeletons hung overhead. One belonged to a serpentine creature that had to span at least fifty or sixty paces long. Another had tusks easily as tall as Ilanna herself. The last bore a humanoid resemblance, but with finger bones as long as her legs.

"What are they?"

Graeme shrugged. "Only the Secret Keepers know for sure. Something as old as Einan itself, that's for certain."

Ilanna shuddered at the thought of encountering one of those creatures. Even Errik seemed subdued in the presence of these gargantuan monsters.

Glass tanks lined the walls of the next room. The viscous fluid within the tanks held the preserved figures of ghastly creatures in suspension. The beasts—fish, serpents, furry creatures, and insects far too large to exist— seemed to be motionless, yet not truly dead. Ilanna found herself holding her breath for fear of somehow restoring them to life.

Through the maze Graeme led them, never pausing to stop and admire the marvels within the Temple of Whispers. One room held weapons that appeared older than the stone walls from which they hung, while another chamber was filled from floor to ceiling with small glass jars that held nothing but sand and dirt of every conceivable color and texture. Ilanna had to cover her nose to keep from sneezing as they passed through a smaller room filled with a greater variety of spices than she'd ever imagined.

It seemed as if the Secret Keepers collected everything from every corner of Einan. Each item in their chambers bore a label with indecipherable symbols inked onto the parchment.

"The Secret Keepers' language." Graeme pointed to one of the symbols. "Think of it as an amalgamation of every language on Einan. So complex only the Secret Keepers can understand it. They spend a lifetime learning it, and still they discover new symbols every day."

Ilanna raised an eyebrow. "How do you know all this?"

Graeme gave her an enigmatic grin. "You planning on telling me how you became a thief of the Night Guild?" At her silence, he winked. "We all have our secrets."

The assistant's manner surprised her. He'd seemed so confused, so submissive in the book store. Yet here, in the heart of the most dangerous place in the city, he walked and talked with the confidence that could only come from familiarity. Ilanna wouldn't hesitate to wager that he knew his way around the Temple of Whispers better than anyone outside the Mistress' priesthood.

Graeme held up a hand at the next intersection. "Careful here." He spoke in a murmur so low she had to strain her ears. "We've gone through mostly storerooms, but now we're getting to the section of the temple where the priests live. We have to be *very* careful this next bit. They move without a sound, never speak a word. If one spots you, you won't know they're there until they've put a dagger in you." He winced. "Keep a sharp eye."

Daggers appeared in Errik's hands. Ilanna drew one of her own. Graeme rolled his eyes but said nothing. He thrust his chin down a side corridor and, at Ilanna's nod, led the way.

Graeme's slippers made no more noise on the stone floor than Errik's soft-soled boots. Sweat soaked the leather grip of Ilanna's dagger and trickled down her back. The cool air of the dimly lit corridors held an unnatural stillness. Ilanna found herself counting the beats of her heart just to have a sound to break the ethereal silence that gripped the temple's interior.

Ilanna froze as Graeme's hand flashed up. The balding assistant pressed his back against the wall, his cloak covering the illumination stone. Not twenty paces away, Ilanna saw the backs of a pair of brown-robed Secret Keepers. The stones brightened and dimmed in time with their measured steps. They moved at an unhurried pace, seeming to glide over the stone floor without so much as the sound of a rustling robe or a drawn breath.

When the Secret Keepers finally disappeared around a corner, Graeme relaxed and motioned for them to continue. He led them down the corridor from which the Secret Keepers had appeared. The passage led to a huge chamber. Glassware, stone grinders, alchemical burners, and hundreds of other unfamiliar objects sat on the tables and shelves lining the wall. The noxious scent of something burnt hung in the air, yet the walls, floors, and ceilings held no stains or traces of whatever experiments took place.

"Through there." Graeme pointed to a door on the far side of the chamber.

"Errik," Ilanna hissed. "Keep this way clear."

The Serpent nodded and took up position flat against the wall, black-bladed daggers in hand.

As they threaded through the maze of work tables and shelves, Ilanna clutched her cloak tight around her to stop it from brushing against anything. She'd wager a year's income that the meticulous Secret Keepers would notice even the slightest detail out of place.

Graeme stopped at the door. "You're up."

Ilanna knelt and drew a tension tool. Her heart sank as her fingers counted ten cylinders. "Give me a minute."

"Make it quick. Never know when they'll return." Worry lined Graeme's face. "I've known Secret Keepers that can work for days without pause."

Ilanna forced herself to take deep breaths as she worked. If she held her breath, the lack of oxygen would set her hands trembling. Even the slightest tremor would make working this delicate lock near-impossible.

Errik's hiss froze her in place. Instinct sent her diving under the nearest table. She pulled her dark grey cloak over her head and, heart pounding, fixed her eyes on the door. A minute later, Errik's quiet call came. "False alarm."

Ilanna crawled out from beneath the table and found Graeme doing likewise. The balding assistant grinned and shrugged. "Better safe than sorry."

Ilanna returned to her work on the lock with a grimace. In her hasty flight, she'd tripped five of the eight pins she'd managed to open. A full two minutes passed before the tenth pin finally clicked into place.

As Graeme pulled the door wide, light flared to life within the room beyond. Ilanna's eyes widened as she took in the warehouse-sized chamber. Ten rows of shelves ran the length of the room, each laden with hundreds of bottles, jars, boxes, crates, and containers of every conceivable size and shape. Every one bore the mark of the Secret Keepers.

"How in the bloody hell are we going to find anything in here?"

Graeme grinned. "Well, there's the first of your two items." He pointed to a shelf on the west wall of the chamber. "Derelana's Lance. They've kept it in the same place for the last forty years."

Ilanna rushed across the room, eyes scanning the shelves. "What does it look like?"

"Look for two small clay jars bound together with twine." Graeme's whisper echoed in the cavernous room. "The ingredients are too volatile if mixed. The Secret Keepers have to keep them separate until use."

Ilanna's eyes fell on a neat row that matched Graeme's description. With delicacy born of wariness, she lifted one from as far back on the shelf as she could reach. "What about this?"

Graeme eyed the label and nodded. "That'll be it." He grinned at her extreme caution. "Don't worry. Until you mix them, they're as likely to combust as flour and pepper."

Ilanna grimaced as she stuffed the clay jars into her pouch. "I'll still be careful, if it's all the same with you."

"Smart choice. I can see why you've survived all these years."

Ilanna stiffened. The assistant meant it in jest, but the words pierced deep. He had *no* idea what she'd done to stay alive amidst the thugs and cutthroats of the Night Guild.

"One down. One to go."

Graeme grimaced. "Now comes the real challenge: finding something that may not even exist somewhere in this maze."

Chapter Thirty-Nine

Ilanna's eyes narrowed. "What?" Her dagger appeared in her hand. "You telling me——?"

"Whoa!" Graeme jerked back, his hands flying up to protect his face.

Ilanna gritted her teeth. "You said you knew where to find the things I needed."

"No." Graeme shook his head. "What I said was that I know my way around the Temple of Whispers better than anyone outside the Secret Keepers. I got you half of what you wanted, right?" His eyes never left the dagger.

"It's a start." Ilanna lowered the blade. "But if your Master Lornys wants me to hold up my end of the bargain, you're going to help me find Kharna's Breath."

Graeme's voice turned plaintive. "But I don't know where to find it!"

Ilanna shrugged. "Means we're going to have to *look* for it."

"Among all this?" Graeme waved at the rows of shelves filling the enormous room. "Like trying to find a kernel of wheat in a granary."

"You look like a smart man." Ilanna gave him a savage grin. "Time you quit moaning and start figuring out where to find it." She sheathed the dagger. "Why not start off by telling me what we're looking for?"

Graeme sighed. "It'll be a clear liquid. Seeing as it's an acid, the Secret Keepers would store it in some type of glass vial or jar."

"Good start."

"Yes, but I don't think we'll find it in here."

Ilanna raised an eyebrow.

"Only a fool would store highly unstable liquids near volatile powders." Graeme pointed to the shelves. "This room must be kept bone dry. A single drop of liquid could cause pretty terrifying chemical reactions with some of these powders."

"So if this is the dry storage, where would we find the liquids?"

Graeme's face scrunched in contemplation. "There's another workshop a short distance further into the temple. But I've never been able to get inside. There are *always* Secret Keepers working in that one."

"So we'll find a way in." Ilanna grabbed the assistant's robes and dragged him toward the door. "We're not leaving until I've got what I came for."

"It's not that simple!" Graeme pulled free of Ilanna's grip. "We've less than an hour to get out of here."

"Why?"

Graeme pointed to the illumination stones set into the wall. "At precisely four hours after midnight, the lights will brighten to wake all the Secret Keepers to work. These halls and work rooms will fill with Secret Keepers."

"We can't leave. Not yet."

"I know. I said we've got an hour. We can keep looking a while longer. But first you need to hold up your end of the deal."

Ilanna snorted. "If you think I'm giving you what you want without—"

Graeme folded his arms. "You came to *us*. You asked for *our* help to do something anyone else would've told you was impossible." He gestured around. "Look at where you are. No one outside the Hidden Circle has ever gotten in and out of here alive. I'm the only one that can lead you through this Keeper-damned maze." He bared his teeth, his voice dropping to a growl. "So if you want me to continue helping you, you're going to deliver on your promises!"

Ilanna locked gazes with the assistant. Graeme refused to back down.

"Fine." Ilanna gave a dismissive wave. "What do I need to do?"

"This way." Graeme led her back into the work room.

Errik met Ilanna's questioning glance with a shake of his head. The Mistress' luck hadn't yet turned against them.

Peering through the door, Graeme slipped out into the hall. He moved with a greater urgency, his head swiveling as they passed through the various intersections. Anxiety radiated off him in tangible waves.

Ilanna followed the sweating apprentice, Errik a step behind. She craned her head to look through every door and down every corridor they passed. Even if the apprentice wouldn't help her, she *had* to find Kharna's Breath.

Graeme stopped at a plain wooden door. "In here."

The lock proved even more challenging to pick than the last. She pushed away the nervous anxiety in her mind, forced herself to focus on the sensations of the rake running over the lock's pins. It took her five minutes to set the final pin and snap the lock open.

Graeme darted inside before the alchemical lights blinked to life. He motioned for Errik to pull the door closed and led Ilanna through the room. Scores of locks of hair in every conceivable color—natural and unnatural—

hung on one wall. Lifelike faces peered down at her from a row of dressmakers' dummy heads sitting on a shelf. She shuddered at the empty eye sockets and lipless mouths. *What the hell is this place?*

He stopped at an iron-bound lock box. "Your end of the deal."

Pushing aside her unease, Ilanna knelt and studied the odd-shaped lock. It was larger and thicker than those used in Praamis and looked far more complex. Inserting her rake, she found her fears confirmed. In addition to six vertical pins, the cylinder bore six side pins. The locking mechanism moved too freely, like it rested on a spring. Not only did she have to set the pins, but she'd have to raise *and* rotate the lock at just the right angle to open it.

"Get comfortable." She spoke without looking up. "This is going to take a while."

"We don't have a while."

Ilanna turned now and glared at the assistant. "You know anything about picking locks?"

Graeme shook his head. "It's why you're he—"

"Then shut up, sit down, and let me work." She caught a glimpse of Errik's grin as she returned her attention to the lock.

The vertical pins proved easy enough—she'd set them above the shear line in a matter of minutes. But the side pins frustrated her. Whenever she set one, a pin on the other side popped out of place. Just when she thought she'd gotten them all in place, the tension tool slipped and the vertical pins clicked back into place.

"Damn it!" She flexed her fingers to prevent her hand from cramping. "Errik, get over here."

The Serpent crouched beside her without a word. Ilanna inserted an L-shaped tension tool into the lock. "Hold this, and twist gently when I tell you."

The shape of the tension tool allowed Errik to apply pressure on the lock without getting in her way. Ilanna made quick work of the vertical pins, though the side pins proved no less stymying. However, with a pick in each hand, she could work both sides of the lock at the same time. Finally, after what seemed an interminable effort, she had all the pins set. With a nod, she took the tension tool from Errik and gently worked the locking mechanism up, down, and to the side. She had to find just the right position to rotate the lock and—

Ilanna grinned, triumphant, as the lock gave a satisfying *click*. She threw open the lid. What looked like a simple block of clay sat on a velvet cushion.

Graeme rushed over. "Yes!" With a small knife, he carved a chunk out of the underside of the block.

"What is it?"

Graeme wrapped his prize in cloth. "Alchemically-grown flesh." He grinned at her surprise. "Looks and feels as real as your own skin, yet can be manipulated however you want. Let's just say the right client is willing to pay a fortune for such disguises." He replaced the lump of false flesh and snapped the lockbox closed. "Now, let's get out of here."

Ilanna seized his arm. "What about Kharna's Breath?"

Graeme jerked his head back the way they'd come. "The work room's back that way. But we need to hurry if we want to reach it before the Secret Keepers awake."

Ilanna rushed after the balding assistant. Graeme led them through the maze of corridors at a half-run. The sound of his breathing and the scuff of his slippers on stone seemed far too loud in the eerie stillness of the Temple of Whispers. Ilanna matched Graeme's pace with ease, but something about the urgent celerity of his movements left her uneasy.

He turned at the next intersection. "The workshop's this way. We have to—"

Ilanna's heart froze as the illumination stones flared to life. The corridors filled with a light so bright she had to cover her eyes.

"We're out of time!" Before Ilanna could stop him, Graeme turned and fled.

Ilanna cursed. A simple wooden door stood at the end of the hallway, just ten short paces away. She was so close. She couldn't go now.

"Ilanna!" Errik hissed. "If we lose him, we'll never make it out of here."

Growling, Ilanna sprinted after Graeme. She caught up to the balding assistant in the next corridor and seized his arm. "What are you doing? We have to go back for—"

"No!" Graeme pulled free. "It's too late. These halls will be crawling with Secret Keepers at any moment. We have to get out of here before they see us." Abject terror twisted the assistant's expression. "Let's go!"

Graeme didn't stop running until he reached the secret entrance. He fumbled for the hidden trigger with trembling hands and threw himself down the stairs to collapse onto the stone floor of the passageway, gasping for breath.

Ilanna lit the alchemical lamp as the wall rumbled closed behind her. She stalked down the steps, a dagger in her hand. "I'm not leaving without Kharna's Breath!"

Graeme snorted. "I'll say a prayer for your soul. If the Secret Keepers find you, they won't leave enough of you to bury. Besides, you've got Derelana's Lance. Let that suffice, and thank whatever god you worship that you got out of the Temple of Whispers alive."

Ilanna shook her head. "It's not good enough."

From what Journeyman Donneh had told her, Derelana's Lance could burn through the steel floor of Lord Auslan's vault room. But it wouldn't work for the enormous door. She couldn't risk the fire spreading to the hinges or melting the threaded shaft that retracted the locking bolts. Derelana's Lance was a sledgehammer, Kharna's Breath the chisel of a master stonemason. It would melt a hole into the steel outer door plate and eat through the locking bolt that prevented the wheel from turning. She *needed* Kharna's Breath.

"There's no way I'm going back in there." Graeme climbed to his feet and brushed off his clothing. "I've come close enough to dying for one year."

Ilanna gripped his collar. "I held up my end of the bargain, damn you!"

"And the Hidden Circle thanks you." Graeme eyed her dagger. "But there's not a snowflake's chance in the fiery hell I'm going back in there."

He flinched at Ilanna's snarl, but his eyes filled with stubborn refusal. Ilanna hurled him backward, sending him stumbling into the wall. His fear of the Secret Keepers far outweighed anything she could do to him.

"Fine. Then you're going to draw me a map to help me get where I need to go."

"A…map?" Graeme's eyes widened. "You mean you're going back in there? Alone? That's madness, not to mention certain death! Do you have any idea how many people have died wandering the bowels of the Temple of Whispers? The Secret Keepers built that maze to protect their secrets."

Ilanna shrugged. "Don't have much of a choice, do I? You learned your way around, but it seems you're too much of a coward to help me. So you're going to tell me how to get back to that work room." She bent and spoke in a low, menacing voice. "I'm *not* leaving Voramis without Kharna's Breath. And you're going to help me. Master Lornys owes Journeyman Donneh that much."

Graeme sighed. "Fine. But if you want even the slightest chance of getting out alive, you won't need a map. You'll need to memorize a code."

Ilanna pulled him to his feet. "We've a long walk ahead of us, and you'll find I'm a quick learner."

* * *

Graeme rushed through the streets of Lower Voramis without a backward glance. Ilanna gave a mocking one-fingered salute to the assistant's retreating figure.

Errik eyed her askance. "You sure about this, Ilanna?"

Ilanna shook her head. "Not even a little. Not much of a choice, though."

"You really trust the code he gave you?"

She pondered it. The assistant had no reason to lie to her, nothing to make him want her to fall into the Secret Keepers' clutches. "I'm not exactly going in without a plan." She tapped her temple. "I've got a pretty clear memory of the route we took. With his code, I should be able to get in and out."

Errik didn't look convinced.

"I know you don't like it. But it's what has to be done."

After a moment, Errik gave a stiff nod.

She pulled a satchel from the place she'd stashed it hours earlier. "Come on. Let's get into these merchant's clothes and find that inn." The idea of a warm bath, hot meal, and a few hours of sleep held a lot of appeal.

Ilanna slipped the plain woolen dress over her dark grey work clothes. The long sleeves hid her bracer from view, but she'd slit them so she could reach her daggers. A false pocket on the left side of the dress' waist gave her access to the hilt of her slim fencing sword.

Ilanna stepped out of the tunnel's hidden entrance and pulled up her hood to ward off the pre-dawn chill.

"The port's this way." Errik thrust his chin to the southeast. "We'll be at The Iron Arms just before daybreak."

Ilanna nodded and followed the Serpent. She had brought Errik because he knew his way around Voramis. She'd spent her one visit to the city holed up in the Blackfall District, enjoying the comforts of The Arms of Heaven for a few days before returning to Praamis for childbirth.

With every step deeper into Lower Voramis, Ilanna's distaste for the city grew. Piles of detritus and rubbish littered the streets. Dust covered the buildings around her, washing everything a pale color that shouted of decay and neglect. She wished she had a scarf to block out the odors of filth that hung thick in the streets.

"Ilanna." Errik's murmur came so quiet she nearly missed it. "Company."

A moment later, six figures stepped from the shadows of a nearby alleyway. Ilanna's heart sank as she caught sight of gleaming steel daggers and wooden truncheons.

The Bloody Hand had found them.

Chapter Forty

Errik caught Ilanna's hand before she drew her dagger. "Don't," he hissed in her ear. "They don't know it's us."

Ilanna paused. The Serpent's words confused her for a moment. Then things clicked into place. The Bloody Hand had no idea anyone from the Night Guild had come to Voramis. The thugs advancing on them saw them as marks to rob. With a tiny nod, she relaxed.

"Evening, folks."

Ilanna gave a high-pitched shriek and clung to Errik's arm. Errik, playing the role of a merchant, stammered. "G-Good evening." His head swiveled and his eyes went wide in a convincing pretense of fear.

The first thug to step from the shadows had a dark, bristling beard that hung down his barrel chest. "A bit late to be out on the streets just the two of yous." His crooked smile revealed teeth the same brown as the truncheon in his hand. "Lower Voramis ain't the safest of places this time of night."

Another man came to stand beside the first. This one had long, wispy, blond hair and a pathetic beard to match. "All sorts of rough types around. Lucky you, we're here to offer you a safe escort home."

A glint of silver caught Ilanna's eye. The thug's cloak pin bore a long-fingered hand tipped with razor claws. *The Bloody Hand.*

The man hefted his short dagger. "No one'll mess with you so long as we're here."

The first thug spoke up again. "All for the modest sum of two imperials." Another smile, another glimpse of rotten teeth. "S'a bargain, if you ask me."

"Of course, some people find the price a bit high." Another voice spoke from behind them, and both Ilanna and Errik shifted. "If you're not inclined to agree, perhaps we'd best leave you to whatever fate the gods have in store for you." Judging by the way he hefted the cosh, he had a definite idea of that "fate".

The other three thugs remained silent, but their weapons—a motley collection of daggers and clubs—spoke volumes.

"I-I don't have t-two imperials." Errik managed a convincing stammer, his voice quavering. "All I've got is a silver drake and a few copper bits." He produced his purse.

The first thug snatched it and peered inside. "Not even an imperial." He shook his head, tsking. "Not quite enough."

"It's not *all* you've got, merchant man." The second thug stepped closer to Ilanna, eying her with a leering grin. "I can think of another way for you to earn safe passage."

"Darling!" Ilanna gripped Errik's arm tighter. "Give the man your purse before he hurts us!"

"She speaks." The second man leaned over Ilanna's shoulder and drew in a deep breath. "Ahh! Smells prettier than she looks, this one." He ran a finger along the back of Ilanna's neck.

Ilanna's jaw clenched and she dug her nails into Errik's arm. "Please, Relin *dear*, the purse!" The thug's touch sent tendrils of disgust slithering through her gut.

"Please!" Errik pulled out another money bag from a hidden pocket. "There are three imperials in here. It's all we have."

The first thug's eyes darkened. "You was holdin' out on us, eh?" He shifted his grip on the truncheon and drove it into Errik's gut.

The Serpent doubled over, and Ilanna let out another shriek. "Relin!" Errik let out a strangled gasp and, groaning, straightened. His eyes met Ilanna's and he gave a tiny shake of his head.

"Seems like we'll have to teach you a lesson about lying to the Bloody Hand!" The thug hefted his club again.

Ilanna raised a hand. "There's no need for that."

The bearded thug stopped, his eyes widening in surprise.

"You have your money." Ilanna spoke in a tone of perfect calm, without a trace of hesitation or fear in her voice. "Let it be done."

The second thug's hand tightened on the back of her arm. "What's this? A bit of backbone, eh?" He leaned in close and whispered. "I like women with a bit of fight in them. Makes it more fun."

Ilanna's knuckles grew white. A lump of ice formed in the pit of her stomach. The man's hot, fetid breath sent a shudder down her spine. His hand slid down the front of her dress, and his breathing came faster as he pressed himself against her side.

Errik spoke up. "Don't do this, please!"

The first thug slapped Errik hard. "Your begging won't stop us from having our bit of fun."

A cold, hard smile spread Ilanna's face. "He wasn't talking to you."

Her right hand slid the dagger from her bracer and brought it across and up. Blood sprayed from the second thug's neck, and the lust in his eyes transformed to an expression of abject horror. He gurgled and clutched at his torn throat.

Beside her, steel whispered on leather, followed by the wet, sucking sound of a blade sliding through flesh. She turned in time to see the bearded thug drop to his knees. Errik pulled his dagger free of the man's chest with a vicious twist.

A gasp sounded behind Ilanna, followed by a yell of rage. She turned to meet the two thugs charging from behind. Both towered a full head over her and were far broader in the shoulder. She couldn't hope to meet them with nothing more than her slim bracer dagger. She hurled the blade at the man on the right. He batted it aside with his truncheon. Ilanna slipped beneath the cross-body strike of the other thug's club and brought her knee up into the first man's groin. He grunted and dropped like a felled oak.

"Bitch!" The second thug swung for her head. Ilanna retreated from the fast, powerful strikes. She couldn't risk drawing her slim sword—it wouldn't survive a battering from the thick truncheon. She danced out of reach and fumbled in her pouch. Her fingers found glass and she hurled the jar of dust. It shattered on the man's face, spraying shards and grit. The thug coughed and fumbled to wipe his eyes. Drawing a push dagger from her bracer, Ilanna drove her fist into the man's throat. The man gasped and slumped.

Behind her, someone gave a wet cough. Ilanna ripped her rapier free of its sheath as she whirled. The blond thug, the one who'd fondled her, lay sprawled on the muddy streets. His breath came in shallow pants, his hand pressed against the tear in his neck. Ilanna stalked toward him, heart hammering against her ribs.

"You know what I did to the last person who laid hands on me?" She pushed the tip of her sword between his knee joint. His weak scream ended in a gurgle. Pulling her blade free, she crouched beside his head and seized him by the silver cloak pin. "Your death is a kindness compared to his."

Ilanna drove her blade into his eye socket. The man twitched and jerked. A dark stain spread through his britches, and Ilanna cringed at the scent of his bowels loosening.

She glanced over at Errik. The Serpent crouched over the body of a thug, wiping his dagger on the man's jerkin. He raised an eyebrow at Ilanna as she pulled her sword free. "You hurt?"

She shook her head.

Errik nodded. "Let's get out—"

A piercing whistle shattered the night. Ilanna whirled, heart sinking. In her rage, she'd forgotten to dispatch the first thug. The metal whistle in his lips was, no doubt, meant to summon more of his comrades.

"Night Guild scum!" The man struggled to stand, hands clasped between his legs. "Your Praamian accents give you away, and only Serpents fight like that!"

Ilanna darted toward him, but Errik caught her arm. "We need to go. *Now!* There's hundreds of Bloody Hand in Lower Voramis. No way we can fight them all."

Rage burned in Ilanna's chest. Just killing the man who'd laid hands on her wasn't enough; every one of the bastards deserved to die.

"Now, Ilanna!"

The rational part of Ilanna's mind took control and set her feet moving. She found herself stumbling after Errik.

The thug's voice followed them. "We've dealt with your kind before! You won't escape us."

The sound of booted feet echoed all around them. Errik ducked into an alley to avoid a group of thugs. He pulled her down the twisting, turning back streets, heedless of the muck and refuse splattering their clothes. Ilanna allowed him to drag her along, trusting him to lose their pursuers. She had no desire to contemplate what would happen if the Bloody Hand found them.

* * *

The first rays of morning light revealed the pale cast of Errik's face. The Serpent peered out the shuttered window, worry written in tightness around his eyes.

"It's bad, Ilanna." He turned to her. "The Bloody Hand isn't exactly known for being forgiving. They're more the 'beat you to death first, ask questions never' types."

Ilanna shook her head. "What did you expect me to do?"

Errik held up his hands. "I'm not saying it's your fault. I'm just saying we're up to our eyes in shite." He paced the room. "They know we use Lord Beritane's carts, so that plan's out the window. They'll be watching the wagonyard. No way we're going to risk it now."

Ilanna leaned against the wall, eyes fixed on the silver cloak pin in her hands. It had torn free as she drove her sword into the man's eye. The blood that covered it had begun crusting.

Errik seemed not to notice. "So I'm going to have to find another way out. But I won't be able to leave the inn until the late afternoon at least. Probably better if we go after dark. We're going to have to abandon the plan to go back into the Temple of Whispers."

"No!" The words snapped Ilanna from her trance. "No. I'm not leaving Voramis without Kharna's Breath."

"Ilanna, we need to get out here before the Bloody Hand—"

"We're. Not. Leaving!"

Errik's jaw muscles worked. "Do you have *any* idea what'll happen if the Bloody Hand catches us? We'd be lucky to get out with nothing more than a painful death."

"It doesn't matter. Are we safe here?"

Errik looked around the tiny inn room and shrugged. "As safe as anywhere in the city, I guess. Goodman Haldrin's as close to a friend as Master Serpent has in Voramis. From what I've heard, he's not likely to sell us out for anything less than a King's ransom in gold. Unless the Bloody Hand pushes him too hard, we should be safe."

"Good." Ilanna nodded. "Then we'll stay here until the sun's nearly down. The entrance to the tunnels isn't far from here. I'm sure I can get in and out without trouble. Think you can handle our escape?"

Errik stroked his chin. "I think so." He drew out a hidden purse and checked its contents. "It'll take a pretty sizeable bribe, but I'm sure I can figure a way out of the city."

"Then that settles it." She stuffed the silver pin into her pouch. "We rest."

Errik stood. "I'll get us something to eat." He eyed her bloodstained clothes. "Take the time to clean up."

Ilanna glanced down. Splotches of crimson stood out on the simple woolen dress. The crusting on her cheek told her the spray of arterial blood had covered her from head to toe.

As Errik shut the door, she slipped the dress over her head and hurled it into the corner. She ignored the chill of the water in the basin as she splashed it over her face. It seemed no matter how much she scrubbed her hands and face, the blood wouldn't wash away. But, as with Sabat's blood, she didn't mind. The Bloody Hand thugs had gotten what they deserved.

Chapter Forty-One

Ilanna's stomach clenched as she climbed the steps to the hidden entrance into the Temple of Whispers. The journey through the tunnels had unnerved her. Something about the way the eerie wind broke the dead silence brought to mind an image of walking through the Long Keeper's halls. She half-expected eyeless, rotting corpses to leap out at her.

Yet the hardest part lay ahead. She had only her memory and Graeme's code to navigate the maze of the Secret Keepers' temple. One wrong turn and she'd wander forever. Delay too long and she'd have no choice but to flee Voramis empty-handed. With the Bloody Hand out for their heads, she had *one* chance to get what she'd come for.

Not for the first time tonight, she regretted leaving Allon in Praamis. His flawless memory would come in handy in the twisting maze of the Temple of Whispers. He'd have retraced their steps to the work room with ease.

The thought of entering the temple alone left her mouth dry and her palms sweaty. She'd need to be on full alert to spot the Secret Keepers before they spotted her. *If only I had another pair of eyes.* Willem would be the perfect partner. The Hawk's ability to move silently rivaled any Serpent or Hound. *It would be nice to have someone I can trust at my back for this bit.*

She pushed the thought aside. Lem had his own duties to attend to. She had to get in and out with haste. Errik would be waiting for her at the south gate two hours before dawn. *Not a bloody lot of time, but it'll have to do.*

Taking a deep breath, she drew out the little hawk figurine. She'd stolen it for Kodyn's first nameday. His fingers had worn away most of the detail, but the solid feel of the wood stilled the slight tremor in her hand. *For my little hawk.* She pressed the hidden trigger. The door slid open without a sound, and Ilanna stepped into the pale, cold tunnels in the bowels of the Temple of Whispers.

Graeme's final words of warning echoed in her mind. *"Leave no trace of your presence. The Secret Keepers will notice even the slightest thing out of place."*

Ilanna tugged on her gloves, tightened the straps on her leather vest, and checked her gear one last time before slipping down the dimly lit corridor. As she walked, she repeated the sequence of numbers Graeme had made her memorize.

3-1-2-2-1-3-3-2-1-1-2-3. "1" meant a right turn, "2" meant straight ahead, and "3" meant left.

She turned left at the first intersection. At the end of that passage, she entered the high-ceilinged room with its enormous skeletons. The familiar sight bolstered her confidence. Between her memory and Graeme's code, she could retrace their steps the previous night.

Her path led through the room lined floor to ceiling with glass tanks, and her eyes strayed to the gruesome creatures floating within. Her certainty increased with every chamber she traversed. Within half an hour, Ilanna had reached the room filled with spices. The next intersection, she knew, was the one where Graeme had warned them to be cautious. She'd reached the part of the Temple of Whispers that housed the priests.

Her heart hammered as she slipped through the shadowed corridors. The dim illumination of the alchemical light stones gave her few hiding places. She had to stay away from the walls; the stones brightened with her body heat. She couldn't move too quickly for fear of making noise, but had to get out of the temple in time to meet up with Errik.

At the far end of the next tunnel stood the room where she'd found Derelana's Lance. She grinned. *I can do this.* Just a few more intersections and she'd reach the work room Graeme had pointed out.

She crouched low and peered around the next corridor. Her heart leapt to her throat at the sight of two brown-robed figures gliding toward her. *Damn it!*

She threw herself back into the work room and ducked beneath a bench. She huddled motionless, her eyes fixed on the door. Blood rushed in her ears.

Two dark figures glided through the chamber—directly toward her. Moving slowly, she reached for the dagger in her bracer. The sandaled feet drew closer with each pounding heartbeat. Every muscle in her body coiled as she prepared to launch an attack.

The Secret Keepers moved past without pause. Ilanna forced herself to take long, slow breaths. The tension in her body drained and she sheathed her blade when the two figures disappeared into the corridors beyond.

Bloody hell, that was close! She remained still for a few minutes as the frantic racing of her heart slowed. The trembling hadn't quite left her hands when she resumed her journey to the work room where she hoped to find Kharna's Breath. She repeated Graeme's sequence of numbers in her mind. The near run-in with the Secret Keepers had shaken her; it took her over a minute to be sure she had it right.

The pressure in the back of her mind mounted. She was running out of time. But she couldn't hurry, not so close to the Secret Keepers. She'd barely escaped one encounter. Would she get lucky a second time?

She forced herself to maintain a slow pace. In her preparations to attempt the Black Spire, she'd spent hours learning to stalk in silence. Though she'd never be a Serpent or Hound, she held her own. The ability to move without a sound required her to maintain a steady, calm pace. Hurrying only increased the chance of an accidental noise: the scuffing of boots on stone, the swish of cloth, or the clank of steel.

Her pulse quickened as she made the final turn and her eyes fell on the door Graeme had indicated. She rushed down the corridor, all but abandoning silence, and reached for the latch. The door slid open with ease.

Darkness met her eyes. Relief flooded her. She slipped into the room and pressed the door shut, leaning against it as she fought to control her breathing. After a moment, she placed her hand against the nearest illumination stone. Light flared in the room, revealing a work room similar to the other. Shelves and cabinets held the same assortment of glass bottles and jars, alchemical burners, and tools of iron, steel, and silver.

A door stood at the far end of the room. *That has to be the storage!*

The illumination stone dimmed as she moved away, but she threaded through the work benches without fear. The Secret Keepers maintained absolute precision in their organization. Not a single glass bottle or jar stood out of place. The metal tools lay in neat rows, ready for use.

She drew out her lockpicks and set to work. Two minutes later, the final pin slid into place. The lock *clicked* open.

Her eyes widened. Glass bottles filled with liquid of every conceivable color lined the storage room shelves. Her heart sank. *There must be a million bottles in here!* Her chances of finding what she sought bordered on impossible.

She called to mind the conversation she'd had with Graeme on their trek through the tunnels beneath Voramis. According to the assistant, Kharna's Breath would be indistinguishable from water. On the plus side, that meant she could skip over any bottle that contained liquid with even a hint of color. On the downside, she had little over an hour to search the warehouse-sized room.

Reaching into her pocket, she drew out the scrap of parchment and quickfire globe Graeme had given her. She held the parchment up to the nearest illumination stone and studied it. The assistant had scribbled a pair of odd-looking symbols onto the scrap: one representing the name "Kharna's Breath", the other for the storage section where he expected she'd find it.

She walked down the rows, studying the signs hanging on each. Her heart leapt as she spotted the first symbol on Graeme's parchment. Turning down the aisle, she scanned the thousands of glass bottles. The vast majority bore colored liquids. She studied those few with clear-colored contents more carefully. She paired one of her quickfire globes with the one Graeme had given her. According to the balding man, Kharna's Breath would show up red under the light of that particular globe. Graeme had blathered on about light wavelengths for far too long. She'd lost interest once she knew the light would reflect off the antimony in the acid. *All that matters is that it works!*

Her stomach tightened as she reached the end of the row. She hadn't spotted the Secret Keeper symbol, and none of the bottles she held up to the light turned red. *Either Graeme's instructions are wrong, or I'm missing something here.*

Thousands of bottles filled with what looked like blood stood on the row of shelves to the left, while the row on the right held liquid metals. She returned to the first aisle. *It has to be here!*

She slowed her steps, moving only when she was certain she hadn't missed a single bottle or sign. The indecipherable symbols on the labels meant nothing to her, but they made her head swim and her eyes ache from comparing them to the symbol on her parchment. Her frustration mounted every time the clear-colored liquid in a glass bottle failed to turn red.

Had Graeme made a mistake? Had he given her the wrong symbol to look for? Would his alchemical light even work? She should have hesitated when he'd said it should *"In theory"*. Her mind raced as she tried to figure out what to do if her plan didn't—

She nearly missed the symbol. Her eyes slid over it without recognition, but something made her glance back. She'd made the same mistake a dozen times. But no! This was the symbol she sought.

It sat on the top shelf, out of reach.

Keeper's teeth! In her mind, she heaped curses on the Bloody Hand. Because of them, she'd had to enter alone. Errik would've had no trouble reaching the top shelf.

Graeme's words thrummed through her. *"The Secret Keepers will notice even the slightest thing out of place."* No way she could climb without making noise or knocking bottles out of place. Even if she moved them aside, she'd have to be certain to put them back in their precise location else risk discovery.

Damn this! She *had* to climb to reach the glass bottles on the high shelf. She'd come this far; nothing would stop her now.

She moved as quietly as she could, pushing aside bottles to make space for her feet. Clinging to the support beam, she clambered onto the middle shelf. She winced at the *clink* of glass on glass. A few bottles fell with a rattle. Icy feet dancing down her spine, she crouched and thrust a hand toward a vial rolling toward the edge. A heartbeat later, her fingers closed around the smooth glass.

Ilanna heaved a sigh and replaced the bottle in its place. She straightened slowly, careful not to shake the shelves. Her eyes fell on the familiar symbol and the clear-colored liquid filling the vials sitting on the shelf. With her free hand, she drew out the quickfire globes and held them up to the bottles. The liquid turned a bright scarlet in the dim light leaking from the little glass spheres.

Smothering a triumphant cry, Ilanna set the quickfire globes on the shelf and reached for one of the bottles. She'd just lifted one from its velvet cradle when she heard the *click* of the door lock. A moment later the light of an alchemical lantern streamed into the storage room.

She froze, bottle in mid-air. The Secret Keepers walked in utter silence, with only the lamplight to mark their presence. Ilanna's gut lurched as the light grew closer. Every shred of willpower went into keeping her movements slow and controlled as she slipped the bottle into her pouch. Panic dug icy fingers into the base of her neck. She had to separate the quickfire globes before their dim light revealed her presence, but she couldn't move more quickly and risk the Secret Keepers hearing the rustle of cloth. She did the only thing she could: she tapped the nearest alchemical globe with her chin. The ball rolled toward the back of the shelf. The light faded.

The Secret Keepers' lantern moved beyond her row, toward the one holding the vials of blood. Moving without a sound required all Ilanna's self-control. She wanted to leap down from the shelf and flee before the priests found her. But any quick or sudden movement would give her away. She had to hang on and hope the Secret Keepers left.

Time slowed to a crawl as Ilanna waited. At any moment, the priests could turn the lamp beam toward her and she'd be caught. With the patience of a stalking predator, she pocketed the quickfire globes and slithered down the shelf support without a rattle of glass. She tugged the bottles back into place, precisely as she'd found them. Heart hammering against her ribs, she slipped away from the lantern light and toward the door.

The Secret Keepers had left it unlocked. She opened it enough to squirm through, then shut it silently behind her. The darkness of the work room enveloped her, bringing a sense of comfort. She had what she'd come for. *Time to get the frozen hell out of here.*

She glided through the corridors like a wraith. Her dark grey cloak blended with the shadows of the poorly-illuminated tunnels. Her memory led her back to the first work room and toward the door beyond. *Just a little more to go, and I'll be free of—*

Light suddenly flared in the room. Ilanna skidded to a halt two strides from the door. Two Secret Keepers entered and stopped short at the sight of her. Ilanna's heart sank as one opened his mouth to shout.

Chapter Forty-Two

Ilanna moved on instinct, drawing the throwing knife from her bracer and letting fly. The blade sliced through the priest's neck, just above the collarbone. Without a sound, he clapped a hand to the gushing wound and collapsed against the wall.

The second priest's mouth remained open as if to cry out. Ilanna's gut clenched as she caught a glimpse of the stump where his tongue had been. Only a faint keening issued from the man's mouth. His right hand darted into his robes.

Pulling another knife, Ilanna closed the distance in two strides and thrust the blade at the priest's gut. Her blow went wide as the Secret Keeper slipped aside. She pursued him, slicing and stabbing with the blade. Frustration rumbled in her throat. The priest twisted, dodged, and retreated to avoid her attacks. Time and again, her blade struck only air.

Then the priest did the last thing she expected. Instead of retreating, he stepped toward her, caught her forearm, and batted her strike wide. His fists became a blur, pounding at her face and gut. She staggered beneath the force of a dozen lightning punches. The impact knocked the breath from her lungs and set her vision wobbling.

She backpedaled to avoid the next onslaught of strikes. The priest's hands and feet flew at her from all sides. He moved with the fluidity and grace of flowing water but struck with the terrible strength of a charging bull. She grunted as the priest's heel caught her beneath the ribs. Had she not twisted aside at the last moment, his kick would have hurled her into the work benches and tables behind her.

As she doubled over, his hand cracked into the back of hers. The nerves went dead and the muscles of her hand loosened. Her knife clattered to the floor.

Ilanna had a moment to think before the priest hurtled toward her, his slippered feet silent as death. She threw herself to the side, rolling around the nearest table. If she could clear enough space to reach for another dagger—

The Secret Keeper's feet flew as he leapt onto the bench and vaulted the table. His flying kick caught her in the side of the head. Darkness swam in her vision. When her eyes cleared, she found herself on the floor. Her skull ached from the blow and from striking the stone floor. Blood and dust filled her mouth.

She cried out as a strong hand closed on her hair and dragged her to her knees. The Secret Keeper's arm snaked around her neck, cutting off her breath. Her strangled shriek sounded so weak, so pathetic. She pounded at the arm, but it had no more effect than the wind buffeting a mighty mountain. Her mind shrieked in panic. Her lungs begged for air.

Her fingers fumbled for another dagger from her bracer. The Secret Keeper caught her arm between his legs. She gave another pitiful gasp as the pressure of his knee on her shoulder strained the joint. The edges of her vision wavered and grew dark.

She had one hope. Fumbling in her pouch, she drew out the thug's cloak pin. She gripped the silver ring in her fist and gave a desperate punch up and back. Something hot and warm gushed over her hand. The grip on her throat loosened, and she slipped free with a gasp of air. Her throat ached, her head rang, and her left shoulder had slipped free of its socket, but she didn't stop to catalogue her injuries. She drew another dagger from her bracer—her last—and, whirling, drove it into the underside of the Secret Keeper's chin.

The priest's mouth hung open, giving Ilanna a clear view of the mangled stump of his tongue and the length of steel piercing the roof of his mouth. His eyes widened and his hands fumbled at her cloak. She ripped the blade free, spraying blood. The Secret Keeper crumpled.

The priest's clothing muffled the sound, but Ilanna recognized the *crack* of glass. A terrible hissing rose from beneath the corpse. A moment later, a cloud of noxious smoke seeped out from beneath him. Ilanna leapt back, but the tendrils of olive green slithered toward her.

A sudden ringing of bells filled the temple, setting Ilanna's ears rattling. She whirled. The first Secret Keeper, the one she'd felled with her throwing knife, pressed a shining blue gemstone to the alchemical illumination stone set into the wall. Even as light flared in the room, the priest gave a faint gasp and slid down the wall, leaving a trail of blood behind him.

Bloody hell!

Without hesitation, Ilanna ripped her throwing knife free of the man's throat and kicked the stone from his lifeless hand. Though the light of the gemstone dulled, the clangor of the alarm bell continued.

Damn, damn, damn!

She whirled toward the door that would lead her back to the hidden exit. A thick cloud of noxious smoke hung in her path. She hesitated only a second.

She didn't have time to wait. At any moment, the Secret Keepers would find her.

Covering her mouth with her sleeve, she drew in a deep breath and charged through the cloud. For a heartbeat, the world disappeared and she lived in a world of smoke. The vapors seemed to cling to her clothes, face, and hair. A thousand tiny fires sprang to life beneath her skin.

Then she was through and sucking in a deep breath of clean air. Fingers of green wrapped around her, seeking to pull her back into their embrace. She barreled the last few steps through the room and into the corridor beyond.

The tunnel spun and wobbled. She staggered against a wall, her gut lurching. She pawed at her burning face with hands that burned and throbbed. A thin, oily film clung to every bit of exposed flesh. Every breath drove daggers into her ribs.

She stumbled onward, fighting to keep her feet. She imagined she could feel the noxious chemicals seeping into her body. The world slowed to a crawl. Though she knew her heart pounded a frantic beat, it seemed an eternity passed between each pulse.

I'm dying, she realized. Her lungs shrieked for air. Her mind grew sluggish, unresponsive to her commands. She watched from behind her own eyes as her muscles drove her onward like one of the Illusionist Clerics' clockwork creations.

Darkness passed before her eyes. She floated in a haze, numb, unseeing, helpless. With only the loud *thump, thump* of her pulse for company, she waited for the inevitable. The Long Keeper would come for her.

The face of her son flashed through her mind. She pictured him as she'd seen him last: laughing, smiling, the food stains on his face a perfect match for the mud coating his hands. The chill of sorrow seeped into her numbness.

I'll never see him again.

He would grow into a man without her. Who would teach him the skills he'd need to survive the world she'd condemned him to? Could he remain hidden from the Night Guild forever, or would all her efforts be for naught? In the end, when hunger, cold, and misery inevitably took him—as they took everyone—he would become just one more tool for the Night Guild to use.

Another face came to mind. Ria's. The dark-skinned girl's eyes sparkled with tears, but the fire of strength burned deep within.

Ria will take care of him. She will turn him into a man his father would be proud of.

His father. Not the bastard Bloodbear whose vile actions had brought Kodyn into the world. Ethen, the tyro who had brought her a crust of bread when Master Velvet punished her. The voice of encouragement when she'd been a breath from giving up. The happy Scorpion who had sat with her in her garden and made her forget her troubles. She had always wanted to tell Kodyn stories of the man who, in her heart, she considered his true father.

I'll never get that chance now. The beating of her heart stopped. She hung in the void, bathing in the peace enveloping her. In the arms of the Long Keeper, she'd never feel pain again. All her suffering, the misery she'd lived for the last fifteen years of her life, gone forever.

But she wouldn't see Kodyn again, wouldn't feel the warmth of his arms wrapped around her neck. She had no desire for peace if she couldn't have Kodyn beside her.

And Ria.

The realization struck her with enough force to jolt her out of the numbing haze. Her heart gave one desperate beat, then another.

She held Ria's face in the forefront of her mind. Ria had smiled just once, but Ilanna clung to that memory of happiness with every shred of willpower. She had to get back to Ria and Kodyn. Her son needed her. Ria needed her. And she needed the both of them. Kodyn had given her something to fight for, but Ria gave her something to hope for.

The girl had brought a spark of light into her life in a way her son never could. She'd seen the look in Ria's eyes in that perfect moment in her kitchen. There had been recognition there, the understanding of what they shared, what bonded them in a way no one else understood. The two of them had endured a lifetime of horrors and suffering. Yet through it, they had found each other. Ilanna had hoped to provide the strength and protection Ria had needed. Ria had given her a greater gift: a home. And perhaps something more, something she thought she'd never have after Ethen's death. The nascent feelings had insinuated themselves into her mind and heart during the journey to Voramis. She had no idea if they would lead anywhere, but by the Watcher, she'd live long enough to find out!

With a groan, Ilanna dragged herself up the wall. Her head felt stuffed with wool. The ringing of the alarm bell set her ears ringing, but she welcomed the sound. Her gut cavorted and twisted like an unbroken stallion. Swallowing the acid rising to her throat, she poured all her strength into taking one step. *Just one!*

One step became two, then four, then ten. Ilanna drew in a ragged, gasping breath. Her chest ached and her lungs burned, but sensation slowly returned to her limbs. She stumbled as fast as her legs could carry her.

She stopped at the first intersection. Her sluggish mind struggled to remember the sequence of numbers.

3-1-1… She cursed. *No, that's not it!*

Panic welled in her mind, but she forced herself to take deep breaths. She had to be calm to remember.

3-1-2…2-1-3-3….2-1-1-1-2. No, 1-2-3. Hope surged within her. *3-1-2-2-1-3-3-2-1-1-2-3. That's it!*

She turned left but stopped. *No, that can't be right.* But why? The fog filling her head made it so hard to think.

That…that was the way in. She had used the sequence of numbers to find her way from the hidden entrance to the work room. To get out, she had to do it all in reverse.

Damn it! She shook her head to clear the lingering effects of the smoke. After a moment of struggling, she corralled her thoughts enough to think clearly. *Do it all in reverse,* she repeated in her mind.

She turned right and rushed down the corridor as fast as her unsteady legs allowed. She had to pause at the next intersection, but understanding came more quickly. After a few turns, she reached the first of the familiar rooms. She didn't pause in her flight. The Secret Keepers had to be close on her heels.

Elation surged in her chest at the sight of the gargantuan hanging skeletons. She wanted to cry, to laugh, to shout out in joy as she sprinted through the high-vaulted room. *Just a few more minutes, and I'll be out of here!*

Graeme's code ran through her mind as she took the next two turns. Now she sprinted down the corridor where she'd find the hidden entrance. She stopped cold in horror.

I never asked how to find the secret door.

The tunnel stretched at least a hundred paces, every stone in the wall as nondescript and unremarkable as the rest.

Think, damn it!

She racked her brain. How many steps had she taken from the hidden entrance to the first intersection? Twenty? Thirty? Fifty?

Had to be at least thirty. Maybe forty. She couldn't remember!

She glanced over her shoulders. The alarm bell hadn't ceased its toll. At any moment, the Secret Keepers would come gliding around the corner and find her. She didn't have time to waste searching for a hidden door but had no other way out.

She shuffled down the corridor, counting each step. When she reached thirty, she ran her hand along the wall in search of any dip, crack, or malformation that would point to the hidden door. For ten heart-pounding steps, she found nothing.

Then her questing fingers encountered an almost imperceptible scratch in the stone. She shone the light of the quickfire globes on the spot. *Could it be?* Either her mind played tricks, or that was the faintest remnant of a symbol—one that matched the symbols etched into the walls of the tunnels beneath Voramis. She had to try.

She pressed on the symbol. Nothing happened. She pressed again. The stone remained unyielding. *No, no, no!* So close—she couldn't fail now.

She bent to examine the symbol and groaned as she saw a hair-thin crack just above it. *The trigger.*

She pressed, and the stone wall slid aside. Without hesitation, she darted inside and pressed the trigger that shut the door. It seemed to close far too slowly. Ilanna half-expected the face of a Secret Keeper to appear at the opening at any second. Yet only blank stone met her eyes until the darkness of the unlit tunnels swallowed her.

* * *

Ilanna drew in a deep breath. After the thick, stale air of the tunnels beneath the city, she welcomed the miasma of odors that filled Lower Voramis.

The whicker of a horse greeted her. Errik stiffened, his hand dropping to his knife.

"It's me," Ilanna hissed.

Moonlight played off the worry lines in Errik's face. "'Bout time. You got it?"

Ilanna nodded. "It was a close thing, though."

Errik's eyes widened. "You mean…?"

"They found me, almost caught me. I killed two of them."

"Shite!" Genuine fear twisted Errik's features, and he fumbled at the horses' reins. "Ilanna, we need to get out of here *now*. The Bloody Hand was bad enough, but the Secret Kee—"

"Easy, Errik." She laid a hand on his arm. "I left the priests a little present from our dear friends of the Bloody Hand."

Errik's jaw dropped. "The pin? You didn't!"

Ilanna grinned. "Damned right I did. Anything to keep them occupied and out of Praamis, right?"

Errik gave an incredulous shake of his head. "Watcher's beard, Ilanna. You don't do anything by half-measures. Next you're going to tell me you've convinced the King of Voramis to take care of the Bloody Hand for us."

"Sorry, not this time." She seized one of the horses' reins. "Now tell me how we're going to get out of here."

Errik shook out of his surprise and thrust a chin at the horses. "We're going to ride slowly through the city like two normal people going about their business. We'll have no problems with the Heresiarchs."

"And if the Bloody Hand finds us?"

"We're going to ride like the demons of old are at our heels!"

They mounted up and turned the horses toward Voramis' southern gate. Going through the Blackfall District—the Bloody Hand's seat of power—to reach the eastern gate would be suicidal. That meant a trek halfway across Lower Voramis. At least they had the horses to make the journey faster.

Errik slouched in his saddle, a scarf wrapped around his face—both to keep out the late night chill and to hide his features. Ilanna mimicked him, letting her head hang low, but kept her gaze darting around. She tensed at every alley they passed, every sound that echoed in the night. Sweat trickled down her back and soaked her clothing.

Once, she thought she caught a glimpse of black on the city rooftops. It had to be her imagination. The Bloody Hand kept to the streets for fear of the Hunter.

As they rounded the corner, three men stepped into the street ahead of them. One held up a hand. "'Ere now, what's yer business so late at night?"

A second man shone the light of an oil lantern on Errik's face. "Where ya off to at this hour?"

"Just getting in from the north. Malandria." Errik spoke in an accent Ilanna had never heard before. "Visiting relatives near the Port of Voramis." He scratched the stubble on his cheek. "We *are* headed in the right direction?"

"Aye." The first man nodded. "A few more turns down that way, and ye'll—"

"Oi, shut up, you idiot!" commanded the third man. He was a dark-haired man whose weasel face looked odd on such a large, hairy frame. "We're meant to ask *them* questions, not the other way around."

The first man reddened and turned back to Errik with a scowl. "Pull down yer scarf and let me get a look at ye."

"My good sir!" Errik's accent reeked of the noble class. "We are Lord and Lady Mudicas of Malandria, come all this way to visit your glorious city, and this is how we are received? Accosted and questioned like common rabble?" He gave a haughty sniff. "King Gavian shall hear of this, just you wait!"

"The King?" The weasel-faced man laughed. "That fool's about as useful as tits on a bear! He and his precious Heresiarchs ain't gonna do nothin' if we decide to pull ye down from that Watcher-damned horse and teach that pretty mouth of yers a lesson." He hefted a club. "Now show me yer face before I have to break it."

Sighing, Errik reached up and slipped his hands around the back of his head. A moment later, both hands came hurtling forward. Two throwing knives glinted in the lamplight. One buried in the eye of the lantern-bearing thug. The other took the weasel-faced man in the thigh.

Ilanna's sword whispered free of its sheath. She thrust it into the open mouth of the last thug. The razor blade severed the tip of his tongue and sliced his cheek open to the ear. With a yelp, he dropped his club and fumbled at the loose flaps of skin.

"Go!"

Errik's shout galvanized her to action. She dug her heels into the horse's flanks and the beast leaped forward. Ilanna kicked out. Her boot slammed into the bloodstained face of the thug, snapping his head back and knocking him into a nearby horse trough.

The clatter of the horses' hooves tore the silence of the night. Shouts of alarm and cries of anger echoed behind them. Lanterns appeared in the alleys all around, but the streets remained empty of thugs. She clung to the horse's back, trusting Errik to lead them out of the city.

Fear dug sharp claws into her mind. According to both Journeyman Donneh and Graeme, Kharna's Breath was a highly volatile liquid. Though she'd wrapped both the glass vial and the twin clay jars, she half-expected to hear the *crack* of glass shattering, feel the stinging burn as the acid ate through the cloth wrapping, her pouch, and her flesh.

But her fears never materialized. A dim part of her mind questioned if she'd found the right vial. Perhaps Graeme hadn't given her the right symbol, or she'd taken the wrong glass bottle. She pushed the worries aside. It was too late to go back now.

The first rays of light shone over the eastern horizon as they approached the southern gate. A handful of yawning Heresiarchs worked at the capstan that opened the enormous steel and wood gates. Before the half-asleep guards thought to stop them, Errik and Ilanna had passed under the portcullis, through the gateway, and into the plains beyond.

Chapter Forty-Three

Ilanna leapt from the saddle before the horse had stopped. "Take care of them and meet me in the warehouse as soon as you can."

Errik nodded and kicked the horses into motion.

Ilanna turned toward the Merchant's District, cursing with every step. She never thought she'd miss the wooden wagon seat, but the return journey from Voramis had been harder than expected. Her training in the Aerie hadn't included lessons on how to sit in a saddle for eight to ten hours a day. Between saddle sores, aching muscles and bones, and the biting sandstorms of the Windy Plains, their trip had taken an extra three days. That gave her just two days until the Labethian Tournament. Two days to prepare everything.

Cutting it damned close! She forced her legs to move faster. She had to reach the warehouse and test the Secret Keepers' mixtures. Either they worked and she'd found her way into the vault, or she'd have two days to find another solution.

She burst through the door of the warehouse. Light streamed in from a window set high into the wall, shining on the steel vault door standing in the middle of an empty space.

"Jarl? Darreth?" Her voice echoed off the rafters, startling a flock of nesting birds. "Allon? Ves? Joost?" Silence met her ears.

Damn it! She stalked toward the rooms Darreth and Jarl had converted into temporary sleeping quarters. The stuffed couches remained, but no blankets or pillows. *That means they're back to sleeping in the Guild.*

She muttered a harsh curse. She didn't have the time to waste crossing the city to the Guild, finding her crew, and returning here. *We need to get working on this now, or else—*

"Ilanna?"

Ilanna whirled. Joost stood at the entrance of the warehouse, a bottle of wine and a roasted chicken in his hands.

Veslund bumbled in behind his comrade. "Hey, Joost, did ye know that—?" He stopped short at sight of Ilanna. "Ye're back?"

"Damned right I am!" Ilanna strode over and snatched the wine from Joost's hands.

"Hey, that's—"

Ilanna popped the cork and emptied half the bottle's contents before the Fox could stop her. She passed the wine back to Joost and ripped a drumstick free. "Haven't eaten more than trail rations in the last week." She bit into the chicken, not caring that it burned her tongue and dripped grease down her chin. "Now, I need you to bring Jarl and Darreth here as quick as you can. And Allon, if you run into him."

Veslund nodded, but Joost looked ready to protest. Ilanna didn't give him a chance. "As soon as you deliver the message to Jarl and Darreth, go buy as much food and wine as you can get for this." She flipped a golden imperial to the lanky Fox. "And hurry! The Labethian Tournament is just two days away." She gave Joost a sweet smile and plucked the chicken and wine bottle from his hands. "I'll take those. Don't want anything slowing you down."

Joost shook his head. Veslund gave a wry smile. "Aye, I told ye she'd come back, didn't I, Joost?" He held out a hand. "That'll be a half-drake."

Scowling, Joost handed over the coin.

Ilanna tsked. "You ought to have learned by now, Joost. Never bet against me."

* * *

Ilanna leapt to her feet as the door to the warehouse swung open an hour later. A very flushed and sweaty Darreth rushed toward her. "You're back."

Ilanna grinned. "Surprised?"

Darreth gave her a crooked grin. "Yes." He drew out a cloth and dabbed at the perspiration streaming down his forehead. "Calling your chances of survival slim is somewhat like saying the Black Spire is 'a big building'. But I'll admit I'm glad to see you beat the odds."

"Damned right! Now get over here and help me test this out."

She turned to her hastily constructed work bench. A section of Odarian steel roughly as long and wide as her arms sat on a pair of saw horses she'd dragged out of a dusty corner.

Ilanna produced the glass bottle and held it up for the Scorpion to see. "Kharna's Breath."

Darreth rubbed his hands together, an eager light glinting in his eyes. "It looks so innocent, but not even *I* have any idea of its true power." A frown pulled down the corners of his mouth. "Not a whole lot of it, is there?"

278

Ilanna grimaced. The bottle was as round and tall as her little finger. In her hurry to flee the Temple of Whispers, she hadn't thought to grab a second one. "It's what we've got to work with. So we're going to have to make it work."

Darreth inclined his head.

Ilanna held out the bottle. "Want to do the honors?"

Desire, excitement, and curiosity lit up Darreth's eyes. "Are you certain?"

Ilanna returned his smile. *This* was why she'd chosen him from all the others in House Scorpion. Just as she sought to push the bounds of her abilities as a thief, Darreth sought the new and marvelous in his own way. He'd bent to the puzzles and problems she'd presented with as much determination and gusto as she had. He lived for a challenge of the mind, just as she lived for a challenge to her skill.

The bottle was made entirely of glass—the only thing that could resist the acid, Graeme had explained. The hands that had crafted it could only belong to a master craftsman. Not a drop of liquid seeped between the walls of the lid and the outer rim of the bottle. After a moment of tugging, Darreth snorted and twisted the lid to unscrew it.

Darreth met her eyes and gave her an eager grin. "Here we go!"

With a steady hand, he tilted the bottle to allow a single drop of the liquid to fall onto the plate of Odarian steel. Acting on instinct, Ilanna stepped out of range of whatever reaction the acid would have with the metal. Nothing happened. The acid sat on the piece of metal like a drop of rain on a leaf.

Horror whirled in Ilanna's thoughts. Had she gotten the wrong bottle? Had Graeme sent her to the wrong section? Her heart sank. The trip to Voramis had been nothing but an enormous waste of—

"It's working!"

Darreth's breathy whisper snapped her back to the moment. The single droplet of acid had begun to bubble. Steam rose from the plate of steel, carrying a noxious odor that stung Ilanna's nose and made her eyes water. Covering her mouth with her cloak, she retreated a few paces to watch from a safe distance.

Darreth, however, moved closer to the steel plate. He squinted at the reaction, his face close to the steel in defiance of the smoke and stench. "Marvelous!" His laughter—a high-pitched sound like a donkey braying—rang out in the warehouse.

The steel smoked for a full minute more. Finally, the last of the acid sizzled, and the final drop of melted metal dripped to the stone floor.

She met Darreth's gaze. "Watcher's teeth, it works!" Triumph rang in her voice.

"So it does." Darreth stared at the glass bottle in his hand. "I'd've said it was impossible had I not seen it with my own eyes."

Ilanna eyed the fingernail-sized hole in the steel plate. "All that from one drop! Think we've got enough to do the job?"

Darreth frowned. "It'll take me some time to figure out how much acid you'll need to melt through the door's outer plate and the steel locking mechanism. I'll need to run a few tests."

"You've got until tomorrow afternoon."

The Scorpion thought for a moment, then nodded. "I think I can make it. But I'll probably need to test Derelana's Lance as well." His eyes darted to the clay jars.

Ilanna grinned. Darreth's eager expression reminded her of the way Kodyn's face lit up whenever she visited. The memory of her son's smile sent a pang of sorrow through her. She ached to go home, even for just a few minutes, but she had too many things to do before tomorrow night and nowhere near enough time to do them. She'd have to wait until she finished the job.

Just three more days, she told herself. *Three more days until I can hold Kodyn once more.* Ria's face appeared in her mind, sending warmth rushing to her stomach. The thought of seeing the dark-skinned girl held a different sort of appeal.

"Ilanna?"

"What?" Her eyes regained focus. "What did you say?"

"Derelana's Lance? The test?" He frowned. "If you're too tired, I can do this alone."

Ilanna sighed and rubbed her eyes. The journey from Voramis had taken a toll on her mind and body. She'd nearly fallen asleep waiting for Darreth to arrive. But she didn't have time to stop. She could rest later.

"No, let's do this." Drawing her belt knife, she cut the ring of wax around the clay jars' wooden lids.

Darreth set the lids carefully aside and peered into the jars. He held out a hand for her knife. "May I?" Using the tip, he scooped a small portion of red powder from the first jar and grey powder from the second. "You might want to stand back for this one, too."

Ilanna took a step back as he mixed the two powders together. "D'you have any idea what you're doing?"

"As much as anyone." Darreth didn't look up from his work. "Journeyman Donneh and I did some research of our own while you were away. I don't have all the facts, but I think this mixture should work." He met her eyes now and gave her a wry grin. "Good thing you've got enough for me to experiment with."

Ilanna quirked an eyebrow. The clay jars were smaller than her fists and only three-quarters filled with powder.

Darreth finished his mixing and produced an alchemical firestriker. "Now, if I've got this right, I simply apply a bit of fire and—" He jerked back as the powder flared to life. Ilanna's eyes widened at the pillar of fire reaching toward the roof. Waves of heat rolled over Ilanna, and she had to take another step back to avoid the sparks spat forth by the blaze.

"Welcome back, 'Lanna."

"Jarl!" Ilanna spun, a smile broadening her face at the sight of the huge Hawk. "Damn, but you've been busy."

"You've no idea." Jarl wiped a muddy hand across his even muddier forehead. "We got a problem."

Ilanna rolled her eyes. "Of course we do." The moment things started to look up, something always went wrong.

Jarl peered over her head. "Busy?"

"Darreth's playing with his new toys. Tell me what's wrong."

The Hawk's face tightened. "It's bad. We've hit granite. Can't get through."

Elation and frustration mingled in Ilanna's gut. On the one hand, the presence of granite meant Jarl and his team had located the foundation of the vault. According to Master Lorilain, the steel room would require a foundation of slate or granite to support the weight. The map of Lord Auslan's mansion had proven accurate. Yet granite was among the hardest stones on Einan. Stonemasons specialized in techniques for cutting and shaping the stone, so difficult it was to manage. No way a team of Grubbers could get through a solid layer of it.

"Keeper's teeth." She raised a questioning eyebrow. "Have you made any progress at all?"

Jarl shook his head. "Been working all day and barely scratched it."

Ilanna's shoulders slumped. She muttered a string of curses. She'd done the impossible to pull off the job: broken into the hidden vaults of the Reckoners, dodged the Bloody Hand, even stolen from the Secret Keepers. Yet she had no clever solution to deal with a solid slab of stone. The look in Jarl's eyes spoke volumes. He knew they wouldn't reach it in time.

"Uh, Ilanna, I think you'd better take a look at this."

"Not now, Darreth. I need to think."

"Ilanna." The Scorpion's voice grew more insistent. "You'll *really* want to see this."

With a huff, Ilanna whirled and stalked over to the Scorpion. "What?"

Darreth stabbed a finger at the floor. "Look!"

Ilanna crouched. Shock washed away all trace of frustration and anger. "Sweet Mistress!"

The alchemical mixture lived up to its name. It was as if the hand of Derelana herself had driven a fiery lance into the floor. Cracks spread from a hole scorched deep into the stone. Ilanna lifted a shattered piece of masonry, only to have it crumble in her fingers.

Her gaze darted to Darreth. "What did you do?"

Darreth held up his hands. "I spilled a bit of the powder. When a spark hit it, it blazed up and just *melted* the stone. But it was an accident, I swear!"

Ilanna leapt toward him and threw her arms around his slim shoulders. "Darreth, you beautiful, beautiful man!" She spun him around despite his protests. "You've found our way into the vault."

Chapter Forty-Four

Ilanna groaned and sagged onto her bed. As if her travels hadn't exhausted her enough, she'd spent the last six hours trudging through the sewer system learning the escape route Jarl crafted for her. Now, she wanted nothing more than a few hours of undisturbed sleep.

A tap sounded at her door. "Ilanna?"

Ilanna stifled a curse. *Not Allon, not now.* She'd dreaded seeing the Hound again. The thought of his hands on her body made her insides curl, but she didn't have the patience or energy to do what had to be done. Besides, she still needed his help to finish the Lord Auslan job.

She forced a smile and opened the door. "Come to welcome me home, Allon?"

"I wish." The Hound's face showed no hint of mirth. "Uncle Jagar…er, Master Hawk sent me to fetch you."

Ilanna raised an eyebrow. "You?"

Allon nodded. "I was on my way here already. But after what he told me…" He swallowed and his eyes slid away.

Ilanna's brow furrowed. "What is it? What's wrong?"

"Master Gold has called a meeting of the Night Guild." He met her gaze now. Heavy bags, the mark of many sleepless nights, hung under his worry-filled eyes. "It's bad."

* * *

Confusion echoed in the mutters and whispers filling the Menagerie. Ilanna stood near the front of the crowd, just behind Master Hawk. If her House Master's posture—slumped, head hanging down, fingers pinching the bridge of his nose—gave any indication, things were worse than Allon had let on.

She glanced around. Allon stood with his fellow Hounds. Errik, still covered in the dust of the road, nodded to her as he slid through the crowd of Serpents. Darreth's fingers twitched, and even the imperturbable Jarl shifted. He, like she, sensed the aura of dread that hung thick in the high-vaulted room.

Time and again, his eyes darted to the tarp-covered object in the heart of the Menagerie.

Ilanna's curiosity burned. *What the twisted hell is under that thing?*

Master Gold climbed to his feet and turned to the assembled Journeymen. "My brothers, sisters, friends, and fellows of the Night Guild. Welcome."

It seemed the Guild Master had aged a decade in the weeks Ilanna had been gone. He wore clothing far simpler and duller than his usual bright ensemble, and his face appeared haggard in the alchemical lamplight. Even the ornamental hawk pinned to his breast had lost its luster. The sight only added to dismay creeping into Ilanna's mind.

"I call you here with a heavy heart." Master Gold clasped his hands behind his back. "As you know, our professions carry certain…dangers. Far too many of our number have met untimely ends at the hands of Duke Phonnis and his Praamian Guard. We all understand the hazards of what we do and we do it nonetheless, for better or worse."

"Though many would name us criminals, we have a certain honor, a code that dictates what we do. The laws of the Night Guild keep us in check and maintain the status quo in Praamis. For hundreds of years, it has been thus."

He swallowed and shook his head. "The Night Guild has weathered many threats in the past, yet I fear this new threat is one we will not survive if we do not band together. The ones who threaten us are without honor, and there is nothing they will not do to achieve their ultimate ends."

At his signal, two Grubbers tugged on the tarp. Hundreds of gasps and curses rose from the assembled Night Guild. Ilanna's jaw dropped in horror.

"Behold!" Master Gold swept a hand at the grisly object. "A message from the Bloody Hand."

A gruesome assortment of lacerated flesh and shattered bones hung on a wooden cross. Threads of crimson dripped from what had once been the body of a human—man or woman, she couldn't tell, so mangled was the corpse. Blood stained the long, dark hair sprouting from the crushed skull. Strips of charred skin mingled with deep, jagged gashes.

Acid surged in Ilanna's throat. The sound of retching echoed in the Menagerie, accompanied by the reek of vomit.

"Look well, brethren of the Night Guild." Master Gold's voice held an edge of fury. "The men of Voramis came to us with smiles and offers of fraternity, but see how they act when they are denied. Is *this* what you would wish upon our fair city?"

Thick, oppressive silence settled over the Night Guild. All eyes remained fixed on the butchered remains hanging in the middle of the room. For long minutes, nothing moved in the Menagerie. Master Gold returned to his seat. He had no need to speak; the Bloody Hand's message was eloquence enough.

Then, without a word, the Journeymen of the Night Guild filed from the room.

"Ilanna." Sorrow tinged Master Hawk's voice. "Come."

Ilanna fell in step behind her House Master. Dread added to the roiling in her stomach. Every part of her wanted to deny it, but she knew the truth: this was *her* fault.

* * *

Entar said nothing as Master Hawk and Ilanna strode into Master Gold's office. The Guild Master motioned for her to close the door. Heart thundering, she obeyed and took the seat opposite Master Gold. Her stomach clenched as the two men stared at her.

Master Hawk spoke first. "It's Prynn."

It felt as if someone had driven a mailed fist into her gut. Ilanna struggled to breath but no air filled her lungs. Her mind reeled, fighting to make sense of Master Hawk's words.

After what seemed an eternity, she found her voice. "Are…you sure?"

Master Hawk nodded. "So was the hand they sent a few weeks back."

The words drove a dagger home in Ilanna's chest. An immense weight settled on her shoulders. Prynn had disappeared almost two years earlier. Had he been in the Bloody Hand's clutches all this time? She shuddered to think of the horrors inflicted upon him. The misshapen lump of flesh and bone hanging on the cross had ceased being human long before its final breath.

Memories of Prynn flashed through her mind: the sandy-haired youth with freckled skin and shy smile welcoming her to House Hawk; the confident apprentice with quick fingers teaching her to wield a knife; the young man who'd laughed at her exhilaration running across the rooftops of Praamis; the Journeyman of House Hawk greeting her as an equal.

Pain filled Master Hawk's eyes as well. The loss of Werrin, Denber, and now Prynn weighed on him. He cared for his Journeymen. Perhaps too much. It was why he hadn't selected another apprentice after choosing her, she believed. Ilanna reached out and squeezed his hand. He looked up, surprised, and returned the grip. For a long moment, they sat in silence, sharing each other's sorrow.

With a nod, Ilanna released the House Master's hand and rubbed her face. No tears welled in her eyes, but the heat of rage—and regret—burned in her head.

Damn the Bloody Hand. She'd fled Voramis the night after killing the thugs. *The bastards move fast!*

She turned to Master Gold. "Are you sure it's them?"

For an answer, the Guild Master drew a bundle from his desk, unwrapped the bloodstained cloth, and placed what looked like a strip of untanned leather on the table. Ilanna's sides heaved as she recognized the brand of the Bloody Hand—a hand with too-long fingers tipped with bestial claws—burned into a section of flesh. "By the Watcher!"

Master Gold quickly covered it. "I thought the body would be message enough."

Ilanna swallowed a surge of acid. "It's my fault this happened."

Master Gold raised an eyebrow. "Why do you say that?"

Ilanna drew in a breath. "The Bloody Hand tried to rob us—Errik and me—while we were in Voramis. We gave them our purses, but they wanted…more." She balled her fists. "We killed them."

"What?" The Guild Master jerked upright.

"We killed them. All but one." She sat back, shoulders drooping. "He called for help before we could deal with him. We had no choice but to flee."

Master Gold muttered a curse. Master Hawk's face grew grim.

"It gets worse. That man recognized us as Night Guild."

Two pairs of eyebrows shot skyward. "Impossible!" Master Gold blurted. "You went in disguise, didn't you?"

"Of course!" Ilanna snorted. "But he recognized Errik's fighting style and our Praamian accents."

Master Gold's stream of curses went on for a full minute. Even Master Hawk's jaw dropped at the color of the Guild Master's profanities.

Ilanna made no excuses. She had gone to Voramis knowing of the danger she'd face—the Bloody Hand as well as the Secret Keepers. She and Errik had done everything they could to avoid trouble. But she wouldn't apologize for defending herself. Sabat had taught her what happened to weak women.

When Master Gold's invectives trailed off, Master Hawk spoke. "This is worse than we thought." His fingers toyed with the scar running across his face. "It's not just a message to the Night Guild—it's revenge for the deaths of their men. It's personal now."

"But doesn't this work in our favor?" Ilanna leaned forward. "Once the other Houses see what the Bloody Hand is capable of, they'll *have* to realize that their only choice is to turn them down. No way any sane person would want that in Praamis."

"I wish it were that simple." Master Gold shook his head. "If I know Bernard, he'll use this to his advantage. He'll insist that the only way to prevent something like this from happening again is to give in to their demands."

"Surely no one is *that* foolish!"

"Fearful men do foolish things, Ilanna," Master Hawk said in a quiet voice.

"Indeed." Master Gold fingered the falcon brooch. "A few of the wiser, older Journeymen will understand which way the wind is blowing and join our side. But I fear we will lose many allies in the days to come. Too many will fall prey to their terror of the Bloody Hand. Master Hound's camp will grow stronger—perhaps strong enough for him to call for a new Master Gold."

Ilanna stood. "I won't let that happen."

Master Gold raised an eyebrow. "Lord Auslan's job?"

"Tomorrow night."

The Guild Master steepled his fingers and leaned back in his chair. "Then may the Mistress' luck go with you, and the Watcher guide your path."

With a bow, Ilanna turned and strode from the room.

* * *

Ilanna's heart sank as she rounded the corner and caught sight of Allon leaning on her door.

"Please not now, Allon."

The Hound stood. "Come on, Ilanna. I haven't seen you in almost a month. At least let me come in and—"

"Allon!" Ilanna cut off his words with a slash of her hand. "I haven't slept well since leaving Praamis. I'm tired, sore, and hungry. That body on the cross was once a friend of mine. And, to top it all off, I've got just three hours before I have to meet Darreth in the warehouse. Not. Now!"

Allon backed off, his face tightening. "I understand." His voice held a strain.

"Thank you." Ilanna squeezed his hand, resisting the urge to strike him. How dare he pester her now? "Let me rest and recover. Let me mourn my friend. When this is all over, I'll make time. I promise." *Time to let you know I'm done with you,* she left unsaid.

"Fair enough." He gave her a halfhearted grin. "I'll see you at the warehouse tomorrow."

"Rest well." Hurt filled Allon's eyes, but Ilanna couldn't bring herself to care. Too many thoughts whirled in her mind to make room for his feelings.

She pressed the door shut and relief flooded her at the sound of the lock clicking. The problems of the world waited outside, but in here she was safe. She could hide from everything, even if only for a short while.

She climbed into bed fully clothed and pulled the blankets over her head. The darkness brought a sense of peace. She drew in deep breaths, fighting the lump in her throat. Prynn's face—a happy, smiling face, not the mangled lump of flesh hanging on a cross—refused to leave her. She squeezed her eyes shut, desperate to be free of the memory of her friend, and crushed Kodyn's stuffed hawk to her chest, as if the reminder of her son would somehow banish the gruesome image.

It didn't. Exhaustion soon won the battle for her mind and body, and she slipped into a deep sleep.

Chapter Forty-Five

"Gentlemen, today is the day." Ilanna smiled at the eager faces around the table. "Everything we've done over the last weeks has led to this."

Veslund's face scrunched. "Uh, ain't the Labethian Tournament *tomorrow*?" He shot a questioning glance at Joost.

Ilanna rolled her eyes. "It is. But our work starts now." She turned to Jarl. "All is in readiness?"

The Hawk shook his head with a frustrated grunt.

"Will it be ready by tomorrow?"

After a moment's hesitation, Jarl gave a slow nod.

Ilanna stifled her irritation. *Off to an auspicious start.*

"The whole plan hinges on you, Jarl."

"I know." He shrugged.

She let it rest. He knew what he had to do; he'd come through. He *had* to!

She shifted her attention to the Foxes. "Ves, Joost, I want the two of you stationed outside Lord Auslan's mansion. The Labethian Tournament runs all day long, so we should have plenty of time to get in and out. But if Lord Auslan decides to return early…" She drew out two hunting horns. "I'm counting on you to give us warning."

Joost gave the horn a skeptical glance, but Veslund took his with gusto. He clapped it to his lips and would've blown had Jarl not closed a massive hand around his forearm. The Fox, a big man in his own right, stared up at the hulking Hawk and decided his health would be better served by *not* making noise.

"Errik, I want you to come in with me."

The Serpent nodded, but Allon bristled. "Now wait a moment! If anyone should go in, it's me." He counted on his fingers. "First, I've spent close to a month studying that map you gave Jarl. *If* the map is accurate—"

"It is." Ilanna glared. "It comes from a very reliable source."

Allon inclined his head. "So be it. My point is that I've spent hours poring over that map. Has Errik even seen it?"

The Serpent shrugged.

"Second," Allon drove on, "I'm the one who's going to get you into the mansion."

"You mean you—?"

"Found us a way in. Damned straight! It's near the walls, but far enough that we won't be spotted."

Elation surged in Ilanna's chest. *One more piece in place.*

"I'm the one who found it, so I should be the one going in with you. Besides, if we have to flee for any reason, who else knows their way around those sewers better than me?"

Ilanna couldn't argue that. His flawless memory made him the perfect guide through the labyrinthine tunnels.

"I'm just as suited to the task as Errik is!" He darted a glance at the Serpent. "And I'm not exhausted from weeks of travel."

"And what if we find ourselves facing off against the Duke's Arbitors? I've no doubt of your skill, but in a fight…"

Allon's face tightened. "I'm no Serpent, but I can hold my own."

Ilanna looked to Errik. The Serpent's brow furrowed. "I've watched him train with Ullard. He's easily the best among the Hounds." He gave Allon a nod. "Almost as good as a Serpent."

The tension in Allon's face relaxed and color rose to his cheeks. Errik counted among the best of House Serpent; coming from him, those words were dangerously close to high praise.

Ilanna persisted. "But good enough to handle the Duke's Arbitors?" She held up a hand to forestall Allon's protest. "I'm not doubting your skill, Allon. But you can't fault me for wanting to keep you from ending up dead."

Let him think I'm doing this because I care, not because I'd rather have Errik at my side in case of trouble.

"But most of the Arbitors will be gone with Lord Auslan. And your plan is to *avoid* a fight."

Ilanna shook her head. "Always be prepared for the worst, Allon." She turned to Errik. "What do you think?"

Errik spoke after a moment of thought. "Take him. Your plan is solid. There should be few enough Arbitors that you'll be able to handle them between you."

"Between us?" Allon's eyes widened a fraction.

The shock in the Hound's expression made Ilanna's lip curl. She'd kept her training with Errik as secret as anything could be in the Night Guild. But it seemed as if Allon dismissed even the possibility that she could match his skill with a sword.

To hide her irritation, she turned to Darreth. "How go the experiments?"

The Scorpion's head rested on his chest, a quiet snore rising from his mouth.

"Darreth!"

"Wha—?" His head snapped up, and he blinked at the people around the table.

Ilanna chuckled. "The experiments?"

"Experiments?" Darreth seemed lost, struggling to break free of slumber. "The...experiments. Ah, yes." He rubbed his face with one hand and produced a few sheets of parchment with the other.

Ilanna glanced at the notes. The top of the page was covered with Darreth's neat handwriting, but by the bottom, the precision had degenerated into barely legible scribbles.

"Maybe you just show me, eh?"

Darreth yawned in response.

"But first, Errik, seeing as Allon's coming with me, you'll be taking his job."

Errik raised an eyebrow.

"You're going to the Labethian Tournament."

A rare smile broadened Errik's face.

Allon's jaw dropped. For a moment, Ilanna thought he'd protest. The disappointment in his eyes seeped into his expression. The vicennial games were the most anticipated event in Praamis. Only a handful of the Night Guild had ever attended. And now Allon would miss out on his chance to see the spectacle because he'd insisted on going with her. She'd intended the assignment as a way to placate him for taking Errik to Voramis over him.

She reached into the satchel she'd brought and drew out the clothes Allon had worn into the Coin Counters' Temple. "You'll be going as Lord Beritane's private clerk." She glanced at the Hound. "Alten Trestleworth, I think you called him?"

Allon nodded, his face glum.

Ilanna handed the clothes to Errik. "I need you to keep an eye on Lord Auslan. He should stay all day long, but if he leaves early, you send word to Veslund and Joost. See if Garrill wants the job. If not, Elmar or Alun."

"Got it."

She met the eyes of Jarl, Veslund, Joost, and Errik. "You all know your jobs. Do them well, and by this time next week, you'll be the wealthiest Journeymen in your Houses. I'm counting on you."

Ilanna watched the four go. *No turning back now.*

She turned to Allon. "You say you've been studying the map, right?"

"Yes." Allon's skill at hiding his displeasure left much to be desired.

"Good. I've found a way through the mansion grounds." The note she'd found in the dead drop this morning had solved the problem for her. "Between the two of us, we ought to be able to find the fastest route to Lord Auslan's vault."

She drew out the crude map and spread it on the table. "The mansion's built like a fortress, but even the mightiest castle has weaknesses." She tapped the servants' entrance. "This is where we get in."

Allon's forehead wrinkled as he bent over the map. "A good plan, but there's a problem. Beyond getting through rooms packed with household servants." He tapped the enormous room at the center of the mansion. "Everything goes through here. If we're trying to get to Lord Auslan's bedroom, we'll have to go up the main staircase and through the corridors. If there's even *one* Arbitor on guard, we're doomed."

Ilanna nodded. "I know. The mansion was designed well. For all the wide open spaces and ornate ballrooms, there're two choke points: the staircase and the entrance to Lord Auslan's private quarters. But I've got a plan for that."

Allon raised an eyebrow, but she shook her head. "I'll tell you once we're inside." She wouldn't risk even the slightest detail of her plan getting out.

The Hound frowned. "Are we good?"

"What's that mean?"

"Last night, I understand. But planning to take Errik into the mansion, and now this? Do you not trust me?"

"It's not about trust, Allon." Ilanna's jaw clenched. "There are far too many things that can go wrong with this plan. Too many moving parts that have to fall into place at *just* the right time. One word to the wrong person and everything goes to shite."

"Yes, but—"

"Allon." She narrowed her eyes. "This isn't about you and me. It's about doing what's best for the job. Can you trust *me*?"

Allon hesitated. "As you say."

"Good." Ilanna's fingers uncurled. "Now's the time to make any last-minute preparations. We go in tonight."

"Tonight?"

Ilanna nodded. "It's the only way we'll be in position when Lord Auslan leaves."

Confusion twisted Allon's face.

"There's too much open space around the mansion. If we try to cross that in daylight, the sentries on the walls or at the front gate will see us for sure. So we *need* the cover of darkness if we're going to get close enough to slip in when Lord Auslan leaves tomorrow."

Allon gave a slow nod.

"I've had weeks to think about this, Allon." Ilanna gave him a wry grin. "Not much to do while riding a horse or wagon but think." *And hope to the frozen hell you don't fall off.* She winced. She had learned the hard way that she was *not* a horse person. "Return here just before sunset. I'll be ready to go."

With a nod, the Hound slipped from the warehouse.

One thing left. She'd have just enough time to return to House Hawk for her supplies, a fresh change of clothes, and a quick meal. Though it sent an ache of longing through her, she knew she couldn't spare even a few minutes to spend with Kodyn and Ria. She'd need a mind free of distraction tonight.

"Darreth, time to show me your magic!"

The Scorpion scowled. "Magic?" He sniffed.

Ilanna rolled her eyes. "Oh, you know what I mean. Show me your *science,* then."

Mollified, Darreth produced a fresh sheet of parchment. "I've calculated the thickness of the vault door and how fast the acid eats through the steel. This is what you need to know."

Ilanna studied the neat handwriting. "You're sure?"

"I've tested it as many times as I could without risking running out. Even then, it'll be close."

Ilanna took the glass bottle of Kharna's Breath, now more than half empty. The clay jars of Derelana's Lance, however, retained most of their contents.

Darreth produced two slim glass tubes. "These are called pipettes. We use them to transport small, measured quantities of liquid between containers. Very handy for making potions."

He pointed to the shorter of the two. "See that marking?" Someone had etched a line into the glass a fingernail's breadth from the tip. "Stick the pipette into the bottle of acid and place your finger over the other end." He demonstrated. "This will create suction and trap the acid in the tube. When you place the full tip against the door and remove your finger, you break the suction and release the acid. Want to give it a test?"

Ilanna nodded. "Good idea."

Darreth led her over to Master Lorilain's vault door. "Take this." He handed her a length of the thin black rope used by House Hawk. He pointed to the knot tied at one end. "See this? You're going to use it to measure the precise location to apply to acid."

Ilanna eyed the hole burned into the steel door. "Show me."

Bending, he placed one end of the rope on the floor and used his foot to hold it in place. When he pulled the string tight, it reached the height of his chest—directly over the hole. "Mark your place using this." He drew a line using a wax stick. "Now, see this second knot partway down the rope? This marks the distance from the wall. Hold this."

He left the knotted end in her hand and pulled the rope tight to the door frame. Once again, the knot hovered over the hole. "Make sure the two marks meet, and you've got the spot where you'll apply the acid."

Darreth shone the light of a beamer lamp into the hole. "Can you see the locking bar?"

Ilanna squinted. "I think so."

"Good. You can also use the longer of the two pipettes to feel for it." He pointed to the second glass tube in Ilanna's hand. "Notice how the mark is closer to the tip? You won't need as much acid to melt through the locking bar."

Ilanna eyed the half-empty bottle. "You're sure this is enough?"

Darreth nodded. "According to my calculations, you should have a bit to spare. Just in case." He scratched his pointed nose. "But you'll only be using it for the door. For the vault, you've got Derelana's Lance." His eyes brightened as he led her back to the work bench she'd constructed the day before.

A ring of blackened stones surrounded the saw horses. The piece of Odarian steel bore narrow holes from Kharna's Breath, but Derelana's Lance had melted entire sections of metal.

Darreth drew a tiny metal spoon from his pocket. "Use this to measure out one scoop of red powder and one grey." He poured the powders into a metal cup. "Make sure they're fully combined, else it won't work."

He dumped the mixture onto the only undamaged section of steel. "All you need is a firestriker and—"

Ilanna leapt back as a gout of fire shot up from the metal. The fire burned for a full minute, leaving a gaping, blackened hole.

"Do the same with the stone beneath and you'll have your way out." He passed her the spoon. "Fair warning: the heat'll be bad in that metal room. It's best if you wait outside while the powder's burning."

Ilanna nodded. "Thank you."

Darreth met her gaze. "No, Ilanna, thank *you*."

The earnestness in the Scorpion's face surprised her. "You've more than earned your share of the—"

"It's not about the money." Darreth shook his head. "You trusted me enough to include me. This," he waved around, "all of this. To be out of House Scorpion and challenge the minds of the Secret Keepers, Reckoners, and Duke Phonnis himself. That is the gift you've given me without even realizing it."

He reached out a hesitant hand and gave her shoulder an awkward squeeze. Shocked, Ilanna could only stare. Darreth loathed physical contact as much as she. Coming from him, it was a gesture beyond words.

"You're welcome," she said when she finally found her voice. "I couldn't have done it without you. Go, rest. Your part is done. The rest is up to us."

"I will. But first, a word of caution. You saw the inner workings of the vault door, right?"

"I did."

"Master Lorilain scoffed at the design—'heavier than clever', I believe she said. But she was wrong."

Ilanna raised an eyebrow.

"The locking bar is directly above the threaded shaft. One drop of acid slips out of the pipette—"

"—and I melt the shaft." She cursed. *It can never be easy, can it?*

"And whatever you do, do NOT let the acid come in contact with any moisture. Your hands have to be absolutely dry. Sweat, saliva, rain, any moisture…"

"Bad news." Journeyman Donneh had said the same thing.

"With that, I take my leave."

Ilanna's eyes followed Darreth from the warehouse. His gratitude had caught her off guard. She'd included him because she needed his cleverness, never thinking of how he would feel about it.

Her revenge against Duke Phonnis mattered less and less with each passing day. Her hand stole into her pouch, fingers tracing the faded outline of the wooden hawk figurine. Her share of the take would buy her freedom from the Night Guild. For that, no risk was too great.

Chapter Forty-Six

"What in the Keeper's name is that?"

Ilanna chuckled at Allon's surprise and confusion. "Our way in." She threw one of the odd-looking garments to Allon. "Put it on."

Allon eyed the garment with confusion.

"Here, you put it on like this." Ilanna pulled the loose cloak over his shoulders and cinched it at his waist. "These," she said, pointing to the strips of cloth, burlap, and twine hanging off the cloak, "make it harder for any watching eyes to spot you. The colors—green, black, and brown—blend in with the shadows of bushes and trees. Hell, it'll even move with the wind, making it look like regular grass and leaves."

"And are these real bits of grass, leaves, and bark sewn on?"

Ilanna nodded. "If we move slowly, we'll be all but impossible to see in the dark. Even during the day, provided none of the Arbitors get too close or stare directly at us."

Allon shook his head. "How the hell did you come up with this…*thing?*"

Ilanna shrugged. "We all have our uses." He didn't need to know Errik had suggested it. If yesterday was any indication, Allon believed the Serpent to be his rival for her affections. *Better keep the two apart.* Though, after this job, it didn't matter what either thought. She would be gone forever.

She slipped into her own camouflaged cloak. "Good thing is that they'll keep us warm, too. Trust me, by sunrise, you're going to be bloody glad for this thing."

Allon gave her a skeptical expression but said nothing.

"Let's do this."

With a nod, Allon climbed the metal ladder rungs set into the stone wall. The shaft ascended for three or four man-heights. Allon lifted the steel grate at the top with a grunt. Ilanna winced at the gentle *clang* of metal on stone. He disappeared into the darkness above, then appeared a moment later and beckoned for her to follow.

Ilanna emerged into the oppressive blackness of an enclosed space. "Where are we?" She spoke in a voice pitched low. The harsh sibilance of whispers carried farther than a quiet murmur.

"Gardener's shed." Allon allowed a faint glow of his quickfire globes to illuminate the shovels, rakes, wheelbarrows, sacks of potting soil, and other items stacked on metal shelves lining the walls. He grinned. "Made it easier to cut through the grate lock—no chance of being overheard."

Ilanna crossed to the door in two strides. She opened it and peered out. The wall around Lord Auslan's property cast a shadow to her right, but the walkways and gardens spread out to her left. Shutting the door, she turned back to Allon. "Well done."

He grinned and inclined his head.

"Now put that away before someone sees the light."

Allon stuffed the quickfire globes into his pouch, plunging the shed into darkness.

"Keep a sharp eye for the Arbitors. Any sign of light and we stop dead in our tracks. The cloaks should hide us if we're still."

"We've been over this a half-dozen times, Ilanna," Allon grumped.

"I know." She did it more for *her* sake than his. His flawless memory had captured the entire plan the first time she'd laid it out, but she needed to be sure they both had every detail correct. Everything hinged on their timing.

"You've got a clear idea of the route we're taking? Only one way through that blackthorn hedge."

"I've got it." Frustration echoed in Allon's voice.

"Then let's do this. Stay close."

She opened the door and peered through the crack. The sound of boots echoed from atop the wall, accompanied by the *clank* of a swinging lantern. She waited until the light and noise faded before slithering into the darkness of Lord Auslan's gardens.

A narrow path led away from the garden shed, running along the inner circumference of the wall. She ignored it and slid into the foliage surrounding the wooden building. The path led to the guards stationed at the front entrance.

Whoever designed the layout of Lord Auslan's garden had chosen security over beauty. Perhaps flowers and fruit trees had flourished during the days of Lady Auslan, but no longer. Ornamental vines grew in abundance throughout the property. More than once, Ilanna and Allon had to pause in their advance to find a way around or through dense stands of thorn-covered bushes.

A glimmer of light in the darkness sent Ilanna to her belly in the shadows of a spindly beech tree. She tugged the hood of the cloak over her face and peered through the two holes cut for her eyes. Her heart thundered as the beam of an alchemical lantern drew closer. *Now to see if these damned things do what they're supposed to.*

The clanking of the Arbitors' silver breastplates grew louder with every heartbeat. The light slithered toward her, dancing over the contours of the bushes, trees, and earth. Blood rushed in her ears as the edge of the beam slid along her side. She clenched her fists to stifle the nervous twitching in her fingers. At any moment, the Arbitors would spot her and cry out.

But the light moved past. With agonizing slowness, the sound of their marching boots faded. Ilanna waited a full minute before climbing to her feet.

She glanced around. The thin sliver of moon provided little illumination. *Where in the fiery hell is Allon?*

Her heart leapt as the ground beside her shifted. Her hand flashed to her bracer dagger, but she caught herself before she drew and ran Allon through.

At least we know the cloaks work.

Not waiting for the Hound to rise, Ilanna moved on. They had to hurry to reach the next hiding spot before the patrol passed in four minutes. Every sound—the crackle of a dry leaf under her boots, the rustle of the bushes she passed, even the *thump, thump* of her heart—seemed to echo in the night's ethereal stillness. The wall around Lord Auslan's property blocked the sounds from the city beyond.

She hurled herself into the shadows of a mighty oak tree as the next patrol passed. She'd resigned herself to making slow progress, but it seemed they'd barely traveled a few dozen paces from the garden shed. She glanced up and winced.

When the Arbitors' lantern light disappeared, she waited for Allon to join her. "We need to pick up the pace. Midnight's not far off."

"I'm right behind you."

Ilanna moved with as much haste as she dared. The swish of cloth and the patter of her boots on the hard-packed earth sounded far too loud, but she had no choice. They had to reach the blackthorn hedge within a quarter-hour.

With her eyes fixed on the blackness ahead, she nearly missed the next patrol. Allon dragged her to the ground beneath a thick stand of creeping vines. The scent of damp earth filled her nostrils. She forced herself to take slow, steady breaths, yet her heart pounded not from fear, but excitement. Even after years, the thrill of the job hadn't dimmed.

She moved before the patrol had disappeared into the night, gliding through the shadows of bushes and trees, searching the darkness for any sign of the hedge.

There! The faint moonlight shone on the wall of thorns that rose thrice her height. With a quick glance around, she sprinted the remaining distance to slide into the shadows of the hedge.

Allon followed a few steps behind. "Now what?"

"This way." Ilanna led him along the hedge. Every few steps, she tested the resistance of the thorns. The barrier held firm.

The Lady's Bells tolled out midnight. *Damn it!* Her stomach tightened with each failed attempt. *Come on!* The note in her dead drop had contained clear instructions on where to go. *It has to be around here.* She had to get through the barrier now.

Relief flooded her as her hand passed through the blackthorn hedge. *Right where he said it would be!*

She pulled the cloak tight around her shoulders and slithered into the narrow gap. Spiny branches blocked out even the faint moonlight, forcing her to feel her way through. Thorns sliced her flesh and tugged at the fabric of her clothing, but she gritted her teeth and moved on. After what seemed an eternity trapped in the oppressive embrace of the briar, she emerged into the darkness beyond.

Blood trickled from her palms, both cheeks, and her forehead. Her dark grey clothes bore holes and tears. But she was through.

Allon stumbled from the hedge a full minute later. He'd suffered far worse than she but made no complaint as he crouched beside her.

A broad swath of lawn stretched between them and the mansion. They had at least a hundred paces to cross, but lanterns arranged at intervals flooded the open space with light. If they moved out of the shadows of the hedge, the guards stationed on the balcony would spot them. Worse, this close to the mansion, the Arbitors passed at two-minute intervals.

She slid to a seat. "We wait."

"For what?"

She gave no reply. He wouldn't understand. Had she not seen it with her own eyes the previous night, she'd have believed it insane.

Time seemed to drag as she waited. Her eyes scanned the lawn for anything out of the ordinary. *Any minute now.*

Fingers of mist seeped from the ground like ghosts rising from the grave. The fog grew thicker with every heartbeat, until she could no longer see the mansion. The light of the lanterns lost the battle against the obscuring gloom.

Ilanna climbed to her feet. "Let's go."

Mouth agape, Allon took a moment to move. Ilanna hid a grin. She'd had the same dumbfounded reaction watching from atop the neighboring mansion last night.

"Stay close."

Ilanna dove into the bank of fog. Pinpricks of light indicated the presence of the lamps. She clung to the shadows between the pitiful patches of illumination and broke into a run. The mist would cover any sound she made. She had only to watch out for any guards and—

She stopped cold, her hand snatching Allon's arm and gripping hard.

A muffled voice came from the shadows that moved through the fog a few paces away. "Every damned night this week!"

"I said I'm sorry, Bort," another voice responded. "It's just a few more nights."

"*Just a few more nights.*" Bort mimicked his companion. "We're stuck out in this miserable cold, wet fog because you're too stupid to know not to piss off Captain Shem after a few drinks."

Ilanna didn't catch the next muttered words. She retreated at an agonizingly slow pace. Even the slightest motion could attract the guards' attention.

The shadows of the Arbitors melted into the mist, but the pinprick of their lantern light and the muffled sound of their voices marked their presence. Giving the guards a wide berth, she pulled Allon toward the mansion—she hoped. The bank of fog made it impossible to see more than a few steps in any direction.

Twice more they had to stop to avoid Arbitors. A knot formed between Ilanna's shoulders, sending twinges down her spine. Anxiety set her hands trembling. The fog would dissipate within a few minutes. They *had* to cross the lawn before that happened.

From one moment to the next, the shrouds of mist gave way to cool, clear darkness. A pair of Arbitors stood less than twenty paces away, backs turned to her. The circle of torchlight ended less than a hand's breadth from her feet.

With speed born of fear, Ilanna sprinted the remaining distance to the shrubbery that grew along the side of the building. She slid on damp grass, caught her footing, and stumbled into the shadows of a flowering bush. Heart thundering, she lay face-down on the wet earth and sucked in as much air as she dared.

Allon slithered to the ground beside her a few moments later. He gave her a wild-eyed smile, and she felt laughter bubbling up from her chest. *They'd done it!*

She pressed her lips to his ear. "We rest here. I'll watch first. Your turn in four hours."

He shook his head. "No way I'll sleep now."

Ilanna grinned. The excited tremor in her hands had traveled down her body to her legs. He spoke the truth—there was no way she could sleep either.

* * *

Not for the first time in the last few hours, Ilanna cursed herself for coming up with this plan. The cloaks kept out much of the night's chill, but the moisture from the earth had soaked her clothes. Not even the rising sun had driven back the cold. They lay in the shade of Lord Auslan's mansion, and morning dew covered the leaves of the bushes and trees around her. She couldn't remember being this miserable in her life.

Judging by Allon's expression, he wasn't enjoying the experience either. More than once, he lost the fight against the chattering of his teeth. They couldn't rub their hands for warmth—couldn't move a muscle. They could only lie on the cold, damp earth and pray for Lord Auslan to depart.

Ilanna nearly wept when the Lady's Bells tolled out the sixth hour of the morning. The Labethian Tournament would begin at the seventh hour. After what seemed an eternity in the frozen hell, the clatter of hooves and carriage wheels signaled the nobleman's departure.

Most of Lord Auslan's Arbitors had ridden with him. According to her inside man, no more than fifteen would remain to guard the front gate and watch the grounds, wall, and riverside. After the next patrol passed, they'd have plenty of time to reach the servants' entrance and slip into the house.

Time moved as sluggishly as the chilled blood in Ilanna's veins. The sound of Allon's chattering teeth sent shivers down her spine. She abandoned caution long enough to bring her icy hands to her face and blow on them.

She froze as the sound of tromping boots approached their hiding place. She'd chosen the thickest patch of bushes she could find, but the gardener kept the foliage near the mansion trimmed and neat. The overhanging trees provided far less cover than she'd like. If even one guard looked too closely, he would see the odd outlines of their cloaks.

Every muscle in her body went taut. *The moment of truth.*

The Arbitors didn't pause in their patrol. They moved at the steady clip of men determined to complete their duty and get out of the cold. Ilanna relaxed and let out a long, silent breath.

She nudged Allon's shoulder and rose to her feet, wincing at the stiffness in her muscles. But, oh, how wonderful it felt to move again! She poked her head from the concealment of the bushes. The mansion hid them from view of the guards on the wall.

With a quick glance around, she ran the thirty or so paces to the servants' entrance as fast as her body permitted. She tapped thrice, waited two seconds, then tapped thrice again.

A moment later, the door swung open, revealing the worry-lined face of Willem. "They know you're coming!"

Chapter Forty-Seven

"What?"

Willem pulled the door shut behind him. "It's the only thing that makes sense."

"Lem, what are you talking about? How do they know we're coming?"

Willem stabbed a finger toward the mansion. "Since yesterday, there's been a flurry of activity. I overheard one of the Arbitors saying they were preparing for something—what, I don't know, but it can't be a coincidence that they bring in a score more Arbitors the night before your attempt."

Horror twisted like a knife in Ilanna's gut.

"What's *he* doing here?" Surprise edged Allon's voice.

In her shock, Ilanna had forgotten about the Hound. "He's been working for Lord Auslan since the beginning." Yet another use for Lord Beritane. The nobleman's recommendation had secured Willem the position. "He's the one who drew the plans of the mansion's interior."

"And if you saw those plans, you'd know we have to find another way in." Willem shook his head. "They've got fifteen Arbitors stationed in the ballroom to guard the stairways, and another ten outside Lord Auslan's bedroom. There's no way I can sneak you in unseen. Our only hope's to go in through the skylight in the bedroom."

Ilanna cursed. "We don't have any gear!"

Willem pointed toward the wall. "There's rope in the garden shed. I'd have gone for it the moment I found out, but they've had us confined to our quarters all night. I just managed to sneak out a few minutes ago, once the Arbitors all headed to their positions." He shook his head. "I'm sorry. I wanted to warn you."

"Nothing you could've done." Ilanna's mind whirled. *What in the Keeper's name do we do now?* "Say we get our hands on the rope, what then?"

Willem winced. "I can try to sneak it up to the roof and drop it down here."

"Ilanna," Allon interjected, "if they know we're coming, they'll be prepared for that. We have to reconsider."

Ilanna ignored him. "But what about the guards? Won't they see you?"

Willem took a deep breath. "I'll have to risk it."

"Think about this, Ilanna." Allon stepped between her and Willem. "We're going to be sneaking into a mansion guarded by Arbitors who know we're coming. That's suicidal at best! We have to try this another time."

"No!" Ilanna bared her teeth in a snarl. "We're going Lem's way. It's the only way we do what needs to be—"

The servants' entrance door opened and a pudgy, balding man appeared. His eyes widened at the sight of Ilanna and Allon in their odd outfits. He whirled on Willem with a glare. "You bastard! I knew your story was a lie. Gutter scum like you can never pass for a true—"

Willem laid open his throat with a casual slash of a hidden blade. The fat servant gasped, choked, and gave a wet cough, clapping hands to his neck. Willem drove his dagger into the base of the man's skull and shoved. The rotund corpse toppled into the bushes beside the entrance.

Willem spat. "Rot in hell!" He met Ilanna and Allon's gazes with a disgusted grunt. "Fat cunt had me beaten. 'Insubordination', he said when I told the majordomo what he was doing to the scullery maids."

"Willem!" Ilanna gaped at the Hawk's bloodstained servants' clothing. "You can't go back in looking like that."

At that moment, a patrol of Arbitors appeared around the corner of the mansion. Willem muttered an oath. "Run!" He took off without waiting.

Ilanna and Allon followed a heartbeat later. They sprinted across the open ground, heedless of the shouts and cries echoing from the patrol. Thankfully, the guards on the wall responded slowly. By the time they turned to see what was going on, Lem had dived into the gap in the blackthorn hedge. Ilanna pushed through without pause, not caring that the brier tore at her hands, face, and clothing. Allon's grunting sounded behind her.

She nearly ran into Lem, crouched in the shadow of a thick oak tree. "What now?"

He turned to her, eyes wide. "I don't know! I didn't expect—"

"The garden shed!" Allon hissed. "We flee through the sewers."

Ilanna stabbed a finger at the guards on the wall. "They'll see us."

Lem shook his head. "Follow me. If we go through the thickest part of the garden, we can get into the shadow of the wall without being spotted. From there, we sneak into the shed."

"Go!"

Ilanna followed Willem as he slithered through thick groves of trees, dense stands of bushes, and walls of flowering vines. The cries of alarm grew fainter as they moved away from the blackthorn hedge. *If we're lucky, the guards won't discover the opening Lem carved for us.*

The Hawk had been serving in Lord Auslan's mansion for weeks. He'd explored every nook and cranny of the enormous complex for the purpose of drawing the map he'd delivered. If anyone could find another way in, it would be him.

Willem dashed across a clearing in the foliage and pressed himself against the base of the wall. After a moment, Ilanna and Allon followed suit.

"Shed's this way." Clinging to the wall, he half-crouched, half-ran toward the wooden building. Only when they were safe within the garden shed did he pause to catch his breath and give her a huge grin. "Good to see you, Ilanna."

Ilanna threw her arms around her friend. "And you, too, Lem. How'd servant life treat you?"

He grimaced. "Never again! Too much hard work."

Ilanna chuckled.

Allon shook his head. "We'll have time for that later. We need to go now!"

Ilanna nodded and lowered herself into the mouth of the access shaft. She clambered down the metal rungs, switching on the alchemical beamer lamp they'd left the previous night. Willem leapt to the tunnel floor and moved aside. A quiet *clang* echoed above, and Allon appeared a few seconds later.

"Think they'll check the shed?"

Willem shrugged. "Can't say. They're thorough, that's for sure."

Ilanna cursed. "They'll be on high alert for anything. We can't go in this way again." She drove her fist into the stone wall of the tunnel.

"What if we go in the back way?"

Ilanna whirled on Lem. "What? Through the Field of Mercy?"

Willem nodded.

"Are you insane?" Allon's shout echoed in the tunnels. He winced and spoke in a quieter voice. "No one gets across the Field of Mercy."

"He's right, Lem." Ilanna gave a dismissive wave. "You know how dangerous it is." She gave him a meaningful look.

Willem's face darkened. "I know what you're *not* saying, Ilanna. Yes, the Field of Mercy took Werrin, but surely we can find another way."

"Let's say we somehow manage to get across." Ilanna rubbed her eyes. "We're still going to have to deal with whatever guards are on patrol."

"I don't think so." Willem screwed his face into a frown of concentration. "As you say, no one's ever crossed the Field of Mercy. The Arbitors are too smart to waste manpower patrolling a part of the mansion that doesn't need guarding. Besides, whatever Arbitors aren't waiting for us inside will be busy scouring the estate to find us. They know they've got all the exits covered, so they'll think we're just hiding out. They've a lot of ground to cover."

Ilanna's mind raced. She'd spent hours studying the patrol patterns of the Arbitors inside the estate. Lem's idea held merit.

"Two problems." She held up two fingers. "The Praamian Guards in Watcher's Square and—"

"Watcher's Square will be empty."

Ilanna raised an eyebrow.

Lem grinned. "You told me to listen to the Arbitors. One of them was boasting that the Duke was bringing him in to guard the Labethian Tournament. Evidently there weren't enough Praamian Guards to handle the crowds. Said the Duke had to pull the guards off Watcher's Square."

"That still doesn't solve the problem of how to cross the Field of Mercy."

Allon sighed. "I think I might have a solution."

* * *

"You going to tell me how you knew about the mist?" Ilanna whispered to Lem as they waited in Watcher's Square for Allon to return.

Lem grinned. "Shows up every night. Leah told me—"

"*Leah,* eh?" Ilanna dug an elbow into his ribs. "Is that a sparkle I see in your eyes, Lem?"

Lem blushed. "She says it's something to do with a creek running beneath the ground. Like the water's absorbed through the ground, up into the air." He shrugged. "Truth be told, I couldn't make sense of it. But I figured it'd come in handy."

Ilanna clapped him on the back. "More than you know." She glanced at the sun. "Noon and Allon's still not back." She cursed.

"If he don't hurry, we're never going to make it in and out in time."

"We?" Ilanna's eyes narrowed. "No one but me's going in."

"Get stuffed, Ilanna. This is as much for me as it is for you. Not a chance you're doing this without me." He gave her a wry grin. "Besides, you'll need me in case you run into a few Arbitors." The dagger—still stained with the fat servant's blood—appeared in his hand.

Ilanna eyed him, then glanced at the expanse of quicksand stretching between Watcher's Square and the wall of Lord Auslan's mansion.

"Ilanna." Willem's tone grew grim. "For Werrin."

Ilanna sighed. "Damn you, Willem!"

He grinned. "That's the spirit. Now, if that Hound of yours will hurry up and—" He trailed off as Allon appeared down the street. "Bloody hell, that's a big crossbow."

Indeed, the crossbow in Allon's arms had a longer stock and broader arms than those used by the Praamian Guard. Judging by the perspiration streaming down his forehead, it had to weigh more as well.

"That our way in?" Ilanna asked as he drew near.

Panting, he nodded and set down his burden. "Saw this…on a job I did…at a loggers' camp." He leaned on his knees to catch his breath. "Lumberjacks use it to…climb into high treetops."

"But how's that getting us across?" Lem pointed to the Field of Mercy. "Not a lot of trees around."

Allon rolled his eyes. "With this." He produced a bolt with a metal tip as long as his hand. "This is an expanding head. The impact will drive the bolt into the wall and push out four hooks built into the tip. Give you a good grip." His brow furrowed. "Problem is, it's built for wood, not stone."

Ilanna squinted across the expanse of quicksand. "How's your aim?"

"Not the best, but I've seen worse. Have a target in mind?"

"Well, I'm thinking you aim for that section of crumbling wall. The bolt should drive through the stone enough that it will give you a solid anchor."

Allon studied the section she pointed out. "Could work." He bent and set a windlass to the cord. His arms pumped furiously, pulling the bow taut.

Just then, a man in the dull, orange-trimmed clothing of House Fox rushed up the street. "Hound here said you needed some Foxes."

Ilanna nodded. "Diken, right? I need to send word to Veslund and Joost out front of Lord Auslan's mansion, and to whichever Fox is working with Errik of House Serpent."

"That'll be Elmar."

"Good. I need you to tell them to delay Lord Auslan's return by whatever means possible." The Labethian Tournament would be finished before the Lady's Bells struck the third hour after noon. "Lord Auslan can't be home any earlier than the evening bell. Use as many Foxes and Grubbers as you need. I'll cover the day rates."

Diken nodded. "So be it." He sped off down the street.

Ilanna returned her attention to Allon. The Hound had finished winding the cord. He threaded a length of black rope through a loop at one end of the bolt and tied a knot before settling the bolt into the groove. He grunted as he lifted it to his shoulder. "Damned thing's heavy! Only way to get the power needed to drive the bolt into stone."

He nestled his cheek in the stock of the crossbow and squinted down the sight. Taking a deep breath, he squeezed the trigger. The bolt arced across the distance, the rope trailing behind. A *thunk* echoed as the metal tip sank into the crumbling stone.

"Yes!" Allon blew out his cheeks. Willem clapped him on the back.

"Good! Lem, secure this."

"Where?"

Ilanna cast around. Her eyes fell on the gallows before the Royal Palace. "There."

With a hesitant nod, Willem raced to tie off the rope. Ilanna shrugged out of her grey cloak and her leather vest.

Allon's eyes widened. "What are you doing?"

"I don't want to risk breaking the rope."

Allon shook his head. "That won't be a problem." He twanged the line. "This'll hold my weight with ease."

"You think you're coming?" Ilanna shook her head. "It'll just be Lem and me."

Allon thrust out his jaw. "You need me. Unless you have another way to get onto the roof." He produced a bolt with a grappling hook tip and another length of rope. "Besides, the chances of running into Arbitors just got a *lot* higher."

Ilanna scowled. She hadn't wanted to take Lem into the mansion, and now Allon refused to let her go alone?

"Fine!"

"Good." Allon tied the length of rope to the crossbow's stirrup and looped the other end around his waist. "I'll go first. That way, I can drag this thing across and get our way onto the roof set up as you're crossing."

Ilanna eyed the forty paces of quicksand between them and Lord Auslan's wall. "Think you can make it? It's harder than it looks."

Allon snorted. "You're not the only one that can do this sort of thing."

With a shrug, Ilanna stepped aside. She glanced at the nearby Royal Palace. "Go quickly. The more time we spend doing this, the greater the chance someone will catch us."

Chapter Forty-Eight

Allon's crossing seemed to take far longer than it should. The Hound grunted and struggled for every hand's breadth of progress. Ilanna cursed herself for allowing him to accompany her. She would need him in case she ran into Arbitors, but did he have to take so damned long?

The rope swayed, bounced, and sagged beneath his weight. More than once, he nearly slipped. Ilanna caught her breath as he hung by his hands, his feet hovering just above a grassy patch growing on the quicksand. She couldn't help admiring his determination. He moved with the relentlessness of the canines for which his House was named.

As the Hound went, Ilanna sliced a length of rope and tied a metal carabiner to each end. She clipped one to her belt; the other would clip onto the rope.

Finally, he reached the wall of Lord Auslan's mansion. He clambered up onto the stones and heaved himself over the top. Sighing, Ilanna turned to Lem.

He shook his head. "You're next. I'll follow once you're across." He grinned. "Someone's got to watch your back."

Ilanna checked her gear one last time. The slim fencing sword sat in its hidden sheath on her hip, and her bracer held a trio of throwing daggers, a push blade, and her favorite knife. The twin jars of Derelana's Lance rode on her hip, secured by a leather thong Allon had produced from his gear. The glass bottle of Kharna's Breath rested in a pouch, alongside the pipettes, measuring spoon, and firestriker Darreth had given her, and a few of the tools she'd need to get into the mansion.

She gripped his arm. "See you on the other side." She leapt up, wrapped her ankles around the rope, and clipped her impromptu harness in place. Hand over hand, she pulled herself across the Field of Mercy. Though the rope swayed and bounced, she never slowed.

The jars of Derelana's Lance swung beneath her. She winced at every clatter, cursing herself for not bringing her pouch. One wrong move and the clay would crack, spilling the precious powder onto the Field of Mercy. She forced herself to a slower pace to reduce the risk of jostling the jars.

Her hands and arms soon ached from the effort. Sweat streamed down her forehead and dripped into her eyes. She swung down, resting her weight on her harness, and wiped away the stinging perspiration. Taking a deep breath, she flexed and relaxed her hands to loosen the muscles. After a moment's rest, she continued the crossing.

A quiet *thump* sounded beneath her. Ilanna craned her neck to see. There, on the unbroken surface of the Field of Mercy, lay the twin jars containing Derelana's Lance, the frayed end of the leather strap still attached.

Damn it!

Releasing her hold on the rope, she reached for the clay jars. They lay far out of her grasp. She unclipped her harness, wrapped her legs around the rope, and tried again.

She cursed. *Still too far!*

She hung from her hands, scrabbling for the jars with her feet. Her toes came so close, but she couldn't quite reach.

Willem's voice drifted across the Field of Mercy. "Get across, Ilanna. I'll pick them up on my way."

Ilanna hesitated.

"Go!"

With a frustrated sigh, Ilanna clipped her harness onto the rope and hauled herself the last fifteen paces to the wall.

Allon peered up at her and held a finger to his lips. Ilanna nodded. Even in the unguarded section of Lord Auslan's property, they couldn't risk alerting the Arbitors to their presence.

She motioned for Lem to come. The Hawk clipped his makeshift harness to the rope and began the crossing. His hands and feet fairly flew—years of training in the Aerie and on the rooftops of Praamis served him well. The knot in Ilanna's stomach loosened as he approached the clay jars. With his longer arms, he'd have no trouble reaching them.

Four men in olive-colored uniforms appeared at the far end of Watcher's Square. Ilanna's heart stopped, her mouth suddenly dry. *Praamian Guards.*

She couldn't cry out for fear of alerting the Arbitors within the estate, but she had to warn Willem. "Hurry, Lem!" she hissed.

Willem gave her a confident grin and winked. Unclipping his harness from the rope, he hung from his hands and scooped up the jars between his feet.

Ilanna's gaze went to the Praamian Guards in the same moment they saw Willem hanging over the Field of Mercy. Everything slowed to a crawl as the guards rushed toward them. Ilanna wanted to shout for Willem to hurry, but her mouth refused to form words. Unaware of the danger, Lem shoved the jars into a pouch and, clipping his harness onto the rope, resumed the crossing.

Every heartbeat brought the Praamian Guards one step closer. They rushed toward the post to which Willem had secured the rope, swords drawn. Ilanna's mind whirled. What could she do? She couldn't hurl a dagger across the Field of Mercy. Allon's crossbow would work, but he had just one bolt. She glanced down, desperate for anything.

Her eyes fell on the leather strap curled around her right wrist. *The sling!* She hadn't used it in years—not since Ethen's death—but it was the only thing she could do for Willem.

She tugged the sling free and fumbled in her pouch for ammunition. She cursed. She'd stopped carrying the lead balls years ago. She had only her quickfire globes.

Without hesitation, she fitted a glass globe into the sling cradle and set the sling whirling above her head. Her position straddling the wall made it nearly impossible to work up momentum. It didn't matter. She had to try to help Willem.

The quickfire globe hurtled toward the Praamian Guards, crashing to the ground a dozen paces ahead of them. Glass shattered and the alchemical liquid within sprayed the stones in a colorful arc. The guards paused, their eyes darting around. One caught sight of her and shouted at his companions. Even as they continued their stampede toward the rope, Ilanna dropped the other globe into the cradle and hurled it.

The moment it left her sling, she knew her aim was true. Her projectile slammed into one guard's chest. He staggered and dropped, clutching at his gut.

Ilanna's elation died a moment later. She had no more ammunition, nothing to slow down the other three guards. Lem still hung a dozen paces from the wall.

Desperate, she seized a chunk of crumbled masonry, fit it into her sling, and hurled it at the guards. It covered less than half the distance to the scaffold before clattering to the ground. Again and again she tried, but the shards of sandstone lacked the weight of her lead bullets or the quickfire globes. None of her projectiles came close to her target. She could only watch, helpless, as the Praamian Guards rushed onto the scaffolding and raised their swords.

The rope *twanged* and fell slack. Willem's confident grin turned to a look of horror as he fell. His feet broke the surface of the Field of Mercy. Mud surged up to his waist, clinging at him, tugging at his legs and torso. He clung to the rope, his face twisted in a mask of fear.

Ilanna reached for her end of the rope in a desperate attempt to pull him free. She heaved and strained, but she fought a force far beyond her strength. Every breath dragged him deeper into the clutching embrace of quicksand.

He fumbled for the jars on his belt, tried to pull them free. His arm came up and forward, sending the clay jars hurtling toward her. The jars fell far short of the wall, landing on the unbroken surface of the Field of Mercy with a clatter of clay.

She never took her eyes from her friend. He held her gaze as the quagmire enveloped first his chest, his neck, his head. With a wink and that Willem grin she knew so well, he was gone. The Field of Mercy gave a horrendous belch and fell still.

"Ilanna!" Allon's voice seemed to come from a thousand leagues away.

Ilanna couldn't look away from the spot where Willem had disappeared. She had to stay. If she didn't, he would be gone forever. She didn't want him to be gone.

"Ilanna!" Allon leaned on the wall beside her. Horror stained his face. "We have to go."

She turned now, her body and mind numb. "Lem…" she croaked.

"There'll be time for grief *after* we're done." Allon lifted her from the wall and set her down on the rocky ground. "The Praamian Guards saw you. We've got less than half an hour before they get a message to the Arbitors at the front gate. We need to move *now*."

She turned back to the wall. Her mind refused to believe Lem was gone. If she looked over, she'd see him clinging to the rope with that confident grin of his.

Allon shook her. "Ilanna!" He gripped her face. "Now's not the time. We have to—"

She pushed his hands away, met his eyes. "I know." The ice in her voice matched the numbness creeping through her. "Have you finished yet?"

Allon stepped back, shocked at the change that had come over her. He nodded.

"Then let's go."

Ilanna wanted to scream, shout, to rail against the gods' cruelty. They'd taken another friend from her out of spite. Yet she would have time to mourn him later. She had a job to do.

A rope dangled from the roof. "Is it secure?"

Allon nodded. "It'll hold my weight easily."

"Good."

The four-story climb took her less than a minute. She welcomed the fire in her muscles. The pain pushed back the numbing chill that had come over her. She didn't bother waiting for Allon but slipped across the flat rooftop, hugging whatever contours hid her from the guards patrolling the walls. She called to mind the image of Lord Auslan's mansion interior. If her memory served, the skylight in Lord Auslan's private bedroom lay on the far side of the roof.

An enormous glass dome rose in the center of the mansion. Ilanna peered inside, careful not to cast a shadow. She snarled at the sight of blue-clad Arbitors waiting in the ballroom four stories below. They were waiting for her. But how had they known?

Cloth rustled beside her and she whirled, snapping out an arm to stop Allon in his tracks. "Wait. Don't let them see your shadow."

Nodding, he peered into the ballroom. His face paled. "Bloody hell, that's a lot of 'em!"

"Damned straight. And they're there because someone tipped them off." She clenched her fists. When she got her hands on whoever alerted Lord Auslan, the fate of Reckoner Tyren would seem a mercy by comparison.

"Think we can get past?"

"According to Lem—" Her voice cracked. She cleared her throat. "They're waiting for us in the ballroom and right outside Lord Auslan's bedroom. But we've got the skylight in the bedroom itself."

Confusion screwed up Allon's face. "Won't they hear us breaking the glass?"

"Which is why we're not going to break it. Just trust me."

With a muttered curse for the Arbitors below, Ilanna set off across the roof. She found the skylight thirty paces away, on the far side of the house, overlooking the river. She peered in. The doors to Lord Auslan's bedroom remained closed. No one stood within the room, not that she could see at least.

She crouched beside the skylight and, drawing a knife, set to work on the caulk holding the pane of glass to the iron frame.

She froze as Allon's hand gripped her shoulder. "What?"

"Where's Derelana's Lance?"

Instinctively, Ilanna reached for the clay jars on her belt. Horror twisted in her gut as she remembered. "It's...gone."

"What?" Allon flinched as if struck. "What happened?"

She held up the frayed leather cord still hanging on her belt. "It broke, and the jars fell onto the Field of Mercy. Lem tried to get them…"

Allon's face went pale. "Bloody, twisted hell, Ilanna. We can't go in now."

Confused, Ilanna snorted. "Of course we can."

"We've got Kharna's Breath for the door, but how in the Keeper's name are we getting through the vault floor?"

"The acid will—"

"Melt the steel," Allon interrupted, "but it won't so much as scratch the stone."

Ilanna cursed. "It doesn't matter. I'll figure something out." She hoped she sounded more confident than she felt. She had *no* idea what to do now that she'd lost Derelana's Lance. She only knew she'd come too far to give up now.

Allon shook his head. "I want this as much as you do, Ilanna, but I can't think of any way we make this work. Not without Derelana's Lance." He cast around. "Look, we can make a run for the river and get away before the Arbitors catch us. Wet and cold is better than dead."

"You're willing to throw all our work of the last months away?" Her fists clenched. She wanted to unleash her sorrow and rage on someone—the Hound's fainthearted caution set anger churning in her stomach.

"If it means I survive another day, you're damned right I am."

"So be it." Ilanna gave him a dismissive wave. She couldn't lash out for fear of alerting the guards, but she couldn't wait. "Go if you want, but I'm not leaving until the job's done. I don't need you with me if you don't want to be."

Whirling, she crouched and set to work on the windows again. For long seconds, only the *scratch, scratch* of her blade on the glass broke the stillness of the rooftop. Then, without a word, Allon knelt and set to work on the other side of the skylight.

316

Chapter Forty-Nine

Together, Ilanna and Allon lifted the pane of glass and set it to one side. Ilanna stuck her head through the hole in the skylight and peered around the room. Finding it empty, she squirmed feet-first through the opening, hung from her hands, and dropped to the marble floor without a sound. She winced as Allon landed with an ungraceful *thump*.

Lord Auslan's bedroom lacked the ostentation common among the nobles of Old Praamis. The gauzy curtains hanging from his four-poster bed were made of simple cotton instead of silks, linen, or lace. A utilitarian writing desk and chair occupied one wall, with a plain oaken armoire and shelf on the other. Soft slippers sat atop the luxuriously deep-shag mohair carpet that surrounded the bed.

The single ornamental flourish in the room hung above the nobleman's headboard: a painting of a smiling woman sitting amidst hundreds of red, pink, and white roses. Lady Auslan had been beautiful before the ravages of time and illness.

Ilanna glided across the carpet and slid the three deadbolts home without a sound. The double doors were built from Ghandian blackwood rather than the bloodwood prized by those with more coin than good sense. Blackwood didn't quite match the hardness of its crimson cousin, but proved easier—and cheaper—for craftsmen to shape. Though the door wouldn't quite hold out a battering ram, the guards outside would be hard-pressed to break in.

She studied the room with a practiced eye. *If I was Lord Auslan, where would I hide the secret entrance to my vault?* There was only one place it could be.

She moved the painting of Lady Auslan aside and grinned at the lever beneath. *The nobles of Praamis really need to start coming up with more creative ways to keep their valuables hidden.* The fact that they believed themselves safe from theft played to her favor. It was why she always chose to obscure her visit to wealthier denizens' homes. If they never knew she'd stolen from them, they'd never improve on their flawed security systems.

Allon reached for the lever. She slapped his hand. "Not yet," she hissed.

317

"Why?" He jerked a thumb at the door. "All the guards are out there."

"You don't know that." Ilanna thought back to the Coin Counters' Temple. The Reckoners used locks to secure the entrances and exits, but relied chiefly on Praamian Guards to protect their most valued treasures. "Only a fool would go in without preparing for the worst."

Allon scowled. "So what do we do?"

For reply, Ilanna drew the fencing blade from its hidden sheath. "Just in case." She had no desire to face Duke Phonnis' hand-picked guards, but she wouldn't be caught unprepared.

Allon hesitated before pulling free his own sword. "You want to fight the Arbitors?"

Ilanna shrugged. "I'd rather not, but if I have to, I'll be the one to walk away from this."

With a sigh, Allon nodded. "So be it."

Ilanna tugged on the lever. A muffled *thunk* sounded within the wall, which slid to one side a moment later. Mounted alchemical lamps flickered to life, illuminating descending stairs. Ilanna cast a nervous glance at Allon, who nodded, then proceeded downward.

According to Master Lorilain, the steel vault would need to be built on a solid foundation of granite. It would be on the ground floor or even underground. That meant they had to go down four floors.

With every step, the tension in Ilanna's muscles increased. She half-expected to trigger some hidden trap or set off an alarm. The lack of security measures didn't ease her nervousness; if anything, her anxiety grew as they stepped onto the third set of stairs.

Ilanna held up a hand. Allon paused, raising a questioning eyebrow. Ilanna mouthed the word, "Listen."

She crouched and stilled her breathing. Closing her eyes, she attuned her ears for even the slightest hint of sound. Nothing. For a full minute, she waited and listened.

There! Below, a throat cleared. A few seconds later, someone coughed.

Her heart sank. *Gods, how I hate being right.* Armed men awaited them below. How many, she had no idea. To make it worse, they'd see her feet on the stairs before she could see them.

She turned to Allon with a grimace. He winced and tightened his grip on his sword. *Too late to turn back now.*

Ilanna passed her sword to her left hand and drew a throwing dagger from her bracer, pressing it against the inside of her forearm. Taking out one of however many men she'd face below would improve their chances of survival.

"Ready?" she mouthed.

Allon shrugged.

She continued her steady descent, expecting at any moment to hear the shout of alarm. It came a few seconds later.

"Who goes there?"

She moved, leaping down the stairs toward the four blue-clad Arbitors waiting there. Her arm went up and forward. Her dagger hurtled through the air and plunged into the throat of one guard, just above his burnished silver breastplate. She shifted the sword to her right hand as the Arbitors stared wide-eyed at their slumping comrade.

The three remaining Arbitors reacted faster than she expected. One rushed her, his heavy long sword swinging for her knees. Another darted toward Allon, while the third fumbled for something in his coat.

Ilanna didn't wait to find out what. Instead of retreating, she leapt to the side and took two quick steps along the wall. The movement carried her past the first Arbitor, and she flicked her blade out. The man hissed as the tip laid open a bloody line along the back of his hand. Whatever he'd been reaching for clattered to the floor.

She whirled and ducked beneath a high swing from the first Arbitor. The clash of steel rang out as Allon met the third guard on the far side of the staircase.

Only now did the foolishness of Ilanna's actions sink in. Two Arbitors faced her, murder in their eyes and naked steel in their hands. She had the wall and the steel door of Lord Auslan's vault at her back. She was trapped.

Instinct honed over years spent training with Errik kicked in. Her mind analyzed the Arbitors' stances, their weapons, and her surroundings in the space of a single heartbeat. She had just one way to get out of this alive.

She moved even as the first Arbitor raised his sword to strike. His horizontal chop, intended to cut through her shoulder or neck, went high as she ducked. The lightning thrust of her thin fencing blade caught the injured man above the knee, just below the hem of his leather jerkin, severing the tendon. He cried out and sagged.

She leapt backward to avoid the other Arbitor's blade. Her back slammed into the wall and she winced as the sword opened a line of fire along her shoulder. His next blow struck sparks off the stone where her head had been a moment earlier.

Ilanna couldn't trade blows with the Arbitor. Her slim fencing blade would shatter under the weight of the long sword. She had to catch him off guard, distract him long enough to get in close and use her dagger.

His next strike came low and fast, a thrust intended to skewer her. Ilanna twisted aside and slapped the blade wide. She flicked her light blade across his face. Blood trickled from a cut in his forehead, dripping into his right eye. Her gaze never left his face. When he squinted at the sting of blood, she executed a perfect fencing lunge.

The Arbitor knocked the attack wide with contempt and brought his weapon back for a riposte. But Ilanna hadn't followed through on the lunge. Instead, she'd released her grip on her sword hilt and pulled a dagger. Before the Arbitor could bring his blade around, Ilanna buried the dagger to its hilt in his neck. The man groaned and coughed, spraying blood. He tried to attack, but Ilanna stepped out of range of his weak strike. The gush of crimson from his neck sapped his strength. He collapsed, twitched, and lay still.

Her gaze went to the second Arbitor. The man had retrieved whatever item had fallen from his hand in her initial attack and was moving toward the wall behind him. The alarm in the Temple of Whispers in Voramis flashed through her mind. Was he trying to alert the guards above to their presence in the mansion?

She leapt over the dead Arbitor and lashed out. Her slim blade laid open the back of his hand. He shrieked and dropped the item—a glass stone identical to the one set in the wall. Ilanna silenced him with a thrust through the back of his skull.

Allon's grunt drew her attention. Both Hound and Arbitor's swords lay on the ground, and the two men fought with bare fists. The Arbitor's heavy armor gave him the advantage, and he had Allon pinned to the stone stairs.

Ilanna drove her sword into the back of the man's knee. The Arbitor screamed and whirled on her. She stepped back, out of reach of his flailing fists. In that moment of distraction, Allon slipped out from the Arbitor's grasp and seized his sword. He slammed the pommel into the guard's temple, and the man sagged.

Gasping, Allon wiped blood from his nose and mouth. His jaw dropped as his eyes fell on the two dead Arbitors. "Damn!" His gaze went from the corpses to Ilanna and back again. "Damn!" he repeated.

Ilanna turned to the vault door. After spending hours studying the replica built by Master Lorilain, she felt as if she knew every rivet and joint of the enormous steel construction before her.

From her pouch she produced the length of rope and wax pencil Darreth had given her. Allon followed her terse instructions with alacrity, as if the fight had driven home the true danger of their job. She measured the position twice just to be certain she got it right. This was no practice run—if she failed now, there was no way out.

Stowing the measuring rope, she drew out the glass vial of Kharna's Breath and the shorter of the two pipettes.

"Careful," Allon breathed.

Ilanna shot him a glare.

"Sorry!" He held up his hands—knuckles raw and covered in his and the Arbitor's blood. "I'm nervous, is all."

"Keep your nerves to yourself," Ilanna growled. "I've more than my fair share already."

With a wry grin, Allon stepped back. "I'll give you space."

Ilanna drew in a deep breath and, with trembling hands, pulled the cork from the glass bottle. She dipped the pipette into the clear liquid, placed her finger on the other end, and drew it out. Holding her breath, she set the tip of the tube to the door and released the suction.

She cursed herself for a fool as drops of acid slithered down the surface of the vault door. Only after a couple of seconds did it begin to bubble, eating away at the metal. Noxious steam filled the staircase with a gut-twisting odor. Ilanna coughed and stepped away from the door.

When the smoke finally cleared and the metal ceased its bubbling, Ilanna moved closer. Her stomach knotted. The acid had pitted the steel but failed to melt through the thick plate.

An idea struck her. Reaching into her pouch, she drew out Darreth's wax pencil. She pressed the tip against the door and cracked it off. Using her knife, she hollowed out a small bowl in the wax.

That should hold the acid in place long enough to melt through the steel.

Gritting her teeth, she dipped the pipette into the bottle and drew out another portion of Kharna's Breath. The level of the clear liquid had dropped by a quarter.

I've got to get this right.

She let out a slow breath and slowly removed her finger from the tip of the tube. A single drop of acid slid down the door, but the rest remained in the hollow of the wax. After a moment, the metal began to sizzle and bubble. She didn't back away from the stinking smoke, but kept her eyes fixed on the door.

Her heart lurched as the smoke faded, elation surging in her chest. *Yes!* Kharna's Breath had burned a hole large enough for her to insert the longer pipette. After a moment of feeling around, she located the locking bar.

She inserted the second glass tube into the bottle of acid. When she drew it out, barely more than one-third of the liquid remained. *Damn it!*

She'd still have enough to melt her way through some of the welded steel plates of the vault floor. Jarl and his Grubbers waited for her on the other side of the layer of granite. She'd have to find a way to get through that stone, but first she had to deal with the door.

Her hand shook as she inserted the pipette into the hole and felt for the locking bar. She sucked in a deep breath. *You can do this,* she told herself.

An alarm bell shattered the silence of the stairs.

Chapter Fifty

Startled, Ilanna flinched and her finger slipped from the end of the tube, spilling the precious acid inside the door. Metal sizzled and noxious steam poured out of the hole.

She cast a wild glance over her shoulder. The only surviving Arbitor slumped against the wall, a stone in his hand pressed against an identical one set in the wall. Allon spun and kicked at the blue-clad guard. The man's head snapped back, striking stone, and he sagged. The Hound's dagger silenced him forever.

But the alarm had been raised.

Keeper's teeth!

Allon spun on her, wide-eyed. "What do we do?"

Ilanna bared her teeth. "What *can* we do? We've got to keep going."

"But the Arbitors—"

"Will have a bloody hard time getting through that blackwood door. We can be in the vault long before they breach it."

"That doesn't help us get out of here alive! Without Derelana's Lance, we'll be trapped."

Ilanna clenched her jaw. "Then run. I'm not leaving. I've come too far, lost too much to walk away empty-handed."

"But how are you going to get through?"

"I'll figure something out!" Her voice rose to a shout. "I always have. But I don't need you here if you're just going to tell me it can't be done."

Allon eyed her, fear and hesitation mingled in his expression. She could see his mind working. If he remained, he'd be risking the wrath of the Arbitors. But if he fled, she'd think him a coward.

"You've done your part, Allon. I can do this myself."

His jaw tightened in a stubborn frown. "No, you can't." He crossed his arms. "You'll need me if you're going to get out of this alive. Between us, we'll come up with a way out. Now quit wasting time arguing and get that damned door open."

Ilanna returned her attention to the pipette. She dipped the slim tube into the glass bottle and drew out a few drops. She'd decided on a new approach for the locking bar: apply a small amount at a time, just enough to melt into the metal without dripping. She'd wasted too much of the precious acid already. She had none to spare.

Allon hovered behind her, nervous tension rolling off him in waves.

"Allon, go watch the door. I want a few minutes' warning before the Arbitors break through."

With a nod, the Hound dashed up the stairs.

Taking a deep breath to steady her hands, Ilanna inserted the pipette into the hole in the door. She took her time, feeling around until she was certain the tip rested against the locking bar. She hesitated only a moment before removing her finger from the tube.

The hole belched smoke and the sound of bubbling metal a moment later. Ilanna waited for the steam to clear before reaching for her quickfire globes. She needed to get a look inside the hole to see if the acid was working. After a moment of fumbling in her pouch, she remembered what had happened to the glass balls. She stuffed the pang of sorrow deep in the back of her mind. She had to focus on the job; she could think about Lem later.

She bent and squinted into the hole, desperately wishing for a beamer or any sort of lamp. Using the tip of the pipette, she felt along the length of the locking bar. Elation coursed through her as she felt pitting along the smooth metal.

It's working!

She repeated the process, applying only a few drops at a time. The alarm blaring through the mansion grated on her nerves, and the desire to hurry warred with the need for precision. At any moment, Allon would come barreling down the stairs and they'd be out of time. She hated the idea of abandoning the job, but she had no hope of defeating an army of Arbitors with only Allon. But she wouldn't walk away just yet, not without at least *seeing* the prize she'd worked so hard to claim.

The level of liquid dropped with every application. When she dipped the pipette one last time, only a single bead of acid remained in the bottle. Her heart sank. Even if she got through the door, she wouldn't have enough to melt through the floor. She'd failed.

A knot formed in her gut as she applied the last of Kharna's Breath to the locking bar. When the sizzling quieted, she reached for the wheel.

The moment of truth. Everything she'd done rested on this moment. She'd invested months of hard work and a fortune in gold, spent far too many sleepless nights wishing she could hold Kodyn in her arms. She'd killed for this moment, and friends had died in the pursuit of success. It had all been for nothing. Without Derelana's Lance to melt through the granite foundation, she'd be trapped in the vault. She'd have to flee the Arbitors, empty-handed. Her plans to buy her freedom from the Guild disappeared in that instant. A weight settled on her shoulders.

She fueled the force of her anger into her arms and wrenched the wheel. It resisted her efforts to spin it for only a moment. Something snapped within the door and the handle whirled smoothly, without a sound.

The door seemed to open of its own accord. She stepped back as it swung outward. Emotions roiled like a tempest within her breast; triumph at her success mingled with sorrow over the loss of her friends and anger at coming so close only to fail.

Alchemical lanterns flooded the room with light, illuminating bare steel walls and a marble pedestal, upon which sat the golden sarcophagus. A thousand gemstones of every hue and shape twinkled in the lamplight.

Ilanna's breath caught in her throat. She'd come so close. Success lay within her grasp, yet it proved a double-edged blade. She could almost reach out and touch the fortune she'd sacrificed everything to obtain, but without Derelana's Lance, it might as well be a cup of water for a drowning man. She ran her hand along the smooth glass case surrounding—

Wait, what? She rapped on the glass. *This wasn't in the Duke's plans.*

The plans had shown everything: the door, the steel room, even the marble pedestal upon which the sarcophagus rested. But they'd never spoken of a glass case.

If the plans didn't include a case, it means this is a new addition. The glass was as thick as her thumb—far too thick for her diamond-tipped cutter—and without a single seam or opening. *It looks like it's intended to be air and water-tight. But why would—*

"Ilanna!" Allon's voice echoed in the staircase. The Hound appeared a moment later, rushing down the stairs. Panic tinged his expression. "They're almost through, Ilanna. We need to go now if we're..." He trailed off, his eyes going wide. "Sweet Mistress!" he breathed. "It's beautiful. The sort of thing you see once in a lifetime."

Ilanna ignored him. Something nagged at the back of her mind. *Why the glass case?*

Allon recovered from his awe after a moment. "Come on, Ilanna. If we leave now, we can get out through the window and across the roof before—"

She whirled on him. "Shut up and let me think!"

Allon flinched and snapped his mouth shut.

Ilanna paced the length of the sarcophagus, eyes fixed on the glass case. The original plans for the vault had called for the steel plates to be welded together. According to Master Lorilain, the pattern welding was the best way…

"To keep water and air out!" she shouted.

Her gaze darted around the room. Hope surged in her chest as she caught a glimpse of rust on the steel walls.

Of course! Lord Auslan had paid a fortune to embalm his wife, but even the slightest bit of moisture would ruin the preserved body. The presence of rust meant some had leaked through the steel plates. Lord Auslan had added the glass case to protect the body because the room itself would never be truly watertight.

She crouched and studied a spot of rust on the floor. The metal in one section had crumbled, the plates separating. A bead of moisture sat in the hole between the plates.

Willem's explanation of the midnight mist sprang to her mind. He'd said it came from an underground creek. Somehow, it had seeped up through the ground. Lord Auslan had built his mansion beside the river. If a body of water ran underneath the vault room, it would explain the moisture.

"Ilanna, we need to go!"

"Wait." Ilanna spun on the Hound. "Look at this."

"Rust?" He raised an eyebrow. "What's the big—" His other eyebrow shot up. "Wait, isn't this room supposed to be watertight?"

"Yes, which means the design is flawed." She stabbed a finger at the floor. "Maybe the granite beneath is cracked. The water has to come from somewhere. See if you can find anything to pry up the floor."

"We don't have the time, Ilanna! The Arbitors are going to get through that blackwood door any minute now. Without Derelana's Lance, we've got nothing."

Ilanna knelt and studied the section of crumbled metal. The itch remained in the back of her mind. She was forgetting something important. But what?

She replayed every conversation she'd had with Master Lorilain, Jarl, and Darreth about the steel room, every word Graeme and Journeyman Donneh had said about—

Her eyes flew wide. "Moisture!"

Allon cocked his head, his expression growing confused.

"Allon, get behind the vault door."

He hesitated.

"Now!"

The Hound obeyed.

Ilanna produced the tiny glass bottle she'd stolen from the Temple of Whispers in Voramis. A single drop of Kharna's Breath remained in the bottom. *This has to work!*

Unscrewing the lid, she poured the last of the acid into the hole. She dashed across the vault and darted behind the door. For a heart-pounding moment, nothing happened. The fires of her renewed hope dimmed.

The horrible moaning of steel echoed through the staircase. A storm of steel shards whirled out the open door with concussive force, piercing stone like a blade into flesh. Ilanna steadied herself against the wall as the ground itself seemed to rumble and shake. A cloud of noxious smoke boiled from the vault.

Ilanna didn't wait for it to clear. She rushed from behind the protection of the thick vault door and stopped, mouth agape.

The floor had buckled and twisted, the steel plates ripped up by the force of the explosion. Pieces of metal were embedded in the walls, the inside of the vault door, and the stone stairs outside. Allon winced as he stumbled into the vault, tugging at a sliver of steel that had pierced his shoulder.

Glass littered the floor. Bits of metal protruded from the jewel-encrusted sarcophagus. The concussion had ripped free a handful of gemstones, which Allon quickly collected.

Ilanna stepped closer to the twisted section of floor. The sound of clattering rocks echoed from the hole that disappeared into the darkness below. A heartbeat later, light pierced the swirling clouds of dust and a dirty, sweaty face appeared.

"'Lanna?"

Triumphant laughter bubbled from her chest. "Jarl, you beautiful man!"

Her elation died as shouts of alarm rang out, punctuated by the clatter of hobnailed military boots.

The Arbitors had broken through the door. She'd run out of time.

Chapter Fifty-One

"Jarl, get someone up here now! We're out of time."

Jarl disappeared, and the head and shoulders of a Grubber popped through the hole in the floor. Two more followed. A fourth brought up a length of rope, which he and his companions ran around and beneath the sarcophagus. Every sinew straining, they heaved the golden head free of the pedestal and shoved it toward the hole in the steel floor.

"Look out below!" one Grubber called out and released his grip on the ropes.

The enormous sarcophagus plunged through the hole to crash to the ground. Gold twinkled on the edges of the buckled steel plates, and more than a few gemstones were torn free. Ilanna scooped them up as the Grubbers slithered back down the hole.

She turned to Allon, who stood on the staircase. "Allon, time to go."

The Hound rushed into the vault. "You first. I'll follow."

Ilanna didn't argue. She lowered her legs into the hole and dropped to the floor of the sewer tunnel below. Jarl gave her a nod and continued shouting orders.

Ilanna had to give the big Hawk credit. He'd trained his crew well. Two Grubbers hauled a hand cart toward them, while another eight worked to insert ropes under and around the sarcophagus. The fall had damaged the golden casket. It lay in halves, both base and lid twisted and scuffed. A pair of filthy apprentices in ragged, grey-trimmed robes shone beamer lamps around the tunnel in search of gemstones that had broken free. They stepped over the mummified body of Lady Auslan as if she was little more than the crumbled granite and mounds of dirt lying around the tunnel.

Allon dropped into the tunnel a moment later. Ilanna dragged him out of the way of the bustling Grubbers.

"How much time do we have?"

Allon shook his head. "A minute. Maybe two. They weren't far behind me."

Ilanna nodded. She'd prepared for this eventuality. She raised her voice. "Jarl!"

The huge Hawk turned with a questioning glance.

"Arbitors a minute away."

He pointed to the hole, and she nodded. Wincing, he turned his attention to the Grubbers. His shouted orders grew louder and rang with a note of urgency.

A pair of Grubbers rushed past and set to work shoveling the crumbled rock into a pile directly beneath the hole. It would do little more than twist ankles, but Ilanna welcomed anything that slowed the Arbitors down.

"Heave!"

Eight Grubbers strained to lift the golden sarcophagus halves onto the handcart, while two more held the cart steady. The dust-covered men passed ropes over and under the cart to secure the casket in place. At Jarl's terse command, the Grubbers raced off down the tunnel, dragging the cart behind them. Jarl put his fingers to his mouth and emitted a piercing whistle. The apprentices ceased their search for gemstones and rushed after the cart. The two Grubbers who remained reached for sledgehammers.

The big Hawk motioned for them to follow. "Time to go."

He took off down the tunnel, Ilanna and Allon a step behind. The ring of metal hammers on wood rang out behind them. The earth growled and rumbled, shaking underfoot. A cloud of dust sprayed toward them as the tunnels collapsed. A moment later, two grinning, dirt-covered Grubbers sprinted past.

Ilanna risked a backward glance. A pinprick of light leaked from the hole in the vault, but a mountain of dirt, stone, and mud had swallowed the section of tunnel Jarl and his Grubbers had broadened. Though the collapse hadn't fully blocked the way, it would take the Arbitors time to get through. If her luck held, it would be enough.

The tunnel ended at a cliff, with a gap five paces across. Jarl had replaced the plank bridge with a proper construction of wood, steel, and cables. The Grubbers hauled the handcart over the arch and set about unloading the golden contents onto a hoist Jarl had built on the opposite side of the chasm.

Ilanna glanced down as she crossed the bridge. Far below—at least five man-heights—the river rushed with a fury that reverberated from the stone walls of the tunnel. Jarl's crew had anchored a floating platform to the cliff face. Four Grubbers stood on the wooden barge, working the wheel that lowered the hoist.

"Bloody hell!" Allon breathed.

Ilanna's chest swelled with pride. "He's good, isn't he?"

From his place on the bridge, Jarl shouted orders to the Grubbers working the wheel. Two grey-clad Journeymen hung off the sides of the lowering hoist platform, using wooden poles to push off the cliff face whenever the weight of the sarcophagus swung them too close.

When the hoist reached the floating platform, the six Grubbers worked to wrestle the heavy golden casket into place on the boat. Gorin, Jarl's fellow Pathfinder, commanded the crew down below while Jarl rushed across the bridge toward the remaining Grubbers.

"To your stations, lads."

The Grubbers took off down the tunnel leading away from the river.

At that moment, the first shouts of the Arbitors echoed through the passageways behind them.

Ilanna turned to Allon. "Go. Make your way home."

The Hound glanced at the river. "You still need me."

Ilanna shook her head. "Jarl and I've prepared for this."

Allon opened his mouth to protest, but Ilanna held up a hand. "Trust me, Allon."

Hesitation warred on his face, but he nodded. "So be it." He gave her a halfhearted grin. "But don't you go dying on me, eh?"

Ilanna forced herself to smile. "Wouldn't think of it." Dying was the last thing on her mind. She had too much to live for now.

With a final worried glance backward, Allon took off down the tunnel.

Jarl gripped her arm. "You sure about this?"

Ilanna groaned. "Not you, too!" Why were men always so protective?

Jarl shrugged. "It's dangerous."

"Ask the two dead Arbitors above what I think about that." She gave his massive shoulder a push. "Go. You've the most important job here. Far more dangerous than running away."

Jarl, eloquent as ever, grunted. "Be safe." He seized the hoist rope and leapt off the precipice.

Ilanna glanced over the edge. The huge Hawk dropped onto the wooden platform, bounded into the boat, and gave a piercing whistle. As two Grubbers cast off the lines, the small craft shuddered into motion. Though the current ran downstream toward the Stannar River, Jarl's boat began to work its way steadily upstream, towed by a sturdy steel cable.

When the boat had finally cleared the wooden platform, Ilanna reached for the axe a Grubber had left leaning against the hoist beam. A steel cable ran

331

from the hoist to the wall, where it was anchored to a wooden beam and secured by a rope. Ilanna brought the axe down hard on the rope, severing it. The hoist toppled off the edge of the cliff. A series of crashes and splashes echoed from below. Ilanna peered over the edge. Jarl's design had worked to perfection. The falling hoist beams had severed the anchors holding the wooden platform to the cliff face. The debris disappeared downstream within minutes.

Ilanna's gaze followed the curves of the river. Jarl had spent weeks designing and building what amounted to an enormous laundry line system attached to a massive waterwheel. The force of the rushing water operated the system of pulleys, dragging the boat upstream. Grubbers were stationed along the river route to hitch the boat to the next set of ropes. The boat would be towed through miles of underground tunnels and waterways until it ended at the hidden landing where Jarl would unload the precious cargo to be transported to the Night Guild tunnels.

The system had one insurmountable flaw: the boat would move *very* slowly. The waterwheel would only turn as fast as the river pushed it. The farther from the wheel, the more power lost. It would take the boat hours to reach its final destination. The subterranean network of creeks and rivers was accessible from multiple places around the city. If the Arbitors spotted the boat, they'd have more than enough time to intercept it.

Ilanna stood at the bridge, in full view of the tunnel leading from Lord Auslan's vault. She had to draw the Arbitors' attention. As long as they were occupied chasing her, they wouldn't think to look at the river below.

As she waited, she ran over the escape route Jarl had laid out for her. They'd spent hours the previous day running over the plan, but it never hurt to rehearse it all beforehand. A combination of excitement and anticipation twisted in her stomach. Against all odds, she'd achieved more than anyone—even she—had believed possible. They had come to the final stretch in a long, grueling journey. All that remained was to outrun a dozen pissed off, sword-wielding Arbitors.

She gave a sarcastic snort. *Should be a breeze.*

The first silver breastplate appeared from the darkened tunnel a few moments later. Dust and dirt turned the Arbitor's blue tunic and black trousers a dull brown, staining his hands and face. But the steel sword in his hand looked no less threatening for his disheveled state.

His eyes widened at the sight of Ilanna. He shouted behind him. "I've got her!"

"And it's a good thing you have!" Ilanna called across the bridge. "Gods alone know what the Duke'll do to you if you fail to bring in the audacious thief who breaks into the most secure place in the city. Oh wait, did I say *if* you fail?" She gave him a nasty smile. "I meant to say *when*."

Her plan to enrage them worked. The Arbitor's boots pounded on the bridge. "You won't escape us, bitch!" Four more guardsmen followed, all eyes locked on her. In their single-minded fury, they'd never think to question where in the bloody hell the sarcophagus had disappeared to.

"We'll see about that." Blowing him a kiss, she turned and ran down the tunnel.

Lanterns hung from the tunnel walls, painting her outline clearly to her pursuers. She ran at a steady pace—fast enough to stay out of reach of the Arbitors, but not so fast she lost them. She needed them to stay focused on her long enough for Jarl and the boat to get away unnoticed. It would be a simple matter to lose them in the twisting, turning sewer system.

The clanking of armor and the pounding of hobnailed boots echoed through the stone passages. The enraged shouts grew less frequent as the weight of the Arbitors' gear—long swords and sheaths, silver-plated steel breastplates, and heavy steel-toed military boots—took a toll on them. Before long, the curses gave way to wheezing and heavy breathing.

The Arbitors were the best-trained private guards in Praamis. They spent hours each day engaged in military drills. Indeed, they could march in step, form a shield wall, or advance in a line as tight as any of the Legion of Heroes. But their training hadn't prepared them for prolonged sprinting through a sewer tunnel in pursuit of a thief girl who'd spent her life running, leaping, and climbing.

Ilanna glanced over her shoulder. More Arbitors—a full dozen now—pounded through the tunnels toward her. No doubt more would soon follow. She had to keep them occupied for a while longer to give Jarl a chance to flee.

She slowed at the next intersection, her eyes searching for Jarl's sign. A smile stretched her lips at the sight of the crude image of a hawk scratched into the stone wall down one passageway. Beneath it sat a pair of quickfire globes and a compact beamer lamp. She pocketed the quickfire globes and depressed the button to switch on the beamer; she'd need light for the next stretch.

"Oi, I've got a question for you lot," she called down the tunnel. "What's blue-and-silver and can't find their own arses with a road map and a search party?"

A string of curses answered her taunt. When the Arbitors appeared around the corner, she winked and made a rude gesture before dashing down the tunnel.

The light of the beamer bobbed in time with her steps. The thrill of the chase set her heart thundering and adrenaline rushing through her veins.

She rounded the corner and skidded to a sudden halt. Not twenty paces away, the tunnel ended at the river. There, in plain view, floated the boat carrying Jarl, Gorin, the Grubbers, and the jewel-encrusted golden sarcophagus of Lady Auslan.

Chapter Fifty-Two

Damn it! Ilanna cursed. *Jarl was supposed to have passed this section already.* Either the current was stronger than he anticipated, or the pulley system had suffered a malfunction.

Whatever the problem, Ilanna had an instant to react. At any moment, the Arbitors would round the corner and see the boat. She couldn't let that happen.

Gritting her teeth, she dropped the beamer lamp, turned, and sprinted back the way she'd come. Straight into the arms of the blue-clad guards.

She drew her sword as she rounded the corner. The two foremost Arbitors stopped, shocked, less than five paces away. Ilanna shouted at the top of her lungs and rushed the one on the left. She struck out, a graceless slash meant to give the Arbitor pause rather than inflict injury. The man leapt out of her way and she pounded past without pause.

Three more Arbitors rushed her with drawn swords and fury etched into their faces. They slowed and spread out, forming a wall of metal and muscle she couldn't hope to cut her way through.

Ilanna's left hand darted into her pouch. Drawing out one of Darreth's pipettes, she sent the glass tube hurtling toward the Arbitor on the far right. It shattered on the guard's breastplate, and the man flinched and raised his hands to protect himself. In that moment of inattention, Ilanna slid around him.

Grasping hands reached for her, and she was glad she'd abandoned her cloak and leather vest. She sprinted toward the intersection at the end of the tunnel. If she could reach it before any more Arbitors arrived, she'd have a chance of—

A single blue-clad guard appeared around the corner. His eyes widened and his hand went to the sword on his belt. Holding it like a club, he held his position at the intersection.

Ilanna had only one choice: she rushed straight at him. The Arbitor swung for her head. Ilanna didn't bother ducking. She raised her slim sword and blocked the blow. The impact jarred her arm to the shoulder, snapped the fencing blade. But the guard had committed his full strength to the blow. As his body twisted with the follow-through, Ilanna dropped her sword and dived to the left. She rolled to her feet and dashed through the intersection.

Darkness enveloped her as she rushed down the tunnel beyond. She drew out the quickfire globes and held them high. Jarl had plotted an escape route against this precise eventuality, but she'd abandoned it to prevent the Arbitors from discovering the boat. Now she had to find her own way out. Judging by the shouts behind her, the Duke's guards hadn't abandoned their pursuit.

Instinct shrieked in the back of Ilanna's mind. She slid to a halt, her eyes going wide. Not two steps ahead, the tunnel floor ended in a void that swallowed the faint light of the quickfire globes.

She muttered a string of curses. She had seconds before the Arbitors would reach her. *So how in the frozen hell am I going to get out of here?*

Whirling, she raised the quickfire globes high. She stood on a ledge three paces wide and four across. The tunnel ended three paces behind her, and the stone ceiling rose high overhead.

She caught a glimpse of another tunnel mouth near the ceiling. Perhaps she could escape that way. She discarded the idea. No way could she climb out of the Arbitors' reach before they caught up.

Damn it!

Her ears pricked up at the rush of falling water. It came from her left. She sprinted to the edge of the shelf and pointed the pitiful light of the quickfire globes toward the sound. If she could get to the water, the current would carry her downstream to the Stannar River. She'd take the icy, fast-rushing river over capture by the Duke's Arbitors any day.

Stuffing the quickfire globes into her pouch, she felt for hand and footholds on the wall. Moisture turned the stones slick but age had worn cracks into the masonry. She climbed out to the left instead of up. If she could get far enough away, the Arbitors might think she'd jumped.

Her heart thundered in nervous terror. A thick, oppressive blackness surrounded her. She had no idea how far she'd fall and no desire to find out. After a few moments of desperate slithering along the wall, she slowed to a steady pace. She had no need to sacrifice safety for speed. Even if the Arbitors saw her, they couldn't catch her. Not in those heavy boots and breastplates.

Light glimmered to her right, growing brighter and accompanied by the sound of tramping feet and shouted curses.

"She's gone." An Arbitor's voice echoed from the cavernous ceiling.

Another voice answered. "She can't have just disappeared!"

"D'you think she jumped?"

"Dunno." Rocks clattered far below. "Would make our job easier if she did. That's solid ground and a long way down."

The beam of an alchemical lantern swung up and down the wall. The light snaked toward her. "There!"

"Go! Back into the tunnels," the first Arbitor shouted. "We're going to cut the bitch off. No way she's escaping us now."

Ilanna cursed. She couldn't climb any faster, so the Arbitors had plenty of time to spread out through the tunnels ahead of her.

The rush of falling water grew louder, and the reek of sewage filled the air. Ilanna groaned. Jarl had charted her route through the driest sections of tunnel. *Looks like I'll be getting dirty after all.*

A chunk of stone came loose in her hand. She clung to the wall in desperation, heart thundering, digging her toes into a crack in the masonry. Her free hand fumbled for a hold. She jammed her fingers into a notch in the stones and allowed herself a pause to rest and breathe.

After a moment, she resumed her traverse. The ache in her forearms and calves grew, but she knew better than to rush a climb like this. One wrong move would send her plummeting.

The air grew heavy with moisture. Finding a solid handhold, she risked drawing out her quickfire globes. There, not two paces away and above, the slurry of sewage rushed from a hole in the wall. Ilanna's heart leapt. She stowed the globes and clambered up and through the mouth of the tunnel. The reek of offal wrinkled her nose and set her stomach churning, but relief flooded her as the ache in her muscles dimmed.

Now to get the frozen hell out of here!

* * *

Ilanna flattened herself against the wall and swore inwardly. The two Arbitors between her and the tunnel down which she had to go seemed in no hurry to move.

She'd spent the better part of an hour creeping through the tunnels, avoiding the Duke's guards and searching for the tiny Hawk symbols Jarl had etched into the stone walls. Now that she'd found her way out, the damned Arbitors stood between her and freedom.

She reached for her bracer dagger but thought better of it. *No chance of fighting my way through this.* Instead, she drew out one of Darreth's pipettes. Better to get past without alerting the Arbitors to her presence.

The glass tube arced through the air and shattered on the stone wall. The two blue-clad guards whirled toward the sound.

"What was that?"

"What d'you think? It's her, you fool!"

They took off, and Ilanna seized the opportunity to slip behind them. She rushed down the hall, grimacing at the squelching of her sodden boots on the stone floor. The tunnel led toward the escape route Jarl had planned for her. Freedom lay just ahead.

Rounding the corner, she collided with the back of a silver-plated steel breastplate. Her forehead slammed into the metal, setting her head ringing. She staggered against the wall. The world whirled around her. The shouts of alarm sounded faint, distant.

A hand closed around her wrist. She tried to jerk free, but the grip held her fast.

"Oi, lookit this!" The bearded face of an Arbitor stared down at her "She's just a little'un!" The man jerked her to her feet. Ilanna winced at the pain flashing through her shoulder, adding to the ache in her head. She blinked to clear her blurring vision.

Another guard rushed toward her, reaching for her other hand. "Be careful with her. You saw what she did to Dall and Ellis. She's dang—" He never finished the sentence.

The palm of Ilanna's hand drove his nose up into his skull. Even as the first Arbitor sagged, Ilanna twisted her wrist, breaking her captor's grasp. She tore her hand free and drove a knee into the second guard's groin. Air whooshed from his lungs and he sagged with a weak groan. Ilanna took off toward the river without hesitation.

Behind her, the fallen Arbitor croaked, "She's here!"

Cursing, Ilanna poured more speed into her pounding legs. Her boots thumped on the wooden bridge and she was across. Seizing the rope Jarl had left hanging for her, she yanked hard without pausing in her run. The sound of snapping timber and creaking rope echoed behind her. Yet the expected *splash* never came.

She risked a backward glance. The bridge had only partially collapsed. The Arbitors would have to cross one at a time, but they could still cross. Even as she debated whether or not to return and try again, the first blue-clad guard thundered over the bridge.

At the next intersection, Ilanna stooped to retrieve the beamer tucked behind a pile of crumbled stone. The lamp bathed the walls and floor in light. Her gaze swept the tunnel and locked onto the mark of the Hawk. Without hesitation, she turned down the right-hand passageway.

She grinned as the Arbitors' shouts faded behind her. They couldn't possibly match her speed, not weighed down with all that heavy armor. Once she crossed the next bridge, she'd be safe.

Lantern light spilled from an adjoining corridor thirty paces ahead of her. The clanking of armor and the *thump, thump* of hobnailed boots grew louder. *Damn it!* They'd somehow gotten around and in front of her.

Every shred of speed went into fueling her muscles. She pounded past the connecting tunnel a heartbeat before the Arbitors reached it. They gave chase, but she only smiled at their shouts and curses.

Elation flared in her chest at the sight of the bridge at the end of the tunnel. She raced toward it, her boots pounding on the wooden planking, and seized the rope. She pulled as hard as she could, stumbling backward as it yanked free. Jarl's makeshift bridge collapsed. The river swallowed wood and rope, leaving only a yawning chasm between Ilanna and her pursuers.

Laughter bubbled up from deep within, and Ilanna allowed it to burst free. Exhaustion, sorrow, elation, and excitement churned in her gut. She'd pulled it off! She'd stolen from the most secure place in Praamis and gotten away with it.

With a rude gesture to the red-faced Arbitors, she turned and sprinted toward the Night Guild and her newly acquired fortune.

Chapter Fifty-Three

Ilanna slid down the rope, her legs sagging as she landed on the hard-packed earthen floor of the Aerie. *Bloody hell, it's good to be back!*

Her trek through the sewer system had taken far longer than expected. She'd taken a circuitous route back to the exit from the underground tunnels, then clambered onto the city rooftops. She wouldn't take the chance, however small, that a lucky Arbitor had somehow caught up with her. Safety came first, even if it left her exhausted.

But she'd finally made it—hours late, covered in muck and slime, and aching for a bath and hot food. Yet as she looked around the Aerie, all thoughts of comfort fled.

Where the fiery hell is everyone?

The high-vaulted room stood empty and silent. The single lantern hanging beside the huge double doors cast a pathetic radius of light.

Jarl knew to bring the sarcophagus straight here, so where in the Keeper's name is he?

Dread sent an icy chill down her spine. Had something happened to the boat? Had the Arbitors caught up to them and captured or killed them?

She stalked down the passageway that led to her room. After a wash and a change of clothes, she'd find out exactly what—

Her eyes widened at the sight of the figure seated beside her door. Gorin, Jarl's fellow Pathfinder, slouched in a comfortable armchair, a blanket pulled up to his chin. The sound of his heavy breathing echoed through the silent tunnels.

"Gorin!" Ilanna's voice cracked like a whip.

The Pathfinder leapt to his feet. "Wha…?" He rubbed his eyes and blinked at her. "Oh, good, you're back."

Ilanna growled. "Where is it? Jarl was supposed to bring it—"

"Hold on." Gorin held up his hands as she closed the distance. His eyes dropped to her clenched fists, then returned to her bared teeth. "He was bringing it here, but Master Gold stopped him."

Ilanna stopped. "What?"

The Pathfinder crossed his arms. "That's all I know. Jarl told me to come here and wait for you to return. Said to bring you to the Menagerie the moment you're back."

Fury burned in Ilanna's chest. *What the hell is Master Gold thinking?* She'd believed the Guild Master was on her side. So why had he waylaid Jarl and her prize?

Gorin's nose wrinkled. "Might want to think about burning those clothes first."

Ilanna looked down. Muck of odious hues—browns, greens, and greys she didn't know existed—stained her breeches. Splashes of the rank slop spattered her hands, face, and shirt.

"You go on ahead. I'll be there after a quick bath."

The Pathfinder pinched his nose. "Best make it a long one."

* * *

A fresh-smelling, clean, but no less furious Ilanna stalked through the tunnels of the Night Guild toward the Menagerie. Her mind whirled as she tried to decipher Master Gold's intentions. What was he doing?

Master Hawk waited outside the Menagerie, his face as somber as his dark grey clothing. Jarl stood beside the House Master. The tension in the huge Hawk's face sent a chill of fear racing through her.

"What's going on?"

Without a word, Master Hawk and Jarl swung the doors open. Journeymen and apprentices from every House stood within. All eyes turned toward her. A ripple of applause spread through the crowd, rising to a thunderous clapping.

Ilanna turned to Master Hawk. The House Master's lips twitched in an uncharacteristic smile. "Seems right for everyone to share in your triumph." The enormous grin Jarl had struggled to hide now broadened his already thick face. With his usual eloquence, he nodded and grunted encouragement.

The crowd parted as Ilanna entered the room. Hands reached out to clap her shoulders or pat her back. For once, she didn't flinch from the contact. Everything around her faded at the sight of the two halves of the sarcophagus sitting in the heart of the Menagerie.

Master Gold stood beside the golden casket. He beamed and motioned for her to join him. Face burning, Ilanna came to stand next to the Guild Master. The applause rose to a new crescendo when Master Gold turned her to face the assembled Night Guild. Even the House Masters, seated on their ornate chairs at the front of the crowd, applauded.

All save Master Hound and Master Bloodbear. The latter sat with a scowl on his ruddy, red-bearded face, his huge hands white-knuckled as he gripped the arms of his chair. Master Hound's narrow face looked pinched and drawn. She read the truth in his eyes: he knew what this meant for Master Gold's position in the Night Guild. Her success had restored the Guild Master's power and authority. Master Hound's dreams of taking control of the Guild had just gone up in smoke.

Ilanna's gaze went to Lady Auslan's sarcophagus. It bore little resemblance to the shining golden casket that had sat in a glass case in Lord Auslan's vault. The fall through the hole had left the halves bent and twisted, covered in dirt, and missing dozens of gemstones. Shards of steel flooring remained embedded in the soft gold.

But no amount of dust or mud could mask the value of her prize. A pouch of loose gemstones—each worth a fortune—lay open at her feet. The casket radiated a brilliant aura that shouted her triumph.

Master Gold raised his hands and the crowd fell silent. "My brothers and sisters of the Night Guild, this is truly a momentous occasion!"

The Journeymen cheered and shouted until the Guild Master called for silence once more.

"The Night Guild has known many great Journeymen—heroes, in their own right: Kainn, founder of the Guild and the first Master Gold; Novus, Master of House Hound, who is said to have killed one of the demons that once roamed Einan; Journeyman Harrad, a Bloodbear so powerful he once lifted a carriage with his bare hands; Journeyman Mallen, the greatest assassin House Serpent has ever produced. These and more have brought honor and glory to the Night Guild through their exploits. It is because of them the Night Guild holds such power in Praamis that King Ohilmos himself dares not move against us."

His hand came to rest on Ilanna's shoulder. "And tonight, Journeyman Ilanna adds her name to the legends of the Night Guild."

A murmur of approval rose from the crowd.

"You all recall what she accomplished for her Undertaking. Braving the heights of the Black Spire, defeating Duke Phonnis' cleverest traps, and bringing word of the fate of Journeyman Callidis of House Hawk. To say it was a task worthy of the Watcher in the Dark would be an understatement. She overcame the obstacle that proved not only impossible, but deadly, for so many others."

Heat rose to Ilanna's face. The torchlight seemed too bright and hot, and so many eyes on her made her nervous. Only Master Gold's grip on her shoulder held her fast.

"Since that day, can any say that she has not gone far above and beyond what is demanded of a Journeyman? Master Hawk, is it true that she has earned more than any other Journeyman in your House?"

Master Hawk nodded. "It is true."

"It. Is. True." Master Gold emphasized the words. "And is it true that her actions in service to the Watcher and the Night Guild have been beyond reproach?"

Again, Master Hawk nodded. "It is true."

Ilanna hid a grimace. *If only you knew the truth, Master Hawk.* The chest of gold under the floor of her house told a very different story.

Master Gold clasped his hands behind his back and strode to stand between the two halves of the sarcophagus. "You've all seen the fruits of her latest venture. Indeed, standing here, I cannot help but marvel at the courage, audacity, and ingenuity that went into, once again, doing the impossible. Listen close, my brothers and sisters, for today you will hear of marvels beyond your imaginings."

The crowd of Journeymen seemed to lean forward, hanging on Master Gold's every word.

"Our tale begins with a fearless thief who dared to defy the vile Duke Elodon Phonnis."

A chorus of hisses and "boos" echoed in the Menagerie.

"Out of spite, Duke Phonnis sought out her closest companions and sentenced them to the most agonizing death possible. He stood on the gallows, beside the dying bodies of her comrades, and declared his undying enmity for her. Ilanna, refusing to be cowed, leapt onto the scaffolding in a valiant attempt to save her friends. When the accursed Arbitors came for her, the good people of Praamis stood beside her, protected her, carried her to safety."

Ilanna resisted the urge to raise an eyebrow. *Not quite how I remember it.*

Master Gold's fanciful tale hadn't ended. "With his dying breath, her comrade begged her to carry out the Watcher's justice on Duke Phonnis. Thus, Ilanna took on the burden of righteous vengeance."

"But the Duke surrounded himself with a thousand warriors, each sworn to hunt down Journeyman Ilanna. Yet Ilanna had no fear. If she could not send the Duke himself to the Keeper, she would bring his world to ruins. She set about to destroy the one thing Duke Phonnis reveres more than his life: his reputation."

"Her first obstacle was one even the great Tiakin of House Fox would have found impossible. She had to break into the vaults of the Coin Counters' Temple to steal the Duke's secrets buried deep, deep underground."

A collective gasp rose from the crowd. More than a few grumbled at what they perceived as sacrilege.

"Yet not even a league of earth and rock could stop Ilanna from discovering every truth Duke Phonnis wanted to hide. As if wielding the powers of the Illusionist himself, she delved into the vile Duke's mind to understand his most complex creations. The very essence of his thoughts lay open to her, and she turned that knowledge back upon him."

Ilanna smothered a grin. *I can't deny he tells a bloody good tale.* She half-expected him to claim that she produced fire from her fingertips or could kill men with a glance.

"Journeyman Ilanna set to unraveling the secrets of the Duke's cleverest inventions. She chose to strike a blow that would destroy the Duke's hold over the city. She challenged the might of the Arbitors and the impenetrable vault built to hold Lady Auslan."

Gasps broke the stunned silence, and all eyes went to the golden sarcophagus halves. Most had heard the story but few believed it was more than rumor. The casket beside her proved otherwise.

"In his cowardice, Duke Phonnis sent every Arbitor at his command to protect Lord Auslan's property. Every door, every window, every rooftop was filled with those accursed silver-clad guards." His smile turned wicked. "Yet they could not stop Journeyman Ilanna. As if wearing the Illusionist's own cloak of invisibility, she crept past them in broad daylight, under their very noses. The vault door opened at a single touch, and, using the Duke's own secrets against him, tore apart his steel as if it were paper."

That last bit's not quite a lie.

"But the Arbitors lay in wait for her. She fought her way through a score of silver-clad guards, covering the retreat for her companions and prize. Even now, the Duke's men have come to fear the name of Journeyman Ilanna of House Hawk."

I'd much rather they didn't know my name at all.

"And now we bear witness to an achievement the likes of which has not been seen in decades. Nay, centuries. Not since Banc the Bold has a feat of this magnitude been accomplished." He thrust a finger at the sarcophagus. "This is not worth simply thousands of imperials, or even hundreds of thousands. Its value lies in the *millions*."

The words rang out in the eerie stillness of the Menagerie. No one spoke for long minutes. Every eye remained fixed on the golden sarcophagus.

"Journeyman Ilanna has done more than achieve the impossible," Master Gold said in a quiet voice. "She has brought honor to the Night Guild, paid righteous service to the Watcher. She has laid low the greatest enemy to our prosperity and wealth and enriched our coffers many, many times over. The Night Guild continues, thanks to her." He turned to her. "Journeyman Ilanna, we are honored." He swept a deep bow.

The Menagerie exploded in a deafening roar of cheers and shouts. The cries set the very stones of the walls trembling.

"Journeyman Ilanna!" they said. They cheered for *her*.

Chapter Fifty-Four

Ilanna's face flushed, heat spreading through her chest.

Master Gold raised his hands to silence the crowd. "Today begins a new era of prosperity, of plenty. Journeyman Ilanna has shown us what it truly means to belong to the Night Guild. Every one of us, from the newest tyro to the oldest Journeyman, should aspire to such achievements. No longer will we be content to subsist on scraps. Now is the time that we take our futures, our destinies into our own hands. Let us strive for greatness, aim for new heights of accomplishment. Let us go above and beyond the call of our responsibilities to the Guild and the Watcher. We must set our minds to new ways to bring the wealth of Praamis here, within these halls. For only then can we revel in the abundance promised to us by our Founders."

The assembled Journeymen cheered again, though with less enthusiasm. More than a few faces scrunched up in confusion. Master Gold's challenge rang out in the Menagerie. *Clever, clever man.* The Guild Master had promised riches, then placed the onus on the Journeymen. He played the role of magnanimous superior without doing any of the work.

"Go, my brothers, my sisters, my comrades, my friends. Return to your Houses, eat, drink, and celebrate the success of your own. Bask in our accomplishments this day, and challenge yourselves to greater achievements. Once the rewards for our efforts have been tallied, we will send word of our glorious victory."

Bloody, twisted hell. Ilanna shook her head. Master Gold spun the fanciful tale to build up Ilanna in the eyes of the Night Guild, then subtly insinuated himself into her success. His use of the word "our" made it seem as if he had played an equal part in the venture. Just one word and he'd elevated himself to the same legendary heights as her. *He's good.*

She met Allon's gaze, saw the same understanding in his eyes. The smile that had widened his face as he cheered for her a moment ago faded. A line appeared in his forehead. Errik, too, seemed to comprehend the gravity of Master Gold's words.

The Guild Master placed a hand on her shoulder. "Come, Ilanna. We have much to discuss in private before the Guild Council convenes."

* * *

Ilanna toyed with the rim of the silver goblet, not caring to drink the wine Master Gold had served her. The Guild Master sat across from her, his mouth pressed into a thin line, his expression pensive.

Ilanna broke the silence. "You said nothing about my crew. Why?"

Master Gold's eyebrows rose, but he chuckled. "Have you ever heard of Journeyman Smolder?"

Ilanna shook her head.

"Smolder was the first full Journeyman in the Night Guild, the boon companion of Kainn, the Guild's Founder. In fact, most of Kainn's greatest achievements were actually carried out by Smolder. It was Smolder who proposed merging the various groups of thieves, assassins, poisoners, and trackers of Praamis into a proper Guild. He conceived of the Guild Houses and orchestrated the successful unification of the gangs. But do you know why Kainn's name is remembered and Smolder's is forgotten?"

Again, Ilanna shook her head.

"Because Kainn was the *face.*" Master Gold's smile grew cold. "Smolder was the mind, but Kainn was the charismatic leader who put Smolder's plans into action. He may have been dumber than a sack of very dense rocks, but he knew how to talk to people. He knew the value of building relationships, using them to get what he wanted. And all of Smolder's hard work and vision added to the legend of Kainn."

Ilanna quirked an eyebrow. "So that's what you're doing here? You're using me to build your legend?"

Master Gold gave a dismissive wave. "I care nothing for legends or legacy. No, I plan to build *your* legend. The legend of Journeyman Ilanna, greatest of House Hawk, queen thief of Praamis." He smiled. "Has a nice ring to it, doesn't it?"

Ilanna pursed her lips.

The Guild Master sighed. "Everyone knows you had a crew working with you. The fact that you kept your enterprise such a tightly guarded secret inflamed the curiosity of every House. You've no idea how many times I've been questioned about you. You've been the talk of the Night Guild for weeks."

"But?"

"But the fact that you had help doesn't take away from the fact that *you* were the one who conceived of this plan. On your own." He toyed with the falcon brooch on his vest. "You came to the Guild Council with the idea and you assembled the crew to work for you. No matter the input from the others,

348

it was *you* who made this happen. And you will find that it's easier to build a legend for one person than for a group."

"Easier to *use* one person as well." She met Master Gold's gaze. "You're going to use this to keep Master Hound and the others in check. This will be your tool to keep the Bloody Hand at bay. You've turned this into *your* political victory."

Master Gold inclined his head. "But is that such a bad thing? If it keeps the Voramians from ripping apart our city, is it not worth it?"

"You've failed to take one thing into account."

"Oh? What's that?"

"Me."

Master Gold raised an eyebrow.

"You remember why I did this, do you not?"

The Guild Master's face darkened. "Surely you can't be s—"

"I will be free. The Night Guild has owned me for fifteen long, brutal years. I have sweated, cried, and bled for the Guild, lost friends and companions. I look around and see nothing but sorrow, misery, and suffering. All this started because Duke Phonnis executed the one true friend I had in this place. Yet throughout this venture, I've come to realize that he did me a favor. He severed any ties I had to the Night Guild."

Anger darkened Master Gold's face.

Ilanna didn't give him time to protest. "You may tell yourself you are my *friend*, that you care for me. Perhaps you do, but what matters most is that you can use me to achieve your ends. Do you deny it?"

Master Gold opened his mouth, hesitated, then shook his head.

"It is no less than I expected from the Master of a Guild that values gold over human lives. You, Master Gold, wear a kinder face than most, but you hold the same dagger behind your back. I have no doubt that you will continue to find ways for me to be useful, to serve your purposes. You will not discard me like others, not now that I've proven my worth to you and the Guild."

Her grip on the silver goblet tightened. "I do not hold it against you. The Night Guild has made you who you are. It has warped and twisted your mind until all that remains is desire, and you will do whatever you must to obtain it."

She bared her teeth. "But the Guild has done the same to me. I will do whatever I must to obtain my desire, and there is nothing I hold more valuable than my freedom." She thrust a finger toward the door. "*That*, Master Gold, is the proof of what I am willing to do. The laws of Praamis, the Duke and his men, the Bloody Hand, even the gods themselves—none of them will stop me from obtaining my desires. When the Guild Council convenes to hear the value of that golden casket, I will be free of this place."

As she spoke, a series of emotions flashed across Master Gold's face. Anger at the sting of her words faded to grudging acknowledgement, replaced a moment later by surprise at her intensity.

She hadn't finished. "I have taken your orders for too long, but now I will decide my own actions." For too long, she'd lived in fear of the notes appearing at her bedside table. No longer. "I am done stealing for you. You can coerce someone *else* to earn your gold."

A new emotion appeared: desperation.

"But you cannot!" A hint of panic widened the Guild Master's eyes. "You are all that has stopped the Bloody Hand's advances into Praamis. Think of what will happen if you leave."

Ilanna inclined her head. "Master Hound will continue to gain power in the Night Guild until the day comes when he calls for a vote to replace you."

"He will welcome the Bloody Hand with open arms. You went to Voramis. You've seen what they've done to the city. Can you truly say you would wish that on Praamis?"

Master Gold's question pierced to her core. She sat back, her fingers toying with the bowed wine glass while her mind whirled.

In her life, she'd known hardship and cruelty beyond what anyone should have to endure. Her father, blaming her for the deaths of her mother and baby sister, had sold her into slavery. The Guild had beaten, starved, and abused her in their efforts to mold her into a thief. She had suffered physical, emotional, psychological, and even sexual torments at the hands of Sabat. She had killed out of fear and a need to survive. She had lost friends and comrades to the King's justice, rotten fate, and the vengeance of the Bloody Hand. The death of Ethen—sweet, gentle, kind, and friendly Ethen—and Denber had made one thing very clear: she wouldn't die a thief.

The Night Guild had shaped her into a confident, capable, dangerous woman, but it had stolen her life. She would be free, and she would have the life she wanted. With Kodyn. With Ria. And without risking death every time she left her house.

With the money she'd earn from this job, she'd have enough to leave Praamis and start a new life somewhere else—anywhere else. A hundred thousand imperials—her share of the take—would suffice to set her up with a comfortable existence in any city on Einan. She'd never have to steal again. She could forget the Night Guild and Praamis entirely.

Yet could she condemn Praamis to the same suffering she'd endured? Her time in Voramis had shown her what happened when the Bloody Hand dug their claws into a city. They would do to Praamis what she had done to the silver goblet in her hand, leaving it just as mangled, twisted, and ugly.

She had suffered, but she had also found kindness among the people of Praamis: Master Umlai the butcher, who had given her and her mother extra bits of meat when they couldn't afford it; Daria, the nobleman's wife who took pity and fed her when she lay starving in the street; Ethen, Denber, Jarl, Werrin, Willem, Prynn, and Bert, the apprentices who had been like her family.

She could leave Praamis, but good people would suffer. It felt so ridiculous, so unfair for all of this to rest on her shoulders. She was just one thief among hundreds. Yet she couldn't shake the burden of responsibility that Master Gold's words had placed on her.

The Guild Master's words came out in a whisper. "Praamis needs you."

Ilanna slammed her fist onto the arm of her chair. "Damn you, Master Gold!" She stood and stalked around the room. Try as she might, she couldn't bring herself to say the words.

"What if we could come to an arrangement?" Desperation tinged Master Gold's words.

She turned to him, raising an eyebrow. "What sort of arrangement?"

Master Gold's face grew pensive. "You want your freedom from the Night Guild? So be it. I believe I can convince the Guild Council to release you from any responsibilities to your House."

"But?" There had to be a catch.

"But," Master Gold spoke in a slow voice, "you operate as an independent in service to the Guild. Any jobs you want to pull, you run them by me or Master Hawk. You have total autonomy to do as you please, provided you follow the rules of the Night Guild. In return for access to Guild equipment and resources, you pay a percentage of your earnings—say seventy percent?"

Ilanna snorted. "Such generosity, Master Gold! How could I refuse?" Her lip curled into a sneer. "You'll have to do better than that."

The Guild Master held up his hands. "Fifty percent. Half your earnings. Surely that's a reasonable—"

"I've no doubt the pencil-pushers will find all sorts of fees and expenses to tack on. By the time they're done, I'll walk away with next to nothing for all my hard work." She crossed her arms. "For fifteen years, the Guild has given me one imperial for every ten I earn. Let's see how you like it."

"Ten percent?" Master Gold shook his head. "The Guild Council will never agree." He stroked his chin. "What if I bring them down to one quarter? Twenty-five percent."

Ilanna pondered the offer. It held appeal. If she accepted, she wouldn't have to leave Praamis. She could lead a normal life, only stealing when she needed the gold. She'd have the freedom to do as she pleased and ply her skills however she wished.

But something stopped her from accepting on the spot. She couldn't make the decision alone, not any more. She had to talk to Ria first.

"I make no promises," she said in a slow voice, "but *if* you can convince the Guild Council for those terms, I will consider it."

Relief washed across Master Gold's face. He sat back in his chair, his shoulders relaxing, and reached for the goblet.

A knock sounded at the door. It opened to reveal Entar. "It's time, Master Gold. The Guild Council has convened."

Chapter Fifty-Five

A strained silence thickened the atmosphere in the Guild Council chamber. The eyes of twelve men and two women remained fixed on her as they waited for the results.

Ilanna didn't turn her head as the door opened. Journeyman Bryden appeared beside her, his angular face more puckered than usual.

Bryden cleared his throat and shuffled the papers in his hands. "Masters of the Night Guild, I have here the assessment results of the bounty brought in by Ilanna of House Hawk."

Ilanna couldn't miss the tightness of his voice, or the fact that he left out the "Journeyman". *He's definitely not happy.* The thought put a smile on her lips.

"The Guild's official gold and gemstone dealers have drafted up their valuation of what they believe the casket is worth."

He shuffled the papers again, and nodded as he held one up.

"As you know, the sarcophagus of Lady Auslan is well known in all of Praamis. Indeed, stories of the priceless resting place of Lord Auslan's wife has spread around the south of Einan. There is simply no way for the casket to be sold whole. With the damage inflicted upon it during transit"—he shot a sidelong glance of disapproval at Ilanna—"there is no other choice but to melt it down and sell the gold for its melt value."

"However, such a vast quantity of gold will require months to move without attracting suspicion. The Guild's dealers will have to transport a good deal of the metal to Voramis, Malandria, perhaps even farther north in order to sell it off in small batches. It would not surprise me if an entire year passed before all of the gold has been exchanged for goods, coinage, gemstones, and metals of equal value, to be added to the Night Guild's coffers."

Ilanna grimaced. *It must be a lot if it'll take a whole year.*

"As for the matter of the gemstones, the dealers believe they will be able to dispose of the majority in Voramis. Most are unremarkable and indistinguishable from the stones currently held by our contacts. A handful will be distributed around Praamis, though only in a limited selection to once again reduce the chance of discovery."

"Among the lot, there were a few gemstones—diamonds, rubies, garnets, and sapphires among them—with unique properties: cut, coloring, flaws, and clarity. These will be transported to Drash and Nysl."

"Yes, yes." Master Gold gave a dismissive wave. "We can dispense with all this." He glanced around the table. "Unless any of you somehow managed to forget how we deal with our more recognizable prizes?"

A few of the House Masters chuckled, but most shook their heads.

"On to the good part, Journeyman Bryden." Master Gold steepled his fingers and leaned forward. "What's the sum total?" Greed glimmered in the Guild Master's eyes, and in the eyes of every House Master and second-in-command around the table. Even Master Hound couldn't mask the curiosity on his narrow face.

Bryden cleared his throat again and drew out another parchment. "Between the melt value of the gold and the estimated value of the assorted gemstones, the casket of Lady Auslan will earn a little over two million imperials for the Night Guild." After a deliberate pause, he added as an afterthought, "And Journeyman Ilanna."

Two million imperials! Ilanna could scarcely believe her ears. She'd known the value of the sarcophagus would be well into the millions, but hadn't counted on *this* much. Even after selling the gold for scrap and no doubt losing a small fortune in shattered and scattered gemstones, she walked away from the single heist with more money than she'd dared believe.

"Sweet Mistress!" Master Serpent echoed the sentiment of all in the room. He stood and, flaring his cloak out to the side, swept a deep bow. "Journeyman Ilanna of House Hawk, I salute you."

Master Grubber, Master Scorpion, and Master Hawk pounded their goblets on the table, and even Master Fox joined in. Master Hound gave her a nod. Though her actions had cost him politically, he could grant the grudging respect of one Guild member to another. Only Master Bloodbear and his dark-eyed second-in-command, a brute named Pialden, remained unmoving, a pair of matching scowls aimed her way.

Bryden's nasal voice broke into the tumult. "There is, however, the small matter of debts."

The room fell silent. Ilanna turned to Bryden, a snarl on her lips. "What debts?"

Despite the impassive expression on his face, Bryden's eyes shimmered with glee. "Why the debts owed to your crew, and to the other Houses for the loan of their Journeymen."

Ilanna's eyes narrowed.

Bryden turned back to his papers, and his voice held a note of triumph. "First, there are the shares of the take promised to your crew." He held up a parchment and read aloud. "To Jarl of House Hawk, ten percent. To Allon of House Hound, ten percent. To Darreth of House Scorpion, five percent. To Errik of House Serpent, five percent. To Veslund and Joost of House Fox, one percent each for a total of two percent."

Master Hawk's eyebrows rose, and Master Hound actually smiled. The Masters of House Scorpion and Serpent looked less pleased, and Master Fox's face darkened.

"A total of six hundred and forty thousand imperials is to be spread around the Houses from which Journeyman Ilanna selected her crew."

The House Masters, even Master Fox, grinned at this number. Master Bloodbear's face drained of color. He wouldn't see a single copper bit of Ilanna's haul.

"Next comes the matter of the equipment and materials purchased for the construction of…" He squinted his eyes and read from the parchment…"one Voramian steel vault door." He shot a quizzical glance at her. "The cost of materials, the use of the Guild warehouse, and the services of Master Lorilain comes up to a total of one hundred thousand imperials."

Ilanna's eyes widened. "What?"

Bryden met her anger with a sneer. "Voramian steel doesn't come cheap, *Journeyman*." He spoke the last word as an oath. "And don't get me started on the cost of procuring Odarian steel. The steelmakers of Odaron have priced their wares so high not even the gods themselves could afford them."

Ilanna swallowed. *Still well over a million imperials,* she told herself. She'd have enough to buy her freedom. She *had* to.

"There is, of course, the day rates owed to Houses Hound, Fox, Serpent, and Scorpion. According to my records, Journeymen from these Houses have been contracted by Journeyman Ilanna for weeks. So busy were they in their pursuit of Journeyman Ilanna's ends that they neglected their House dues. By Guild law, these dues and fees are to be covered by Journeyman Ilanna."

Heat flared in Ilanna's chest. "Explain this, *Bryden*." She spoke through gritted teeth. "Why would they be earning day rates while simultaneously pulling in a share of the profits?"

Bryden shrugged. "Damned if I know. If only someone had made the arrangements clear at the onset of the job, all this confusion might have been avoided. As it stands, the aforementioned Journeymen of the aforementioned Houses are owed day rates for the weeks since they began working for you."

Ilanna turned to Master Gold for help, but the Guild Master shook his head. "When you initially contracted the Journeymen, it was agreed that you would pay their day rates, correct?"

Ilanna nodded.

Bryden spoke up. "They made the arrangements with their respective Houses, but since that day, have they notified any of you about the change in their earnings?"

Anorria of House Scorpion peered down at her ledger and shook her head. Eburgen of House Hound responded in kind.

"I thought not. The same goes for House Hawk." He failed to hide his malicious delight. "So, as Guild law clearly states, they are owed day rates for as long as they participate in your enterprise. The fact that you offered them a share of the take is truly generous of you. You are a paragon for all Journeymen to emulate." The sneer echoed in his voice.

Ilanna clenched her fists. "How. Much?" As expected, the petty accountant had found a way to dig his greedy fingers into her fortune.

"Together with the day rates owed to House Grubber for the use of twenty-five Journeymen, House Hawk for the services of the Pathfinders, and apprentices and House Fox for five Journeymen, that comes out to a hundred thousand imperials."

Ilanna drew in another sharp breath. She knew Jarl had hired Grubbers to dig the tunnels and build the hoist, floating platform, waterwheel system, and the escape route, but she hadn't given thought to how long they'd been working down there. She'd told him to bring in Gorin and the other Pathfinders. Errik must have hired Foxes to help him keep an eye on Lord Auslan at the Labethian Tournament. All of this added up to one hell of an overhead cost.

"We must not forget the small matter of the materials used by Journeyman Ilanna and her accomplices over the course of the enterprise. Building materials, Guild equipment, the use of space in House Hawk, and so on. A sum total of fifty thousand imperials."

Ilanna's gut tightened. Bryden had whittled her fortune to nearly half. Any more expenses and her arrangement with Master Gold would be for nothing. Had she come this far only to fall short?

"Is that all?" Her words came out tight, clipped. "Or is there anything else you'd like to charge me for? Perhaps the air I'm breathing belongs to the Guild as well."

"Journeyman Ilanna." Master Hound's voice cut off Bryden's retort. "You undertook what is undoubtedly the greatest endeavor the Night Guild has witnessed in decades. Centuries, perhaps. For your efforts, you have claimed a prize of breathtaking value." The look in his eyes told Ilanna he knew *exactly* what that prize meant for his plans, yet he kept the fury from his voice. "I can say in all honesty that *no* Journeyman in recent history, not even Journeyman Mallen, has brought in a fortune to rival this. Is it any surprise that the cost of such an endeavor is equal to its audacity?"

Much as Ilanna hated to admit it, Master Hound spoke the truth. "As you say."

Bryden gave a harsh chuckle, which earned him a reproachful glare from Master Hound. "As for you, Journeyman Bryden, perhaps you cease your petty torments and simply get on with your duty." He folded his arms over his chest. "What is the final tally of profit for this endeavor?"

The sour expression returned to Bryden's face. He cleared his throat, hemming for a moment before reading. "One million, one hundred and ten thousand imperials."

The words hung in the air, seeming to echo around the room. Ilanna's heart soared. All eyes remained fixed on her, and she returned the gazes of the Journeymen and House Masters with confident calm. Against the odds, she had pulled off the impossible. She'd earned her freedom.

She caught Master Gold's eye and raised an eyebrow. With a nod, the Guild Master stood.

"Gentlemen, the last time Journeyman Ilanna stood before us, she came with the request for her freedom from service to the Night Guild. We set before her a task worthy of the Watcher himself. She stands before us with every obligation to us met, every debt paid off. Is there any reason why she should not be granted her request?"

Master Hawk's expression grew grim, his eyes filled with sorrow.

Shock showed on Master Hound's face. Ilanna could almost see the inner workings of his mind as he absorbed and processed Master Gold's words. His face brightened after a moment of calculation. "Indeed, I would say she has more than earned it." In his surprise, he failed to hide the eagerness in his voice. Her departure from the Night Guild would deprive his political opponent of a valuable ally—likely his *most* valuable ally, after the fortune she'd just delivered. He would love nothing more.

Master Gold's smile reminded her of a cat preparing to pounce on a mouse. "But I believe I have found a way to meet her request *and* ensure the continued prosperity"—he shot a smug grin at Master Hound—"*and* safety of the Night Guild. What I propose is this…"

Chapter Fifty-Six

"Is it true?" A rumbling voice echoed in the silent Aerie.

Ilanna whirled. "Is what true?"

Jarl's massive frame filled the tunnel that led away from House Hawk's main room. "You really leaving us, 'Lanna?"

Ilanna swallowed. "I…" What could she say to him? He'd been there from the beginning, had been kind to her from her first day as an apprentice. Her plan to buy her freedom had succeeded largely thanks to him. The hurt and sorrow in the big, bearded man's eyes tore at her.

"I have to, Jarl," she said, her voice quiet.

"Why? We're your House, 'Lanna."

"I know, but…" She drew in a deep breath. "All this, the life we lead, I can't do it any longer. I need more than a House, Jarl."

The Night Guild had hardened her, had shown her how to be strong. But they'd taken the thing that mattered most: her family. Her father, her mother, her baby sister—they'd all died because of the Guild. She'd spent the last four years determined to keep Kodyn free of their clutches.

"I thought we was…" He trailed off, his eyes dropping. "…family," he whispered.

She gripped his enormous forearm. "*You*, Jarl, are among the few good things the Night Guild has ever given me." She swallowed the lump in her throat. "And if you think I'm going to forget you, you're a bigger fool than I thought."

He chuckled, a sad sound.

She took his craggy face in both hands and kissed his bearded cheek. "I may be leaving the Guild, but you're not going to get rid of me that easily. You will always be my friend."

* * *

Ilanna leaned against the cool tiles of the rooftop and tipped the wineskin to her lips. The mild, fruit-heavy flavors of the Nyslian rose wine enchanted her palate but brought back memories tinged with sorrow.

Denber always loved this wine. Werrin and Willem, too. She drew in a deep breath. The taste of rain hung thick in the chill night air. The moon hung high in the sky, but the shadows across the Praamian rooftops seemed more forlorn than usual. Even the towering onyx dagger of the Black Spire emanated a solemnity and sorrow to match Ilanna's mood.

She'd spent hours on this very rooftop, drinking, eating, and talking with Denber, Werrin, Willem, Prynn, and Bert. It felt so empty now—her alone, the last apprentice of House Hawk. Five years as a Journeyman couldn't erase the memories of those few bright moments with her friends.

She raised the wineskin in a salute. She'd come to their once-favorite spot to say farewell. After today, everything changed.

The House Masters had been bickering when she left. Master Gold had laid out his proposal with his usual eloquence. Masters Fox and Grubber, flushed with their newfound wealth, had agreed without reservation. Master Bloodbear, as spiteful and hate-filled as any of his House, had refused to hear any argument. Master Hound's stance had seemed more reasonable—after all, the Guild certainly couldn't allow anyone to operate outside of their control— but lacked real substance. He argued for tradition, while Master Gold offered a chance at continued prosperity that no sane House Master or Journeyman could dismiss. Faced with the Masters of House Scorpion, Serpent, and Hawk and the Guild Master himself, he'd soon cave.

Snorting, she took another pull of wine. *Let them quibble over terms and caveats.* In the end, she would tell them what she wanted and they'd give it to her. Master Gold needed her, and he'd use all his influence to keep her working for the Night Guild. He would have no control over her—either by blackmailing her through the mysterious notes or using his influence as Guild Master. He'd have to cater to her demands for once.

That's if I choose to stay, of course. She hadn't yet decided. And the decision wouldn't be an easy one.

If she bade the Night Guild farewell, she'd leave the only life she'd known. She'd been a Hawk for fifteen years. She'd spent countless hours training to acquire the skills she'd need in her service to her House. She couldn't imagine life without the thrill of racing across the Hawk's Highway, the heart-pounding exhilaration of slipping in and out of noblemen's homes without leaving a trace. Where else could she find such a test of her mind and body? Her latest enterprise had made one thing crystal clear: she lived for the challenge.

She couldn't imagine never seeing Jarl or Master Hawk again—the only members of her "family" remaining—or racing up the Perch. The journey to Voramis had reinforced her bond with Errik. The Serpent had endured the abuses of Master Velvet beside her, but they hadn't broken his spirit. He'd survived the Menagerie and his training as an assassin with his sense of honor and decency intact.

Darreth, the odd Journeyman from House Scorpion, had reminded her of Ethen. He had the same love of learning, the same quick mind. His quirks never bothered her; if anything, they made him a more curious companion. He'd grown on her.

She'd even be sorry to say goodbye to Allon. Her relationship with him had only been one of convenience and necessity, in *her* mind, at least. But he had a few qualities—a bright mind, an innate curiosity, and a desire to test his boundaries that rivaled hers—that made him a suitable comrade. Perhaps in another life, there could have been something real between them. But, like with everything else, the Night Guild had poisoned that.

She remembered very little of her life before the Night Guild. She'd lived, breathed, and dreamed thieving for so long. The thought of leaving it all behind filled her with an unexplained fear.

She knew one thing for certain: she would *never* return to her old life. The Night Guild no longer owned her. Though it had taken fifteen years, she had bought back her life. And *she* would decide how she wanted to live it.

If she decided she couldn't give up her life as a Hawk completely, Master Gold's offer gave her the perfect solution. She'd have total freedom to operate independent of the Night Guild. She could do as she pleased. That was a feeling she'd never experienced, and it filled her with exhilaration. She was free.

The warmth that spread through her had little to do with the wine. From her pouch, she drew out an ornate figurine. The hawk, carved from a garnet as dark as Ria's eyes, seemed to hover in the air, twinkling in the moonlight. She'd bought the bird the day she petitioned the Night Guild for her freedom. Kodyn wouldn't know its true value for years, but it would always remind her of the high price she'd paid for her life.

The image of her son's face brought a smile to her lips. No longer would she have to hide his existence from the world. She wouldn't have to worry about his being conscripted into the Guild ranks. The Night Guild had no claim on him. He could live a normal life, do whatever he wanted. She had more than enough gold to give him everything. He could be a smith, a butcher, a clerk, or any mundane profession he chose. Everything she'd done had been for him. She'd bought his freedom, too.

Tomorrow, she'd take him to the Old Town Market, the way her mother had once done with her. They'd buy something nice for Ria.

The way she felt about the Ghandian girl left her confused, yet excited. Ria had become as important as Kodyn, yet in a different way. She couldn't imagine her future without Ria. Perhaps she didn't have to. Her gold could buy Ria whatever life the girl wanted. She just hoped it would include her.

She raised the wineskin to her lips one last time: a farewell to her past, a salute to her future. The memories of her friends—Denber, Werrin, Willem, Prynn, Bert and Ethen—would remain a burden of the life to which her father had condemned her. Yet she would form new memories. *Happy* ones.

She stood and glanced at the moon. If she hurried, she could be home before daybreak. She'd have time to prepare a breakfast before Ria and Kodyn awoke. She had nowhere to be. She could simply sit and enjoy a meal…with her family.

Excitement lent wings to her feet. She flew across the Hawk's Highway, the city of Praamis a blur beneath her. The city seemed aglow with moonlight. A weight had lifted from her chest, and she reveled in the intoxication of her freedom. It seemed as if Old Town Market had come alive in the night, beckoning her home. She raced toward the brilliance.

A profound sense of wrongness hit her. *That can't be moonlight.*

The wind brought the scent of smoke a heartbeat later. Old Town Market burned. Fire engulfed the shops, stalls, and houses around the marketplace, spreading outward in a terrible wave of death and destruction.

Ilanna's heart stopped. *No, no, no!* Horror twisted a knife in her gut. She raced over the rooftops, abandoning all caution.

She had to get home, had to get to Ria and Kodyn before…

Her world crumbled as she saw the raging inferno devouring her house.

End of Book 2:

* * *

Ilanna's thrilling journey concludes in Queen of the Night Guild

Queen of the Night Guild

**<u>Her life burned to ashes. Her city under siege. She will sacrifice
everything for bloody vengeance.</u>**

Ilanna has lost everything: her friends, her home, her family, her dreams of
freedom. All that remains is a burning desire to find the bastards who burned
down her city and tried to kill her.

But a traitor hides among the ranks of the Night Guild, poisoning her friends and allies with lies. Amidst cutthroats and thieves, even the truth can be twisted and turned into a weapon of betrayal.

Cast out and hunted by her former comrades, Ilanna has no choice but to turn to old enemies to save not only her life, but her Guild and city in the process.

Queen of the Night Guild is the breathtaking, heart-stopping conclusion to the Queen of Thieves epic fantasy series. Fans of Sarah J. Mass, Scott Lynch, and Sabaa Tahir will love Ilanna.

Click now if you love a gritty tale of revenge and treachery that will keep you reading into the night!

More Books by Andy Peloquin

Queen of Thieves

Traitors' Fate (**Queen of Thieves/Hero of Darkness Crossover**)

Hero of Darkness

Heirs of Destiny:

Different, Not Damaged: A Short Story Collection

About the Author

I am, first and foremost, a storyteller and an artist--words are my palette. Fantasy is my genre of choice, and I love to explore the darker side of human nature through the filter of fantasy heroes, villains, and everything in between. I'm also a freelance writer, a book lover, and a guy who just loves to meet new people and spend hours talking about my fascination for the worlds I encounter in the pages of fantasy novels.

Fantasy provides us with an escape, a way to forget about our mundane problems and step into worlds where anything is possible. It transcends age, gender, religion, race, or lifestyle--it is our way of believing what cannot be, delving into the unknowable, and discovering hidden truths about ourselves and our world in a brand new way. Fiction at its very best!

Join my Facebook Reader Group
for updates, LIVE readings, exclusive content, and all-around fantasy fun.
Let's Get Social!
Be My Friend: https://www.facebook.com/andrew.peloquin.1
Facebook Author Page: https://www.facebook.com/andyqpeloquin
Twitter: https://twitter.com/AndyPeloquin